I0657937

WE STARTED OUT AS FRIENDS

Marjorie Dawn Tulloch

Toronto, Canada

Copyright © 2011 by Marjorie Dawn Tulloch
Cover design by Malikah Tulloch-Jack
www.novelthelist.blogspot.com

All rights reserved.
No parts of this book may be reproduced, scanned, or distributed in
any printed or electronic form without permission.

ISBN: 978-0-9878868-0-4

Preface

W omen love fiction. To be lost in a world of drama, intrigue, love and loss is an exhilarating and uplifting experience. Muslim women are no different.

My intention in writing this piece of fiction is to share a story that will affect the hearts of my readers. I hope to educate them and give them positive examples of conduct, within a story that gives Canadian Muslim women an opportunity to see characters that they can relate to in print.

Rachel, Fatima and Ali take readers on a journey in which many subjects surface that will inspire deep thought and discussion.

By the end, readers will learn that many issues transcend faith and religion, but with the correct focus we can rise above challenges, creating and maintaining successful relationships.

We Started Out as Friends is about love; the love between friends, husband and wife, parents and children, brother and sister, and just how far reaching that love can be.

It is my hope that by the end of this book, readers will have expanded their own capacity for loving all those in their lives.

Acknowledgments

A dear and heartfelt thanks to all those who helped to make this possible. Many thanks to Serah Daya and Andrea Bryce, who helped me with the first drafts by reading and giving their raw feedback. Thanks to Nasreen Razvi, Sharmaine Brissett and Rozmine Merchant who read the first completed draft and helped me with the initial edit. Thanks to Kawther Hamed, Ginella Massa, Shanice Grocia, Malikah Tulloch-Jack and Laila Hasib for editing. Thanks to Malikah Tulloch-Jack for her work on the cover. To my children, Malikah, Muhammad Husayn and Tahir, for their encouragement, excitement and positive energy, a deep and resounding, thank-you, I love you.

Rachel Covered Her Mouth To Prevent Herself From Speaking.

Fatima, breathing heavily, stood at the bottom of the porch stairs, looking up to Rachel's level. "That is exactly why you are in the situation you're in. You don't even know what love looks like."

Rachel saw Ali approaching before Fatima did.

"Fatima, it's time to go inside." Ali's deep voice cut through the night air and the building tension between the two women. All that could be heard was the rustling trees and their breathing.

Fatima and Rachel stood staring at each other without speaking. Rachel spoke first. She had to take a cleansing breath and clear her throat to do it. "Your husband is speaking to you."

Fatima shook her head and turned to walk away. Rachel watched Fatima and Ali walk across the street and enter their home before she retreated and slowly locked her door.

Chapter One

ℑ

"You're going to be all right. You have to be."
Rachel blinked her eyes and squinted under the hospital lights in the sterile white room. She couldn't stop shaking. Still groggy, she closed her eyes again. *No, I will never be the same again,* she thought. The warm words of the petite brown haired nurse touched her and hurled her even deeper into the well of shame that engulfed her. *How could anyone care for me and treat me with such compassion after what I've just done?* Rachel wondered.

It didn't help that the doctor had also been sympathetic. Tall, young and entirely too good looking for this job, he had smiled warmly while trying to distract Rachel with some frivolous conversation about allergies. Rachel had tried to reciprocate, but could not have been more humiliated if a billboard with her on it had been posted in front of the hospital.

She could see the hospital staff moving around but was not sure what they were doing. She couldn't focus on anything. Fresh tears ran down her face, into the tracks of the not so old ones. The tears followed each other in a steady stream, promising to drown all her sorrow, but they could not. Tears flowed as though they could wash away the act; wash away the shame and indiscretions, making Rachel new again. They could not.

Rachel had gone under anesthetic in tears and had come out in tears. She wondered if she had cried throughout the procedure. *Was that even possible?* She could remember the hospital staff being so cheerful and kind. *Did they treat everyone like this?*

They had made every effort to cheer Rachel up. The nurse closest to her head had been humming. "You're going to be fine sweetheart. Really..." she had said, all too knowingly.

Had she done it too? Who were these people? *Didn't the nurse know I was about to be struck with a sudden and complicated death as punishment for this grievous sin, this hideous act that I had done, not once but twice?* Rachel thought. She could only think about the possibility of her dying during the relatively safe and simple procedure. *Safe for me, certainly not for my baby.* She knew she would have deserved it. She was so grateful when her eyes opened.

The anesthesiologist had told her to count to 10, and then she would be out. She had willed herself to stay awake as she searched herself for the answers. *Did she really want to do this? Was she doing the right thing? Did she want to abort another child?* As she reached three the answer came to her, *NOOOOO!* She wanted to scream. *Let me go home!* It was too late. Now, she was awake.

Where was her baby? What did they do with it? *My.* God. *How could I end up in this position again?* She had promised herself she would never do it again. Now, this was a pattern.

She was 24 years old with two children and two abortions under her belt. Not to mention countless trips to the clinic for emergency contraception. *Wasn't that the same thing?* But this time wasn't her fault. She couldn't think about it now. She had to get home, before her mother returned from church.

Rachel pressed her eyes together attempting to squeeze out all the tears, the pain and sadness. When the nurse returned she brought with her more love, more soothing. Didn't she know she was an accomplice? *How many more would she assist today? This was a job? These people are sick.*

"I need to get out of here." Rachel hadn't realized she had spoken out loud.

"No honey, you have to rest. I'll bring you some food when you get to the recovery room."

Rachel glared at the *accomplice*. "How long have you worked here?" she charged.

"A few years."

"And you like it?" Rachel demanded, with her eyes wide.

"It's my job. I like to help people."

Rachel almost choked, trying to hold back a wicked laugh.

Help people? She doesn't know herself either.

Rachel looked around the recovery room at the other patients. The walls were a soothing green, and the burgundy leather chairs were well cushioned, but nothing could comfort Rachel. One of the other two women had a man with her. *Sickening. You actually let her go through with this. And you call yourself a man?* Rachel couldn't even look at them.

Rachel was alone. Of course, it was her choice. She had not told Jamie. Indeed she would never tell him this.

"He would kill me," Rachel whispered to herself. She suddenly felt a new chill and drew her blanket tighter.

After 30 minutes Rachel was led to the area where she would get dressed. She held her head up and tried to look casual as she passed staff, patients and visitors. She wondered if they knew what she had just done.

"Here you go, honey." *Wasn't honey sweet?* Rachel stepped into a small room that had several cubicles for dressing. She entered one and closed the door. She thought about her life and where she was going. Nowhere she was proud of.

This month she would turn 25. Her sons were four and five.

They had been born 10 months apart and would both be five in December for two months. They got a kick out of that. Jonah was excited at the prospect of catching up to his brother. Joshua thought they were going to be twins for two months.

Rachel let out a weighted sigh. Imagine if they knew what had happened today. It was for the best, wasn't it? What would she do with three kids? She thought back to her time in the recovery room.

Rachel had heard soft footsteps on the hospital tiles. The *accomplice* had come to check on her. Rachel was feeling fine, aside from terrible cramping. She had not experienced that before. Of course this time was different. Rachel had read that when people were being operated on, their bodies often tensed under the touch of the scalpel. She wondered, in her emotional condition, what her body had done.

What about her baby? *What did they do with it?* She wondered. *She had to do it.* She couldn't have another child. Not like this. Not for Jamie. Yet she was so sick with grief that she couldn't think about it anymore. It was over and she would go on. She was not going to let it get to her, stay with her. Not like the first time. This baby would not haunt her like the first one.

She got dressed, washed her face and finger combed her jet black hair. Last year she had cut it into a short bob, but it had long since grown out of the style, and now hung past her shoulders. She powdered her face and put on her signature raspberry lip-gloss. Her mocha skin was flawless, as always. She was ready.

The hospital would not permit her to leave alone, so Rachel had taken a cab to the hospital and called her best friend to pick her up. She hadn't told Fatima why she was going to the hospital. She knew Fatima wouldn't want any part of this. Indeed, Rachel didn't even want any part of this.

When she came out of the dressing room, Fatima was waiting. By the look on her face, Rachel knew she had figured out what was going on; and she was mad.

Rachel signed the release papers at the nurses' station and quickly turned to leave. Fatima was steps ahead of her.

"Fati, please, I can't keep up." Rachel complained as she weaved through the people. She counted the steps until she would land on the carpeted section of the floor closer to the door. She felt like a child who only started to cry as soon as her mother appeared.

Even though she was a few months older than Fatima, she always felt like Fatima was the mother or big sister. She just had that way about her. Rachel stepped gingerly as her cramps intensified. Just before she reached the sliding doors that would take them outside, Fatima turned to face her best friend of 19 years.

"Where is Jamie?"

Rachel pressed her lips together and then blurted out, "He doesn't know. I couldn't tell him this. He'd kill me if he knew."

"Why? Because he wants one more child for your mother to support?"

"Fatima come on, you know I work. I take care of my kids." Rachel had never burdened her mother financially, but did still live in the house where she had grown up.

"Maybe you should start taking care of yourself," Fatima fired back.

"What did you say to me?" Rachel stepped aside to let a wheelchair enter the lobby.

"Let's go. I parked out front."

The two women walked in silence, and when Fatima opened the passenger door, Rachel slid herself into the white Acura MDX with difficulty.

Rachel watched as Fatima entered the car. She wore designer blue jeans, as usual, a baby pink top and matching headscarf, with pink sunglasses on top of her head. The pink complimented her complexion, which matched Rachel's complexion perfectly. Due to frequent headaches, she wore sunglasses year round. Still, she hated them. Fatima always felt like she couldn't see when she wore them.

They drove most of the way in silence until Rachel couldn't take it anymore. "Fati, say something."

"Do you need anything before we get home?" Fatima was a health sciences student, with an eye towards medical school. She knew exactly what Rachel would need.

"I need to pick up this prescription at the pharmacy." Rachel took out the prescription and held it in her hand. When they arrived in the store parking lot, Rachel handed it to Fatima. "Could you get it for me?"

Fatima's eyes widened as she glared at her friend in astonishment. This was too much for Rachel. She knew what she had done, she was grieving, she was in pain and her best friend in the world thought she was garbage. She crumbled under a heap of hot tears.

"Please Fati, I can't *walk*." She started sobbing as she dropped her hand. She didn't even care if she got the medication or not. Indeed, she would have been happy to be left on the side of the road. She deserved to suffer and she was not going to fight it.

Fatima snatched the paper from her hand and, while Rachel fumbled in her purse for money, left the car without saying a word.

Rachel leaned back in the car and let out a heavy sigh. Although she was grateful to have Fatima, she was relieved to be alone for a few minutes. She knew Fatima was upset with her now, but she still would never let Rachel down. She could always depend on Fatima. They had been best friends since kindergarten.

Rachel had been new to the neighbourhood and entered school in senior kindergarten. Her parents had moved several times before settling into Fatima's neighbourhood.

On the first day of school Rachel had been very nervous. The first day of a new school was always the worst. Fatima had been in her class. She had been so small and cute, and had walked right up to Rachel saying, "Hi, I'm Fatima. Do you need a friend?" She had known then. And she knew now. She always knew what Rachel needed. She always knew what was going on with her, even when it was not clear to Rachel herself.

The two girls had gelled instantly and were inseparable. Fatima was the kind of friend that was just like a sister. The kind you loved sometimes and hated sometimes. You just couldn't stand a day without her, but sometimes wished she would get out of your hair and off your back.

Yes, she loved Fatima, but Fatima had her really ticked off right now. Fatima couldn't possibly understand. Rachel hadn't intentionally made a mess of her life.

"Here you go." Fatima returned with the medication. "There are two bottles in there. The little pink ones you take twice a day, 12 hours apart and the large white ones you take three times a day with meals. The insert will give you all the details." Fatima slid behind the wheel again.

"I don't know what you're all puffed up about. I only asked you for a ride home." Rachel was hurt and embarrassed but still needed to hear Fatima talk. Anger was still better than the silence.

"Why didn't you tell me what was going on?" Fatima asked softly.

"Would you have come?"

"That's beside the point."

"That *is* the point." Rachel laughed at her friend, indignantly, as she wiped away the last of her tears. She needed someone and Fatima was the only one she could call. Fatima knew it.

Fatima sighed. "What about before today. Why didn't you tell us you were pregnant?"

Rachel looked down at Fatima's expanded middle. "I didn't want to burden you with my problems."

"It didn't have to be a problem. We're all here for you. We

9

love you. We would have worked it out. We would have helped you, Rachel."

They stopped at a red light. Two women pushed strollers and another elderly man pulled two toddlers in a wagon. *Where did all these kids come from?* Rachel wondered.

Rachel wrinkled her brow and scowled. "We? You mean you, your husband and your truckload of kids? I think you have enough to deal with."

"You know it's not like that."

"It's been done. Just forget it."

"I know it's not the time, but we will talk about this."

"Yah, whatever."

Rachel closed her eyes and leaned back, trying not to think about the pain. *I deserve it*, she thought. *I'll probably be infertile after this.* Why she was thinking about fertility, when she was the single mother of two boys, was beyond her. Maybe she still had the dream of meeting Prince Charming. Maybe then she could have a family of her own, a real family, like Fatima.

She thought about everything Fatima had said. She knew she had given Fatima a hard time, but Fatima was right. Rachel could have turned to them, all of them. She knew that. But how could she tell her why she hadn't? How could she tell her that she was so ashamed that they were both pregnant but under such different circumstances? How could she expect Fatima to understand, while she excitedly made plans for her baby with her beloved husband, that she was pregnant *again*? No she just couldn't tell her. She had made the only decision that she could. She needed to block Jamie from her life. She couldn't allow him to have any excuse to come around more than he had to.

"When did all this happen anyway?" Fatima was speaking again, and Rachel really couldn't take anymore. Sinking further into her seat, Rachel exhaled and rolled her eyes under her closed lids.

"I thought you said this wasn't the time?"

"Answer me, Rachel. I haven't seen Jamie in months."

"Yes, it's been a while." Rachel exhaled slowly and braced herself for what was coming.

The full realization of what Rachel was saying sank in. Fatima hadn't seen Jamie in the neighbourhood since December. It had been at least four months. Fatima glared at her friend in shock. "Why did you wait so long?" Fatima could barely whisper.

"Hey, keep your eyes on the road." Rachel eagerly tried to change the subject.

"Why, Rachel?" Fatima gripped the steering wheel and signaled.

"I didn't know for a while. Then I didn't know what I wanted to do."

Fatima pulled the car into a gas station and parked. "What are you doing?" Rachel asked.

Fatima put her hand on her own abdomen and dropped her head as tears welled up in her eyes. "You should have come to us. We would have helped you. I mean, you came this far, why not just have the baby? We would have helped you. Rachel, you know we would have helped you."

Fatima was crying now. She was always emotional when pregnant, but she rarely cried. Rachel knew she was heartbroken, and she felt guilty about involving her, but she wasn't going to let Fatima get the best of her. Rachel wasn't going to break down again. She had been through enough.

"Please, I don't need this now." Rachel ran her fingers through her hair clutching the roots and looked out the window to try and remain composed. Fatima's crying was shaking her up.

"You? You? Is it always just about you? You had no right!" Fatima was having difficulty containing her anger.

Rachel decided to be *more* angry. "Excuse me? Who has the right then? It's my life, my body."

"You're sitting in my car talking about your life? Didn't you call me to pick you up? Doesn't your life affect everyone around you? You don't live in a bubble. You have a lot of talk for someone who couldn't even find her own way home." Rachel avoided looking at Fatima and did not respond.

11

Fatima continued, "You want to talk about your right? You had the right to use your head. You had the right to choose wisely. You had the right not to throw yourself around and abuse yourself! You had the right to make choices that were good for you long before today." Fatima sobbed while she rested her head in her hands, her elbows on the wheel. "You had no right. You had no right."

People looked inside the car as they passed by, but Rachel rolled on without a second thought. Fatima just didn't know who Jamie was. "That's fine for you to say, *Miss Perfect Life*. Sorry I don't have the ideal, professional-basketball-playing husband to take care of me."

"Give it up! You're no different from me. You chose your path. I can't believe you could do this. Is it even legal this late?"

"Uh, well, it was in a hospital," Rachel snapped back, as Fatima started up the car.

"This is disgusting. I can't even hear this." She pulled the car into traffic.

"Fatima please, I'm sorry, I can't handle this now. I just want to go home." Rachel started crying again too. She was not surprised at Fatima's reaction. She hated involving her, but she had had no choice. She had no one else to call.

"Does your mother know about this?" Fatima softened her voice but kept her eyes and head straight ahead. The traffic was getting heavy as they approached rush hour.

"What? Mrs. Thou Shalt Burn in Hell? I don't think so."

"You really underestimate Naomi. She's more understanding than you think."

Rachel fanned her hand in front of her face. That was a signal to Fatima that she had had enough. She was finished now. She had no more energy for this topic.

They turned onto their street, the street they had both grown up on. It was early April and the mature trees that lined their street were budding. There had been heavy rains in the last week and the sprawling lawns were green. Many houses had early spring flowers already in their gardens. The neighbourhood had primarily older residents and the lawns were always well kept. Most of the children had grown up and moved away. Houses didn't often go for sale on this street.

Rachel and Fatima had lived one house away from each other, Rachel at 108 and Fatima at 112. A few years after Rachel had moved in, another family moved into number 110, with a boy that was destined to come between them forever.

"I thought Ali was away?" Rachel had spotted Ali in his driveway, stepping out of his black Range Rover. Ali and Fatima had married shortly after Fatima's high school graduation. Ali had already been playing professional basketball for one year and had bought the house across the street because they both wanted to stay close to their parents.

Fatima always said she wanted her children to be close to their grandparents and with Ali on the road so much, it was a big help. If Fatima wanted to travel with him, their three girls had more than enough people to take care of them.

"Actually, I thought he was coming back on Friday," Fatima said, as she pulled into Rachel's circular driveway and curved around the flower bed island.

"Humph, maybe he's checking up on you. No telling what you're bound to do with your growing belly and all." Rachel's attempt at a joke had no effect on Fatima. Ali had noticed them and stood waiting in his driveway for his wife.

Fatima temporarily parked in Rachel's driveway; the same driveway that they had played hopscotch and spud in thousands of times. In spite of her anger Rachel sensed that Fatima was happy to be there for her. She did seem happiest when caring for others.

After Rachel left the car, Fatima drove out and into her own driveway. Rachel slowly walked towards her front door. Yes, she had made some bad decisions in her life. One really. Jamie. She just kept on paying for it. She couldn't change the past. She had to deal with the present. The abortions were history. There was nothing to do but take care of herself and her sons. Whatever decisions she made had been best for her. She was sure of that.

Rachel paused before she reached her front door. The street was quiet, and she could hear Ali's and Fatima's conversation. She knew Fatima would not tell Ali anything about the events of the day, but she still felt compelled to listen anyway.

"*As-salaam alaikum*-peace be onto you," Fatima greeted her husband. "Am I confused, or are you home early?"

"*Wa alaikum as-salaam wa rahmatullahi wa barakatu*. Is everything ok?"

"I was going to ask you the same thing," Fatima responded.

"Change of plans." Ali looked past Fatima, across the street.

Fatima usually kept on top of Ali's game schedule, but with her own exams coming up, and being in the last trimester of her pregnancy, she had been too preoccupied.

"I didn't sleep too well last night. You sure everything's all right?" Ali's gaze settled back on Fatima.

"Everything's fine." Fatima turned to look across the street at Rachel. The two women's eyes met before they turned away and entered their homes.

Once inside her door Rachel leaned against the heavy wood frame. She hated this house since her father had died. Nothing was the same anymore. She felt like she was on a fast downward spiral. What had really happened to her today? How is it she had made a promise to herself that she could not keep? She had promised she would never terminate another pregnancy. Yet she had. Who was she really?

She knew Jamie would come around again, maybe tomorrow, maybe next week, or maybe weeks from now. He would continue to float in and out of her life until she put a stop to it. She was definitely ready to end it. She had been at the lowest point in her life today. Things had to change.

Chapter Two

ॼ

Fatima stretched in her bed and looked up at her ceiling. She still smiled every time she saw it. Ali had written a poem on the ceiling in their bedroom when they had bought the house. She still had no idea how he had managed to do it, but he had, and it had been completed before they moved in. Whenever he had out of town games it comforted her in his absence. She always slept peacefully as a result.

Today she woke up feeling the weight of the world on her shoulders. How could her best friend have been going through something so serious and not have confided in her? Yesterday it seemed that she was so angry with Rachel, and she definitely was, but she was also angry with herself. If she had been the kind of friend that she should be, she should have known something was wrong. Rachel should have felt comfortable to turn to her. She was partly to blame for this whole mess. How could she not have seen the signs? Was she so engrossed in her own family that she had neglected someone close to her who was in need? She could never let that happen again.

Fatima heard the front door and knew Ali was returning from his parent's house. Every morning he joined his father for *fajr*-morning prayers and often had breakfast with Mama and Papa before returning home. In good weather Fatima would go with him and bring their daughters, but on days like today she was very happy that the best place for a woman to pray was her bedroom. She smiled and snuggled under her duvet.

Her room faced the front of their house, and with the window open she could clearly hear the birds playing. They were lucky enough to have blue jays nesting nearby. She loved the beautiful blue birds and had one in particular that she was trying to teach to talk. She imagined them splashing in the backyard fountain in between the trees.

Ali had planted a fruit tree each time a child was born. He had planted a cherry tree for five-year-old Masuma, an apple tree for three-year-old Laila and a pear tree for her twin sister Batool.

"Ali, should I put Fatima's food in the fridge?"

Fatima could hear the voice of Rahma, Ali's younger sister. She often came over in the morning to help with the children, use the computer and socialize.

"No, just leave it on the table. I'll see if she's up."

"Ali, do you think I'm a good friend to Rachel?" Fatima hit him with the question as soon as he walked through the bedroom door.

At 6 feet 4 inches, Ali had an undeniable presence. Many people were intimidated when first meeting him, due to his serious demeanor. Only those closest to him knew the warm and loving man he could be. Though he indeed viewed and approached life seriously, anyone who was fortunate enough to catch one of his smiles knew there was more to him than appearances revealed.

"Of course you are. The best. Who else would do all that you do for her?" Ali replied.

"Do you think I'm trustworthy?" Fatima sat up surrounded by white bedding, her current favourite colour.

"I trust you with my life," Ali said as he sat on the side of the bed. "What's this about?"

"Well, do you think I'm too hard on her? You know, maybe I make her feel bad sometimes?"

"I knew something was up." Ali straightened his back. "What is it? Jamie?" His voice flattened. They all felt the same way about Jamie. They had seen how he had treated Rachel over the years, and how much her two sons suffered because of his neglect. No one was a fan of Jamie, and he and Ali had had more than one confrontation in the past.

"No. No, she's ok. I was just thinking, that's all."

The look on Ali's face let Fatima know that he understood there was more, but he wasn't going to press her. He knew when to give a woman her space. He stood up and walked towards the walk-in closet that connected their bedroom to the bathroom.

"How are Mama and Papa this morning?" Fatima asked, with a smile on her face. She loosened the scrunchie she had holding her dark hair and let the long layers fall down her back. She loved those two people dearly.

"Great. Mama made her traditional welcome home breakfast for me."

"She is so funny. She does that every time. Shouldn't it be reserved for when people return from long trips?"

"Hey, who's going to argue with Mama?" Ali tilted his head, raising his eyebrows over eyes that were the colour of iced tea. He flashed his signature smile revealing a dimple in his left cheek.

Mama was from a small village in Rwanda and Papa had been an Italian missionary when they had met. He had spent 15 years in Rwanda building churches and schools and ministering to the people of Mama's village. He and Mama had married and built a fairly large following. After the massacre in 1994, many people had their faith shaken when they saw Tutsi and Hutus in the same church turn against each other. Some churches had ministers who had preached and supported the killings from the pulpit.

Mama and Papa had been sheltered by Muslim neighbours who had refused to get involved in the violence. Their brotherhood through faith was more significant than ethnicity. Many people were protected in Muslim neighbourhoods until the unrest had ceased. After 100 days, Mama and Papa had emerged to a broken country. They eventually made their way to Canada.

Naturally, their interest in Islam had been stimulated, and after a period of diligent study they had taken *shahada*, declaring themselves Muslims. Ali had been 10 years old at the time. Rahma was born soon after.

Both children were a beautiful combination of their dual heritage. Ali was definitely his father's son, but with the perfect bronze skin that gave homage to his African ancestry. Rahma had the small neat features of her mother, combined with an olive skin tone much closer to her father's complexion.

"Well, I'm going to make some porridge." Fatima turned down her duvet and moved to get out of her bed.

"Don't bother. I have breakfast for you in the kitchen." Ali usually brought her breakfast in the morning. When he was away his parents delivered her food or sent it with Rahma. Mama's welcome home breakfast was a favourite of Fatima's because she knew the love and care that went into it. It consisted of traditional Rwandan foods prepared in Mama's special style.

Fried sweet potatoes, beans and sweet cornbread were always served with fruit salad topped with homemade whipped cream and, of course, tea.

Mama kept a secret mixture of spices for her "*save your life*" tea. She claimed that if you were on your last leg, this tea would bring you back to life. They had all tried to recreate it but could never get it right. She had promised to reveal the recipe in her will.

"I'll eat it. The porridge isn't for me," Fatima said.

"Ah, it's for Rachel," Ali said.

Fatima smiled. Her mother was Jamaican, and they had a running joke in the family about the way Jamaicans used cornmeal porridge as an all-purpose cure. If you were sick you needed cornmeal porridge. If you were healthy, fat, thin, pre/post-surgery, during pregnancy, after childbirth, had an underweight baby, big baby, loss of appetite, digestive problems, hungry or thirsty, all conditions and situations called for cornmeal porridge.

"But she's ok?" Ali did not sound convinced. "That's fine. I'll let you ladies have your little secret. I'm going to the gym and then I have practice."

"Remember, Joshua starts soccer tonight." Fatima stood and started to stretch.

"Of course I remember. I'll be back by five."

Rachel's oldest son was starting soccer and Ali was one of the coaches. They were all so excited to see Joshua growing up. Fatima had always felt a little guilty about the way events had unfolded for her and Ali. They all had been best friends growing up. They had done everything together. Fatima was an only child and Rachel and Ali were like a brother and sister to her. When she became Muslim and married Ali, everything changed. She always felt that she had stolen Rachel's best friend. Then Jamie turned out to be a dead beat and Rachel was left alone. Fatima just felt obligated to share Ali, at least for the sake of the boys.

"Ali, you're going to the gym on a full stomach?" Fatima asked.

"I have a few errands to run first. That should give me enough time to digest Mama's meal." Ali winked and disappeared into the closet.

Fatima prepared to shower and change into her workout clothes for her daily yoga routine before heading to the kitchen. Rachel usually came over in the mornings. She wanted her porridge to be ready.

Fatima's kitchen had been renovated to include stainless steel appliances, floor to ceiling cabinets and an over sized double sink kitchen island where she dreamed of making bread and pastry. She had just turned off the stove when she heard the doorbell.

"Ooh, baby blue, how cute is that? Does that mean you might actually have a boy this time?" Rachel teased Fatima about her blue yoga outfit that barely covered her growing belly.

"Will you get in here so I can close the door?" Fatima stood behind the door, the way she always did when she answered the door with no *hijab*-covering.

Rachel stepped into the foyer. It was a large space decorated with mature plants. Islamic calligraphy hung on the walls and, in the centre of the foyer, a vase of flowers rested on a tall round marble table. To the left, a winding staircase led to the upper level of the house. "Who told you to come to the door exposed?" Rachel joked with Fatima.

"Nobody wants to see you anyway," Rachel continued. "Now that husband of yours, that's another story."

Fatima looked at Rachel and almost felt like she was looking at herself. The two were often mistaken for sisters. They often sported the same haircut; though Fatima's hair grew fast when she was pregnant and was now well past her shoulders. They had similar features and skin tone. The only major difference was height. Rachel was at least three inches taller than Fatima. Still, on more than one occasion someone had actually mistaken Rachel for Fatima or vice versa. They always got a kick out of that, especially since Fatima wore *hijab,* and Rachel didn't.

"You don't stay down long," Fatima replied. She looked at her friend intently. She certainly looked better than yesterday, and her spirits seemed up. One could never tell with Rachel though, she used her sarcastic humour as a defense mechanism all too often.

Rachel came in and took a seat at the kitchen table.

"How are you feeling?" Fatima asked.

"Fine. I really am sorry about yesterday. I just didn't know who else to call."

"I know. I'm glad you called me. We'll talk about it later, ok?"

"Thanks," Rachel replied. She then looked down at her hands resting on the tiled tabletop. "I know I shouldn't need to ask, but you didn't say anything to Ali, did you? I can't imagine what he would think of me."

Fatima was shocked. "Of course not. No need to worry, on both counts. You know he would never judge you. If anything, I think it would just make him angrier at Jamie."

At the mention of Jamie's name, Rachel shifted nervously in her seat. Fatima noticed and changed the subject.

"Are you hungry?"

"What's cooking?" Rachel tilted her head.

"Porridge," Fatima said as she tried to suppress a smile.

"Cornmeal?" Rachel asked

"Of course."

The two ladies burst into laughter. "Fati, I am so sorry, forgive me?"

Fatima held Rachel's face and kissed both sides. "Of course. I just wish you had told me everything. I just wished I could have been there for you. I still don't understand why you did it. It doesn't make sense to me. And why are you still allowing Jamie so much access to your life?"

"Well, it's over now. We can move on." Rachel, eager to change the subject, looked towards the front door and commented on socks that were stuffed into Ali's shoes. "What's with the socks?"

"He always puts his socks in his shoes when he takes them off. Sometimes one pair will become like a storage place. He'll have three or four pairs of socks in a shoe. You never noticed?"

"No, have you talked to him about that?"

"A million times. Anyway, that's nothing. Try looking under the couch, beside the bed, in the computer room, you name it. He says it's an illness he's had since childhood. Finally, he suggested that we each be allowed one bad habit."

"You actually agreed to that?"

"Sure. I used to get so irate about it, then one day Mama was here, and after I told Ali off about it, she looked so hurt I could have died. I actually think the suggestion came from her."

"What's your bad habit?" Rachel leaned over the table.

"I would never tell you!" Fatima was aghast.

Rachel looked back at the socks. "Girl, that would drive me mad."

Fatima smiled mischievously. "You have a man that comes around once every six months, doesn't support his two sons, has you all hospitalized, and you're complaining about socks?"

"No, but come on, that's crazy! You know I'm a neat freak."

"You're crazy." Fatima turned away from Rachel and reached for the pot on the stove.

"No girl, that's crazy." Rachel insisted as she pointed at the shoes stuffed with socks. "Thank goodness he has at least one fault. He was making the rest of us look bad."

Fatima raised her eyebrows. "One? He has many. I just don't talk about them. You know that as well as I do. You practically grew up in his house." Fatima served Rachel her porridge and sat down across from her with a cup of herbal tea. She would eat her breakfast after her workout.

"So, where is everybody?" Rachel asked.

"The girls are still sleeping, and Rahma is probably in the computer room, as usual. Ali is getting ready to go out."

Rahma was taking online courses for one semester while working with her father's non-profit organization as a co-op assignment.

"Make sure Ali knows I'm here. I wouldn't want him to come down indecent or anything." Rachel started to eat.

"He knows you're here. He'll let me know when he's coming down. Anyway, how are you feeling today? You seemed to be in a lot of pain yesterday. Is that normal?"

"I don't know, I'm not an expert or anything, but I do feel better, although the cramping is pretty bad."

"You should call the doctor, just to be sure. How is the bleeding?"

"Heavy."

"Clotting?"

"Don't ask. I was brave to come over here. I feel like I should just spend the day in the washroom."

"Hmm, make sure you at least call them," Fatima said.

"Fatima," Ali called from the second floor. When Fatima indicated that it was all right for him to come down, he descended the stairs and entered the kitchen, where he greeted Rachel.

"Rachel, how are you doing?"

"Good. Where are you off to so early?"

"The gym."

Rachel eyed him from head to toe. "You're not dressed for the gym." Ali wore casual pants and a knit top.

"I have some errands to run first. Is that all right with you?"

"I'm just saying you *are* a ball player. It's not like you're not used to going around in sweats. It must be something special." Rachel continued eating.

"Fatima, I'll call you later." Ali bent to put on his shoes.

Rachel moved to stand in the double doorway and called after Ali as he walked across the stone porch, "Don't be mad, Ali, you know Fati is my girl. I just have to make sure everything is on the up and up over here." She then turned to Fatima. "Don't you have a gym downstairs?"

Fatima laughed and shook her head. "Did I mention you were crazy?"

"Look, you've got mail." Rachel took the mail from the box and handed several envelopes to Fatima.

"Thanks." Fatima flipped through the letters and junk mail and stopped at one piece of mail addressed to Ali. It was from a lawyer's office. She didn't recognize the name or address. It was not even from their city. *Strange.*

"Why don't you open it?" Rachel had not left Fatima's side after giving her the mail.

Fatima dropped her hand, removing the letter from Rachel's line of vision. "Girl, do you always have to be in my business?"

"I'm just saying, I'm standing right here. You want me to pretend I don't see it? You know I can't lie. Me, I would open it."

"I can't do that. I'll just give it to him later." Fatima turned the envelope over in her hand.

"What could it be about?" Rachel pressed.

"I don't know," Fatima admitted.

"And you're the wife, so you know I don't know." Rachel stepped aside allowing Fatima access to the kitchen. Fatima continued to look at the envelope as if the answer could come through the paper. "Strange."

"Fati, are you ok?"

"Sure," Fatima answered absentmindedly.

"Are you sure?"

Fatima didn't respond. She placed the letter with the rest of the mail in the mail holder and returned to finish her cup of tea.

"So, what plans do you have today?" Rachel asked.

"After I work out, I have a meeting with your mom."

"Really, what about?"

"She's having some of the ladies from her church group over for lunch. They wanted to meet some Muslim women and talk about Islam. I guess they have a lot of questions."

Naomi was a devout Christian who had family roots in Canada for generations. Her great-great-grandparents had travelled through the Underground Railroad to settle in Southern Ontario. Rachel's father had been from the Caribbean.

Naomi had raised three children by herself after her husband's death. She had suffered through depression and had lost her two older children to foster care because she had been unable to care for them. Mama, who had seen the writing on the wall, had taken legal guardianship of Rachel just before the Children's Aid Society had become involved. Rachel had lived with Mama for a few years until Naomi was able to reclaim custody of her. By then, the older children were living independently. Rachel's elder brother and sister had moved to different cities and rarely kept in touch, aside from the occasional phone call.

Naomi had developed diabetes in later years and was legally blind as a result. In spite of all her problems, she was a ray of light and full of love and happiness. Fatima loved her as much as she did her own mother and Mama.

Fatima's mother was also a single parent, and her work as an archaeologist took her around the world. Dana had named her daughter Fatima, after the famous Portuguese city where she had met her husband while he was working on a project for a British Museum.

Due to her frequent travel, Dana's house remained empty most of the time. Living across the street enabled Fatima and Ali to watch over it. As a result of Dana's absence, Fatima often turned to Naomi and Mama when she needed motherly support. Today Fatima was happy to spend time with Naomi's church sisters, and was always thrilled to have the opportunity to talk about Islam, especially if it meant dispelling myth's and misunderstandings. Mama would attend the meeting with her.

"Remember you need to see the doctor, or call, or something," Fatima reminded Rachel.

"Yes, I will for sure. I better get out of here and let you get ready." Rachel finished her breakfast and stood to leave. "See you later. Thanks for everything."

"Let me know what happens."

After Rachel left the house, Fatima cleaned up the kitchen and started her yoga routine while her girls were still sleeping. Fatima was not going to wake them up if she didn't have to. Rahma would stay with them while she went to Naomi's.

Chapter Three

𝕵

When Fatima arrived the other ladies had already been seated and were engaged in chit-chat. Naomi's home, as usual, smelled sweet. When they were kids they regularly made excuses to go inside. They had to use the washroom, or they were hurt. Then they would start sniffing. "Hmm, I smell something," would always be the standard line.

Naomi would smile her knowing smile and say, "I wonder what it could be? Maybe it's window cleaner. I just did the windows."

"No, that's not it," the child would say.

"Maybe it's laundry soap? I did the laundry this morning."

"No, I think it's something to eat?" they would reply.

"Oh." Naomi would put her hand to her head as though the answer had just come to her. "Could it be this?" Then she would lift a cover from a dish to reveal her treat of the day. It might be cookies or cake or her special tarts.

Whatever it was they all loved them just as much as Naomi loved making them, but they knew Naomi got the greatest joy from seeing people eat her food. She was the same way now. As

Fatima entered the house the same familiar sweet aroma, coming from Naomi's kitchen, comforted her immediately.

"Ms. Naomi? It's Fatima."

"Come on in. We're all waiting for you," Naomi called from the upper level.

Fatima climbed the stairs from the small foyer to reach the living room. "Sorry I'm late." She kissed Naomi on the cheek and hugged her. She then took a seat beside Mama and turned to greet the other ladies.

There were three women in Naomi's living room. Sister Harrison, Sister Charles and Sister Barclay were all seated and ready to start the session. Sister Harrison, about 30 years old, was the church secretary and the mother of three small children. She was cute and perky, with what Fatima liked to call a ski slope nose. She had her black hair cut in a chin length bob. She was the first to greet Fatima.

"Hi, just call me Susan."

Sister Charles was in her late 40's and very stern. It was said that when you got to know her she was the warmest, most generous person, as long as you made sure not to get on her wrong side. She ran all the children's programs, and was part of the visiting committee. She was said to have a firm but loving hand.

Sister Barclay was about 60 and very friendly, in a grandmotherly sort of way. Fatima knew her well. She was often in the neighbourhood visiting and taking Naomi to appointments when the rest of the family was not available. "Fatima darling, it's so good to see you again," Sister Barclay said.

"Thank you, Sister Barclay. It's good to see you too."

Sister Barclay looked at Naomi. "I noticed your lovely garden. I can't wait to see all the flowers come in. They were so beautiful last year. I was admiring the yard before I came in. Lilies are my absolute favourite. I just love them." She then turned to Fatima. "Naomi told me about the mystery gardener."

"Yes, that's my Ali," Naomi said with pride. "He planted everything just the way I told him to. Even though I can barely see, when the sun shines just right, I can see them." Naomi smoothed out her blouse over her trousers the way she usually did when she had finished making a point.

"We're expecting a few others, but we can get started. I know the ladies have a lot of questions. Maybe we can start by introducing ourselves. You all know me. I'm Naomi and I have three children. I live with Rachel, my youngest, and her two sons, the lights of my life, Joshua and Jonah. I arranged this meeting because the sisters in my ladies group have a keen interest and curiosity in the lives of Muslim women, and who better to ask than Muslim women."

The ladies all introduced themselves as some of Fatima's and Mama's friends arrived. Lena was the divorced mother of an autistic boy. She was pursuing her PhD in education. She rushed to hug Fatima as soon as she entered. She rubbed Fatima's tummy and said, "Look at you! I'm so jealous!"

Fatima pushed her playfully. "Don't say that! Take it back."

"Ok, I take it back. You know I'm happy for you."

"I know, and don't worry, your turn will come."

"When? When?" she asked spiritedly.

Saniya entered holding her youngest child, a six-month-old girl. "Fatima, are you trying to catch up to me?" She was 31 and the mother of six.

"I think you would have to stop for me to do that. It doesn't look like that's happening soon!"

They were about to get started when the last lady made her entrance. "I'm here!" They all looked at each other.

"Nahla," the ladies said in unison. Nahla ran a theatre company that performed in the schools as well as in her downtown playhouse. She was known for making an entrance.

When they were all seated, the questions started.

"Do you guys have arranged marriages? Are you allowed to choose your own husband?" Susan was the first to start talking.

"Absolutely, you choose your own husband. You should take advice from parents. We all want our parents' blessings. Also, parents or friends may introduce potential partners, but in the end it is the choice of the couple," Saniya responded.

"Can you date?" Susan continued.

"No, there is no dating in the usual sense. You can talk and get to know the person that way, but there is no relationship before marriage."

"Then how would you get to know each other?" Sister Charles asked.

"There are many ways. First you need to know what you are looking for. Then, if you know the kind of questions to ask and how to judge the answers that is a big help. Also, talking to people who know them, people who live with them, have travelled with them and done business with them will help determine their true character. It's more accurate than trying to figure out if the person they are presenting to you is the real deal."

"What's the difference between Muslims and Islam?" Sister Barclay asked.

"Islam is the religion, belief in one God and the belief that Muhammad(saw)-may Allah honour him and give him peace) is His last Prophet. A Muslim is the person who practices the religion of Islam," Lena said.

"How do you become a Muslim? Can anybody be a Muslim?"

Fatima was tickled at the eager questioning of the ladies. With all the information available about Islam it still amazed her that the same basic questions were always asked. She was happy for the opportunity to share with these charitable and open-minded ladies.

"Yes, Islam is for all people and for all times. You become a Muslim by declaring that there is no God but God, and Muhammad(saw) is His messenger."

"Who is *Allah*?" Sister Charles asked.

No matter how many times this question had been answered,

Christians had the most difficulty accepting the answer. "*Allah* is the Creator of the Universe, the God of Adam and Eve and all the Prophets including Jesus(as) and Muhammad(saw). The Arabic word for God is *Allah*. Christian Arabs also say *Allah*."

"So you believe in Jesus?" Susan sat forward in her chair. Fatima sat back and let another sister tackle this question.

"Yes, absolutely we do. We love and revere Jesus(as) very much and believe he will return at the end of time. The *Quran* tells us that he did not die on the cross, but *Allah* made it seem so to the people. *Allah* rescued him and took him up to heaven."

The questions continued until noon. The ladies asked about family and children and friendship with non-Muslims. They were particularly interested in Mama's experiences in Rwanda, becoming Muslim and being married to Papa.

"How did you survive during the war?" Susan asked gently.

"The tensions had been growing for weeks. Of course, no one imagined that it would end the way it did, but Tutsis were being harassed constantly and even beaten in the streets on a regular basis. We started to get very nervous at the beginning of April," Mama replied.

"Then we heard that the killings were starting in the villages. My friend told me that we should come to her neighbourhood. It was a Muslim neighbourhood and there were both Hutus and Tutsis living there, as in many areas, but these people had vowed not to let anyone enter their neighbourhood and harm anyone.

"My husband had agreed that I should go, but he headed to one of the village churches because we heard that many people had gathered there for sanctuary. He decided to stay with them, if necessary, thinking he might be able to reason with the death squads if they came." Mama scoffed at her own mention of the death squads. "Reason with death squads? Can you imagine? How wrong he was. He barely escaped with his life."

The women hung on Mama's every word. "He was actually able to keep them off for hours, since they were not targeting foreigners, but eventually negotiations were up, and they just started chopping everyone in sight. Papa got his left leg badly injured but was able to escape to the bush, where he hid for days, until he was able to make his way to my hiding place, with a few other parishioners."

"How long did you stay in hiding?" Susan asked.

"100 days."

"What happened during that time?"

"Several times the death squads came, but our neighbours protected us. They went out with rocks, knives, bows and arrows. They would not permit the squads to advance one inch. There was even a case of death squads setting fire to a *masjid*-Muslim place of worship but being too afraid to enter and kill the people. They thought the Muslims had some kind of magic." Mama laughed. "It was no magic, just *Allah*."

"Why didn't the Muslim Hutus join in the massacre also?" Sister Barclay joined in the questioning.

"Their bond in faith was just more important than ethnicity. They understood clearly what it means to serve God. They not only protected Muslim Tutsis but non-Muslims as well." Mama sat calmly in her seat as she related her story. "It was well-known that the safest place to be was in a Muslim neighbourhood. They stood together in those neighbourhoods.

"You know, after the massacre some of those murderers even converted to Islam so they could hide, from prosecution, in Muslim areas. Some of them were sincere of course. They really wanted to seek purification and ablution from their sins."

"So no Muslims ever came to harm you?" Susan questioned.

"Yes, there were a few. And you know what they were told? 'If you dare come to hurt anyone, first tear the *Quran* and denounce your faith.' Do you think they could do it? Never. They turned away, every one of them."

"They would not tear the *Quran* and denounce their faith?"

"They could never do it."

"Wow." Susan thought of her own small children and wondered how she could survive something so horrendous. "How old were your children?" she asked.

"Rahma wasn't born yet, but Ali was ten at the time. That's when he got the name Ali. Our friends started calling him Ali because every time the men would go out, Ali would cry and cry because he wanted to go too. The men had organized a system for watching the neighbourhood, and they needed to work in shifts. Ali had made his own bow and set of arrows, and he would beg to patrol with them.

"They said he was as brave as *Imam Ali (as)*. So we called him Ali from then. When we came to Canada he insisted on taking martial arts, archery, everything. He said never again would he allow people to be hurt while he stood by." Mama wiped a tear from her cheek.

"What about the rest of your family?" Susan asked. The whole room fell silent while they waited for Mama's reply. All that could be heard was the ticking of the kitchen clock. Fatima who was seated beside Mama moved closer, put one arm around her shoulder and held her opposite hand.

"Most of them, dead. My mother is still missing." Mama rose to her feet and left the room.

"Oh, we are so sorry," Susan whispered through her hands that now covered her mouth.

"It's ok. You didn't know." Fatima cleared her throat and adjusted her clothes as she thought of Mama's anguish not knowing if her mother were dead or alive and what had happened to her.

Mama's family had been miles away from the church that she and Papa had been working at. When the killings started there was no way to get to them or even get information about them. It was something that had haunted Mama all these years.

Naomi let out a heavy sigh. "Let's have lunch."

Fatima, eager to change the mood of the room, jumped to her feet and offered to help, but when she entered the kitchen she realized that Naomi had already prepared all the food.

"Ms. Naomi, you did everything."

"With my new kitchen, everything is easy now." Naomi came close to Fatima and patted her hand.

"Wow Sister Grant, this kitchen is amazing. Look at all these gadgets. It must have cost a fortune." Susan stood behind Fatima.

"Yes, I'm sure it did. With all these bells and whistles I can cook gourmet meals all by myself." Naomi's new appliances all had ridges and Braille overlay, and the stove had special easy to use timers along with a sound system to alert the user if the stove was on, off, on high, medium or low heat. Everything had large knobs with loud clicking sounds. There was even a master switch, in case of emergency or doubt, to turn off everything in the kitchen at once. The floor had special markers to remind her where she was without having to touch anything.

The ladies helped themselves to an assortment of finger foods, casseroles, desserts and, of course, Naomi's famous fruit tarts.

"So Fatima, your husband is a point guard for the Razors?" Sister Charles inquired.

"Yes, he is." Fatima was used to having people ask her about her husband and his basketball career.

"Oh, I've seen him, such a handsome boy," Sister Barclay said, as she returned to her seat, just steps away from the kitchen.

"Thank you, he looks just like my husband." Mama had re-emerged from the back room looking refreshed. She was a pretty woman. Her dark skin was smooth and youthful, and her brown eyes were round and soft. She was about 5'7", with a small frame. Still, her presence was unforgettable.

"That's not all true, Mama," Fatima said. "He's a lot like you. He may have Papa's height and some of his features, but he has your bone structure and your voice. He has your beautiful rich voice."

Mama indeed had a beautiful voice. Although Papa had taught their children the basics of *Quran* reading, she had taught them to recite *The Holy Quran* and *dua*-supplications in the most breathtaking way. No matter how many times Fatima heard Ali recite, it still touched her heart and brought tears to her eyes.

"Either way, *he is gorgeous*. How do you deal with all the groupies?" Susan asked, as she bit into a tart.

"Well..." Before Fatima could answer, Mama interrupted.

"There are no groupies," Mama answered in her definitive way. "We have trained our son well, and we could send him safely to the moon. I am sure of that." No one dared to disagree.

Susan cleared her throat. "I see," she said in her perky little way.

"Well," Fatima added carefully, "in his first year of playing his father travelled with him all the time. He was so young; his parents wanted to make sure he was all right on the road. After we got married, Papa insisted that I travel with him. It was tough, because I had just started university, but it worked out. We actually had a lot of fun that first year."

"What about now?" Susan raised her eyebrows over her cup of tea.

"It is harder now, with three little ones, but we're all pretty comfortable with the arrangement. Still, if he needs me, I'm there. I have so much support here, it's fairly easy to pick up and go if I have to."

"Does that happen? Will he just call and ask you to come?"

"Sure. Not often, but it has happened," Fatima replied.

"And what, you just drop everything and go?" Susan pressed.

"No questions asked." Fatima shrugged.

Susan chuckled and lifted her tea cup. "I would too, if I were you. You just never know."

"Now, leave the girl alone. Enough about her business; this is not a meeting to discuss her marriage," Naomi interrupted.

"Oh, but it's so interesting. A young Muslim basketball player and his family right here in the neighbourhood. You know I need all the details," Susan squealed.

The women continued to eat and talk for one hour, then started to leave. "Well, thank you all for coming." Naomi seemed truly pleased at the success of this first meeting.

"We should do this again. There is so much more I want to know. It was so much fun," Susan piped up.

"Yes, it certainly was informative. How about next week, same time?" Sister Charles suggested.

"Sounds great. Let's consider it confirmed. Fatima, could you stay for a minute? I want to talk to you," Naomi said.

"Sure."

After the ladies had left, Fatima sat beside Naomi. "Did you want me to help you clean up?"

"No, no, I just wanted to talk to you." Naomi paused, and then turned her face towards Fatima. "Is Rachel all right?"

Fatima, a little nervous, responded with a question, "What do you mean?"

"She didn't go to the swim club this week, and you know how committed she is to coaching." Naomi paused as if wondering if she should continue. "And a few weeks ago, Jamie was here." Naomi nervously folded her hands in her lap.

"A few weeks ago? Are you sure?" Fatima thought Rachel had said it had been months since the last time she had seen him.

"Yes, I saw him," Naomi insisted.

Fatima widened her eyes and looked doubtful. "Ms. Naomi, you saw him?"

"Yes, my sight comes and goes. Sometimes I can see a little. The doctor thinks it's my imagination, but I know it was Jamie that day."

Fatima kept listening.

"After that day she was acting strange, you know; real quiet and sulky. Then yesterday, after you dropped her home, she went straight to bed. She was real sick last night."

Fatima smiled. "Ms. Naomi, how did you know that I dropped her home?"

"Fatima please, you know I know your car. I heard you drop her off, and I heard her sneak in and go to her room. I also heard her crying all night." Naomi's face became red and she flared her nostrils.

Fatima knew how difficult it had been for her since her husband had died. She had become a completely different person after the accident. Naomi never fully recovered after the shock of losing her husband and always felt guilty that she had not been emotionally and psychologically available to help her children during their mourning.

Now she wanted only to connect with Rachel and help her raise her sons, but Rachel always seemed like she was avoiding spending any real time with her mother. Fatima knew this caused Naomi deep sadness.

Fatima remained silent, trying to avoid a response. Naomi waited. "I'm sure she'll be fine," Fatima finally said.

"You're a good friend, Fatima." Naomi patted her hand. "I know you won't betray her trust. Just make sure she gets what she needs, please?"

"Of course." Fatima was embarrassed by Naomi's comments. Naomi knew that Fatima was withholding information, but what choice did she have? She couldn't tell Naomi about what had happened to Rachel. It wasn't her place to do so.

Naomi wagged her finger. "I told her if that boy comes around she should just call the police. He is up to some trouble. I can just smell it. He usually comes at night. No shame that boy has, no shame I tell you. She has enough reason to get a restraining order. I don't know why she won't do it. Talk to her, please Fatima, maybe you can get through to her."

"I will," Fatima promised, and she intended to keep it. She would talk to Rachel later in the day.

Fatima smiled as she walked home. How did these old people know everything? You couldn't put anything past them at all. Well, it was good. *We all need people looking out for us*, Fatima thought.

So, Jamie had been here. Fatima couldn't get that out of her mind. Rachel hadn't told her that. Why not? What had happened? Why was he here two weeks ago? *Why didn't we see him?* He usually made a big production out of his visits. It stayed on Fatima's mind for the rest of the day.

Chapter Four

꒲

Fatima returned to find that her children had eaten lunch and were ready for their nap. Rahma read them a few stories and put them to bed. After Rahma left, Fatima tried to study, but she was exhausted and fell asleep too.

When she woke up it was after 5 p.m., and the house was quiet. The girls never slept this long. Fatima went to check on them and saw that they were not in their rooms.

Realizing Ali must be home, she went to look downstairs and found him in the kitchen. "*As-salaam alaikum*, where are the girls?" Fatima rubbed her face to help herself wake up.

"*Wa alaikum as-salaam*, Papa came over. He wanted to visit with them. I told him you were sleeping, so it would be better to keep them at his house."

Papa never needed a reason to take the girls. He lived for them. He often came by to play with them or help take care of them in some way. He had built a huge playground for them in his back-yard and they spent many days out there. He also taught them regularly. All the girls had started reading *Quran* and the oldest had already memorized much of the 30th part of the Holy Book.

"Did they eat?" Fatima had prepared dinner before going to Naomi's house.

Ali leaned against the black marble of the kitchen island. "Are you joking? You think I would feed them if they're going over there? What would happen if they refused Mama's food? She would probably think they're sick."

Fatima laughed. "You're right. They'll have more than enough to eat over there. Did they use the washroom?"

"Yes, yes, Fatima, they're fine. Relax. Here sit." She looked behind Ali and could see that the letters were missing from the letter holder.

Fatima was eager to find out what was going on, but she was hoping that Ali would tell her voluntarily. She slid into the bench of the booth where they usually took their meals. "So what time did you get home?"

"About 45 minutes ago." Still leaning against the island, he watched her closely. Fatima knew that look. He had something to tell her and was trying to find the right way to do it.

"How was your day?" Fatima's eyes scanned the kitchen in search of the mysterious letter.

"Good, nothing special. Coach worked us hard though."

"You look tired. Are you hungry?" Fatima started to get up to prepare his food.

"Actually, I am, but I can wait. Come, I need to talk to you."

Fatima's curiosity was at its peak. She followed Ali to the family room at the back of the house and sat beside him as he indicated.

"I need to go out of town." Fatima remained silent waiting for the rest. "I'll be back by tomorrow afternoon."

"What's going on?" she finally asked.

"I need to go to Ottawa." Ali's face was blank. Fatima couldn't read anything from it, and she was trying hard.

"Why?"

"I just need to take care of something. Nothing to worry about. I'll be home tomorrow." Ali's gaze shifted from one of Fatima's eyes to the other, gauging her response.

"When are you leaving?" *Why is he being so cagey?*

"Tonight. I have a flight for 9:45 p.m. I'll leave right after the soccer game."

"That's cutting it kind of close, isn't it?" Fatima couldn't understand why he was not more forthcoming. This wasn't like him at all.

"It is, but I think it'll be ok. I have a meeting in the morning. I'll try to do it as early as possible then head back home. I'll be home before dinner." Ali rubbed his chin. "Maybe you should all stay with my parents tonight, or I can ask them to come over here."

"No, I'll be fine." Fatima shook her head. Papa treated her like a top priority, especially when Ali was away. He personally made sure she had whatever she needed or wanted. She didn't want to pressure him more.

"At least Rahma should come, in case you need anything." Ali was never comfortable leaving Fatima alone, especially while she was so advanced in her pregnancy.

"If she wants to. Whatever. So, are you going to tell me what this is all about? Or am I to die in suspense?" Fatima tried to make her voice sound light, although she didn't think she could be convincing.

Ali looked quickly around the room and let out a heavy sigh. It was clear he was not going to talk about it. "I can't right now, but I will as soon as it's all sorted out."

Fatima sat stunned. She hadn't really expected him not to tell her. She couldn't believe it. Ali was sitting in front of her telling her that he was about to fly to Ottawa, stay overnight, be back home tomorrow by dinnertime, and he was refusing to tell her why.

"This doesn't make any sense. You're making me nervous. Ali, is something wrong?"

"No, no, I don't want you to worry about anything."

"Then you need to tell me something that makes sense."

"I'll handle it, and I'll be back before you miss me." He looked up and tried to smile.

The phone rang, breaking the heavy silence that had fallen between them. Fatima walked across the room and down two steps, to the lower level of the family room, to pick up the phone on her desk.

"Hi Rachel, what's up? What happened?" Fatima remembered that Rachel was going to call her doctor.

"I'm at the hospital. I guess the procedure wasn't done completely so I had to have an emergency D&C.

"What! Oh no." *What else could go wrong today*? Fatima wondered.

"I'm ok, but I'm exhausted, and this nurse really ticked me off, and now I'm being discharged, and I'm really sorry Fatima, but could you pick me up? I'm really sorry."

"Of course I'll come. I'll be there right away."

"Oh, and Joshua and Jonah are at the daycare. They need to be picked up before 6 p.m."

"Ali is getting them today. Remember, Josh starts soccer tonight?" Fatima glanced up the stairs to see Ali watching her. She turned her back and continued listening to Rachel.

"I forgot. I don't think I can make it tonight." Rachel sounded on edge.

"Don't worry. Ali can manage. Papa has the girls, so he'll just have your guys. It'll be fine. I'm leaving now. Bye"

"What's going on?" Ali stood up and approached Fatima.

"It's nothing." Fatima deliberately sounded more nonchalant than the situation called for.

"It sounds like something's wrong." Ali reached the top of the steps.

"Don't worry. I can handle it." Fatima stepped past him and left the room. When she arrived at the storage bench beside the front doors she grabbed her *hijab* and her purse from one of the three rattan baskets underneath and slipped into her shoes. Ali stood at the end of the hall watching her. She turned and left without saying goodbye. When she was finally outside she put her sunglasses on and groaned in frustration. She felt like screaming.

This was the first time Ali had ever kept anything from her. He certainly never stayed away from home unless he was playing ball. Even then he always preferred that she go with him. Fatima racked her brain trying to figure out what could be making him so anxious. She couldn't help wondering if it had something to do with the letter. *But why the secrecy?* She had a very uneasy feeling about the whole thing.

Rachel waited for Fatima to arrive, and when she saw Fatima's car she tried to rush to it. Fatima came out of the car to help her.

"Take it easy, girl. Here...let me help you. Where is your car?" Fatima looped her arm with Rachel's and helped her to the door.

"It's still in the shop. I should get it back tomorrow."

Two people entering the hospital stepped aside to let Rachel pass and looked back at her as she walked by. Fatima smiled at her friend. "Even on your worst day you still turn heads."

"Ha, they're probably wondering why I'm being let out." Rachel eased herself into the car. Fatima stood beside the door after closing it for her.

"At least someone is humble around here."

Rachel knit her brows and shifted her eyes. "What do you mean?"

"Ali doesn't even pretend not to notice the attention he gets."

Rachel leaned back and closed her eyes. "He would have to be mentally impaired not to notice, but you know he doesn't care."

"I guess." Fatima walked to her side of the car. After entering and getting buckled she turned her attention back to Rachel. "I can't believe this. Is this the height of incompetence, or what? How could they not have completed the procedure properly? Who was the doctor?"

"Dr. Simms, but I think it happens sometimes. I don't know. I really don't have the energy for this. Anyway, there was this nurse."

"Oh yes, you mentioned the nurse. What happened?"

Rachel relayed the story. She had been sitting waiting for her examination and the nurse that had attended her was young, about Rachel's age. Rachel thought she would like her, until she opened her mouth. After looking at Rachel's chart she turned to Rachel and asked, "Did you go to the University of Toronto?"

"Yes," Rachel had replied, while she searched the nurse's face for some familiarity.

"And you have two boys, right?"

"Right."

"Are you Jamie's girlfriend?" the nurse had asked.

Rachel turned to Fatima. "Now, do you think I really wanted to hear his name?"

"What did you say to her?"

"Oh please, I still haven't answered her."

"How does she know you? Who is she?" Fatima questioned.

"I don't know. Did you hear me say I know her? She said she's a friend of Jamie's and she heard he had kids. My name sounded familiar and I fit the description. Whatever that means. She ticked me off, that's all I know."

Rachel fumed at the thought that someone who knew her knew her business, especially a friend of Jamie's. Maybe she was upset at not knowing what the relationship was between Jamie and this woman. The whole situation was so humiliating, and again Rachel was angry with herself. *What had she done wrong to deserve this? Why did Fatima end up with the perfect life? What was the difference between them?* Even though she kept trying to put her life right it seemed like obstacles kept being thrown in the way.

"Why do you care? Who cares?" Fatima interrupted her thoughts. "Just worry about yourself and your kids and stop thinking about what everyone else is thinking, because they're living their lives and it has nothing to do with you."

"The whole situation is just so embarrassing." Suddenly another reality gripped Rachel. "What if she tells Jamie?"

"What? She can't do that. What about confidentiality?"

"Oh, wake up Fatima, not everyone follows the rules. I mean, obviously she knows why I was there. Jamie will kill me."

"I am so sick of hearing about Jamie. Stop making decisions in your life based on him! Where is he now? Where is he when your kids are sick or lonely or hungry or dirty or whatever? Tonight Joshua is starting soccer for the first time. He is so excited, and where is his father? Nowhere, that's where. Just forget that loser and move on, Rachel. For God's sake, what is it going to take for you to get it?"

Fatima didn't understand. Jamie wasn't the same guy they had known in high school. He wasn't just a small time hoodlum anymore. He had graduated. He had connections. He really knew some serious people, and he could do a lot of damage, to all of them.

"Move on to what? I don't see any knight in shining armour riding around here. If there was, you grabbed him quick enough. Anyway, I have two kids; that definitely reduces my value on the market." Rachel felt emotion building and that made her angrier than ever.

"What are you talking about? You can have anything you want. You know that. You've made good things happen in your life. Remember the scholarship?"

Rachel had received several scholarship offers, but the one she was really interested in was the swimming scholarship to a top university in the United States. She had been so excited to go, but had changed her mind at the last minute, because Jamie had convinced her that their relationship would not survive the distance.

"I didn't want to leave Jamie." Rachel shook her head. "That was stupid, wasn't it?"

"Jamie didn't want you to leave *him*. You were ready to go. He was threatened by you moving forward when he wasn't. What did we tell you then? If you two were meant to be together then you would be and if not you would meet someone better. You didn't go and now look, where is he?"

Rachel remembered everything. Fatima and Ali had worked hard to convince her to go. She had almost thought that they were trying to get rid of her. They had told her all the right things, she just hadn't believed them.

"Rachel, you have to start believing in yourself again. And you have to listen. *Allah* sends you messages through the people around you. You miss them if you don't listen. You have so many people giving you good advice, people who really care about you. Get back on your life and start moving forward, one step at a time."

Fatima was right. Rachel knew it, but there had been so much going on at the time. Ali had recently signed with the Razors, and he and Fatima were planning to get married.

Papa had insisted that they wait one year to get married. He wanted to see how Ali handled himself on the road. He always said, "Every daughter is my daughter, and every son is my son." He would not give his blessing for Ali to marry Fatima until Ali proved that he was responsible. Ali had agreed. He didn't want to get married without the approval of both his parents.

Rachel had felt like she was losing everything. Jamie just felt safe and familiar. He didn't become controlling until she was pregnant with Joshua. Or so she thought. Talking her out of the opportunity of a lifetime was certainly a controlling move. Two girls she had competed with had gone on to swim on the Canadian Olympic Team. Rachel knew she could have been there too.

"You don't understand. You're married. It's different for you." Rachel turned to look out the window.

"You could have been married too. Ali knows so many people, good guys, who would be great for you."

"Who said I want to marry a Muslim?"

"It doesn't have to be a Muslim…and what's wrong with being married to a Muslim?

"I just don't know if I can be that good little wifey, that's all," Rachel replied in an animated way.

"It's all up to you, honey. Just be the good little baby-mother then," Fatima shot back.

Rachel turned to look at Fatima in shock. She usually was straight forward, but this was harsh, even for her. Maybe Rachel was wearing her out. She was certainly exhausted too. They pulled up in front of Fatima's house.

"Hey, did you forget about me?" Rachel joked.

"No, I want you to come over. You need to rest, and Naomi might get suspicious."

They entered the house and Rachel gingerly stepped on the tiled floor of the foyer. She immediately headed straight for the kitchen and slid into the booth. Fatima walked to the family room to turn on the *adhan*-call to prayer. "I have to pray, and then we can have dinner," she said over her shoulder.

"Aren't you going to wait for Ali?" Rachel asked.

"No," Fatima said flatly, and continued walking.

"Ok, I won't ask."

Rachel stretched her legs and made herself comfortable. She loved Fatima's kitchen. It was large enough to have several people working comfortably in there at once. Ali and Papa had built a wonderful restaurant-style booth that was perfect for the kids. They could easily slide in and out, and it was convenient for the adults as well. The seats and back were cushioned and exactly what Rachel needed right now. She stretched her legs out and put her feet up on the opposite bench.

From her seat she could see outside through the front window. She was looking directly at her house and wondering what her mother was doing right now. She knew her mother was worried about her. Fatima was right to have her come over. Naomi had a way of sensing things.

Rachel laughed and shook her head. She had told her mother that she could probably go into business. With a sign outside, 'Naomi Knows', she could make real money telling people all about themselves. That's why Rachel had to keep her distance for a little while.

The *adhan* finished and Fatima started to pray. Rachel always felt relaxed at the sound of the *adhan*. She had been hearing it for over 15 years and it had the same effect on her every time. She also enjoyed watching Fatima and her family pray. The movements had such beauty and grace. They all seemed so united when they prayed together.

Thinking about Fatima, she wondered how she kept her balance in her condition. She was just weeks away from having her baby, yet her prayer was still as smooth as ever. Fatima finished and returned to the kitchen.

"How do you manage all that up and down with that huge belly in front of you?" Rachel asked, to lighten up the mood. She was expecting Fatima to hit her with a ton of questions and was willing to use any delay tactic necessary.

"I do yoga every day. I'm flexible, fit *and* strong." Fatima flashed a smile.

"Ooh, I'm scared! I wouldn't want to come around here late at night," Rachel joked.

Fatima heated the food she had prepared earlier, placed it on the table then brought up the subject of Jamie. "Ready to talk?"

Rachel knew Fatima was not going to let her off the hook again. "What do you want to know?" Rachel picked up her fork and jabbed a piece of stewed chicken.

"Well, what happened? Why did you decide not to have the baby? Why didn't you tell us? It just doesn't sound like you," Fatima asked.

Rachel sighed. She had hoped to put this all behind her. She certainly didn't want to discuss this with Fatima. But she felt she owed her some explanation after Fatima had done so much to help her. *Should she tell her about the night that Jamie had come a few weeks ago?* She looked out the window. Night was falling and she wondered about her boys. They would be on their way home soon. She was so sorry she had missed Joshua's big day.

"I was going to have it, I guess. I just really wasn't thinking about it."

Fatima listened carefully while Rachel completed her story. "Then Jamie came by unexpectedly and I tried to tell him and he started going off. He acted like he didn't believe it was his child. I don't really get it. I guess it's because he doesn't come around that often. Then he said he heard Ali was spending a lot of time with the boys, and he said maybe they weren't his either. It was so weird."

"That's it? You had an abortion because Jamie was being himself? Who cares? You see him two or three times a year."

"You don't understand. How was I going to have another child for such a loser? Josh and Jonah already suffer so much because of him. I couldn't do that to another baby. I just couldn't."

"No." Fatima shook her head. "This doesn't make sense. It's not adding up. There has to be more to it." Fatima was not accepting this line of argument at all.

"I know it's my own fault, but you don't know what it's like carrying and having a baby for someone who is such a big stress in your life. You have no idea what that feels like." Rachel dropped her head in defeat.

Fatima thought about how impossible it would be for her to get through her pregnancies without Ali's love and support. She also knew how vulnerable she felt when she was pregnant, even though she was secure in her marriage. "I do understand. I just feel so sad about it. No matter what, Joshua and Jonah are such beautiful boys and a blessing to all of us. I just think that with all the support you have you could have made it work."

"For some things there is no substitution," Rachel said as she played with her fork.

Fatima knew that was definitely true.

"I just wanted to cut ties with him completely. I figured this was as good a time as any. I actually thought I might move," Rachel added.

Rachel did not want to tell Fatima how scared she was of Jamie. It was better if she just moved away and got as far away from him as possible. Everyone would be better off, she thought.

"Move? Where? Why? What about the boys?" Fatima's confusion and concern showed in her eyes.

"I haven't figured all that out yet. I just think it might be best. I need to put distance between me and Jamie. Maybe if he doesn't know where to find me for a while that will change things. I'll take the boys with me, or not. I don't really know yet."

"Running is not going to solve your problems. It's not the location that's all wrong. It's just you, Rachel. You have to fix you. You might think it will be easier if you go, but it will be much better to do it right here, with all of us here to support you. You can't just get up and go to *I-don't-know-where*; and leave the boys? No. You definitely can't take them away from everyone and start all over. Who will help you take care of them?"

"I'm a big girl now. I can do it." Rachel knew she didn't have a plan, just a desperate need to start her life over, get away from Jamie and make sure that her friends and family did not get caught in the middle. She had a decent job working with Bell Canada, but she could find another job. Maybe she could get transferred to another office.

"Fatima, Jamie is not small time any more. He knows some serious people. And they're not all street people either. They're professionals, business people, and politicians. He can make a lot of trouble."

"Rachel, he's nothing. He can't do anything. Stop giving him all this power. Where are you, Rachel? This is not you. Has he threatened you? We can call the police. You know you should have done that a long time ago. You can get a restraining order. I can't believe the nerve of him. Threatening the mother of his kids? Not that he cares about them anyway.

"I don't even know why he shows his face around here. He's just trying to mess with your head. He's slowly taking more and more control because you're letting him. Only you can stop this, Rachel. Maybe I should go and talk to him. Why, I'll just go to the police myself. Or maybe I'll call Shawn. He's a lawyer. He'll know what to do." Fatima went on and on. She was like a faucet that had been left running. She didn't even notice Rachel's growing agitation.

"Stop!" Rachel put her hands to her face, and then let out all the breath in her lungs as she fully relaxed. "It's not me he wants to hurt." She paused, not knowing how to tell her best friend the truth. "It's Ali."

Chapter Five

𝔍

"What are you talking about? He actually said that? Why would he want to hurt Ali?"

"You know their history. He's so jealous of him. Jamie knows I never really loved him. He just can't handle it. I guess it's an ego thing. Now, with Ali playing such a big role in Joshua's and Jonah's lives, it just eats him." Rachel's eyes lit up. "You should see how excited they are when they talk about all the things that Ali does with them. It's killing Jamie. And, of course, Ali is successful in a way that he's not." Rachel was nervous telling Fatima all of this. The last thing she wanted was for Fatima and Ali to get involved in her problems. And whether Fatima wanted to see it or not, Jamie was a big problem.

"It's his choice not to be in their lives. What does he want? For them to have nothing? Just sit around waiting for him to show up whenever the wind blows him this way? That's no life for those boys. He should be grateful someone is taking an interest in his kids and giving them some positive life experiences." Fatima pushed her cold plate away.

"Maybe *someone* would be ok, but not Ali. Anyway, he says

he's not around for the boys as much as he wants because he's busy building their future." Rachel knew how pathetic that sounded, but she wanted Fatima to calm down and hopefully move onto another topic.

Fatima scoffed at Rachel's comments. Rachel was too embarrassed to even reply. She knew everything Fatima said was true and she wanted nothing more than to walk away from Jamie permanently, but he was so persistent. When he was away she was fine. She didn't even think about him, but when he came around with his sad story she just felt so weak. If she ever tried to resist him he would get explosive. She just couldn't handle the outbursts.

But what if he could change and be a good father to her boys? Did she have the right to give up on that? Didn't her boys deserve a chance at having a family? Then there was always the fear that he would move on to someone else. Then she would look like the idiot, stuck with his kids while he went off and had a new family. She knew it made no sense but these were the issues she had to get over before she could truly move on in her life.

Fatima was silent as she processed everything she had heard. "Rachel, did you make the list?"

Fatima was always talking about her prayer list. Mama had one and they had even gotten Naomi to start one. Fatima insisted that if Rachel made a list and prayed over it every day, she would be amazed at the miracles that would happen in her life. "I promise you, if you pray on that list, one by one, you will be crossing things off and thanking God for hearing and answering your prayers."

"Maybe for you, but not me." Rachel started to pick at her food again.

"Why not you? It works for me, and everyone else, but not you? You really think you're that bad?" Fatima teased.

"Fatima, you know it's just not my thing." Rachel took a bite of her food.

"If that were true, you wouldn't be my friend." Fatima smiled at Rachel with tenderness.

"Next topic." Rachel cut Fatima off abruptly. This was one area she was not going to get into now. Praying was hard for her since her father had died. She had prayed so hard for him to recover from his accident and come back home. It hadn't happened. Now they had to live a life without him. They had suffered so much since his death that Rachel just had a blockage when it came to prayer. She knew it worked for some people, but she just didn't know how to make it work for herself.

"Ok, next topic." Fatima reached across the table and held Rachel's hands. "I'm going to ask you something, and I want you to tell me the truth, no matter what it is, ok?" Fatima sounded so serious that Rachel felt uneasy.

"Yes."

Fatima took a deep breath. "Your baby, was it Jamie's?" Fatima kept her eyes on Rachel's face.

Rachel heard the key in the door behind her and felt relief. She didn't like the direction of this conversation. On the other side of the door Ali paused. When Fatima gave him the ok, he entered the house.

"*As-salaam alaikum.*"

"*Wa alaikum as-salaam,*" Fatima replied, without taking her eyes off Rachel.

"Hey Ali, how was the game?" Rachel was eager to hear about Joshua's first day on the field. She was so grateful that Ali had stepped up and taken on the responsibility of her sons. At least she had made one good decision in her life, having him as a friend.

Ali bent to take off his shoes. "Incredible! I just dropped them home. They must be talking your mother's ear off right now. They were so excited. Joshua is good! You should see him handle the ball. I think you have a little star on your hands." Ali was beaming with obvious pride. "*And*, he got the only two goals."

"Really? I should go see them." Rachel tried to get up, but Fatima would not release the grip on her hands.

Ali winked at Fatima before turning and heading up the stairs.

"Ali," Rachel called to him as he mounted the first step.

"Yes, Rachel." Ali paused and looked back.

"Mom loves her kitchen. It's amazing."

He smiled. "I'm glad," he said, and then disappeared up the stairs.

Fatima pulled Rachel towards her across the table and whispered, "Answer me."

"I shouldn't even answer you," Rachel replied in an angry whisper. "Of course he is. What kind of a person do you take me for?"

Fatima released her grip on Rachel. "Just forget it. I don't know what I'm saying."

"I can't even believe you could ask me something like that. What are you really suggesting? You know what? I don't even want to know. I'm just going home." Rachel stood up. "My life is getting crazier by the minute."

"Listen, forget it. I just, I don't know, so many things have happened in the last two days that I don't feel like myself." Fatima blushed.

"I guess you're entitled. You are hormonal." Rachel was happy to drop the subject. She didn't even want to imagine what was going through Fatima's mind. "Just don't go getting freaky weird on me." Rachel's voice softened.

"I'm sorry, I feel really stupid. I don't know what I was thinking." Fatima was obviously embarrassed.

"I *have* dumped a lot on you too. That wasn't fair." Rachel reached out and touched Fatima's shoulder. "This was really bad timing. Look, my boys are waiting for me, and your husband is waiting for you, so I'm going home."

Fatima nodded.

"You get some rest and take care of Mr. Abati's baby." Rachel allowed herself to smile again. "I don't want him blaming me for stressing you out."

"Good night, Rachel. Kiss the boys for me."

"Bye." Rachel touched Fatima's cheek and left. Fatima closed the door behind her.

"What is happening to my life?" Rachel thought, out loud, as she walked across the street to her house. She dreaded going there.

Everything reminded her of her father. She felt guilty leaving her mother alone as much as she did, but nothing was the same without him. Naomi wasn't even the same. Rachel really missed him now. If only he were here she would know what to do. She had always felt so safe with him. Now, nothing was right, and nowhere was safe. Rachel reached into her pocket and pulled out a piece of paper. She had some things to add to her list.

Inside the house Fatima could still feel her cheeks burning. What had she been thinking asking Rachel such a question? She really needed to rest. Leaving the girls with Mama and Papa was starting to sound like a good idea.

She stood at the bottom of the stairs and looked up. Ali was likely packing a bag and getting ready to catch his flight. Rachel had been a timely distraction, now back to her life. She looked up the stairs, but she didn't think she had the strength to climb them. It was getting harder for her these days. Sleeping on the couch was sounding good. She hated sleeping alone anyway. Ali appeared at the top of the stairs, with a bag over his shoulder. He wore blue jeans, a button-down shirt and a brown suede jacket.

"Do you need a hand?" He smiled warmly at her, but she was not in the mood for his pleasantries.

"No, actually I was heading towards the couch." Fatima turned and made her way to the family room and sat in the arm chair closest to the entrance. The pressure of the last two days coupled with Ali's impending departure was too much for her. She leaned back and closed her eyes.

"It's not what you're thinking." Ali's voice came from the doorway directly behind Fatima.

"And how do you know what I'm thinking?" Ali pulled up an ottoman to sit by her side. Fatima opened her eyes to look at him.

"Because of these." He curled his fingers and gently pressed them to the corner of her eye. "And these." He repeated the action on the other eye. When he pulled his hand away, his fingers held the moisture from the tears Fatima was trying to hold back.

"You know how I am when I'm pregnant. I'm just a little emotional." She was embarrassed. He could always read her so well.

"I know. That's why I don't want you to worry about anything."

Fatima stared straight ahead and through the back window. "I hate to think that we have secrets between us. If there's some kind of problem, I should know."

"We have no secrets. I don't want you to think that." Ali pulled his seat closer. "Listen, I have never had to ask you this before, but I'm dealing with something right now, and I just need you to give me some time. Can you do that?"

Fatima looked straight ahead. "You're going to miss your flight."

"I need to make sure you're all right."

"And if I'm not?" She turned her head to look at him again.

"Then you should tell me."

"I'm fine." Fatima continued to look at Ali, and in spite of all she was feeling, she started to smile.

"Why are you looking at me like that?"

"Like what?" Fatima asked innocently.

"You tell me."

"I was just remembering something; something the ladies were saying about you today."

"Oh? Ladies talking about me? What else is new?" Ali smiled, although his clear brown eyes still held the heaviness Fatima had seen in them when he had first told her about his trip.

"Aren't we modest?" Fatima hit him with a cushion.

"Look, I have to go. Let's go get the girls." Ali stood up and held out his hand.

"No, I think I'll wait a few minutes. I want to rest a little."

"I don't feel good leaving you alone. Let's go. We'll move slowly."

"Really, I just want a few minutes by myself," Fatima insisted.

Ali reluctantly agreed. "Fine, I'll call you in a little while."

"*Inshallah*-God willing." Fatima closed her eyes and leaned back again. "Ali, did you tell your parents you were leaving?" Fatima called out to him before he went through the door.

"I spoke to Papa, but I had to duck out before Mama caught me. You know she would drill me." Ali smiled and Fatima couldn't help but smile back. After he had left she relaxed and fell asleep.

The telephone rang waking her up. Ali was calling from the airport to say he was about to board his flight and was suggesting that Fatima leave the girls with Mama and Papa and pick them up in the morning. He had already spoken to them about it. She agreed.

After hanging up the phone, Fatima prayed, transferred to the couch and pulled a blanket over herself. When a piece of paper fell out of the blanket, she lifted it, and her tension slipped away. Fatima knew immediately what the paper was.

Ali always left notes around the house when he travelled. The couch was one of his regular spots. He never forgot this ritual. Fatima wondered how he always managed to do it without her noticing. She opened the piece of paper. *I'll miss you*, it said. "I'll miss you more," she whispered. She pulled up the blanket and went to sleep.

Chapter Six

ℑ

The next morning when Fatima opened her eyes, the sun was shining. She had woken up for *fajr*-the first prayer of the day, prayed and gone back to sleep. She had no problem waking up early these days. When she was pregnant she found it very difficult to sleep in, and she was usually up bright and early.

She had spoken to Ali when he had called from Ottawa at 6 am. He had tried to sound normal, but Fatima had thought he sounded preoccupied. She didn't ask him about his plans and he didn't offer any information. He just made sure she was all right and reassured her that he would be back in the evening, as he had promised. He wasn't impressed that she had slept on the couch. "That can't be comfortable."

Nothing about this is comfortable, she had wanted to say, but instead had just said that she had been so tired she really didn't want to tackle the stairs, and she had felt lonely. "It's not the same when you're not here," she confessed.

"You didn't look for the notes," Ali mentioned.

"How do you know?"

"Because, I left instructions and if you had found them I would have known."

Fatima really appreciated these rituals. They made life feel somewhat normal. Even though their life was hectic, there were a few things she could always count on. Ali leaving notes around the house when he travelled was one of them.

He was not a talkative person. She admired that about him. She was impressed with his degree of reserve. He was open with her, but with few words. She had also learned to be more silent as a result. She often had to figure out what Ali was thinking and feeling by paying attention to his actions as much as his words. When he was in the company of others he was more of an observer than a talker.

Fatima detested men who had to be the centre of attention. Her opinion was that if you were talkative, eventually you would say something that you shouldn't. The more you talked the more likely that was to happen. Ali was rarely in danger of that. When he spoke it was valuable, otherwise he wouldn't bother. So, she really cherished these heartfelt little messages. They gave her more insight to the man she shared her life with.

He was right about her not looking for the notes. She was tired yes, but she was also upset and just didn't feel like playing with him. She was confused by his behaviour. She had an active imagination and could not help trying to come up with possible reasons for his trip. It was frustrating not to have any good possibilities.

Anyway, it was daylight now and she would go get her daughters and start the day. Since it was Saturday, and she had no specific plans, she would just play it by ear.

When she arrived at number 110 the house seemed uncharacteristically quiet. She tried the door and found it open. It often was at this time of morning. During April, after *fajr*, Mama often spent hours in the garden. The door would be unlocked to facilitate her going and coming.

"*As-salaam alaikum, ya Rasoolullah,*" Fatima said, as she entered the house. Rahma was the first to greet her. She ran to Fatima, hugged and kissed her, using her special pet name for Fatima, the

Italian word for sister. *"As-salaam alaikum, Sorella.* We were worried about you. I don't think Papa slept all night. Come see."

Fatima followed Rahma into the living room which the family used as a prayer room. There was nothing in it except wall to wall carpet, large cushions lining the walls, a wall of book cases at one end of the room and a low table at the other end that held a stand for reading the *Holy Quran.* The room was painted in a beautiful earth tone and decorated with a few large plants.

"He fell asleep right after *salah*-prayer."

Papa was lying on the floor with the three girls on top of him. Laila and Batool were on his chest and Masuma rested with a pillow on his leg.

"Figures Masuma would think to get comfortable. How were they last night?"

"Fine, they were all played out so they slept pretty well. They got up at *fajr* time, but I guess they were still tired because they conked out immediately after." Rahma waved her hand at the sleeping girls.

Fatima stood in the doorway watching them. "I'm torn. Should I wake them or let them sleep?"

"Leave them, for sure. Let's go to the back."

As they approached the sunroom at the back of the house they could see Mama working diligently in the yard. It was a warm and sunny day, and the girls laughed and chatted for a while, enjoying the fresh morning air. When Mama heard them, she left her work and came to keep them company for a while.

"Did you speak to Ali this morning?" Mama removed her gloves and placed them on the chair in front of her.

"I did."

"Hmm. He snuck out of here without seeing me." Fatima could tell that she was not pleased, but she didn't go on. Mama was extremely careful around Fatima when she was pregnant. She always insisted that the happiness of a pregnant woman should be the top priority of the family. She believed every experience, emotion and thought that the mother had would have a physical manifestation and impact on the unborn child. It became a part of him or her. She was adamant that Fatima should be cared for and stress free during this time.

Rahma quickly changed the subject. "Mama, you should see Papa. He's sleeping and the girls are all around him. It's so cute, I should take a picture."

Mama smiled. "You know, I think he was in that room all night. He said he couldn't sleep knowing you were alone."

"*As-salaam alaikum, Piccolina*." Papa had called Fatima *Piccolina*- little doll, from the first time he had met her. He entered the sunroom and stood beside Fatima's chair.

Wa alaikum as-salaam, Papa. I'm not so tiny anymore. I think I grew overnight."

"Yes, I see, but you are still a doll. *Come sta lei, mio caro*?"

"*Alhamdulillah*, I'm fine thanks."

"So, when is your husband's return?" Mama interjected.

"Mama, you know he said this evening," Papa replied while giving her a scolding look.

"I wanted to hear from his wife, since he didn't bother to tell his mother anything." Mama pursed her lips, showing her discontent.

"Oh Mama, he didn't want you to worry." Papa hugged Mama and gave Fatima and Rahma a wink. Fatima was reminded, in that moment, how much Ali was like his father, and she was grateful that he had such a good role model.

"He's a grown man. He'll be just fine," Papa said.

Mama sat at the wrought iron table. "I'm not worried about him. It's not right for him to leave Fatima like this. She's due any minute. He spends enough time away as it is." Fatima could see the wheels in Mama's head turning. She wasn't saying much, but Fatima knew she was running through all the possibilities, just as she had. The thought made her uncomfortable.

Papa insisted, "We're all here. She has everything she needs."

"Except her husband."

"What are you all doing today?" Fatima wanted to talk about anything but Ali's absence.

Papa rubbed his greying head and sighed. "I have a lot of work to do."

Papa worked for a non-profit organization called *Children of Rwanda*. It was based in his homeland, Italy, but he was able to do much of his work by internet and on the phone. During the massacre, many Rwandan children had been air-lifted to Italy and placed in homes with Italian families.

Many had been adopted, and in the years after the massacre the Italian and Rwandan governments had ongoing negotiations about the status of the children. Rwanda said the adoptions were illegal. The Italian families had no permission from family members or the government to adopt the children. Italy had insisted that the adoptions were in order.

Unfortunately, many of the children had no family to return to. Those that did have families who had demanded their children back posed another problem. Having left as babies many of the children knew only the Italian families as their own. It had been a very sensitive situation.

In the years since the genocide, some children had been returned and many had remained in their adopted families after returning to Rwanda to perform the adoptions satisfactorily. Still, there were ongoing issues, such as maintaining cultural identity, keeping in contact with living family members, trips home and dealing with the integration of the Rwandan children into Italian society.

Hundreds of thousands of children had been orphaned following the 1994 genocide. According to statistics from the Ministry of Gender and Family Promotion in Rwanda, the number of children who had been orphaned or were otherwise considered vulnerable was anywhere from one to three million. Papa was currently working on an assessment to determine the number of children living on the streets and their needs.

Papa had been active in the cause from the beginning, and continued to build a large organization that also offered sponsorship and support to children and their families in Rwanda.

"You know what I have to say about that." Mama's eyes sparkled.

"Yes, Mama." They all repeated Mama's famous line, "If they want African babies, let them make their own."

"Not everyone is as lucky as me," Papa was always quick to reply.

He was lucky indeed. Italy had one of the lowest birth rates in the world. With two children and a fourth grandchild on the way, Papa was rich beyond imagination.

Fatima spent the day talking to Rahma and watching her daughters play outside. She even helped Mama with some of the gardening, where she was permitted. It was still early to start planting, but Mama would prepare the soil and spend time in her greenhouse, where she had seedlings waiting to be transplanted when the fear of frost was over.

Fatima couldn't think of going back to an empty home, so she happily passed the time with Ali's family. The day flew by quickly, and when Papa emerged from his study Fatima couldn't believe that it was already 4 p.m. Ali would be home soon.

"Mama, maybe I should go home and wait for Ali."

"Why not eat with us, and then go? It's only another hour. Go have a nap. I'll wake you when he gets here."

"Are you sure? The girls are pretty wound up. I don't want to burden you."

"Papa is free now. You know he's at their service. Go. They won't even miss you." Mama was right. Fatima looked out to the backyard where Papa was chasing the girls. They squealed as they ran around. Papa still walked with a slight limp from his injury during the genocide. Although he wasn't able to run fast, the girls didn't know the difference. They just knew that he was their Papa, and he was all theirs.

Fatima went into the guest bedroom on the main floor behind the kitchen. This is where she usually slept when she stayed over. It was hard to get comfortable these days, but she would try. Ali must have been in the room recently because his scent was on the bedding. She sank into the pillow and took comfort in knowing that when she woke up he would likely be home.

"Daddy! Daddy! Daddy!" Fatima woke up to the sound of her daughters' voices. Ali had arrived and they were thrilled. They had not seen him since the afternoon before. Fatima sometimes worried what effect having their father absent so often would have on them. During the regular season he was typically away from home for about 100 days. It was a significant amount of time for the girls and for Fatima. Sometimes it put a heavy strain on family life.

Ali and Fatima had recently been discussing his possible departure from the league. Ali felt that he needed to spend more time with their daughters, and if Fatima decided to pursue a degree in medicine the girls would definitely need one full time parent. He was thinking of developing a camp and recreation site on land that they owned outside of the city. Work was already being done on a main house for their family.

Fatima came out of the bedroom and stood watching Ali interact with his family for a few seconds.

He had the same easy comfort with everyone wherever he was. It was as though he belonged everywhere. Ali stood beside Papa. Papa was a tall man, but Ali had grown past him by the time he was 17. He really did look like his father, a younger, darker version of Papa. They both had strong lean features, a firm jaw, serious eyes and an easy smile.

The family was thrilled to see him. Rahma jumped up and hugged him around his neck. Masuma and Batool hugged one leg each.

"Where's Laila?" Ali asked.

"She ran to hide as soon as she heard you. I think she wants you to find her," Rahma answered.

Ali bent over, peeled Batool and Masuma off his legs and removed his shoes. "I better get on it before she falls asleep somewhere."

"That certainly has happened before," Fatima interjected.

Ali noticed her standing in the doorway of the guest room for the first time. "Fatima, *as-salaam alaikum*. How are you?" Ali greeted her.

"*Wa alaikum as-salaam*, I'm good, and you?" *Why does this moment feel so awkward?* Fatima wondered. She hated everything about the last 24 hours. Quickly, she decided to put everything out of her mind and enjoy her evening. Worrying never helped in any case. Ali was home now, they were all together and whatever was happening outside would remain there, at least for tonight.

"Glad to be home. I think we should find Laila," Ali said.

Fatima moved towards him. "For sure. I'm right behind you."

"You know I can't wait for you," he said, teasing her about her slow movements. Ali always had a way of interjecting humour even in the most serious moments. It was good to have someone to lighten things up once in a while. They searched for Laila and found her in a doll house in the family room. Just like the others, she was delighted to see her father.

Laila and Batool, the three-year-old twins, were replicas of their mother, while Masuma resembled Ali. At five years old she took her role as elder sister very seriously. She often tried to be bossy, but the twins would not allow her to get the best of them. Laila always wanted to play and was often up to some mischief; likely because she thrived on attention, the more the better. Batool was the helpful one. She needed to make sure everything was in order. She also loved to eat. She always headed straight for the kitchen when arriving at Mama's house or anyone's house, for that matter.

Ali sat with Laila on the carpeted floor for a few minutes, to play with her, while Fatima looked around the family room. It was filled with books, toys and dozens of Ali's trophies and medals. He had outstanding achievement in archery, judo, tae kwon do, mixed martial arts, swimming, track and field and, of course, basketball. Fatima had wanted to keep some of them at their home, but Ali had refused.

"Do you think she planned this, to get you alone, all to herself?" Fatima sat on an exercise ball.

Ali rolled over, taking Laila with him. "Do I think? I'm sure."

He didn't seem to mind. It warmed Fatima's heart to see him play with their children. At these moments she would think of Rachel. She and her boys didn't have any of this. They all loved Rachel's family and were there for them, but it couldn't be the same.

"How is Rachel doing?" Ali asked.

"What?" Fatima was surprised that he seemed to have read her mind.

"Rachel. I've been thinking about her. She hasn't been looking well," Ali replied.

"You noticed?"

"Yes, I noticed."

"Oh well, you know, woman stuff." Fatima tried to make light of the situation.

"No, I don't." Ali was not prepared to give up easily.

"She'll be ok. She has me."

Ali nodded. "You look tired. I should take you home," he said.

Fatima stopped her movement on the ball. "No, your mother made dinner. We have to eat first. We can't leave now. She waited for you."

"Yes, ma'am. Whatever you say." Ali rose to his feet with Laila in his arms.

They made their way back to the kitchen. "You're in trouble, you know," Fatima said.

"Me? Why?"

"Mama's upset you didn't tell her you were going." Fatima watched closely for Ali's reaction.

"She didn't say anything to me." Ali stopped in the hallway before reaching the kitchen.

"You know she wouldn't in front of me."

Ali looked pensive for a moment and then smiled. "It's fine, I'll make it up. I know how to take care of her."

"Daddy, what did you bring?" Laila turned Ali's face so he could only look directly at her.

"You'll have to wait until you get home to find out." He nipped her forearm and when she pulled it back, he gave her a kiss on her neck.

When they arrived at the kitchen, Ali paused to allow Fatima to pass him and take her seat at the table. He placed Laila in her seat beside her grandfather and took his seat beside Fatima and his mother.

They had a pleasant dinner, laughing and talking about the girls, Rahma's studies and her plans for the summer. They guessed about the exact birth date and weight of the baby, and suggested possible names. No one mentioned Ali's trip. When they finished dinner Ali and Fatima said goodnight and took their family home.

Ali had bought three dolls for his daughters. Each doll had one of their names stitched on the front of its dress. "I can't believe you had time to do this. They're beautiful," Fatima said.

The girls danced around their parents' room with their dolls. Fatima watched them, feeling so happy for their joy. She remembered how much she had wanted this kind of attention from her own father. It never came.

He had always wanted a son, and Fatima had felt that if she had been a boy maybe he would have stayed. She had tried to show interest in the things her father loved, but he just didn't think cars and sports were for girls. It was too bad, because she really was interested.

She had taken mechanics in high school and was one of the best in her class. She could fix just about anything in or outside of the house, although Ali never gave her the chance. Her father just couldn't see past the fact that she wasn't a boy. Or so she thought.

He currently lived in British Columbia, and though they talked often enough, she was hurt that he never visited her after any of the girls were born. She was sure if she had had a boy he would have come.

"And for you." Ali handed Fatima a gift bag. She recognized the scent immediately.

"Rose oil, thank you so much." It was 500 ml of pure essential oil. "Ali, it's too much. It must have been so expensive," Fatima insisted.

"Do you like it?" Ali asked.

"Of course, I love it. You know I do." Rose was Fatima's favourite scent and one that she always kept in the house in some form, whether flowers, oil or spray.

"That's all that matters." Laila stayed close to him, weaving in and out of his legs, while he stroked her head.

"Open it, Mommy, open it." Fatima opened the bottle and the smell filled the room. She put one drop on a tissue and waved it in the air. The girls wanted some on them, so Fatima opened her drawer and pulled out a bottle of almond oil. She put a few drops in her palm and mixed in one drop of the rose oil. She touched the mixture, rubbed her fingers together and touched each girl behind their ears.

Ali watched from the doorway. "Ok, the party's over, little ones. Time for bed."

"Daddy, can we have a bed story?" They never said *bedtime*.

"Go pick one, I'm coming." He turned back to Fatima. "I'll just be a few minutes."

"Take your time."

"Can you read *The Night Prayers*?" Fatima could hear the girls asking. It was their favourite story and they asked for it almost every night.

"Sure. In bed you go." Ali followed them into their room.

Fatima prepared herself for bed. She showered and mixed some of the rose oil in a small bottle she kept in her drawer. It was so soothing for her stretched skin, and the smell was incredible. She felt elated instantly.

She adjusted her pillow, and when she slipped her hand underneath she felt a small piece of paper. She knew it was one of the notes Ali had left for her yesterday. She was ready to read it now. She pulled out the paper. *Call me* it read. She suddenly felt sad thinking of Ali waiting for her call that never came.

"They fell asleep before I even finished," Ali said, as he returned to their room.

"Lucky you. They wear me out with their stories."

"Hey, look what I got for Josh and Jonah." Ali pulled out two identical soccer balls.

"Uh, how many kids do you have?" Fatima smiled. She was pleased that he loved Rachel's boys. They really needed him.

"Believe me, sometimes I wonder," he replied with a smile.

"Do you wish they were basketballs instead?"

"They're still a little short for that game. I'll warm them up and switch them over later." Ali winked to let her know he was joking.

She couldn't help but notice how Ali beamed when he talked about Joshua and Jonah and their sports activities. She knew she shouldn't, but she had to ask. "Do you ever wish you had a boy?"

"What do you mean, instead of the girls?" Ali sat down on the edge of their bed.

"Yes." Fatima really wondered how he would answer.

"What are you talking about? Of course not. Where is this coming from?"

"I don't know. You're so into Joshua and Jonah, I just wondered if you ever thought about it."

"I guess most men would like to have a son... and the first time, sure I thought about it. Not since then. It's such a gift to have these children, any children, am I going to quibble about boy or girl? It really doesn't matter to me anymore. *Allah* gives us what is best. He is All-Knowing, All-Wise. Who am I to suggest that He is wrong? How rude could I be?"

Ali suddenly became somber, running his hand over the sheets. "You know what my family has been through. Just to have healthy, happy, safe kids, sleeping peacefully in their beds, means more to me than anything else."

"Are you sure?" Fatima could not get her father out of her mind.

"Fatima, I would not trade one of my daughters for one thousand sons, I promise you."

"Not even Laila? You know how she can be."

Ali chuckled at the mention of his mischievous little daughter. "*Especially* not Laila."

"What if this baby is a boy?" Fatima raised herself on her elbow.

"What if it is?" Ali crossed his arms.

"Will you be happy?"

"Would you want it any other way?"

"Would you be especially happy?" Fatima pressed for an answer.

"Yes, to have yet another child, healthy and perfect, *inshallah*, I would be *especially* happy." His eyes indicated he was teasing her, and she was annoyed. It was a serious topic for her. She knew she shouldn't care, but sometimes emotion took over rationale.

"You know what I mean, happy because it's a boy."

Ali paused, staring at her so long Fatima wondered what he was thinking.

"I'm not your father," he finally said.

Fatima was caught off guard. Was she that transparent? She didn't know how to respond. She knew that Ali was a different man from the one she had grown up with, but sometimes the doubts just overpowered her sense of reason. It was so difficult to keep her focus on what was real instead of the pain of her past. Flustered, she stumbled over her answer. "I know that...I do...I was just thinking."

"Well, stop doing that, ok? I love our family. I love Laila, I love Batool, I love Masuma; I don't need anything else, except a healthy baby." He stopped to look at Fatima chewing her lip. "And a happy wife. Ok?"

"Ok."

"You're stuck with me," he added gently.

"What do you mean?"

"I am never leaving you, or our girls. No matter what."

Fatima turned her attention back to the piece of paper that was in her hand. "Did you check the doors?" she asked Ali.

"I'll do it right now."

When Ali left the room she opened the paper again. "Call me." She reached for the phone and dialed Ali's cell phone.

"Is that my phone ringing?" Ali asked, as he re-entered their bedroom.

"It is." Fatima hid the house phone and pretended to be settling in to sleep.

"Who could be calling me now?" Ali asked as he reached for his phone. He checked the caller ID before answering and almost laughed out loud. He pressed 'answer' and in his most professional voice said, "Ali Abati. May I help you?"

Across the street Rachel looked out her window. She spent many nights like this. Indeed, all night sometimes. She would sit and remember the last time she had looked out for her father. When she was small she would come to this room because it gave her the best view of the street. She could see when he was approaching before anyone else in the house; until the last time, when he didn't come back. Sometimes she sat here wishing she could turn back the time. Believing that if she thought about it hard enough it would happen; she would see him driving down the street and realize that this had all been a bad dream.

When the lights went out in Fatima's house she shook her head in amusement. "He is so predictable."

Ali always went to bed at the same time. Routine was important to him. He didn't make a big deal about it; it just was his way naturally. He usually woke up at the same time and often once during the night.

Although she was across the street, many nights that routine gave her a strange sense of comfort and security. She knew when the lights would go out and she knew when they would go on. Ali never turned on the bedroom light during the night or early morning, but he may turn on the hallway light or a lamp on the main floor.

Rachel felt as long as everything was ok in Fatima's house, then she was ok too. Sitting in her chair next to the window, she thought about her life and her father. She clearly remembered the last day he was home.

It had been her tenth birthday, and a small group of friends and family had gathered at her house. They had been waiting for her father to return from work. They had decorations and cake, and Naomi had made all Rachel's favourite foods.

They waited and waited. Late at night, after most guests had left, Papa started calling around to see if they could locate him. Finally, the police had called to say he had been in a car accident. Rachel never saw him again. They wouldn't allow her to see him at the hospital, and they had had a closed casket.

Naomi had put away all his pictures, and Rachel sometimes had a hard time remembering what he looked like. He was fading in her mind. His voice and his laugh, everything was fading. It scared her to death to think about losing him again.

"Mommy." Jonah stood at her bedroom door. He was almost the same height as Joshua who was a little small for his age.

"What is it, honey?" Rachel turned to face her son. Jonah came and sat on his mother's lap.

"I don't like it when you go away."

"I'm not going anywhere, honey."

"When you go away I have bad dreams," Jonah insisted.

"It's ok, honey, I'm here. What kind of bad dreams?" Rachel asked.

"Bad men come."

"I'm so sorry, honey. You're ok. Mommy's here now."

Jonah often had bad dreams. He spent many nights in bed with Rachel. Due to his sensitivity, he worried excessively. Whenever Jamie came around, the dreams became worse.

She rocked him in the chair Jamie had bought her when she was pregnant with Joshua. She had wanted a rocking chair so desperately. One day he had just surprised her with it. She had rocked her children here and Fatima's too.

"You don't know, Mommy; there are bad men out there. Don't leave me. They come when you leave me."

"I won't leave you. I'm right here. I love you, Jonah." She held him tightly and kissed the top of his head.

Jonah fell asleep in Rachel's arms, and she continued to rock him through the night. Even when she knew he was deep in sleep, she just didn't want to let him go. When she saw the light come on Fatima's main floor, she knew it was 4 am. She put Jonah in her bed and kissed him again. "I won't ever leave you, as long as I live."

She returned to her rocking chair and pulled out her list.

Chapter Seven

꒓

Sundays were usually an easy day at Fatima's house. They tried not to go anywhere or have any specific plans. It was just a day for the family to relax and enjoy each other. The girls did whatever they wanted and that usually meant starting the day by jumping on whoever was still in bed.

This morning the bed was empty. Ali had gone for a run, and Fatima was studying at her desk in the family room.

The room was comfortable, with walls painted a soft earth tone and decorated with soft pink couches and armchairs. Cashmere pillows and throws helped to create a serene setting. Two large windows on either side of the fireplace were draped in fabric that matched the couches. Framed nature scenes hung on the walls.

Fatima's desk was neatly tucked in the corner to the right of the entrance. She often came to this room to relax. On winter nights she loved to unwind in front of the fireplace.

She didn't usually study on Sundays, but she felt restless today and needed to do something to occupy her mind. She decided to put in a few hours early and relax the rest of the day.

Usually when Ali returned from a trip, the girls were interested in him exclusively, for at least a few hours. Fatima would take advantage of that time to do something for herself.

Her exams were starting in two weeks, and she had to push herself to study. At this stage in her pregnancy she could not care less about course work. She just wanted to prepare for her baby, although there wasn't much for her to do. They already had the major things, and she would do most of the other shopping after the baby was born. She had help to clean and do laundry once a week, and she really didn't have to cook if she didn't want to. That definitely made it a bit easier to study, but with three active little girls, it was still chaotic most of the time.

Suddenly, Masuma came running down the steps into the lower level, giving Fatima an excuse to take a break. "I'm telling on you!"

Laila screamed behind her, "It wasn't me!"

"Yes, it was!" Batool was crying.

Fatima turned to face three very upset little girls. "What happened?"

All three girls were yelling and crying while Masuma waved a piece of paper in her hand that had red and green crayon scribbled on it.

"Laila was drawing on Daddy's paper."

"Give it to me. Where did you get this? Fatima asked.

"In his drawer, but it was an accident!" Laila was hysterical now.

The girls knew that Ali usually kept treats for them in his bedside table.

"It's a bit early for sweets, don't you think?" Fatima took the paper from Masuma's hand and realized, too late, that it was the letter from the lawyer that had arrived on Friday.

As she tried to process what she had read, she suddenly felt her heart racing, and her breath became hard to catch. She stared at the paper so long it no longer seemed real. When she heard Ali enter the house, she told the girls to go to the basement and watch a movie.

"We want to see Daddy." They all started jumping.

"Get in the basement!" Fatima yelled.

The girls froze. She had never yelled at them before.

She softened her voice. "Masuma, please take them," Fatima pleaded, as she tried to control her trembling.

The girls quickly and quietly disappeared while Fatima sunk her face into her two hands. When she looked up Ali was standing in front of her, wearing a beige track suit with baby blue lines along the sides.

"What's going on?" he asked in a soft but concerned voice. He couldn't imagine what would cause her to yell at the children.

Fatima couldn't get the words out. She held up the paper. "Masuma found this in your drawer."

Ali slowly took the paper from her hand.

"So this is what's going on? Someone is filing a paternity suit against you?"

Chapter Eight

ℑ

Ali stared at the paper in his hand. Fatima remained speechless. As the initial shock started to dissipate, she waited expectantly for Ali to give the explanation that she knew would clarify everything.

"What is this?" Ali looked up.

"Notification of a paternity suit." Fatima pressed her temples with her fingertips.

"This was in my drawer?" Ali asked.

"This is the letter that came on Friday. The one you took and obviously put in your drawer." *He is not going to act like he doesn't know what he's looking at.*

"I never saw this," he said, shaking his head.

"Ok, so it walked to your drawer." Fatima's frustration started to grow.

"No, I took the mail to our room to read it, and then the girls woke up, so I just put all the mail in the drawer. I never actually read anything."

"It's open, Ali." Fatima linked her fingers behind her head and leaned back into her chair.

"Where's the envelope?" Ali asked.

Fatima lifted the envelope from her desk. "It's right here."

Ali took it from Fatima. "I would open mail like this? Obviously the kids opened it. Fatima, this is the first time I'm seeing this, really."

"Whatever. That's beside the point." Fatima fanned her hand in the air. "What's this about a paternity suit?"

"I have no idea what this is about." Ali looked at the letter again. "I can't believe this."

"That's not exactly what I need to hear right now."

"Fatima this is not even possible. This is crazy. You have to know that. It's obviously a mistake."

Fatima got up and crossed the floor. When she passed the sun shaped mirror above the fireplace she could see Ali's reflection. He was distressed, as she would expect, but he wasn't saying anything that was helping her at this moment.

"Fatima, come on, sit down. Please, don't be upset by this. You don't think for one second that this could be true?" Ali asked.

"Oh well, I don't know, lawyers don't usually send out mail notifying lawsuits that have no validity. This is a reputable firm. They're not going to risk their reputation on some nut-case. They have to do interviews and see evidence. They need to investigate before they take on a case like this. You're not some Joe Blow. You're a well-known athlete, with money. They're not going to take a chance like this, Ali."

"I know. I know." Ali's voice was reduced to a whisper.

"So, *what* are you saying?" Fatima asked him. "This is some crazy woman who forgot who her child's father is, and just woke up deciding it should be you?" Fatima was starting to feel light-headed.

"Of course not." His voice softened. "Fatima, I hate what this is doing to you. You should calm down. Let me get you some water."

"Don't patronize me, I'm fine. I don't need water. I just need some answers right now."

"I wish I had answers for you. I don't understand this at all. I have no clue what's behind this. I'll call Shawn in the morning and figure this out."

Shawn was Ali's childhood friend. He was a diligent and focused young lawyer who had quickly worked his way up to one of the top law firms in Toronto. Many firms had been vying for him, and he had decided to work for a small but busy firm just outside of the downtown area.

"You'll figure this out. Oh, so easy." Fatima sat back in her chair.

"Fatima, I don't know who this woman is, and even if I did, her child can't be mine." He pointed toward the door leading to the basement. "I have three children, and they're all downstairs." Ali stated in a voice so calm Fatima wondered if they were really discussing the same subject.

"Think Ali, think."

Ali's face dropped. "About what? There is only you. No one else. Not before you, and not after you. Fatima, I don't need to think about that." Ali turned away while Fatima followed him with her eyes.

She knew she should believe him, but with this letter in front of her, how could she?

"Why not call Shawn now?" Fatima looked at Ali hopefully. She needed answers.

"It's Sunday, and he's gone to a wedding." Ali reached out to touch her arm in a reassuring gesture before she pulled away.

"He has a cell phone."

"Fatima, I understand how you feel, but he can't do anything about it today. Really, I'll talk to him in the morning."

"Well, I'm happy you're taking it so lightly." Fatima stepped around him and sat on the steps leading to the upper level.

"You think I'm taking this lightly? I have a family, my wife is pregnant and we get *this*." Ali shook the letter in his hand. "I see this as a threat to my family. Trust me, I'm not taking this lightly, but I don't know anything more than what is on this paper." He looked at Fatima and added, "And that I don't have any kids except ours."

"Why do you think someone would do something like this?" Fatima asked.

Ali sat down on the chair that Fatima had left vacant and

leaned forward. "I don't want to speculate. I don't know what to think. I'll speak to Shawn tomorrow and see where we go from here."

"So, you didn't know about this letter, but the law office just happens to be in Ottawa, and that is where you happened to go the other night and couldn't tell me why? Do you think it's reasonable for me not to draw a connection?"

"My trip had nothing to do with this."

"Oh, that's wonderful!" Fatima threw her hands up in the air. "Another mystery. Do you realize how this is looking to me?"

"Of course I do, but Fatima there is no way this can be true. I have never heard this woman's name before today. I don't know her, or any other woman for that matter, and I'm going to get to the bottom of it starting tomorrow. I promise you."

Fatima held her head up. "It's a boy."

"What?" Ali jerked his head.

"The child is a boy. Look at the letter." Fatima pointed at the paper in Ali's hand.

"It has nothing to do with me," Ali said, ignoring the letter and keeping his attention on Fatima.

"Well, apparently it does, because the letter is addressed to you," she snapped.

"It's not my boy, Fatima." Ali stood to move towards her, but Fatima held him at arm's length. He continued speaking. "Listen, I get it. It's disturbing news. It's enough to jack up anybody, never mind when you're pregnant."

Fatima refused to answer him. She wasn't quite sure what she wanted him to say, but she knew what he was offering was not enough.

He sighed and closed his eyes. "I know how hard it is for you to be married to me. I do. I'm on the road constantly while you're alone at home with the girls, or you have to rearrange your life to travel with me. I know it's not easy. It's hard for me too. Now you're pregnant. I think about it all the time. Honestly, if I could give you something more, you know I would. This is as shocking to me as it is to you."

"The name doesn't ring a bell at all?"

"No, Fatima," he insisted. Ali sat down again and turned his attention back to the letter.

"Swear to me."

As soon as the words left her mouth, she realized the impact that they would have. Swearing was very serious and strongly disapproved of in Islam. In addition to that, the suggestion that she didn't believe him would be very serious to him.

Ali squinted and knit his brow as he absorbed the meaning of her words. "Fatima-" he started.

"Forget it," Fatima interrupted him, flashing her hand in his direction.

"You know what..." Ali rose to his feet. "I'm going to call Shawn. At least I can leave a message."

"Thank you, Ali." Fatima finally felt some relief. At least he was taking some action.

Ali disappeared to the upper levels of the house while Fatima remained in the family room. She knew he was offended at the suggestion that she didn't believe him. Integrity was important to him. If he said it was so, he expected you to take him at his word, and he always gave people the benefit of the doubt until he knew otherwise. She sounded like she doubted him and she knew Ali would not take that lightly.

What did he expect? There were definitely some missing pieces here. After all, this was all being dumped in her lap. She hadn't gone looking for it. She had exams in two weeks, and all this was now on her head. She felt her baby moving as her body started to relax and her breathing returned to normal. What affect was all this having on her child? She was seriously stressed out. She knew she should trust him, but she could not get rid of that nagging feeling that something bad, very bad was going to happen.

Really, how could someone think of accusing the wrong person of fathering their child? DNA would prove them to be a liar, so what could be gained by filing a false claim? There was still the matter of Ottawa; if it wasn't about this case, then what was it about? What was so urgent and secret?

True, Ali had never given her any reason to doubt him. He was always sincere, almost transparent. That's why she had married him. She had always felt secure with him. It was something she had lacked growing up.

From their first meeting, Fatima had spent most of her free time in the Abati household. She didn't have any brothers or sisters, and Ali and Rachel had been like siblings to her. Though Rachel had had an older brother and sister, they never paid much attention to the two girls.

Fatima's mother, Dana, had worked long hours, and her father, who had separated from Dana when Fatima was young, was not very involved in Fatima's life. Fatima was frequently left on her own. The Abati home had had a sense of comfort in it. She had not realized then, but the family had been through the worst experience possible, yet they were still warm, loving, happy and always giving to others.

When they had moved in, they had introduced themselves to all the neighbours and had become parents of all the neighbourhood children. Their door was usually unlocked during the day; people were often in and out of their home.

Ali had been a quiet child. He was a good student, but had put most of his spare time and energy into sports. Fatima later realized that it had been an outlet for him. Physical activity was a way for him to release the pain he held inside. He had lost his grandparents, aunts, uncles, cousins, neighbours and friends. Fatima shuddered at the thought.

What if her girls had lost Mama and Papa, Rahma, Naomi, Rachel, Joshua and Jonah in one sweep? How would they function? How could they ever be happy again? Could they have any joy in life? How could they ever love or trust again?

Fortunately, Mama and Papa had been strong. They had built a life that was stable and full of love. Routine was an important part of their life. Mama was a smart woman and she had insisted that it was what Ali needed to feel secure. He had had all security ripped away from him and she had worked very hard to recreate that feeling in his daily life. So he had healed; or so Fatima had thought.

Sometimes she could see the old pain. At times he would sit for long periods and just stare. She never asked him what he was thinking about. She was afraid to know. She wanted to be supportive, but she just couldn't bear to hear about the horrors that she imagined he had been through. She did feel guilty about it, like perhaps she was letting him down by not being there for him completely.

Still, he continued to be pleasant, positive, warm and kind to everyone. He had once told her that focusing on others helped him to feel alive. It blocked the pain and gave him an excuse not to think about himself. He had been a man even then, and was deeply affected by the fact that he could not stop what had happened to his family in Rwanda. He had vowed that he would never allow anything like that to happen again.

At school he had not taken many close friends. Although he was friendly with everyone, when he left school he preferred to be alone. His classmates were eager to play with him and the boys frequently wanted to fight with him, as a way to test their strength. Ali would usually refuse, but, if he had to, he could definitely hold his own.

He had focused much of his energy on martial arts and had become a four-time champion in mixed martial arts. One of his favourite pastimes was archery, and when he was stressed he usually spent time in that sport. He had introduced Shawn to it so he would have someone to compete with when the mood took him, but he usually practiced alone.

The passion and drive that he put into sports moved Fatima. In his daily life he was calm, controlled, pensive, but when he was on the court, in the pool or on any kind of field he changed. Another person emerged. He was aggressive and intense. It made Fatima wonder about the emotions that he kept inside.

Well, Fatima thought, *it was good that he released his emotions somehow*. His parents had suggested counseling for him, but he had refused, saying he didn't need it.

Though he had often spoken to Fatima and Rachel, he never spoke about the past, only his plans for the future. He talked about how he was going to take care of his parents and his own family, when he had one. Fatima had wanted to take care of *him*. He had seemed so sad.

He had always been serious and disciplined and his parents had given him great freedom because they trusted him. Indeed, he was always where he said he was going to be, doing what he said he was going to be doing. If his parents ever said no to him, concerning something he wanted, he accepted it. During his teenage years, when most kids were going through internal and external turmoil, he just played harder.

Papa had often taken Rachel and Fatima to Ali's events, thus influencing them to become athletes too. Rachel had been on a swim team throughout high school. Fatima had loved running and martial arts. Most of her training had come from Ali, who had started teaching when he was 14.

He had insisted that she pursue at least one form, and she had earned her black belt in Tae Kwon Do by the age of 16. Ali had not been satisfied. He wanted her to be proficient in a variety of forms and he continued to train her. He allowed her three months rest after she had her babies, then it was back to work. He had already started training his daughters. It was important to him that they had the confidence to stand up for themselves when necessary. He knew he wasn't always going to be there to protect them, and the thought seemed to disturb him sometimes.

Fatima walked to the French doors that faced the backyard. They were framed by matching window panes. She stepped into the bay and looked out at the two fountains and the birds that danced in the water daily. She remembered the day her mother had told her that Ali wanted to marry her. He had told his parents of his intentions and they had spoken to her mother. Dana definitely thought Fatima was too young, but Ali's father had convinced Dana that they were good kids and if Ali could prove that he was responsible, he would give his blessing. They would support the young couple and Papa believed they would be fine. "It's better to be with one than many," he had said.

It had not been hard for Dana to accept Ali as a son-in-law. She had loved him already. He was so different from the other boys.

In the end when Dana had seen the path that Rachel had taken, she realized that early marriage and family was not the worst that could happen to a girl. Rachel's children had been born close to Fatima's. Joshua was just three months younger than Masuma and Jonah had followed soon after.

Ali had prepared well for his marriage to Fatima. When he had the chance to play professional basketball, it was an opportunity he couldn't refuse. The freedom and income it would give him would enable him to do all the things he had dreamed of.

He had adjusted well to the rigours of the profession, and he and his father had bonded in the year that they had travelled together. Papa said he was truly proud of the way Ali had handled himself. It was in his contract that he be given time to pray wherever he was, thus his prayers were always on time. He never played on the days of *Eid* or on the *10th of Muharram*. The other players had grown to love him and respect his commitment to his values.

They often congregated in Ali's room after games, where they could escape from the pressures of the road. They knew it was a place where they could find peace and be free to be themselves. Papa had said many of them had not had fathers and had appreciated his presence and guidance. Nowadays, many of the players, even the ones much older than Ali, confided in him and sought advice from him.

The only weakness Ali had was when it came to his wife. He was usually careful about the way he spent his money, but made sure Fatima always had whatever she wanted. Fortunately for him, she thought the same way that he did and was focused on building their future. He always joked that if she had been a more demanding woman, he would have been in the poor house.

The first year of their marriage had been pure fun. While most of Fatima's friends were in university or working, she was travelling across North America with Ali. While her friends were trying to juggle jobs and school and explore new and sometimes dangerous freedoms, she was settled in her beautiful home with her doting husband.

Ali's teammates were initially disappointed to learn that Papa was no longer going to be a regular on the road, and they wondered how their night-time sessions would be affected now that Ali's wife was going to be with him. Many of them were not accustomed to being around a woman in *hijab* and did not know what to expect.

Fatima had immediately put them at ease and had encouraged them to continue to crash with them. Ali always had a room with a separate bedroom suite, to allow her privacy. The rule was that they could come over anytime. They should call first, but if they couldn't, they were welcome to just knock on the door. Fatima saw, firsthand, the trials of the profession, and she wanted them to have a safe place if they needed to get away from it all.

It always moved Fatima to see those big tough guys crash on the hotel room floor and talk about their deepest feelings, fears and wishes. Sure, there was a lot of joking and rough housing too, bragging and game commentaries included, but there were many moments of open sharing, especially when there were only one or two teammates present at a time.

Many of the wives had come to know Fatima, and on occasion a wife had called her to inquire about her own husband's conduct. Fatima never revealed anything. She had a standard answer prepared. She always told them that she understood the pressures of the road and she made it a rule not to mind anyone's business except her own. The players loved her even more for that.

When she had Masuma and couldn't travel as much, they all vowed to keep Ali in line for her. They sometimes even called to check up on her. It was funny the way they treated Ali. They were often just as aware of his duties as he was himself. They reminded him to pray and always let him know that they had their eye on him.

Because of the stories that Mama had heard about life on the road, she had formed a network with the mothers of some of the ball players called *Moms Away*. It was a network of mothers in various cities. The players knew that if they needed a mother while they were on the road, they had one. They could call the mother that was in town to talk, get a home-cooked meal, or just a safe place to stay. Naturally, the Abati home was a favourite.

Now Fatima thought about Ali being upstairs and wondered what he was doing. *He must have made the call by now.* She knew she had hurt him. The worst thing for a Muslim to be was a liar. The suggestion that he may not be telling her the truth was like questioning his *deen*-religion, and that would have been unacceptable to him.

She went downstairs to check on the girls, and found them asleep. "Oh, poor things." Fatima's heart broke. "They must have been traumatized," she whispered. She pulled blankets over them and then climbed the stairs to speak to Ali. She found him in the study in front of the computer.

She walked behind him to see the screen. He usually took university courses during the summer, either in night school or online, towards completing a degree in Leisure and Recreation. Fatima was surprised to see him looking at the course calendar now, because he had said he wasn't going to take any courses this year.

"I thought you weren't going to study this summer," she said.

"I reconsidered," Ali answered without turning around.

"Ali."

"Fatima," he replied, while keeping his eyes on the screen.

"It's never hard for me to be your wife. You're the most important thing in my life. You are my life. I just get scared sometimes."

Ali turned around and pulled another chair close to him. He motioned for her to sit. She sat in the chair and waited for his response.

"I can understand that." He reached for an ottoman for her to rest her feet on, and continued, "What are you afraid of?"

"Just losing everything."

"How would that happen?"

"I don't know. Maybe we'll grow apart. Maybe one day this baller lifestyle will just transform you and we'll end up like all the other players and their wives."

Ali nodded and Fatima could see that he was thinking. He leaned back in his chair. "What do you think I do when I'm away from home?" he finally asked.

Fatima shrugged her shoulders. "Play ball?"

"And?" Ali prompted.

Fatima shook her head. "I don't know."

"I think. I think about my life, my responsibilities and my girls, all of them. I think about you, our babies, my mom and Rahma. My father is not going to be here forever, and then it will all be on me. I have to make sure that everyone has what they need, is safe and happy. That's what I think about, how I'm going to do that, how I'm going to make that happen. Do you really believe I have time to mess with my life, my family, my future?"

"That's not fair, Ali. Don't flip this on me." Fatima resented the direction she felt him going in. He was making it seem like she was in the wrong. "How do you expect me to react under these circumstances?"

"I expect you to be furious that someone would attack our family this way. That's what I expect." When there was no reply, Ali rubbed his face as he watched his wife. "I'm going to be going on the road again, in a few days. How can I feel comfortable to do that if you doubt me?"

"I don't... I'm not... I didn't... I'm not sure what to think right now." Fatima felt completely drained.

Ali let out a short laugh as he stood up. "Do you know how that makes me feel? All of this is for you. My work, the money, the sacrifice, everything is for you. If you're at home and stressed out about me, then it's not worth it. I had no idea you felt this way. I thought we had an understanding. I thought everything was ok. Now I find out that an accusation from someone we don't even know can tear it all apart? How can that be?"

Fatima remained silent.

"I must really be doing something wrong," Ali said

"So what now?" Fatima asked.

"I guess that's on me. I left a message for Shawn to call me immediately and I'm going to move on this tomorrow, but it's not just about the letter. It's deeper than that. Next time it will be something else. How we handle future challenges is going to depend on the foundation we have as a couple. That's what I'm concerned about."

"Ok. So what are you saying?" Fatima stroked the arms of her chair.

"I'm saying I got a wakeup call today. I realize I just can't take anything for granted." He walked around the room.

"I just thought your reaction was kind of strange. You seemed so calm," Fatima said, following him with her eyes.

"Yes, I'm calm. You know why? Because it doesn't matter. None of it matters to me. These issues, these challenges, they come and go. I can handle whatever comes at me. It only matters to me if it affects you. Otherwise, I'll just deal with whatever happens. That's life."

Fatima didn't answer. Hearing him put things like that; she didn't know what to say.

"Let me ask you this." Ali sat in his chair again and pulled it forward. "Take this situation, for example. What's the worst thing that can happen? For *you* what would be the worst thing?"

Fatima thought about it before replying, "Well, if it was true, I guess."

"And so what if it were true? You think *Allah* can't get you through it?" Ali asked her.

"What are you saying?" If he was trying to make her feel better, he was taking the wrong approach.

"I'm showing you how I keep things in perspective. If you realize that your worst fear is nothing, then you can release the fear. Even if the worst happens, you'll get through. You have to trust Him, Fatima. You don't need to work everything out for yourself. I don't even try. I just put it in *Allah's* hands and leave it there."

She felt ashamed. She knew what he was saying was true, and compared to what he had been through in his life, this really was nothing. Why should he react?

Ali continued. "The situation is only as bad as you make it."

"That's fine for you, Ali, but what about me? You're not the only one in this."

Ali had a pained look on his face. "I've called Shawn. There's nothing more I can do right now."

Fatima thought about what Ali had said but could not understand where he was coming from. "What would be the worst thing for you, in this situation?" Fatima asked him.

"The worst thing would be if it upsets you and if it hurts our marriage. Still, no matter what happens, I have to deal with it. Part of self-building is being the master of your emotions."

Fatima remained silent. Ali certainly was getting good at mastering his emotions. She was having difficulty reading him right now. Was he trying to tell her that she didn't have anything to worry about, or was he saying that she might, but she should choose not to worry? She wasn't quite sure.

Fatima fixed her eyes on Ali. She needed to be able to see the slightest waver when she asked the next question. "Do you know what I keep thinking about? That one time - I don't know, maybe it was more than one time - that you called, asking me to join you on the road, and I didn't go. I thought I couldn't. I just wasn't feeling well, and I had exams. You just asked me out of the blue, and I never asked you why."

Ali held her gaze. "It was one time, and I understood that. It was not a problem."

"But I never asked you why." Fatima couldn't help wondering if she had made a mistake; made a mistake by not going to him, made a mistake by becoming comfortable with him travelling by himself. She remembered the first year that they had travelled together. She knew exactly what the dangers were. *I have three kids, how can I keep up with him?* She sighed. Ali hadn't wanted to start a family when she did. She had pushed for that.

Ali shook his head. "Why I wanted you to come? There's only

one reason and it's always the same. You're my wife and I wanted you with me, that's all. I just missed you. The same as always. There's nothing else." Ali held out his hands to emphasize his last statement.

Fatima sighed and stood up. She was well aware how much of "nothing" happened on the road. "Ok Ali, I'm exhausted. I'm going to lie down."

"What about the girls?" Ali asked, as Fatima walked towards the door.

"They fell asleep in the basement. You can put them in bed if you want. I would just leave them though. I already covered them with a blanket."

Fatima headed towards her bedroom. Looking over the railing, she spotted the flowers, in the foyer, as she walked down the hall. "Ali, you know your mom has been really quiet these last few days," she said.

Ali turned away, but Fatima could see the tension in his jaw. "Well, it *is* April," he said

Fatima had forgotten. April was the anniversary of the start of the genocide in Rwanda. Every April Mama became very sombre. Her mood usually lasted for a few weeks. At that time she would pour her energy into the garden. The summer would show the fruit of all her work. She had the most beautiful garden on the street. "Ali, I forgot. I am so sorry." She started walking back towards him, but he held up his hand.

"Don't worry. Go rest."

Fatima turned and headed to her room. Before she closed the white double doors, she looked towards the study. She could see that Ali had pulled away from the desk, his elbow resting on his knee. He was rubbing his forehead against the palm of his hand. Now the events of the day really did seem small indeed.

Chapter Nine

ℑ

"Why don't *you* ever get wet?"

"My job is to instruct. Your job is to swim." Rachel walked along the side of the pool, in her flip-flops, while Tracy and the other girls completed their warm-up laps. Every few minutes, she would glide her foot through the water. She could never be this close to a pool and not go in.

Tracy stopped swimming and started treading water. "I think it's about time you feel how refreshing this pool is." Tracy pulled her hand back, threatening to splash Rachel as she continued walking.

"If one drop of water touches me you'll be doing extra laps, breast-stroke."

"After all these years, you're still no fun." Tracy glided forward and resumed her gentle strokes in line with the other five girls on the team. Rachel had been coaching her since she was nine years old and the other girls almost as long. They were all Grade 11 and 12 students now. Though they were silly sometimes, when it came to the business of swimming, they didn't mess around. They held three national records to prove it.

Rachel continued to run the girls through various drills until 8 pm. As they were getting out of the water, Rachel noticed a young man outside the exit door. When Rachel spotted him he stepped to the side. The giggling that was coming from the girls as they headed toward the change room told her that something was going on that she needed to investigate. She walked toward the exit and spoke to the young man in the hall. "Hi, can I help you?"

"Waitin' for Tracy," he mumbled. Rachel raised her eyebrow and quickly processed what she had just taken in about this boy. Extremely saggy jeans rolled over untied sneakers, bandana hanging out of his back pocket, another one on his head, two fitted t-shirts, at least five earrings, and tattoos travelling from his knuckles to his neck.

You can wait a little longer. Rachel thought. She slipped into the office and called Tracy's mother. "Mrs. Taylor, I'll be driving by your house, would it be all right if I gave Tracy a ride home?"

"Of course, but I thought she was planning to go for pizza with some friends after practice."

"Somehow, I think she's had a change of plans," Rachel replied.

Rachel entered the change room just as the girls were getting dressed. Silence fell on the room as soon as she appeared.

"Tracy, I just spoke to your mom. She's expecting me to drive you home. I'll be out in five." Before Tracy could answer, Rachel left. Not on her life was she going to let one of her girls leave with *that*. What was Tracy thinking? The guy couldn't even put a sentence together.

How Rachel wished she had had someone to look out for her when she was that age. Girls just had no clue the kind of fire they were playing with. It's all fun and games, until you're left holding the dirty end of the stick. No matter how you warned them, every girl thought she was the exception. Rachel knew that from experience.

Later that night Rachel rocked herself in her chair. She often sat and looked out her window when she needed to clear her head. The night sky, moon and stars had a soothing effect on her. She loved the sounds of the night – the insects, the wind whistling through the trees, dogs barking and cars in the distance.

She had dropped Tracy home earlier and lectured her all the way. Tracy had told her that *Troy* was no one special, just a guy from the neighbourhood. Nothing to worry about. *Nothing to worry about. These girls had no clue.*

Rachel hugged a stuffed bear that her father had bought for her before she was born. She always held it when she wanted to feel close to him. For weeks, after his death, the bear still held his scent. Then one day she had picked up the bear and could no longer smell him. The last real part of him was gone forever.

Her room was still decorated as it had been in her childhood. Soft hues of pink and purple dominated the space and in one corner of the room a huge mound of stuffed animals reached half way up the wall. The wallpaper was white with tiny pink flowers on it.

Her parents had decorated her room as a surprise Christmas present one year. In all these years she hadn't changed anything. She still slept on a single bed. Many nights one or both of her sons would come to her room. They would all sleep together, or Rachel might leave them in the bed and spend the night in her chair.

Now it was late and she couldn't sleep, as usual. She had so many thoughts running through her head. She hadn't told Fatima everything. She still had to go back to the doctor. The ultrasound had shown old scar tissue. The doctors were not sure how it would impact her reproductive health. Tears streamed down her face. She thought about her sons, and Jamie, and all that she had lost because of him. She knew that it wasn't his fault. She had made the choices, but it had just been so hard. Everything in her life felt so hard.

Outside the street was quiet. They lived on a long street that ended in a circle. It was perfect for the kids, and felt very safe. There was one way in and one way out.

She tried to remember her father's voice, the way he used to talk to her, read to her and sing to her. Life had crumbled after his death, and Naomi had never been the same. The night he died was the last time Rachel had had a mother and a father. She had been orphaned on her 10th birthday and she had refused to celebrate another birthday since.

She had refused to leave the gravesite on the day of the funeral. Even though it had been raining, she had stayed. She was only 10, but her mother had respected her decision. Fatima had insisted on staying with her. Mama and Papa had agreed to stay with the girls, at the cemetery, for as long as needed. They understood death and loss in a way that few others did.

They had stayed for hours in the rain. Rachel had wanted to pray for her father, and Papa had encouraged her to do so. Those memories were so bitter sweet. She had suffered so much, but the comfort, support and strength she had garnered from the Abatis was unlike any other. Whenever she was in need they were there. She had never returned to the cemetery after that day. She couldn't say good-bye twice.

She often wondered how her life might have been different if she had had her father or even her big brother in her life. Would Jamie have pursued her as he did if he had known that she had men looking out for her? She didn't think so.

Ali had disapproved of Jamie from the start and the two had had several confrontations as a result. Yet, Rachel had been weak enough to still let him through. She suspected that one of the reasons he usually came around at night was to avoid Ali. Only when Ali was travelling did he make daytime appearances, and then usually with a lot of bravado attached to them.

Rachel hated those times the most because Joshua and Jonah would see him, and they would be so crushed when they didn't get the attention that they so craved from him. After his departure Joshua would be sullen and withdrawn and Jonah would start having nightmares again.

Recently his nightmares had not been connected to a visit from his father, and Rachel didn't know what to make of that. She wanted to heal her sons, but she didn't know how to heal herself.

She hugged her bear tighter and rested her face on the animal's now wet head. Some days she felt so scared. There were so many things she wanted to do, yet she felt blocked. She saw herself free from Jamie and living a life that utilized her talents and skills. She also hoped for a family of her own, with a good role model for her sons. She knew that there was no reason for it, yet she couldn't get through the wall that seemed to stand between her and her ideal life.

She thought about her boys and wondered how they would grow up to be men without their father. She feared what they would think of her if they ever found out what she had done.

The decision to terminate the first pregnancy had been made quickly. She had been a teenager and stressed out and all she knew was that she could not tell her mother. She had just wanted her life to go back to normal. She had only told Fatima about what was going on.

Of course, Fatima had begged her not to do it. Fatima had not been married yet, so Rachel doubted that she could even begin to understand what she was dealing with. Fatima had pleaded with her to talk to her mother. Rachel had refused. That would have defeated the purpose. She didn't want her mother to know. She already had enough stress to deal with. Rachel could not put an added burden on her. She had turned to Fatima, instead, but had not taken her advice.

She had thought about talking to Ali, to get the male perspective, but she would have been mortified if he had known the truth. Still, she felt if he had told her not to go through with it, she may have listened. She remembered during that time they had all taken a road trip with some friends. She had been sick and Fatima was very attentive. Ali must have been concerned because at one stop when everyone left the van, to get food, he had stayed back and asked her, point blank, what was wrong.

"I'm sick," she had replied.

"What kind of sick?" Ali had countered. His hard stare had really unnerved her. She had no reply. She had been saved by the other passengers returning to the van. She knew he must have considered all the possibilities, but in the end there had been no baby so she assumed he had laid it to rest.

After everything was over Rachel had been surprised that she didn't feel back to normal. Babies haunted her. She saw them everywhere, and within a few weeks she was consumed by guilt. The due date of her baby became an obsession. When the day came, she decided that she had to have another baby, and she had to have one with Jamie. She knew it would not be the same baby, but she had to know what a possibility might be.

Unfortunately, she hadn't spoken to anyone about her feelings. She hadn't realized that she needed help in dealing with her unresolved issues.

When Fatima got married and began travelling with Ali, Rachel had felt so alone. Then came Masuma. Fatima was ecstatic. Ali hadn't planned on starting a family so soon, but he warmed up to the idea quickly. It was all too much for Rachel. She was pregnant almost immediately after Fatima had made her happy announcement. Joshua was born three months after Masuma.

Jamie had only visited Rachel once in the early days after Joshua's birth. When she realized she was pregnant again, she felt like such an idiot she couldn't tell anyone. That's when Jamie had started coming around incognito. Ali had promised that if he ever saw him in the neighbourhood he would make sure it was his last visit. They all took him seriously. No one ever told Ali about Jamie's visits when he was travelling.

The fourth pregnancy had completely caught her off guard. She hadn't paid attention to the fact that she was feeling strange, and when she realized what had happened she was already three months pregnant. She thought seriously about what to do. She sat many times at this same window watching the street and imagining what her life would be like if she had a third child out of wedlock.

She was so ashamed. What would her friends think of her? How could she do this to another child? What if it was another boy? Oh God, what if it was a girl? She couldn't handle it. Yet, she had promised never to do again what she had done before. Jamie had known about the first abortion and he had abused her terribly for it. He had called her a murderer on many occasions. All of that had stopped when she had Joshua.

She knew that no matter what she decided, she could not tell him what she had been considering. Then he had come by that night a few weeks ago and she had tried to tell him. He didn't even want to hear that she might be pregnant. *If* she was, he had said, there was no way he believed it could be his child. He accused her of terrible things.

She pressed her hands against her ears to block out the memory of his harsh voice and stinging words. She had decided right then that she would not have the baby. She was not going down the same road with him, and she was not going to regret it this time. She would just move on. Still, she was devastated that she was in the same position again.

She looked out at Fatima's house. When the lights went out, she knew it was safe to go outside. She needed some fresh air and she couldn't take a chance that Fatima or Ali would see her out alone that late. She placed the teddy bear back on her bed. She would wash her face and apply light makeup, just to feel good.

She laughed when she looked at herself in the mirror. "What's the point? Who's going to see me?" She quietly checked on her boys and her mother. They were all sleeping peacefully. She tiptoed into the sometimes creaky hall and down the stairs.

Outside the cool night air snapped her back to the present. The wind whistling through the trees reminded her of a sad song. She pictured some gothic creature moaning as the wind carried them from tree to tree and she wondered why she, so often, felt driven to come out during the night. She locked the door and when she turned around to step off the porch, her breath caught in her throat.

"Jamie," she said breathlessly. She felt her heart thumping in her chest and she held the railing to steady herself. She was terrified of him, but she was not going to let it show. She straightened her back and asked evenly, "What are you doing here?"

He smiled easily. "I was in the neighbourhood. I came to see you."

He was tall, about six feet. Rachel looked past his broad shoulders to the street. She didn't see his car. She was quickly trying to calculate the best way to get away from him. He was strong, she knew that, and each time he came around he seemed stronger. He had become obsessed with working out in recent years. The stairway was not too wide and his body blocked her escape on one side, while he held the opposite railing with his hand.

"I'm fine, as usual." She tried to push past him, but knew that she could never do it if he did not allow her.

"Not so fast. Where are you off to?" Jamie asked, his voice heavy with insinuation.

"I'm going for a walk. Now move." Her voice didn't sound as strong as she wanted it to. She looked past him to the garden that Ali had planted. *Why did he have to be so regular?* She wondered if she should scream. It hadn't been that long since Fatima's lights had gone out. With the street so quiet, they would surely hear her. No. There was no reason to panic, yet. Everything would be fine.

"You look a little thin compared to the last time I saw you. You stressed out or something?" His eyes travelled slowly from her face to her feet and Rachel had to shake to throw off the chill.

"Single parenting will do that to you. Excuse me." She grabbed his wrist. It felt like warm steel. She wondered what would happen if she grabbed his pinky and pulled it right off. Ali had always told them that when out-matched by an opponent they should not try to match strength, but be prepared to attack weak spots.

"Slow down. Aren't you letting me in?" He stepped up one level.

Rachel glared at him. He was dark. She could see he had recently shaved his head and his dark eyes were piercing. Some would say he was handsome, but she knew the other side of him and she didn't want to deal with that now, not when she was barely coping with all that was on her mind tonight.

"Why in the hell would I let you into my house?" She surprised even herself with her response, but she had to start building her courage sometime.

Jamie was visibly taken aback. She had never spoken to him in that manner, and he obviously didn't like it. He was used to getting his own way and he was going to come out on top one way or another tonight. He grabbed her face and squeezed it between his thumb and his four fingers. She could feel the sweat running down the back of her neck while tears burned her eyes. She would never give him the satisfaction of seeing her cry.

"You better watch your mouth, understand me?" He let go and slapped her face not too gently. "You know if I decide to go in you can't stop me. *Asking* is just a courtesy."

Rachel put her hand to her face to stop her jaw from trembling. "The boys are sleeping," she said in an almost pleading voice.

Jamie stepped closer to her. "That's why you'll be quiet." Rachel clutched the railing so hard that her circulation cut off and her knuckles turned yellow.

Suddenly Jamie let out a harsh laugh. "I'll give you and your nasty little attitude a pass tonight. I understand why you're feeling a little out of sorts," he sneered.

Rachel could feel her heart in her throat. Her breathing became strained. The cool breeze on her sweating body caused her trembling to intensify. What did he know, she wondered? The seconds felt like minutes. She was frozen. Her body was so stiff it ached, as she waited for him to continue.

"I guess you heard the news?"

"What news?" Rachel asked, confused.

"Oh, you *didn't* hear? It's all over the internet. Seems the almighty Ali has finally taken a fall."

Jamie let go of the railing and stepped back. He knew she wouldn't go anywhere now.

"What are you talking about?" She desperately searched his face as if she could pull the answers out of him.

"Seems like good little Ali is only good when he's at home. On the road is another matter."

"What do you mean?" Rachel was angry just hearing Jamie say Ali's name.

"Apparently, he has another kid out there somewhere." Jamie leaned casually on the railing.

Rachel gasped. She would never believe it, and certainly not coming from Jamie. "Shut your mouth. You shut your dirty mouth!" She almost screamed at him, "You don't know what you're talking about."

Jamie glared at her, but he was enjoying the scene too much to get angry. "Ok, see for yourself." He pulled out his phone, found a news site online and thrust the screen into Rachel's face.

"Oh, my God." The article confirmed what Jamie had said. "You loser. You came here just to tell me this?"

"He's not looking so good now, is he? Or maybe only to the likes of you." She knew Jamie was holding back laughter and she just wanted to smack the smug look right off his face.

"I don't believe this. This is garbage." She pushed the screen away from her face. "It's a lie, I'll never believe this."

"Whatever you say, babe. But keep watching. This show is bound to get good."

Rachel's head was reeling. *The letter from the lawyer, this must be what it was about.* Fatima had not mentioned anything. Rachel wondered if she knew about it yet. "Oh, my God. Oh, my God," she kept repeating.

She turned to look at Jamie, who was reviewing the article and smiling. "What do you know about this?" she asked him.

"Unfortunately, not enough, but it looks like he is finally going to be put in his place," Jamie replied. He was smiling from ear to ear. "I'll do some investigation, for sure. Boy, this is juicy."

"Get out of here," she spat the words at him.

"With pleasure." He backed down the steps. "But I'll be back. Just remember who's running things around here." He turned and walked toward the street.

Rachel let out a nervous laugh. "Sure, that's why you parked down the street?" She knew she had said too much. She was still trembling, but after the things Jamie had said about Ali she didn't care. She would put herself at risk to defend him any day. She knew he would do the same for her.

Jamie whipped around at her comment and Rachel swore if he had not been so far away, she would have received a painful reminder of what it meant to cross him. He stood for a minute and the two of them stared each other down. Then he laughed and walked away.

She watched him walk at least 100 metres up the street to his car. When he got close, the car started up. He had not come alone. She shuddered at the thought of being outside, in the dark night, with more than one thug at a time.

When he drove away she collapsed in a chair on her front porch. What was going on? It just seemed like everything was spinning out of control. Now this news about Ali. She definitely couldn't sleep now, and it would be hours before she could call Fatima to ask her what was going on. She just curled up in the chair and waited for the sun to come up. She would call Fatima at the first light of day.

Chapter Ten

A li had already been up for over an hour and *fajr* was approaching. Before going to his father's house he stopped in the kitchen to make a cup of tea. Fatima would be awake in a little while and she loved her tea. He let it cool for a few minutes, then poured it into a thermal cup and covered it. It would be perfect for her now. She had a sensitive mouth, and couldn't eat or drink anything too hot.

He smiled when he thought of how much she still reminded him of that little eight-year-old girl he had met so many years ago. She had been mature, although small for her age. She was as cute as a doll and exceptionally smart. Rachel had followed her everywhere. Of course he hadn't thought about marriage at that age, but by the time he was 15 or 16 he was sure she was to be his wife. His parents had been pleased with his choice, and Rahma had been so excited to have a "sister" that she immediately started calling Fatima *Sorella*.

Fatima had every positive quality he could imagine. If she had a negative quality, it was that she tended to be a little emotional. He didn't quite understand that side of her. It was so unlike the way he handled his life. They had agreed to ignore one negative trait of the other person, so he let it go.

There was one other thing he opted to give her a pass on. It was the thing that really drove him nuts. He hadn't told her, but he never understood how frazzled she would get when they had to get ready to go anywhere. She was usually so organized, but when she had to get dressed, she lost it.

She couldn't ever figure out what to wear. Clothes would be everywhere and she would get irritated with anyone who tried to hurry her. If she had to eat, the kitchen would be a disaster. If she had to get the kids ready or apply make-up, *good night*. Every room she entered would be turned upside-down. Forget about time. He was always ready first and waiting. Ali couldn't get it. *Just get dressed and go.* She looked good in everything anyway. Still, he never mentioned it, lest he amplify the confusion. The last thing he wanted was to slow her down.

Yes, her emotional nature disturbed him, but it also made her more endearing to him. It made him want to protect her. Not just physically, but also emotionally. He wanted to protect her heart. He knew he had failed. He had let her down this time.

In all the years he had known her, he had never seen her hurt or this upset because of him. It was unnerving. He had really messed up and he knew it. If only he had intercepted the mail, this whole thing would have gone down differently.

He shook his head to try and erase the memory of the look on her face when he had walked in the door after his run. Seeing her so disturbed, had shaken him. He had tried to comfort her, but she wouldn't let him near her. He lived to please her, see her smile, know that he had made her happy. Now he was the cause of her distress.

He would fix it. He had already spoken to Shawn. Shawn knew Ali well and he knew Fatima. He would know how to handle this in the best way. Ali trusted that.

Ali pulled a piece of paper from a drawer, and wrote a single number on it. 7. In the corner he wrote 1/9. He placed the paper beside the cup of tea. Fatima would know that there were 9 papers to be found and she would have to find them all to decode the message. She loved this game the most, and Ali loved initiating it. He wouldn't be leaving until the next morning, but he sometimes took a head start with the notes. It kept Fatima on her toes.

Ali moved towards the door and reached for his shoes. Fatima's size 6 shoes were beside his size 12. Even though she was half his size, she was tough. He really enjoyed training her as a result. He knew she believed that he was so adamant about her training because he was concerned about her safety, but that was only a small part of the truth. Ali had complete confidence in her ability to handle herself with or without formal training.

The spirit was the most important, far more important than any physical ability, and underneath her soft emotional exterior, she had the strongest spirit of anyone he knew, apart from his mother. Rachel was the exact opposite. She had the natural physical advantage, but no heart. If she could put the two together she would be an awesome fighter.

Truthfully, training Fatima was pure delight for him. She was a quick study, she listened well and wasn't afraid to try new routines. He had to remember not to push her too much, because she never refused a challenge. She was strong, fast and could hit hard. When he sparred with her she really challenged him, and he loved it. He wouldn't want to be on the wrong side of her fight, that was for sure.

Ali checked to make sure all was straight in the kitchen and headed outside. The air was cool and crisp, and he could hear the birds starting their song. It was one of his favourite sounds. He loved the way the earth slowly came to life at this time of the morning. If he ever happened to miss it, he felt off kilter until the next morning. The entire universe was involved in this ritual. He felt sorry for those who slept through this most precious time of day. He inhaled the morning air as he crossed the street to his father's house.

Ali looked at the front porch of Rachel's house and was surprised to see Rachel asleep in a chair. He approached the house and gently called Rachel's name. She stirred and then opened her eyes.

"Rachel, what are you doing out here? You weren't here all night, were you?" Ali was becoming increasingly concerned about Rachel.

"Uh, yes, no, I just came out for some fresh air and I guess I fell asleep." She sat up and rubbed her arms, indicating she was obviously cold. "What time is it?" she asked.

"About 5:15. Are you ok?" Ali asked.

"I'm fine. I just had a lot of things on my mind. You know how it is."

Ali nodded. He knew that Rachel had a lot of things going on in her life. It hurt him to see what she had been through. Still, he wasn't going to pry. It was better if she talked to Fatima about these things. He could see by her puffy eyes that she had fallen asleep crying. "You should go inside now. It's cold. You'll get sick." He stepped forward and put one foot on the first step of the porch.

"I'm ok. I think I'll do that in a minute." She was still trying to gather her senses.

Ali shook his head. "I'm not leaving you out here, and I'm not staying out here with you either."

"Ok boss," Rachel answered, with mock sarcasm, as she rose to her feet.

"You're welcome to come in with me if you would rather not go home yet." Ali motioned toward his parents' house.

"Oh no, I shouldn't... I mean, I should go, before the boys get up or something, you know. Anyway, I would have to explain to your parents why I was out here in the first place."

Ali shrugged casually. "It's up to you." He waited to see her turn in before he would leave his position at the bottom of the stairs.

Rachel stopped with her hand on her front door. "Ali?"

"Yes."

"Is everything ok with you?" Rachel asked.

"Sure. Why?"

"I just wondered, that's all. Well, in case you ever need to talk or anything, I'm still here." In that moment she realized how much she missed him. They used to have such a free and comfortable relationship.

Since he and Fatima had married, Rachel could not remember having had one real conversation with him; not the way they had before. She always felt like things had changed somehow. Ali had become slightly distant. It was a subtle change, nothing obvious, but she could feel it. They had never discussed it, but the shift made her feel uncomfortable, almost silly in his presence. She hated it and longed for the kind of rapport they had enjoyed before. These few moments were like gold to her.

"Thanks Rachel, I know that," Ali answered.

Rachel fluttered her eyes in surprise. "You do?"

Ali turned his eyes down, and replied, "Yes, I do."

Rachel was caught off guard by his candid response. "Oh, ok then. Well, I'll see you later." Rachel pointed to her door. "I guess I'll just go inside now."

"Good idea." Ali kept his eyes on the steps in front of him, and waited until Rachel was safely in her house before he turned and walked toward his old home.

Inside, his father was waiting for him by the door and they greeted each other with hugs and kisses. Ali noticed that his father held him a little tighter than usual and his mother was uncharacteristically quiet. Still, they were both warm and loving. Rahma hugged him and kissed him as usual. They all prayed, and Ali read a *dua*, as they normally requested of him. Mama cried, as she often did, at the sound of his voice.

As soon as he felt the time was right, Papa led Ali into his study. The study was decorated in the dark rich colours of brown and burgundy. The mahogany shutters matched the bookshelves and large desk that Papa worked from daily. "Sit, Son," Papa said to him.

Ali pulled out a seat. There was one chair in the study reserved for him. It was a large black leather armchair and the one most comfortable for him. Ali and Papa had had many important conversations in this room. Ali stood and waited for his father to seat himself behind his neatly organized desk and then followed suit.

Papa placed in front of him a print-out from the internet. It detailed the story of the pending lawsuit. Ali dropped his shoulders. This was going to get messier than he expected and a lot faster than he could have imagined.

"Rahma does a search on your name every day. Maybe several times a day." Papa chuckled, and then became serious again. "She found this last night."

"Rahma saw this? Oh no. I need to talk to her." Ali was devastated that his little sister had read about the lawsuit.

"Wait, wait. Me first." Papa patiently waited for Ali to speak.

"Papa, I'm going to see Shawn today and take care of this."

Papa clasped his hands and brought them to his face. He looked over at Ali. He stared. Waiting. Finally he nodded. "And Fatima?"

Ali felt his chest tighten. "She's upset." He then detailed the events of the day before.

"How could you let this happen?"

Ali was taken aback. "What do you mean? Papa, you know I didn't expect this, but I'll handle it. I told you I'm going to deal with this."

"You should have protected Fatima from this. How could you let her find out like that?"

Ali stroked the arms of his seat. "I didn't know-"

"It's your business to know what goes on in your house."

Ali remained silent. His father was right. He had messed up and he knew it. His father's disappointment was too much to bear. He looked down at the desk.

Papa continued, "So what now?"

"Like I said, I'm going to see Shawn-"

Papa waved his hand in the air. "No, no, I mean what about your wife? It matters little what happens with this case. Damage has already been done to Fatima. Can you imagine the shock that went through her body when she took that letter from your daughter's hand? Do I need to remind you that she is pregnant and due in days?"

"No Papa. I know. I know everything."

"Hmm, you do? So, what will you do now?"

"I don't know."

He really wasn't sure how to reach Fatima. He couldn't reverse what had happened and he wasn't sure how she would be feeling this morning. It was a delicate situation. He wanted to comfort her, but he wasn't sure if he may inadvertently cause her more distress by doing or saying the wrong thing.

Papa got up from his seat and walked over to his son. Ali started to stand, but Papa motioned for him to remain seated, and then held Ali's face with one hand. He gently, but firmly, shook Ali's head. "Is your name Ali Abati?"

"Yes, Papa."

"Are you my son?"

"Of course."

"Then you will know what to do." He released his hold and firmly patted the side of Ali's face, before walking toward the door. Pausing, he turned and said to Ali, "Remember, your family is your world. Put your focus there."

Ali remained seated for a long time after his father had left. He absorbed Papa's words. "It's your business to know what goes on in your house," he had said.

Yes, Ali was the *imam*-leader of his home and responsible for everyone and everything in it. He had work to do for sure.

"Hey big brother," Rahma said as she peaked into the study.

"Hey you, come here." Ali swirled the large armchair and extended his hand to his sister. Rahma came to sit on his knee, and rested her head on his shoulder. Her mass of curly brown hair fell behind his back. She was tall, but she still enjoyed cuddling up to her brother as she had when she was a small child. "I am so sorry you had to see that stuff," he said.

"Don't worry. I don't believe a word of it. I know they're all liars," she said adamantly.

"Yes, and how do you know that?" Ali was moved by her loyalty.

"Well, I know you. I know you would never do something like that." She looked him straight in the eye.

"You sure?" Ali asked her.

"Yes. I'm sure," Rahma said with confidence.

Ali kissed her head. "I don't want you to worry. I'm going to take care of it." Rahma listened intently. "Now in the next little while you might be hearing a lot of talk about this. I want you to ignore all of it. If you need to know anything you come straight to me. Understand?"

"Yes." Rahma seemed relieved. Her dark brown eyes sparkled with love and admiration for her brother.

Ali continued, "Now, what is this I hear about you doing searches on my name every day?"

"Well, not every single day, but I have to know what's being said about you," Rahma replied.

Ali rubbed her back. "It's the internet and anybody can write anything. It may not all be good for you to read… hey, Mama let's you spend that much time online?"

"She's usually with me, but sometimes she has her own work to do. Anyway, she trusts me."

"Well, I'm going to have to have a little talk with her," Ali replied.

"Great, I think that's my cue to leave." Rahma stood up. "I love you, Ali."

"You too."

After Rahma left the room, Ali leaned forward and closed his eyes. He rubbed his hands over the top of his head. His short hair bristled under the movement of his fingers. He didn't hear her enter, but there was no mistaking a mother's touch. Mama stood behind her son and slipped her hands onto his chest. Ali held her hands and squeezed, as though squeezing them could give him the strength he needed - the strength of his mother, and her mother and father, and all those that had gone before them.

Mama started speaking slowly. "You know, when you were

born, the midwife said, 'This chest, this is the chest of a warrior.' She said she had never seen such a strong, developed chest on a newborn. People walked from all the neighbouring villages to see this baby with the chest of a warrior. I prayed, that day, that God would fill your chest with love, compassion and bravery. Love for all that is good, compassion for all those fortunate to be in your care, and bravery to always do what is right. No matter what the cost.

"When you were given the name *Ali* and I learned who *Imam Ali(as)* was, I knew my prayers had been answered. Connect with your *Holy Prophet(saw)* and your *Imams(as)*, all of them, and follow their examples. You will know what to do."

Ali stood and guided his mother into his seat, then leaned on his father's desk. "Thank-you, Mama. You always know what to say." He paused while he thought about what he wanted to say next. "Can I ask you something?"

"Certainly." Her brown eyes remained warm.

"It might be personal," Ali warned her.

"Go on," she urged.

"If Papa ever hurt you, how did you get past it?"

Mama inhaled and let out her breath slowly. She looked at her son with sadness in her eyes. "It has never happened."

"Really?" Ali was stunned and disappointed.

"Never. I wish I could help you." She was truly sorry. "In 30 years of marriage your father has never hurt me. Confused me, yes. Frustrated me, sure. But he has never hurt my feelings or caused sadness or disappointment to enter my heart. Never. Not once."

"Wow." Ali didn't know what else to say.

"Your father is a man of few words. You know that. He is an excellent listener. He thinks before he speaks and acts." She laughed. "He would rather remain quiet and miss saying the right thing, than to speak and risk saying the wrong thing. It's harder to hurt people when you behave like that."

"What if he had? What would you need to get past it?" Ali asked.

"Honesty, openness, vulnerability." She reached for Ali's hands again. "Fatima loves you. Desperately. Since her childhood. She wants her family. She wants her marriage. She wants you. That's why she was so devastated by this news. Just reassure her that she still has all of that."

Ali stood and hugged his mother, lifting her off her feet. He held her tightly to him. "Thank-you, Mama. Thank-you."

"It was my deepest pleasure, my beautiful son." He put her down and she kissed his chest.

"I think I need to go home now," he said.

"It's about time." Her eyes sparkled.

Before Ali left the house they all hugged him again and sent their love to Fatima. He felt like he could take on the world.

When he arrived at home the smell of roses greeted him at the door. He realized that it must be the oil he had bought Fatima two days before. He walked through the foyer, down the hall and into the family room. When he entered the room he saw that Fatima had fallen asleep where she had prayed *fajr*. That happened to her a lot these days, since she was naturally tired, being at the end of her pregnancy. He moved closer to see the empty tea cup by her side, and one of her hands closed around the paper he had left on the counter. Ali bent and gently lifted Fatima. Even with the added weight of her pregnancy, she felt like nothing in his arms as he climbed the stairs.

She stirred. "Ali?"

Ali pulled back his head to look at her. "Who else would it be?"

"You're silly," she whispered.

"Shhh, shhh, sleep," Ali said.

He brought her to their room, placed her in bed and tucked her in. "Fatima, I am so sorry for everything. I can't imagine what you must have felt when you received that letter. I should never have allowed that to happen. I should have been the one to tell you. I'm sorry I couldn't do or say anything to make it better for you. I was caught off guard too. I didn't really know what to say. I'm sorry I let you down. I am so sorry."

Her breathing remained even, and Ali was not sure if she had heard him or not. Part of him wanted to wake her and repeat everything. The other part wanted to continue watching her sleeping, peacefully, forever.

He stood up to leave the room, and as he walked through the doorway, he heard her ever so softly say, "Thank you."

Chapter Eleven

ℑ

Rachel sat in her living room watching the clock and waiting for the best time to call. Fatima was usually up early. 8 o'clock should be ok. But then she might be alarmed by Rachel calling so early, plus Ali would definitely be home. If Rachel waited until nine then there was a chance he would be on his way out or at least occupied, but Rachel would be at work at that time and wouldn't have the freedom to talk as she would like. The clock turned 8:15. "Late enough." Rachel dialed Fatima's number, adrenaline cursing through her veins. She wasn't sure if the anxiety she was feeling was due to fear of what she would hear on the other end or the memories of the encounter with Jamie during the night.

"Hello."

"Fati?"

"Hey, Rachel."

"How are you doing? Did I wake you?" Rachel started the conversation cautiously. She wasn't sure how much Fatima knew about what was going on.

"Kind of, but it's ok. What's up?"

"I heard some news."

"What news?"

"I read something online about Ali and a lawsuit?" Rachel tried to keep the anxiety out of her voice.

Fatima was suddenly wide awake. "Oh no, it's online already?"

"So you do know?" Rachel leaned back on her couch.

"Yes, it's what the lawyer's letter was about." Fatima sunk into her pillow.

"Are we talking about the same kind of lawsuit here?" Considering Fatima's condition, Rachel certainly didn't want to shock her.

"Yes Rachel, it's a paternity suit." Fatima sat up in her bed and brushed her hair back with her hands.

"Oh Fati! So, what's Ali saying?" Rachel dropped her head into her hands.

"Well, he seemed just as shocked as we are. He says he doesn't know the woman, and doesn't know what this is about."

Relief washed over Rachel. "Oh, thank God. Now I can breathe."

"That's it? Just like that and you can breathe. You're fine now?"

"Well yes, if Ali says he doesn't know her, then... well... you believe him, don't you?" Rachel felt a little confused and wondered if she was missing something.

"I don't know, Rachel. I've been on the road with him. I know how it is. It's crazy." Rachel could hear the creeping despair in Fatima's voice.

"But he's not," Rachel reminded Fatima.

"I don't know."

"Yes, you do," Rachel insisted. "You do know. Fatima, are you feeling ok?"

"Of course. I just have to look at all the possibilities. I can't have my head stuck in the sand or just follow blindly. That's all I'm saying."

"Well, you can't be ok, because what you're saying is not making any sense to me. I'm coming over."

"What? No, I'm fine. You don't have to come over. You have to go to work."

"Oh please, I run that place. I can be a few minutes late. Anyway, I'm already dressed."

"Really Ray, it's not necessary," Fatima insisted.

"I'm there. Just open the door."

By the time Rachel rang the doorbell, Fatima was there to let her in. Rachel looked beautiful and professional in a cream pant suit.

"Oh Rachel, you look great. I can't wait until I can fit into regular clothes again."

Rachel hugged and kissed Fatima. "It's not all it's cracked up to be. I would change places with you in a minute."

"Are you sure? Do you remember the conversation we just had?" Fatima asked.

Rachel waved away the comment. "Piece of cake." She walked towards the back of the house. "So, where is the troublemaker anyway?"

"He's in the workout room." They could hear the clanging of barbells and Ali grunting as he pushed his body to its limit.

"Sounds like he's at war." Rachel took a seat on Fatima's couch and placed her handbag behind her.

"Yes, well, you know how he gets." Fatima sat beside Rachel.

"Shouldn't he have a spotter?" Rachel was genuinely concerned. Lifting heavy weights alone was dangerous.

"Oh, please don't even get me started. We have had the conversation too many times. Obviously, I can't do it, and if I even go down there to see what he's doing, I'm going to have a heart attack. You wouldn't believe the weight he's lifting." Fatima was obviously concerned as well.

"Well, he should just lift you. At least if he drops you, you can move yourself," Rachel teased.

"Barely." Fatima giggled and rubbed her tummy. "Anyway, he would need two or three of me. He can do me with one hand." Fatima paused and then continued. "I know you're in a hurry, so don't worry, I'm fine."

Rachel straightened up. "How is everything over here? Are you guys talking?"

"Yes, of course. We talked about it yesterday, and I heard

everything he had to say." Fatima shrugged. "Now, it's just wait and see." Rachel couldn't miss the sadness in Fatima's voice.

Rachel narrowed her eyes and studied the young woman in front of her. This wasn't the friend she knew. *How could she say these things? Why was she sounding so unsure?* "Fatima, he wouldn't lie to your face. Even if he had messed up, do you honestly think he could carry it on this far?"

"No, I honestly don't, but I never expected to get mail like that, either. I just need to be prepared for anything. I'm not going to be shocked like that again. Ever." Fatima looked down at her hands, folded in her lap.

Rachel finally understood the depth of Fatima's pain. "Oh honey, it must have been horrible for you. Come, hugs." Rachel reached over and hugged Fatima.

"Thanks, Rachel. I do feel pretty lonely right now."

"Please, don't say that. You have all of us, my mom, Mama and Papa. Has Ali talked to them?"

"He would have seen them this morning, but we didn't talk about it."

Rachel remembered seeing Ali in the morning. Now was probably not a good time to mention what had happened during the night.

Fatima folded and unfolded her hands. "Ali's parents are great. They really are, and I love them to death, but they're *his* parents."

"Fatima, they are the fairest people I know," Rachel said. "And they love you. Truly love you."

"I know they do. I love them too. It's just not the same at a time like this."

"Have you called your mom?"

"No, I don't want to worry her."

"Well, she's going to hear sooner or later. Isn't it better if she hears from you?"

"Good point. It's just not on the top of my list of things to tell people, you know?"

"Listen, I know this is going to be ok. Unless Ali is on crack, this cannot be true. I'll never believe it. So, you don't worry about that. But if you need to, you call me every other minute. If you need to talk or anything, you call me, ok?"

Rachel could not count the times that Fatima and Ali had been a support for her and her family. This was the least she could do in return.

"You have to work. I'm not going to bother you." Fatima stretched her legs and shook her head.

"Did I mention that I run that place?" The two women laughed, and then Fatima changed the subject.

"Now, about you, tell me how you've been feeling."

Rachel's face clouded over. "I'm ok, but I still have to see the doctor."

"For a follow up?"

"Yes, but it's a little more involved." Rachel paused and smoothed out the lines in her pants. "There appears to be scar tissue from before, so they have to see what happens. There's a possibility that I won't be able to have any more kids." Rachel's face turned red, and her eyes became glassy.

Fatima took Rachel's hand. "Rachel, don't give up hope so quickly. You know in the end it's not up to the doctors."

Rachel nodded. "It's amazing isn't it? I have two boys, no husband and I'm worrying about whether or not I can have more kids." Rachel wiped the first tears as soon as they fell.

"You have a right to think about your future, just like everyone else. Don't take that away from yourself. Now, regardless of what the doctors say, that's not the end. They don't have the last word." Fatima spoke gently to her friend.

"It seems like the opportunity for me to live happily ever after is slipping further and further away."

"That's nonsense," Fatima said, with conviction.

"Really? Who is going to want me? I have two kids already, and I may be sterile in a minute." Rachel reached into her bag for tissue.

"First of all, you don't know that, and second, your value is not tied to whether or not you can have children. Maybe this man already has his own children. Or maybe he will embrace your boys

117

as his own. Leave that to *Allah*. You just take care of you. Let Him do the rest."

"Yes, I guess you're right. What else can I do anyway?" Rachel leaned back in defeat.

"There's a lot you can do." Fatima raised her eyebrows at her friend.

Rachel knew exactly what Fatima was talking about. Fatima was encouraging her to pray, seek God and forge a relationship with Him. It was an experience Rachel just hadn't had yet.

Rachel's mother attended weekly prayer meetings and Fatima had regular prayer meetings she called *dua* sessions, with her Muslim sisters, but Rachel had never had that experience where she felt her prayers had been answered. She just hadn't developed that level of faith. She wasn't even sure how to do it.

Rachel could see the peace that Fatima had developed over the years. She was so different from other women her age. Rachel knew it was Fatima's experience with God that had done it. Rachel had seen her evolve. So many things had seemed to fall into place for Fatima. Even the inevitable challenges and difficulties of life seemed more manageable.

Rachel knew that Fatima was living her ideal life. She was always content. Sure, she would have liked her husband to be home more, but she never complained. She used his absence to her advantage. She would do something she may not have time to do otherwise. Sometimes, she would rearrange the house or change something about herself. Ali had the good fortune of returning to a new home and new wife, on occasion.

Fatima also used the time to give more direct attention to the children. She had developed some rituals for when Ali was away so that the girls would have something to look forward to that would eclipse the longing they all had for him.

One of their favourite things to do was scrapbooking. Fatima would have the girls record the events of each day, in words and pictures, and put them into a book for Ali to enjoy when he returned home. The girls loved having Fatima record all their adventures, and the things they wanted to tell Ali upon his return.

Fatima would also visit and care for the community or would devote herself to more intense study. She always had a plan and she used her time well. The days would fly by and Ali never knew what adventure he was coming home to hear about next.

Rachel, on the other hand, felt that no matter how she tried to get herself out of a hole, somehow she ended up further and further in. Now things with Jamie were getting more complicated. He was coming around more frequently; just when she had decided to cut him off completely. Her mother didn't seem to be doing well and memories of her father were becoming more difficult to deal with. Then, there was Jonah and his increasing nightmares. With all this on her mind, she couldn't even think about prayer.

"I better go. I've taken enough of your time." Rachel started to stand.

Fatima pulled her back down. "Ok, how about you come over tomorrow and pray with me? I would really appreciate it."

Rachel hesitated. She wasn't ready to take this step.

"For me?" Fatima tried to look as pathetic as possible.

"Fine. I guess you could use some support right now."

"Aahh!" Fatima screamed and almost jumped into Rachel's lap. She grabbed Rachel's hands and squeezed them, all the while bouncing in her seat.

"Calm down. Pregnant lady bouncing around. Not good," Rachel said, as she tried to hold back her own smile.

"Great, I can't wait," Fatima said. Rachel could already see the wheels turning in Fatima's mind.

"You can come over tomorrow morning. Oh, I am so excited!" Fatima knew she should contain her enthusiasm, but this small step was a huge breakthrough for Rachel, and Fatima was planning to take full advantage of it.

"Slow down. You're wrinkling my suit." Rachel pretended to be concerned about her clothing. "What about Ali? I'm going to be all up in his home space." She waved her hands in little circles to emphasize her point. "Do you think he'll mind?"

"Mind? Are you kidding me? He's going to freak, he'll be so

happy," Fatima said.

Rachel laughed. "Forgive me if I can't picture Ali *freaking* over anything."

"He'll be happy, trust me." Fatima couldn't stop smiling.

Rachel stood up. "Well, I better get going. Oh, there's one more thing I wanted to tell you. Jonah has been having nightmares recently, but these ones are different."

"How?"

"Usually, you know, he would go off if something happened, or if Jamie came around, but this time I don't know why it started. He keeps saying, 'bad men come', when I go away."

"Really? That's interesting." Fatima sank deep into thought.

"What?"

"I didn't tell anyone, but I've been having really funny feelings lately too."

Rachel sat back down. They all took Fatima's "feelings" seriously. She was very intuitive and usually dead on when it came to her premonitions. "Why didn't you tell us?" Rachel asked anxiously.

"I didn't know what it was about. Then with all this stuff with Ali, I just thought it was related to him, but maybe it's not."

"Wow. Well, keep me updated," Rachel said.

"Same with you. If you want the boys to spend more time over here, that's fine. It may be good for them. We're going to a wedding next week. We can bring them with us."

"No, it's too much to ask." Rachel felt guilty about all the attention that Fatima and Ali paid to her sons. "It's your family time."

"They *are* our family." Fatima squeezed Rachel's hand. "Ali will love it, and he's going to be the one taking care of them anyway."

"You didn't even ask him," Rachel protested.

"I don't have to ask him this. Really, he'll be fine with it. You can come too. That would be great, actually; I just thought you might want the break from the boys."

"Sure, I'll think about it."

"Good. See you tomorrow?"

Rachel nodded. "How much time do we need?

"Can you come at 7:30 or 8?

"Sure, I'll be here." Rachel stood up and Fatima walked her to the door.

"Hey, I had another idea," Fatima started. "Maybe you and I can do a little retreat. Our house out of town is almost finished and it's beautiful. It's surrounded by acres of undeveloped land, and it's right on the lake. We can go for a few days while Ali is away. I think we both need some 'me' time."

"Ha! In your condition? Yah, right. Tell you what, you talk to him, if he says yes, then I'll drive up there, pay for gas, food, entertainment, whatever. The whole thing will be totally on me, and you can have me praying all night long."

"Why do you have to be like that?" Fatima pouted.

"Because, I know exactly what he's going to say, that's why. Actually, can you call me on speaker when you're going to ask him? I would love a front row seat to this." Rachel was laughing now.

"He's not even going to be here this week." Fatima looked at Rachel who had her eyebrows raised. "He might say yes," Fatima insisted.

Chapter Twelve

ℑ

"No way. Absolutely not. Impossible." Ali flipped a pancake on the grill. Fatima, Masuma, Laila and Batool all waited patiently for breakfast to be served.

"Why not?" Fatima sat on one side of the booth, facing the three girls across the table, who were drinking orange juice and quietly colouring.

Ali kept his focus on the grill. "I'm not going to let you and Rachel drive more than an hour out of town to spend days alone in a deserted area, in an unfinished house, where the closest neighbour, let alone any kind of convenience, is a mile away. Did I forget to mention that you are due next week, which means now? God knows where the hospital is. And what about the lake? There's been a lot of rain recently. What if there's flooding or some other problem? And no phone service yet? There's no way you're going." Ali put a plate of pancakes on the table. Batool was the first to dive in.

"Thank-you, Daddy."

"You're welcome, sweetheart. Eat up."

"That's like telling rain to be wet," Fatima said.

Ali smiled and smoothed Batool's hair while Fatima continued her protest. "Anyway, we won't be alone. The work men are still there." She forked a pancake and placed it on her plate.

"Sure. And I'm going to send you for one minute to stay with a group of strange men?" Ali shook his head incredulously.

"They're not strange men. Hamza is in charge and will be there the entire time." Hamza was a close family friend in charge of construction and development of the property. Fatima took the first bite of her pancake.

"Fatima, he's not responsible for you, I am. Anyway, he would think, no he would *know*, I'm crazy to let you go up there."

Masuma and Laila started a competition to see who could put the most syrup on their plates. Batool just focused on eating so she could have more.

Ali took the syrup from the girls and started to pour for Fatima.

"No thanks. I'll just have some fruit." Fatima put her hand up.

"Counting calories?" Ali raised an eyebrow. Both he and Fatima were health conscious. It was one of the many things that they had in common. Fatima wanted to make sure they were healthy, strong and together for a long time.

"Why not?" Fatima lifted her head.

"You only have a few more days left. Live a little," Ali said as he passed her a bowl of mixed berries.

Fatima couldn't let this opportunity to get a punch in pass her by. "I am trying to, but my over-protective husband is cramping my style."

Ali took his seat on the bench across from her. "Fatima if you need time to yourself, I understand and support that 100%. I can't let you go to the house. There are so many hotels around town that have spas. Why not do that? You can even go downtown if you want." He put another pancake on Batool's plate. "Why don't you check it out and pick whatever you want. I'll go for that. You'll be close to the family, your doctor and the hospital." Ali nodded. "I'm comfortable with that."

"Nothing can compare to being in nature." Fatima pushed the point.

123

Ali looked at Fatima. She was pretending to be stubborn, but he knew she wouldn't go if he didn't agree. For that reason, he really wanted to find a compromise that would suit her. "How about this, after the baby is born and you two get the 'all clear', we can go up there and you can relax, in nature, for as long as you want?"

"We?" Fatima wore a playfully surprised look.

"It's a big house, you won't even see me if you don't want to." He downed his orange juice.

"Going with a new baby is not the same as going by myself," Fatima pointed out.

Ali shrugged. "No, it's not."

Fatima finally gave in. "Ok, I won't go. And I'll think about the spa."

Ali smiled and quietly finished his breakfast.

As he started to clear the plates, Ali said, "Listen, Shawn is going to be here soon. We should get the kids ready."

Fatima's mood immediately changed. "I'll get them dressed. Your mom should be here in about 30 minutes."

The girls had swimming lessons and were then going visiting with their grandmother. That would allow Ali and Fatima uninterrupted time to speak to Shawn about the paternity suit.

Fatima helped the girls get dressed while Ali cleaned the kitchen. When Mama arrived, they ran outside, fully excited about the day ahead of them. After they had left, Ali turned to Fatima.

"Are you ok?"

Fatima stood in front of him. "Sure."

"Shawn will be here soon. You don't have to stay if you don't want to."

"Are you kidding me right now? I can't function if I don't know what's going on." Fatima put her hands on her hips. She wore a blue and white waffle-knit hooded maternity top and matching pants.

"I just don't want you to be stressed out about this. I don't think it's a good idea for you to stay. Just let me handle it," Ali said.

"Ali, I am not going to be in the dark about this. I'll go crazy if I don't know what's happening. Come on." Her eyes were intense as she looked up at him. "I'll be fine," she added.

Ali reluctantly agreed. "All right."

When Shawn rang the door bell Ali was standing by to open it.

"Hey, big guy." Shawn Thomson was Ali's high school friend. They had forged a friendship that had lasted over 12 years. Ali trusted him completely.

"Thanks for coming by so quickly, Shawn." Ali closed the door behind his friend and led him into the foyer.

"No problem, no problem. I understand the urgency. This definitely needs our immediate attention." Shawn stepped forward and stopped when he saw Fatima standing in the hallway. "What's up, Mommy?" Shawn was also close to Fatima and had great affection for her.

"Hey Shawn, how you doing?"

"Good, good. You look like you need to take a seat," he joked with her.

"Funny. I've been waiting for *you*." Fatima turned and walked towards the family room.

Shawn turned back to Ali and lowered his voice. "You sure you want to do this here?"

"Yes, definitely. She insisted. Come on, let's go sit down."

The room was painted a soft green and decorated in green and cream. Fatima had already taken a seat in the corner of the cream-coloured leather couch at the far end of the room when the two men arrived. Shawn sat on the couch closest to the door, removed his suit jacket and put it over the arm of the chair. Ali pulled up a chair facing Shawn. A coral stone coffee table separated them.

"So what do you have?" Ali asked.

"I contacted the office today and received some information."

Shawn looked across the room at Fatima.

Ali encouraged him to continue. "Please Shawn, go ahead. It's fine."

Shawn opened his bag. "The woman in question, Leanne Roy, claims she met you about 18 months ago in Toronto. She says she saw you for about six months. She's documented all the dates." Shawn pulled out a sheet of paper. Ali took the paper from Shawn's hand.

"Does anything look familiar?" Shawn asked him.

"These look like dates that I would have been away, but I would have to double-check to be sure." Ali returned the paper to the table keeping his eyes straight ahead.

Fatima sat silently with her two hands rolled together into a ball. She leaned with one elbow on the arm of the chair and pressed her doubled fist to her mouth.

"Ok guy, talk to me." Shawn sat back and waited.

"I don't know anything." Ali shrugged his shoulders.

Shawn shook his head. "Listen, you have to give me more than that. These are serious allegations, my friend. I need something to work with here."

"I don't have anything. I don't know this woman, never even heard her name."

"Ok, well, there's more." Shawn reached into his bag again. "Pictures." Shawn placed the photos on the coffee table.

Ali picked them up and flipped through. "Pretty good photo editing."

"Is that you?" Shawn pointed to the man in the pictures posing beside the woman filing the lawsuit.

"Of course it's me, but I never posed with her." Shawn looked from Ali to Fatima.

"Maybe it was a fan who wanted a picture with you?" Shawn suggested.

"No. I would never have put my arm around them." Ali rubbed his hand across the back of his neck.

Fatima opened her hands and rubbed her arms.

Shawn reached into his bag again. "Receipts."

Ali picked up the receipts that were placed on the table.

"Is that your signature?" Shawn continued.

Ali studied the receipts in his hand. "Looks like it," he replied reluctantly. Shawn tightened his lips.

"Come on Shawn, I'm in hotels all the time. Anybody could have found these or forged my signature on a new receipt. I don't even know if these are originals."

"Were you in those hotels on those dates?" Shawn pressed.

"It's possible. I would have to check." Ali pressed his fingers against his temple.

"Email transcripts." More documents hit the coffee table.

Ali carefully examined the transcripts. "So, I was hacked," he responded matter-of-factly.

Shawn laughed, and then turned his attention to Fatima. "Fatima, please, could I trouble you for a glass of water?"

Fatima tried not to roll her eyes as she carefully came to her feet. "Sure." Ali kept his focus on the documents on the table.

When Fatima had left the room, Shawn leaned towards Ali. "Listen, you know I'm going to do everything you need me to, but I think the best thing for all concerned is to come to some kind of agreement soon. Otherwise, this will get very messy, pretty fast."

"Agreement? There'll be no agreement. They're liars. A DNA test is going to prove that." Ali's eyes hardened and his voice became harsh.

"Yes," Shawn continued slowly, "we are definitely going to do that, but the longer this drags on, the more publicity it's going to get, and Ali...you have a family."

"I know that," Ali answered sharply, and then looked at the email transcripts again. "Ok, so what's the deal?"

"No matter what the DNA results are, every day that this keeps active causes more damage to your image. All people are going to remember is that your name was associated with a paternity suit." Shawn leaned back in his seat. "It doesn't look good."

"You know, as well as I do, if we meet they're going to want money," Ali said.

"You have it."

"No way. If I pay one cent, I'll never be able to convince Fatima that I'm not covering up something. She'll never believe me."

"Buddy, she's not going to believe you. *Period*. Did you see the evidence on this table?" Shawn gestured toward the documents between them. "Judging by the look on her face and the tension in this place, you're in the dog-house already. I'm choking up in here."

Ali clenched his jaw.

Shawn continued, "And you know what they say. Where there's smoke, there's fire. Everyone, including your wife, will think that even if this is not your child, maybe you did have a relationship with this woman or some other women. Shawn motioned in the direction of the kitchen. "It's what Fatima is thinking right now.

"Trust me, you don't want your family to go through this. We can arrange a meeting and squash this whole thing now. Then you can focus on repairing your marriage."

Shawn straightened up, conscious of the fact that Fatima had returned with the water. "Thank-you."

Ali stood up and walked towards the back window, while Fatima returned to her seat. He looked outside for a few moments while Shawn and Fatima waited for him to speak. By the time Ali turned around to face Shawn, he was resolute. "I am *not* meeting with these people. We're going to prove that they are lying and clear my name. Are you with me or not?"

Shawn held his hands up. "Of course I am. Of course. Let me get back to the office. I have a load of work to do on this. I'll check in with you later today." Shawn finished the water before rising to his feet.

"Sounds good." Ali stepped forward.

Fatima remained seated while the two men walked to the door.

Shawn stopped in the hallway and turned to Ali. "Man, I'm sorry Fatima had to hear all that."

"It's fine, she wanted to be there. We'll deal with it." Ali pushed his hands into the pockets of his track pants.

"Still, I would not want to be you for the next 30 minutes."

"I'll handle it."

Shawn rolled a fist and gently tapped Ali on his chest. "Later, my friend."

Ali let Shawn out and turned to see Fatima at the end of the hallway. The sun shone through the back doors and framed her as she stood in the doorway of the family room. "Fatima…" Ali stepped towards her, but she held up her hand.

"I'm fine. Really, I am." She tried to smile, but her eyes couldn't lie. Even though she had left the room, she had caught enough of the conversation to know that Shawn was taking this as seriously as she had expected.

"Fatima, I know it looks bad."

"Looks?" Fatima shook her head.

"Fine. It is bad, and I have nothing to offer you, except what we've built our life on, not just in the years since our marriage but all the years that you've known me. You know who I am."

Ali continued slowly towards her. She kept her hand steady and closed her eyes. "No. Ali, please don't." When she opened them again, he was standing directly in front of her. "What do you want me to say? 'I trust you? I believe in you? I'll stand by you no matter what?'"

Ali pulled his head back in confusion. "No. I don't need any of that." He placed one hand on the wall above her head. "I just need you to be ok."

Fatima had to swallow her emotion. He always knew just how to get to her. "Everything is going to be fine. I know that." She cleared her throat. "Now, if you will please excuse me." She slipped past Ali and disappeared up the stairs.

When Ali heard their bedroom door close, he turned into the workout room and attacked the punching bag with a ferocity he had not felt in years.

Chapter Thirteen

Rachel transformed when she got into her workplace. She was dynamic and in control. She supervised an office of 12 people, both full-time and part-time customer service personnel. Though most of them were older than her, she commanded respect and was well liked by all.

Today she worked just as efficiently as usual, but her thoughts were on the events of the last 24 hours, and her friends, Ali and Fatima.

Fatima had not told her, but she knew that Ali had been away on Friday night. She did not believe that the lawsuit had any validity to it; still, something was going on. Something did not make sense. She wanted to help them. *But how?* There had to be a way. Fatima was about to deliver a baby, and she didn't need this stress right now.

She thought about the wedding invitation. It would be great to hang out with both Ali and Fatima again. It rarely happened these days. Maybe she should just let them take the boys. They so loved being with Ali.

She really needed to think about pressing charges against Jamie. She knew his aggressive behaviour could escalate. Her greatest fear was that he may attack her or harm her in front of the boys. How would they ever heal from that? She couldn't bear it if her sons witnessed any harm coming to her or violence and aggression from their own father. She was sure that would be the final straw. She would snap. Did she want to wait until that point? Her mother had been pressuring her to press charges against Jamie for some time. Rachel wasn't sure why she hadn't done it. He was her sons' father. She did not want to be the one to bring him before the law. She knew it would not be her fault, but still she couldn't bring herself to initiate the process.

"Hi, Rachel."

"Hey, good morning, Jasmine." Jasmine was a co-worker who was five months pregnant. Rachel couldn't stand the sight of her. She was always bringing in baby books and showing everyone what she had most recently bought for her baby. Rachel could not even walk in the direction of Jasmine's desk.

In less than five months she would have had her own baby. It seemed so surreal. Strangely enough, the first pregnancy was far more vivid and real to her. That child would have been older than Joshua and Masuma. She wondered about that child a lot. Who it would have been? What would have happened to her life if she had had that child or even if she had healed properly after that loss?

"Rachel. Rachel?"

"Oh yes, sorry about that. You were saying?" Jasmine was motioning to the phone.

"Line three," she said. Rachel handled the call and returned to her work.

Thoughts of Jamie kept creeping into her mind. What was he up to? Why was he bothering her so much lately? Rachel worried about what would happen if Ali knew he was coming by or if the two of them got into a confrontation.

His latest visit was so odd. It was really eating her. Anyway, she had much more to focus on than worrying about Jamie. Getting back to work was the best way to pass the time until lunch.

"Rachel, are you coming with us?" one of the workers asked her.

"No, go ahead. I have an appointment. I'll see you later." Rachel gathered her belongings, straightened her desk and headed downstairs. The elevator opened and she stepped out. She was searching inside her handbag for her phone and almost ran over the woman standing in front of her.

"Oh, I'm sorry, pardon me." Rachel looked up and stared into the face of the nurse from the hospital.

"Excuse me, you're Rachel, right?"

Rachel stepped back, resting her weight on one leg. "Who's asking?"

"It's ok, honey, I just want to talk to you. I'm Brigitte, the nurse from the hospital. Remember me?"

How could she forget? "How can I help you?"

Brigitte looked around shaking her head of thick curly hair. "Can we sit somewhere? It's about Jamie." Her light brown eyes shifted nervously.

Curiosity and anxiety mixed together. "Sure," Rachel replied. Brigitte followed as Rachel walked outside and found a private place to sit.

Rachel listened in shocked outrage as Brigitte told her story. She couldn't believe this. She knew Jamie was low, but this was too much. Rachel sat in stunned silence. "Why did you come and tell me all this," she asked Brigitte, the nurse.

Brigitte smiled. "I don't know. I just liked you for some reason. I've seen your boys around. They're beautiful. I just thought that you deserved to know."

Brigitte stood up to leave. "And Rachel,"

"Yes."

"Jamie knows about the abortion. I'm sorry."

Time stopped. Rachel didn't even see when or how Brigitte left or what direction she went in. She felt dizzy and nauseas and weak all at once. *Jamie knows about the abortion. Jamie knows about the abortion.* What was she going to do? She wanted to scream, run, hide, anything to get away from this. "He's going to kill me," she whispered to herself.

The rest of the day passed by in a blur. For the first time Rachel could remember, she did not want the day to end. She didn't want to leave the safety of her office and face the real world and what she expected would happen next.

Jamie had been following Rachel and Ali, Brigitte explained. He was trying to build a case that she was unfit, so he could take her sons from her. He wanted to prove that her mother was unstable and her friends and associates were unsavoury. That's why he was in the neighbourhood so often and how he had known about the paternity case so quickly. *Why? Why?* She knew he didn't want those boys. He just wanted to get back at her for not wanting him. "What am I going to do?"

After leaving her office she got into her car and drove. She had no direction, no purpose. She surprised herself when she ended up at the cemetery. It took her 20 minutes to get out of the car. She sat clutching the steering wheel, fighting the urge to just put the car in drive and burn out of there. She had not been here since the day her father had died. No one had.

Her brother and sister had moved away and her mother hadn't been able to bear it. Rachel closed the car door and slowly walked toward the plot. She wondered if she would remember where he was. She did. It was like a force pulling her, and as she walked her pace quickened.

She found him just where she remembered. The day was so clear in her mind now. The rain. The people. Her refusal to leave. Fatima, Mama and Papa staying with her, for hours, while she cried and prayed. Now she was back.

He had a head stone that she had never seen. "Dearly Missed" it read.

"Oh Daddy, you will never know how much." Rachel moved closer. "Daddy, I'm here. I'm so sorry I left you. I'm so sorry I couldn't come back." Rachel started to sniffle. She had left her handbag in the car, so she had nothing to wipe her face. She sat on the grass beside the grave and noticed for the first time flowers on the two sides of his headstone.

133

She looked around at the other plots. Some had flowers and decorations, others didn't. Obviously, loved ones had left them, but none of Rachel's family had come back to visit her father. Who would have left these? Two beautiful bouquets of spring flowers framed the grave. Rachel smelled them and immediately her spirits were lifted. Her father would have loved them. He had always loved his wife's garden. Rachel remembered that. He preferred to plant vegetables himself, but he did admire Naomi's devotion to her plants. Rachel guessed that the flowers had been there for at least a week. Still, they were holding up pretty well.

Rachel thought about the flowers and how everything in creation had a life span. Everything living eventually would die: flowers, plants, animals and people. That was what they called the circle of life. Then why was it so hard to accept? Why couldn't we just move on? If death was a part of life, then why was it so unbearable?

"Daddy, I'm here. It's Rachel. I miss you so much. I love you so much. I can't imagine you under the ground so far away from me. I can't stand it that I can't see you or touch you or hear your voice...I remember all the care you gave me when I was little...You worked so hard to take care of us."

Rachel remembered the times he went to work with only bread and butter for lunch. She remembered when he opened his wallet to give her or her older siblings his last dollars for some school event or something else they needed.

"You sacrificed so much to give us everything you could. You encouraged me when I was down. You held me when I was sad. You stayed up at night with me when I was sick."

Rachel moved closer and closer until her face was next to the headstone. "Then in your last moments you were alone. I wasn't there to take care of you. You gave me so much and I gave you nothing. I did nothing for you. I did nothing for you."

Rachel broke down crying. She placed her hands in the dirt in an effort to get closer to her father. She wanted to hold him so badly. She needed him so much. She told him everything that had happened to her since her tenth birthday. She told him about Jamie and the babies. All of them. She told him about Fatima and Ali and about how scared she was about her future.

"Daddy, just tell me what to do. Please Daddy, just tell me what to do. I'm so scared…I need you so much. I'll do whatever you say please, please help me, Daddy." Rachel sobbed until her chest hurt. She forced herself to catch her breath. As she continued to stroke the dirt around the plot she felt the first drops of rain. The soft rain turned to heavy rain and Rachel stayed. She sat and talked to her father until it got dark and then she went home.

When she pulled into her driveway, she remembered. "The daycare. Oh no." She shut off the engine and ran into the house. Joshua and Jonah were inside, eating cookies and playing a board game. When Rachel entered they jumped up and ran to hug her.

"Mommy, you're dirty," Joshua said.

"It was raining." She pushed the boys back and called for her mother until she emerged from her bedroom. "How did the boys get home?" Rachel asked her.

"When you didn't get them, the daycare called. I called Fatima and she sent Ali to pick them up."

Rachel stood in the same spot, unable to move towards Naomi. "I'm sorry. I just got caught up and I didn't notice the time. I forgot to turn my phone on. Sorry."

"Are you ok? What happened?" Naomi's voice was full of concern and sadness.

"Nothing, I just had to do something, that's all. Did they have dinner?"

"Yes, I cooked. They've had everything. You just need to put them to bed."

Rachel clapped her hands. "Let's go guys, bedtime." She needed to talk to someone and she didn't have that much time. She quickly put the boys to bed and turned into her room. She had been in such a hurry to send them off that she hadn't even changed out of her wet clothes.

Now she peeled off her clothes, showered and got dressed in a pair of khaki cargo pants and a red stretch knit top. She had no time to dry her hair. She combed it back and secured it in a tight ponytail. There was so much she needed to say. It was Monday, and Fatima had a night class. She wouldn't be back for, maybe, another hour.

"What should I do?" Rachel sat in her chair and rocked herself as she thought. She looked at the clock. It was already past nine. Fatima's kids would be in bed by now. Rachel paced the room. Back and forth. Back and forth. Then she decided.

"Ok, Ok. I'm going." She closed her bedroom door behind her and called to her mother. "Ma, I'm going out for a minute." Then she left quickly, before Naomi could ask her any questions.

She crossed the street to Fatima's house. Standing in front of the doors, she took a deep breath and rang the doorbell. "Oh, shoot. I'm going to wake the kids." When Ali opened the door she almost forgot why she had come.

"Sorry about the doorbell. I forgot the kids are probably sleeping." She tried to keep her hands from moving too much while she looked up at him.

"It's fine. Don't worry." Ali waited for Rachel to say something else. He assumed she had come to address the issue of not picking up the boys from daycare and to thank him for getting them. When she didn't, he finally said, "Fatima's not home."

Rachel shifted. She knew she must look a mess. Her face was still swollen from crying and her eyes were red. "She's at her class, right?"

"Yes." Ali nodded slowly.

"Well, I just really needed to talk." Ali didn't move from the doorway and didn't encourage her conversation. To lessen the awkwardness she was feeling, she asked lightly, "Were you busy?"

Ali couldn't help but laugh. "What's going on, Rachel?"

"I just needed to talk. Could I come in?" After she said it, her face started to burn with embarrassment. She had never been in Fatima's house in her absence. What would Ali think?

Ali narrowed his eyes. "What happened?"

"I can't talk like this." She shifted her weight from one leg to the other.

Ali lowered his head slightly. "Where's your mom?"

"She's home. I can't talk to her about this stuff."

Ali looked over Rachel's head. "Let me see if my mother is home."

Rachel couldn't take any more. She knew she was making a fool of herself. She was standing in front of this man's door, begging him to let her in, and he wasn't budging. She was distressed, confused and scared, and all she wanted was to talk to her friend. She was already boiling with embarrassment and didn't care what came out. "I don't want your mother!" she yelled.

She couldn't tell if Ali was surprised by her or not, but he remained still. "Please Ali?" She couldn't look at him anymore.

After an awkward pause she turned and ran down the stairs.

"Rachel." Rachel stopped but didn't turn around at the sound of Ali's voice. She was too humiliated.

"Come."

She turned enough to see that Ali had stepped aside to allow her to enter the house. She looked around the street, slowly re-climbed the stairs and walked through the doorway.

Ali stepped away from the open door. "No more outbursts. If you wake the kids, I'm throwing you out." His face had softened, and it made Rachel feel a little better.

"I'm sorry. Thanks so much." Rachel took a seat in the booth while Ali poured her a glass of water. He pulled out a stool and sat across the kitchen waiting for her to speak.

Rachel sipped the water while she thought about what she wanted to say. It was so much; she didn't know where to start. "I've been thinking about my father a lot lately. I think all these years I just tried to block it out, but now I can't. It hurts so much I just don't know what to do."

Ali listened without saying a word.

"It seems like no matter what I do, I can't get it right. Even when I try, just one little mistake and it seems like I'm set back in a huge way. I just don't know how to get control of my life."

"What do you want?" Ali asked her.

"I don't know."

"That's the first problem. So, how will you get it?"

Rachel thought about the question. "I guess I just want to be happy, to feel normal. I want to feel something other than this pain."

Ali rubbed the back of his neck. "Rachel, I don't know if I'm the best person to counsel you."

"I don't want a counselor. I just want a friend. Remember that? We were friends once, Ali."

"I understand your feelings of loss," Ali said, ignoring her last statement. Rachel knew that was true. Ali never spoke about all that he had lost in Rwanda, but she knew most of his family members had been killed.

Ali continued. "Death is just a doorway in our life. We all have to cross it at some point. There are no guarantees as to how long we're going to spend on this side." Ali paused, and then continued. "It hurts us when we lose people we love, but the relationship doesn't end. It just changes.

"They've done what they came to do. We have to fulfill our own purpose. We do the best with the time we have. Life doesn't come with a guarantee of how long we will be here or how we will leave."

Rachel tried to process what Ali had said to her. "What if I feel confused? What if I don't really know what to do? Where do I start?"

"Focus forward. Give value to the world. Put your energy into something positive. Start there."

Rachel didn't know what she was really doing here, in Fatima's kitchen. Why had she really come? Ali couldn't help her if she didn't tell him everything. She knew she wasn't going to tell him about Jamie. She was terrified about what could happen if Ali knew what Jamie was up to.

"Easy for you to say, you're happily married." Rachel took another drink of her water.

"You could be too."

Rachel stopped with her glass in mid-air. She had never really thought it was possible for her to be happily married, and she had never realized that she thought that way until now.

Ali continued, "I know your father is gone and you miss him, but he's not the only man that can love you."

Rachel was left tongue-tied.

"Love didn't die with him. It's all around you. Start with those closest to you; your mother, your sons. If you don't learn to love them, how can you love anyone else?"

"I do love them." Rachel was insulted at the suggestion that she didn't love her family.

"Really? How do you show it?" Ali shook his head. "Rachel, if this is how you love people, who would want to be next in line?"

Ali's words were stinging, but she had come for honesty and she knew he would give it to her. Rachel looked at the kitchen clock. It was ten to ten. Fatima's class finished at ten. She had one more question to ask and this may be the only chance she would have. She only hesitated for a second. She had to know.

"Why did you choose her?" Rachel's voice was barely audible. Indeed she couldn't believe she had really gotten the words out, but she had to know.

"What did you say?" Ali wasn't sure he had heard correctly.

"What is it that made you marry Fatima?" She kept her eyes on her water. Part of her wished she could crawl into the glass and drown, but she was relieved that she had finally gotten the question out.

"Are you serious?" Ali folded his arms across his chest.

Rachel glanced at the clock. "Yes. I am."

Ali lifted his chin, speaking slowly. "She's smart. Beautiful. Funny. Kind and honest. She is the best listener, and she understands life the way I do." He paused. "Enough?"

"So, which of those do I lack?" Rachel wanted to strangle herself, but she couldn't stop now.

Ali closed his eyes. "Rachel, come on."

"Ali, please. Who else can I ask these things? You're my friend, my best friend in the whole world. Please, just tell me." She couldn't believe that she had come this far, but she wasn't going to turn back.

Ali rested his elbows on his knees. With his hands clasped together, he rubbed his forehead against his knuckles as he thought about how he should answer her. "None."

"What?" It was almost a whisper.

Ali raised his head. "None of them. You don't lack any of them."

"Then why did you choose her?" Rachel tried to keep her voice from cracking.

Ali thought about the impact his words would have, then very carefully he said, "Until you value yourself, no one else is going to."

"Oh. Wow. You really take honesty to another level don't you?" Rachel covered her face with both her hands. She didn't know whether to feel happy, insulted, relieved or grateful that he had told her the truth.

Ali smiled. "That's what friends are for." He stood up and moved towards the door. Just then there was a soft knock. Sister Charles stood in the doorway holding a pie.

"You must be Ali. I met your wife at Naomi's." She held up the pie. "I believe this is your favourite? I promised Fatima I would bring one by when I was in the neighbourhood. I saw the lights, so I just thought I would try. Otherwise, I would have left it with Naomi."

Ali took the warm strawberry-rhubarb pie from Sister Charles. "Thank-you. Fatima isn't home yet. I'll be sure to let her know that you stopped by."

"That's fine." Sister Charles looked past Ali to see Rachel sitting at the table. "Oh my, Rachel, how are you? You're so quiet sitting there."

"Good evening, Sister Charles."

"Is it still evening?" Sister Charles looked at her watch. "Oh my, it's after ten. Time flies." She peered over her glasses into the kitchen. "Well kids, good night." She threw another glance at Rachel and then quietly left.

"Great. She's going to tell my mother that I was here." Rachel started to feel embarrassed all over again.

"That's the least of your worries," Ali said as he placed the pie on the table and headed towards the stairs.

"Ok comedian. Aren't you going to offer me a piece?" Rachel asked, referring to the pie.

"Help yourself. I'm going to check the girls."

Before he reached the top of the stairs, Batool appeared. "Daddy, I'm hungry."

"Do you want some pie?" Ali moved up the stairs towards her, watching her eyes light up. "Auntie Rachel is in the kitchen. She'll help you," Ali told her.

"Where's Mommy?" Batool rubbed her face.

"She's not home yet. Go on." He continued past her to the bedroom to check on Masuma and Laila.

Rachel and Batool enjoyed Sister Charles' pie, and then Rachel prepared to leave. She kissed Batool good night. "Go up to bed and tell Daddy I left."

Rachel stepped outside, closed the door behind her and walked across the street to her house. Just as she was opening her front door, she saw Fatima's car turn into the driveway.

Chapter Fourteen

ℑ

Fatima parked the car and turned off the ignition. "*Alhamdulillah*". She was home. Her last class of the year was complete, and she only had to prepare for her exams. The first of them was next Friday, her due date. She hoped she would be able to write it. The second one was later in the month and would most likely have to be deferred until the summer. She was not looking forward to the possibility of writing an exam in the summer with a new baby, but at least Ali would be home and available to help with the children and the house.

She wasn't sure if he was going to study or not this summer. Either way, she knew she would have his help, as well as the help of the extended family. She would just wait and see what he decided to do. A long time ago she had learned the value of being silent. It wasn't necessary to resolve every issue by talking. It was the natural female approach, but men didn't appreciate it. Ali was patient, but he was still a man.

Allah had made men the head of the household, and they were capable of so much, but a simple thing like a woman asking a question was enough to mess them up. Early in her marriage, she had learned that many issues could be resolved without saying a word. Time, prayer, patience and compassion could take care of so much.

She got out of the car, removed her backpack from the back seat and headed up the long stone path towards her house. Ali and Papa had completed the landscaping the previous year. The neighbours had questioned why they hadn't just hired someone to do it, but Fatima never did. She understood the need a man had to work with his hands. It was also a wonderful time for father and son to bond. She prayed that Ali could have that experience with his own son one day.

She smiled as she remembered advice Papa had given her when she was newly wed. "When your husband is upset, you be quiet. When he is happy, then you talk." It had come in handy on more than one occasion.

It wasn't always easy to tell when Ali was upset, but these days she knew he was stressed. The baby was coming, he was dealing with the paternity suit, and he knew Fatima wasn't happy about it. He was concerned about what his parents were thinking, he still had to travel tomorrow to complete the final games of the regular basketball season, and on top of it all, it was April.

He never spoke about it, but more than once she had seen him looking at a picture he had of himself and his grandmother, taken when he was a small boy. Fatima ached inside. She wished she could help him, but she didn't know how and she felt like he would not allow her even if she tried.

Fatima stepped onto the first of the porch steps, and one of the front doors opened slightly. She could see the light from inside the house, but nothing else. She took another step and the door opened a little more. She paused. The door remained still. With each step the door opened just a little more.

When she reached the top of the porch, she tip-toed to the door. She was determined to catch Ali this time. She silently slipped through the doorway and looked behind the door. Nothing.

"Boo," Ali whispered from behind her. Before she could turn around, he had taken the backpack from her shoulder. *How did he do that?* Go from behind the door to the other side of the doorway without her seeing him? *If he had been behind the door at all.* She could never figure it out.

She put her hand on her hip and looked up at him. "Don't you have anything better to do than to frighten pregnant women in the night?"

Ali pretended to be thinking. "Right now? No. Nothing at all."

It was Ali's last night home this week. As of tomorrow, he would be on the road until Friday. He always tried to make this time special, just as Fatima tried to make his time away special for the girls. She removed her shoes and her head scarf. "Isn't it past your bedtime?" she asked.

He reached behind her and closed the door. "You know I can't sleep until you're home."

Fatima laughed. "You're going to have a long week."

"As always." Ali stepped aside, allowing Fatima entrance to the kitchen. "How was your class?"

"All I care is that it's over, thank goodness. School is the last thing I want to think about right now." She looked at the pie on the table. "Looks like you started without me."

Ali moved the pie to the island. "Sit." After Fatima sat at the table, he sat across from her. "Sister Charles stopped by."

"I saw her up the street. She stopped my car on the way in. She mentioned that she saw you." Ali nodded. Fatima continued, "So, how was your night?"

"The usual: kids, kids, kids and more kids, kids, kids," Ali answered casually.

"Yeah, I heard you have a lot," Fatima replied.

Ali stretched his legs under the table. "It's my wife, you know, she just won't stop."

"What? Ali, that's not nice."

"I thought we were joking." Ali rested his forearms on top of the table.

"That didn't sound like a joke to me." Fatima moved her hands to her lap.

"I'm sorry." He smiled. "It was 90% joke."

Fatima stood up to leave the table. Ali grabbed her arm.

"What else happened tonight?" she asked.

"Why do I get the feeling you already know?" Ali pulled her back into her seat.

"Why didn't you tell me?"

"You just got home. It's not what I want to talk about right now," he replied, "or how I want to spend our last few hours together," he added as he seated himself across from her.

"What happened? Is everything ok?" Fatima asked, referring to Rachel's visit.

"She just needed to talk."

"What's going on? And why didn't she just wait for me to come home? She was already here."

"It wasn't a big deal, just stuff." Ali brushed some crumbs from the table.

"Naomi is ok...and the boys?"

"Yes, I think they're fine."

"You *think* they're fine, and she just needed to talk about stuff that you can't tell me. Do I have it right?" Fatima was having a difficult time hiding her irritation. She couldn't understand Ali's elusive behaviour these days. She felt like she didn't know who she was living with anymore.

"She just had a bad day, I guess. It seems like she's had a lot on her mind."

"Really? So she needed to talk. Did she forget that I had a class?"

Ali sighed and rubbed his hand over his face. "I can't say. She was just upset. Her dad has been on her mind a lot, and she just needed to talk about it. That's all."

"Why didn't you tell her to come back when I got home?"

"I was going to, but she was all messed up, and I could tell she was embarrassed that I wouldn't let her in. I couldn't do that to her."

"You couldn't? Oh, I see. I'm happy that you're so *considerate*. Well, the three of us have an agreement and if our relationship is going to work out the boundaries have to be respected. Rachel understands Islamic etiquette."

"You're right. It was a special case. You had to be here to see.

She was in bad shape." Ali could see that Fatima's agitation was growing and his focus was keeping the situation from escalating.

"That makes it worse." She motioned with her hands. "Your shoulder is not the one she should be crying on."

"She was nowhere near my shoulder."

"Isn't that comforting?" Fatima answered sarcastically. She stood up, slipped on her scarf and shoes, and then reached for the door.

"Maybe I should go and talk to her."

Ali moved as quickly as she did. He reached over her and put his hand on the door. "It's late."

Fatima pulled the door open. "That didn't stop her from coming to my house."

In 20 seconds flat, Fatima was knocking on the side door of Rachel's house. When she remembered that Naomi was the owner of the house she knocked more softly. She caught her breath and stepped back. How many times had she knocked on this same door during her childhood?

She had knocked when she was desperate to use the washroom and was not able to make it to her own house just steps away. She had knocked when she was thirsty or hurt or needed comfort. This time she was hurt and confused. Ali was keeping something from her. If Rachel had come to speak to him when she wasn't home there must be a reason why, and she wanted to know what that was.

Rachel moved the curtains to look out. The same curtains they had shopped for together, and Fatima had sewn with so much love, putting her trademark F on. Rachel opened the door and asked, "Fatima, what's going on?"

"You were at my house tonight," Fatima said. "Is everything all right?"

Rachel's concerned looked changed. She stepped outside and closed the door behind her.

"Yes," she said and crossed her arms in front of her. She was still feeling a little uncomfortable about her visit and anticipated that Fatima may be annoyed. She was prepared. Ali was Fatima's husband, but Rachel was not going to let Fatima take her to task for a simple conversation.

"You're ok?"

"I guess."

"So what happened? Why didn't you wait for me?"

"I just needed to talk. A lot has been going on lately," Rachel stated flatly.

"Ok..."

When Rachel didn't elaborate Fatima finally said, "You knew I was at school."

"And? What's the problem? I can't talk to Ali anymore? We've been friends since grade three."

Fatima was fuming. She had come to Rachel's house to see what had happened, to make sure she was all right, and all Fatima was getting was this strange attitude from her. What was going on? She couldn't understand what had gotten into Rachel. If she was truthful, at this point she didn't want to understand. She just wanted to make herself perfectly clear. "Rachel, we have boundaries and you know why."

Rachel narrowed her eyes. "Don't you trust your husband?" It was a low blow considering the current issues at hand.

Fatima stepped up to meet Rachel and looked her straight in the eye. "I trust God and can handle whatever comes my way."

Rachel's nostrils flared as she arched her eyebrows. "Well, handle this. Yes, I knew you were at school. Yes, I went to your house at 9:30 on a cold, dark night knowing that you were not there, because I needed something from someone and no, it wasn't you. I needed my friend. My best friend. As I remember, I used to have two of them."

Fatima kept her breathing even and refused to respond. She wanted to hear everything.

"Your beloved husband opened the door, to find a basket case on his front porch, and attempted to call 'everybody and their mother' to deal with it, so he wouldn't have to. After I freaked out and made a total fool of myself, he finally let me in and was gracious enough to allow me a seat at your kitchen table, making sure to sit as far away from me as possible. He gave me cold water and let me babble. Then, when your children needed him, he left me to enjoy Sister Charles' pie by myself, with Batool's help of course. Finally, I let myself out, through the door that was left open the entire time. I think you would have been proud of him."

Fatima should have been furious, but all she felt for Rachel at that moment was sympathy. "Why Rachel? Why do you do this to yourself?"

Rachel was startled by the sudden change in Fatima's approach. "Listen, forget it, ok? It was just a conversation. No big deal."

"Really."

"Look, you have everything. All I wanted was just a few minutes." Rachel leaned on the metal railing while watching Fatima.

"You still don't get it. You have it all too. If you would just stop focusing on what you think you're missing, you might be able to see all that you have. Ali has never stopped being your friend. Anytime you need him, he's there for you. He watches out for your mom and takes care of your boys like they're his. He would lay down his life for you. How many people have friends like that? But somehow that's not enough for you. What do you want, Rachel?"

Rachel shifted her eyes. "He just feels sorry for me."

Fatima laughed out loud and shook her head. "I'm sure if he wanted to give charity there are many easier ways he could do it," she retorted.

Rachel remained silent, but her bottom lip started to quiver. Fatima stepped down into the garden. She picked up the stones that Ali had placed so carefully. She started throwing them at the budding crocuses just pushing their way through the dirt. "Who," she threw a stone, "plants flowers," she threw another stone, "in someone else's garden?"

Rachel released her arms and then crossed them again. "He did that for my mother," she said decidedly.

"Your mother is blind!" Fatima did not realize her voice had increased so much in volume.

Rachel covered her mouth to prevent herself from speaking. Fatima, breathing heavily stood at the bottom of the stairs looking up to Rachel's level. "That is exactly why you are in the situation you're in. You don't even know what love looks like."

Rachel saw Ali before Fatima did.

"Fatima, it's time to go inside." Ali's deep voice cut through the night air and the building tension between the two women. All that could be heard was the rustling trees and their breathing.

Fatima and Rachel stood staring at each other without speaking. Rachel spoke first. She had to take a cleansing breath and clear her throat to do it. "Your husband is speaking to you."

Fatima shook her head and turned to walk away. Rachel watched Fatima and Ali enter their home before she retreated and slowly locked her door.

Chapter Fifteen

The next morning Fatima woke up and looked around as she stretched in her bed. She had intentionally chosen a masculine style for the room. Dark furniture draped with solid colour fabrics brought a strong and comforting energy to the space. She usually used duvets and bedding in solid colours, plaids or stripes.

Ali spent so much time travelling that when he wasn't she wanted him to feel at home. She wanted him to feel completely connected to their room and at peace when he was there. She never encouraged the children to sleep with them. Even when they were babies, they always slept in their own rooms. Ali did feel sorry for them sometimes and allow them in on rare occasions. Fatima only permitted them to hang out on the mornings that the family had time to lounge.

She did have some feminine markers in the room as well. The custom blinds were covered with sheer curtains, and on her side of the bed was a soft fluffy rug. She had a couch decorated with large soft cushions. Salt lamps sat on either side of the bed and she always had candles and aromatherapy oils nearby. It was her favourite room in the house.

The events of last night seemed to be a world away. Ali had not wanted to discuss the confrontation with Rachel when they returned home. He just wanted to put it all aside for the time being. Fatima had agreed to keep her focus on her family when she was in her home and leave the outside world beyond her front door.

She was not going to let the events of the evening rob her of precious time. It was Ali's last night home and no one was going to ruin it. This approach was, sometimes, the only way to keep her sanity and ensure that her and her husband could outride the inevitable storms and challenges that would arise in their relationship.

As she stretched she looked up at the writing on the ceiling.

You are...
The Answer to my Prayers...
The Fulfillment of my Dreams...
The Direction of my Destiny...

Ali had written it for her, but it reflected her feelings exactly. It had always been such a comfort to her whether he was home or not, but somehow today it made her feel sad. Things were not the same anymore. She had not mentioned Ali's recent trip out of town, but it was on her mind. She wondered when she would learn about what had been so urgent. She would not bring it up now, but in time he would have to discuss it with her.

Ali would be leaving this morning and not returning until Friday. It was always hard to say good-bye, but this time would be more difficult. She really felt like she needed him to be with her right now. When he was with her she didn't need to think. His presence would block out all her negative thoughts, fears and worries. When he was gone, all she did was think.

She missed the days of travelling with him, and often wondered if she had had the children too early. Ali had wanted to wait. They were young, he had said, and had a lot of time, but Fatima had been so eager to try and have a son. After having Masuma and facing the realities of parenting, she decided waiting would be a good idea. And then dreams of a boy resurfaced, and along came the twins.

She didn't even want to think about who this baby might be. She had refused to find out the sex of the baby, although the suspense sometimes was unbearable.

She leaned over to look at the table beside her bed. She had already found four of the papers that Ali had placed around the house. The first one had the number 7 written on it. The other three papers had one letter each, an *n* and two *e's*. She had placed the four papers in a line on her bedside table. She still needed to find the others to decode the message. Ali had promised her a special gift if she found all of them before he returned.

Fatima had her week fully planned. She would study in the mornings and then take her daughters out in the afternoon. She had several people she wanted to visit with before her period of confinement started, and she wanted to look for outfits for Rachel's boys, in case Rachel decided to send them to the wedding the following week. She would be with Naomi and her church sisters on Friday, and then Ali would be home.

She glanced at her clock. She wasn't sure if she should expect Rachel this morning, but she would be ready just in case.

At precisely seven thirty, the doorbell rang. Rachel held up a bouquet of flowers as a peace offering.

"Where did you find flowers at this time of the morning?" Fatima asked, as she graciously accepted the gift.

"Oh, I have my ways." Rachel was dressed in a blue, grey and black plaid skirt, a black sweater and a black leather jacket. She wore her hair curly and looked much younger as a result. "I need to talk to you about last night."

"Come in."

When they were both seated in the living room, Rachel started speaking quickly. "You know I would never do anything to hurt you, Fatima. I only came over because I had a really messed up day, and I needed to talk to Ali, that's all. You know he has this different way of looking at things. I just needed to hear what he had to say. I would never do anything to harm you or your family." Rachel looked Fatima directly in the eyes.

Rachel continued, "And I am so sorry about that stupid comment I made about you not trusting Ali. That was so mean and disgusting of me. We both know he is perfectly trustworthy, and you would never have any reason to doubt him. I'm so sorry."

"Never say never." Fatima placed the flowers on the table in front of her.

"Don't say that, Fatima. You guys are perfect, and I can't even handle anything less than that today, so don't even go there." Rachel finally took a breath.

"Oh sure, I wouldn't want to upset you now, would I?" Fatima continued, "So tell me, what happened that had you so upset?"

Rachel told Fatima about the meeting with Brigitte, about Jamie following her and Ali, and Jamie's plans to take the boys.

"So you told Ali all this?"

"No, not exactly."

"Either you did or you didn't," Fatima pressed.

"I didn't." Rachel looked down.

"Why not?" Fatima was shocked and slightly confused.

"I don't know. I just felt kind of overwhelmed. What will Ali do when he finds out?" Rachel glanced in Fatima's direction.

"Well, I don't know, but he needs to know that he's being stalked, don't you think?" Fatima's eyes were wide.

"You're going to tell him?" Rachel chewed the inside of her lip.

"Of course, I'm going to tell him. What if he's in danger? How could you keep this from him? What did you come over for, if not to tell him this?"

"I don't know. I was just babbling, really." Rachel looked down at her lap, folding and unfolding a corner of her jacket.

Fatima furrowed her brow and assessed Rachel. She believed that Rachel's apology was sincere, but she did notice that Rachel suddenly had trouble meeting her gaze.

Fatima didn't have to ask why. She knew Rachel too well. And she would never forget the words that Rachel had said last night.

"... *you have everything. All I wanted was a few minutes.*"

Anyway, that wasn't important now. This news about Jamie was going to have to take precedence.

"Don't you think it's about time you talked to the police, or at least saw a lawyer? You have to do something, Rachel. Shawn is really great, maybe you should talk to him."

"I don't know." Rachel struggled with this issue. She was so afraid of making waves.

"What are you going to do? Wait until Jamie really goes berserk around here? You have two little boys and your mother to think about. It's not just about you. This is not going away. You have to meet it head on, or else it will blow up in your face. We're all here for you. You can do this."

"I'm not like you, Fatima. I can't."

"Yes, you can, and you have to. Things are getting out of hand and you have to take action. I know you're scared. You just move forward anyway. We're going to support you. We have so many resources. You can get the best lawyers. You can have all kinds of security and protection. There is no limit to what we would do for you. You just have to say the word. But it has to come from you."

Silence fell between them as Rachel soaked in Fatima's words. She knew Fatima was right and she agreed it was time for her to do something now. She had to. The first step was just the hardest.

"I went to see my dad."

Fatima eyes misted. "That's wonderful. How was it?'

"Good. It was really good." Rachel dabbed at the tears that were gathering in her eyes.

"You should go more often. Regularly. Maybe it will give you the strength you need right now."

Rachel nodded then quickly changed the subject. "So you're going to tell Ali?"

"Absolutely."

"Ok, I'm going to think about everything you said. Really, I'm going to think about it."

"Good. Anyway, time is passing. Let's get started." Fatima

reached for the *dua* books she had put on the table.

First they started with *Hadith e Kisa* /The Story of the Cloak. Fatima explained briefly to Rachel. "One of the things I love about this *hadith* is the way the family members speak to each other. *Imam Ali(as)* doesn't call his wife, 'Fatima', he calls her 'Daughter of the Prophet,' and she, in turn, doesn't refer to him simply as 'Ali,' she uses his full title, 'Commander of the Faithful.'

"When they speak to their children, it is with so much love and tenderness, it reminds us that those we are supposed to be most respectful to are the members of our household and not the outside people, the way we usually are.

"It is said that whenever this *hadith* is read, the angels come down and encircle the people, praying for their forgiveness until the gathering disperses, and *Allah* answers requests made at that time. So, I really love this."

The two ladies spent the remainder of their hour together reading and listening to various *duas* and *Quran*. Fatima and Rachel both made their own specific supplications, and when Rachel left to go to work, Fatima prepared to give Ali the news.

"I know."

"You know?" Fatima sat on the lounge chair in her bedroom. "How did you know, and when were you going to tell me?"

"I didn't want to worry you." Ali walked into his closet to get his clothes.

"The more things you keep from me the more worried I get." Fatima raised her voice slightly to make sure he heard her.

He stepped back through the doorway. "I just found out last night. Shawn has a private investigator working on my case and this is what he came up with so far."

"That was fast."

"He has good men." Ali disappeared into the closet again.

"Ali, could you just sit down for a second and talk to me?" Fatima hated when he behaved like this.

Ali returned to the room, stopped getting dressed and sat on the bed facing Fatima.

"What else do you need to tell me?" Fatima asked.

"It's just what Rachel said. Jamie is following us in an attempt to stir up trouble. When we have more evidence then we can take action."

"What kind of action?"

"Don't worry, Fatima."

"This is my family, and all you can say is, 'don't worry?'" Do you think that's reasonable? Now, you're leaving. How do you expect me to feel?"

"You'll be safe when I'm away. I've made sure of it," Ali said.

"Oh, when were you going to clue me in to what's going on?"

"I tell you what I think you need to know," he replied without changing his facial expression.

"How manly of you." She was deliberately sarcastic, knowing how much he hated it.

"I am what I am, Fatima. I'm not going to come to you with every little problem, to stress you out, when you can't do anything about it anyway."

"I just want to feel included. If something involves me or the family, I just want to know. It's important to me. And how do you know I can't do anything? I have a brain. I have ideas too."

Ali glanced at the clock. "Ok, what do you want to know?"

"Don't talk to me like that, Ali. I'm trying to communicate with you, here." Ali could be so warm at times and then suddenly shift to being so distant, often with no warning. "Well, did the investigation find anything else? Related to your case, I mean." She could not bring herself to say the word "paternity."

"I studied the photos, and it looks like my pictures were cropped from pictures that we took last summer, when we went on vacation," Ali said.

"How would someone have had access to them?"

"I had emailed them to my cousins, so who knows. If someone got into my email then they could get it, I guess."

"What about the emails?" Fatima questioned.

"They were all sent between midnight and 2 a.m. You know I'm always sleeping at that time."

She knew that was true. She had never known Ali to stay up much past 10 pm. He would sleep even earlier if he could. He always woke up early, extremely early, but never before 2 a.m.

"Well, someone knows your schedule. What about the receipts?" Fatima continued.

"The dates are right. I was at those hotels." Ali stood and walked around the room. "I don't know how anyone got a hold of them or if they are even the originals. The team is still working on that."

"I see. Anything else?"

"No, that's about it for now."

So he is still being tight-lipped about his trip, Fatima thought. She wanted to ask about the paternity test, but the words could not pass her lips. As if Ali could read her mind he said, "I'm still waiting for Shawn to let me know which company we're going to do the DNA test with."

Fatima nodded. "Ok, I just wish you felt comfortable to share with me. You shouldn't be dealing with this by yourself." She was trying to be supportive, although she really wished she could jump somewhere into the future to a time when this would no longer matter.

Ali recalled the way Fatima's mood had changed when he had reminded her that Shawn was coming over to discuss the case. He also recalled the look on her face when Shawn had left the house that day. How could he keep bringing up an issue that he knew disturbed her so much?

"I can handle it." He stood up and pulled his shirt over his head.

"I know you can handle it, Ali. That's not the point. It makes me feel like you don't trust me or value me when you don't tell me things. I'm your wife. I want to be there for you."

"You are. You're there in the way that I need; it just may not be what you think I need."

"What about what I need?"

Ali squeezed his eyes shut and leaned his head back. When he brought it forward his eyes were heavy. "I'm trying, Fatima. I am trying."

"Ok, ok, let's leave it for now. Thanks for telling me everything. I really appreciate it." Fatima smiled as she thought about his impending departure. "Anyway, I want you to leave happy."

Ali smiled back. "Impossible."

After Ali and Fatima had fed and dressed the children, they said their goodbyes and Ali departed amidst a torrent of hugs and kisses from the little ladies of his house. He then crossed the street to say goodbye to his parents. Fatima turned in to start studying. She had a full day ahead of her, but she knew that no matter how busy she was, Friday could not arrive soon enough.

Chapter Sixteen

ॐ

Fatima breezed through her studying. Her first exam was biology, her favourite subject. She kept good notes and always reviewed after classes, so preparing for exams was less difficult. After lunch she put the girls down for a nap, with the intention of doing the same herself.

"Can we go see Papa?" Masuma asked before her head hit the pillow.

"After you wake up," Fatima replied. She was truly grateful for the loving and supportive extended family that she had. There was no way she could get through each day without them. When they all woke up from their naps, they went across the street to see Ali's parents.

"There she is." Mama's friend, Nargis, was visiting and her face lit up when she saw Fatima. She was a nurse and loved anything to do with babies. It was her son, Abbas, that was getting married the following week and the two women were discussing the final details of the wedding.

"Come Darling, sit." Nargis motioned to a cushioned chair next to her. Mama and Nargis sat in the sunroom, surrounded by unassembled wedding favours.

"*As-salaam alaikum*, Auntie." Fatima kissed Nargis on both cheeks.

Nargis belonged to a large Khoja community in the city. The Khoja's were an ethnic community of Indians, some of whom had travelled to and settled in East Africa. She was uncommonly kind and welcoming. She had become fast friends of the Abatis soon after their arrival in Canada. She was thrilled that Ali had agreed to recite *Quran* at Abbas's wedding.

"His voice just moves me. He must be the best reciter in the province, maybe the country," Nargis said.

Fatima squeezed Mama's hand. "The best *male* reciter."

"Of course, of course," Nargis agreed. "So Fatima, how have you been doing?"

Fatima knew that the question was about more than her pregnancy. The lawsuit was all over the news. She was surprised reporters were not outside her house. Maybe photographers were lurking in the bushes. Anyway, she couldn't worry about that. So far they had received enormous support from friends and neighbours. Everyone seemed to believe in Ali's innocence. If anyone didn't, they kept it to themselves. Fatima's phone had been ringing almost non-stop. She often turned the ringer off as a result. Call after call came from Ali's present and former teammates, coaches and managers. They all expressed their support. Ali had told her he would need to do a press conference soon. She remembered the conversation well.

"**I guess I'll** be expected to be there." She had dreaded the idea of being in the spotlight.

"Absolutely not," Ali had said.

"Why? I know in cases like these it usually looks better if the wife stands by her husband's side." Fatima mentally recalled countless cases of women, smiling or stoic, standing by the sides of their husbands while the men faced some scandal or another. She always wondered how the women could do it.

"I don't care how things look. I'll do what's best for my family. I'm not going to parade you in front of cameras just so I look innocent." Fatima had been through enough, he had said. He wouldn't dream of putting her through such a circus. Papa had already warned him about succumbing to the pressure of press agents and managers. Fortunately, everyone knew Ali was his own man, and no one expected to be able to browbeat him into doing anything.

Fatima turned to Nargis. "I'm fine. It's Ali's last week on the road. He has three more games, and then he's home until the fall."

"Perfect timing." Nargis smiled and raised her eyebrows.

"It is. I couldn't have planned it better myself," Fatima added, as she reached for one of Nargis's sweets. She always travelled with some kind of treat. Children loved her because of it. Today she had almond baklava with maple cappuccino syrup.

"Do you miss being out there?" Nargis asked.

"Yes and no. I love watching him play, and I always watch the games on TV when I'm home, but these days I would rather avoid the crowd. *And* I certainly don't miss hanging out with the other wives. They're a piece of work."

"So, when are you due?"

"Next Friday." Fatima bit into her baklava.

"The day of the wedding?" Nargis looked from Fatima to Mama and back to Fatima. "How do you plan to swing that?"

"Well, the other kids were past their due date, so I just figure I'll keep going until I can't."

"You are amazing. I would be sitting at home with my feet up from the beginning of eight months! Are you ready for four children?"

"I guess I'll find out." Fatima smiled and her eyes sparkled. She really loved these last days of pregnancy. She never felt anxious to give birth. She enjoyed each of her final moments to the fullest.

Mama interjected, "She doesn't have a thing to worry about. We are all ready and waiting to take care of her and those four babies."

"Do you know what the baby will be?" Nargis asked.

"No, I didn't want to find out." Fatima slipped a quick look at Mama, who didn't say a word.

"Whatever it is you just be grateful. A healthy baby is the most important. When you have worked in the hospital as long as I have and seen all that I have you understand that." Nargis was a neonatal nurse, so Fatima understood exactly what she meant.

"Have you been reading Surah Yusuf?" Nargis continued.

"Every day." It was said that if a pregnant woman recited this chapter of the *Quran* her baby would be pious, intelligent and beautiful.

"What about names?"

"Ali is going to choose this time. He hasn't told me what he's thinking about." Fatima adjusted herself on the chair.

Nargis's eyes widened. "I would never trust my husband to pick my child's name! I don't even let him pick which restaurant to eat at!" she exclaimed.

All three women laughed. "I trust him," Fatima replied.

Mama smiled silently.

Being with these two women made Fatima miss her own mother even more. Dana was currently in Malaysia working on two buildings that had recently been discovered in northern Kedah state. She wasn't due home until September. Fatima had been fighting the desire to call her; she couldn't bring herself to broach the topic at hand. She just wished Dana could be with her. Fatima knew if her mother could just hold her, everything would feel right. "Oh Mom, where are you?" Fatima whispered under her breath as she looked out on the backyard.

The Abati house had a similar set-up as Fatima's, except for the huge sunroom that the Abatis spent so much time in, and the magnificent backyard. Mama's garden was the envy of the entire neighbourhood. The previous summer they had put in a small pond with a waterfall. In the morning or late evening it was the most soothing sound to hear the trickling water. Mama had even added a few tropical trees to her nursery. Sometimes, if Ali and Fatima had the opportunity to get out at night, they would come and sit in the backyard to enjoy the beauty.

"Ok ladies, let's get these favours wrapped," Nargis said. The women spent the rest of the afternoon filling and wrapping monogrammed mint tins for the wedding guests, chatting, laughing and, of course, eating. Fatima had invited Rachel to meet her at the house after work and Mama was looking forward to seeing her and spending time with her.

The hours flew by quickly. By the time Rachel rang the doorbell Fatima needed to stretch her legs. When she opened the door Rachel rushed past her to greet Mama and Papa, who had recently emerged from his study, and then quickly excused herself. Fatima was still standing at the doorway with her hand on the door knob when Rachel returned.

"What was that?" Fatima asked referring to Rachel's whirlwind entrance. "Where are Joshua and Jonah?"

"Come, come." Rachel closed the front door and pulled Fatima into Papa's study.

"What is it, Rachel?"

"Oh, are we allowed to be in here?" Rachel asked as she looked around the room.

"It's fine, but what has gotten into you?" Rachel just hopped from one leg to the other. "Here Rachel, sit down." Fatima guided her into the large arm chair.

"Nice chair." She twirled around.

"It's Ali's."

"He has his own chair in his father's study? Phew, they love their son."

"Rachel, the news?"

"It's Jamie! He's been arrested," she whispered forcefully.

"How do you know?"

"I have sources, too." Rachel had a few friends who were good at unearthing information and kept her updated on important community happenings.

"Ok, what was he arrested for?" Fatima pulled up another chair and sat beside Rachel.

"Illegal possession and misuse of a firearm!"

"Surprise, surprise. He's a thug," Fatima said matter-of-factly.

"There's more."

"Rachel, will you just spill it?"

"He escaped from police custody!"

"What?! How is that possible?" Fatima hit the arms of her chair.

"I told you he has connections." Rachel's face was blank, but her eyes were moving. It was clear she had more on her mind.

"Ok, so what are you thinking?"

"A man with nothing to lose has nothing to lose."

Fatima was getting very frustrated with Rachel's communication. "The point, Rachel?"

"What if he goes off and comes here or something?"

"You think he will?" Fatima folded one arm across her chest and put the opposite hand under her chin.

"No, I don't think so. The neighbourhood is pretty tight." Rachel was starting to sound erratic.

"What do you mean?" Fatima was having trouble keeping up with her.

"Oh, you don't know?" Rachel put one hand on her hip. "There are security people all over the neighbourhood."

"You're kidding?" Fatima was astonished.

"Did you doubt? Don't tell me I know your husband better than you do? I'm sure Ali has at least three men watching your house alone."

"I had no idea."

"Didn't you wonder why the street was so quiet? Normally, you would expect the press to be hounding you guys, under the circumstances."

"This is really heavy." Fatima dropped her hands in her lap.

"Yes, it is." Rachel said, as much to herself as to Fatima.

"Ok Rachel, everything is going to be fine. I have no idea what Jamie is up to, but *Allah* is greater than all these things. All we have to do is keep praying and take action. It's time, Rachel."

"I don't know where he is. What am I supposed to do?" Rachel answered, with attitude.

"Talk to Shawn and see what steps you need to take to protect yourself and your sons. You're afraid of Jamie and with good reason, I might add. You have enough on him to get a restraining order. Then you have to file for sole custody. It's pretty simple." Fatima waited for Rachel's response.

"Ok, ok," Rachel agreed, but the look in her eyes said something else.

Fatima stood up and pulled Rachel to her feet. "Let's get some food into you. We'll get started after dinner. Where are the boys?"

"They went into the backyard. I'll go get them." Rachel left the room, slipped outside and around the side of the house along the cobblestone pathway to the backyard.

Rachel, Fatima and their children had dinner with the Abatis in the sunroom and stayed until the sun set. Papa lit the large candles that stood on tall stands in each corner. The room was flooded with hues of red, orange and gold. The children wrestled and rode on Papa's back, jumping and rolling around until they were exhausted. By the time they were ready to leave, Rachel was feeling much better. Fatima had spoken to Shawn, who had agreed to meet with them the next evening. Finally, something was taking shape.

"So Rachel, I'll see you in the morning?" Fatima knew she was pushing it, but she hoped Rachel would be open to another prayer session.

"Sure, I'll be there."

"Great. See you then."

They went to their own homes and turned in for the evening. Naomi was at a church retreat and was scheduled to return on Thursday night. Rachel spent the rest of the evening cleaning and organizing her house. She figured she could focus on one area of the house each day until her mother returned. Knowing that Naomi was expecting guests on Friday, Rachel started thinking about what food she could prepare for them. With Rachel's help, Naomi would have nothing to do when she returned. By the time Rachel turned in, well after midnight, she found Jonah in her bed.

"Nightmares again?" she whispered to herself. "What am I going to do, Lord? What am I going to do?"

Chapter Seventeen

ℑ

The next morning Rachel arrived at Fatima's house at 7:30, just as she had the day before. They spent an hour reading and praying. Fatima talked to Rachel about the value of making a list.

"Sometimes, I find we may not know what to pray for specifically. When you write it down, it becomes a physical manifestation of your desires. I think that is powerful. Also, it becomes easy to pray for the same thing over and over, and if someone asks you to pray for them, you can write it on your list so you remember to do it."

"Do you always write a list?" Rachel thought of her own list that she had secretly been keeping.

"Absolutely."

"Isn't it kind of greedy or selfish to always be asking for something?" Rachel had not grown up with this concept of prayer. She had basically learned the Lord's Prayer, and that was it.

"No, no, not at all. *Allah* wants us to ask. When we ask and He answers, it builds our faith. We become more connected to Him. He becomes real and it becomes easier to serve Him. It's not a one-way street. He answers us, so we also have to answer Him."

Rachel thought about what Fatima was saying. She knew that

making her own list had given her more clarity. She knew she needed her mother to be well, she wanted her boys to be stable and happy, she had to shake Jamie and build a bright future for herself. Still, she had so many questions. "What if I ask for the wrong thing? What if it's not good for me?"

"We should always ask God to give us what's best. But don't worry so much. God wants what's good for you. He's not trying to trip you up. When you don't ask, you don't include God in the process. *That's* when you need to worry."

"Ok, so if He wants what's good for us, why do we even have to ask? Why not just accept whatever we have."

"Because He told us to. God told us to ask," Fatima stressed. Rachel was not going to argue with that.

Fatima explained further, "*Allah* wants to have dialogue with us. He wants that relationship. You develop that through communication. When your prayers are answered, you can cross them off and you'll remember to say thank-you. So many times we ask for something and we forget, and then we don't realize when we have been answered. We never say thank-you."

Rachel thought about all that Fatima had said. It made sense. It always did coming from her. She just had this simple matter-of-fact way of saying things. No pressure. No stress. Just the facts.

"Did you pray for Ali? You know, for marriage?" Rachel asked.

"No, I didn't. I hadn't been thinking seriously about marriage at that age. What I did know was the kind of person I wanted in my life. I saw the mess the girls at school were in because of boyfriends and all that. I knew I didn't want that headache. Watching someone like Ali and seeing his family gave me a picture of what a good person should look like, what a good family would be like. I was definitely clear about that. What about you?"

It was a loaded question. One that Rachel had not expected to have turned back on her. She wasn't quite sure how to answer. She wasn't sure what Fatima was asking. "What do you mean?" Rachel ventured carefully.

Fatima did not clarify, she just waited.

Rachel spoke quickly. "I never really thought about the kind of person I wanted. I guess when I did I just thought it wasn't possible for me. I thought my dreams couldn't come true." Rachel smiled shyly.

Fatima nodded. "Do you see the difference? It's completely your choice. What you believe about your life is exactly what you will create, whether you like it or not."

The thought of having anything better than what she had right now was almost impossible for Rachel. *Really* having Jamie out of her life? Feeling confident and capable and deserving of success? She just couldn't see it. Even the thought of it scared her a little. She almost didn't want to try for fear of being disappointed by her own failure. The possibility of having a happy home life and actually feeling content most of the time instead of faking it seemed too good to consider. Having the outside Rachel and the inside Rachel in conflict was becoming exhausting. "So what about after you have already created the mess? Then what?"

"Piece of cake, as you like to say. The hardest part is believing. Once you have that, then you use all the tools in front of you. Prayer is one key thing. Then you have to start seeing yourself in the life you want, and then take steps towards it. It will become clearer to you with each step. The list helps you keep focused."

Rachel rubbed her arms. She suddenly felt chilled. "Why does it hurt so much?"

Fatima reached over and put her arms around Rachel's shoulders. "Those are growing pains. You have to stretch yourself out of your comfort zone. That's when you grow. The rewards are tremendous. You step into a whole different reality. But you can't see it until you are there, or at least close. You need to start moving."

Rachel rose to her feet. It was all she could handle for one day. Fatima was just happy that Rachel was still coming, was still open. She so wanted Rachel to have the benefits of faith that she and her family enjoyed. Fatima imagined they would be even closer then, because they would have more in common.

Rachel headed through the hallway towards the door, with Fatima following her. Rachel paused at the door. "One more question. How do you figure out what you want? You know sometimes you don't even know."

"I think if you don't know, perhaps because you haven't seen it in your immediate family or in your life, through your own experiences, then you have to start looking outside. Look at other people, other stories. Use them as examples."

Rachel straightened her clothing and adjusted her handbag. "Ok, I'm off. What do you have planned for today?"

"Studying, then shopping."

"Sounds good. I'll pop in after work to see how you're doing."

"See you then."

Fatima closed the door and headed to the kitchen to make breakfast. When she heard the knock, she knew Rachel had forgotten something. She never used the doorbell when the kids were sleeping. "What did you leave this time?" Fatima opened the door and stepped back. It took her at least three seconds to process what she was seeing.

"I thought this bird was going to do me in before you opened the door." Fatima's blue jay was chirping wildly.

"Mom!" Fatima completely forgot she was pregnant and jumped into her mother's arms. "Oh Mom, what are you doing here?"

Dana was tall with a medium build. Because of her active lifestyle she was in excellent shape. Today she wore a long skirt and tunic. Her arms were covered in beautiful bangles, and she sported colourful dangling earrings. She kept her naturally curly hair short and looked more like Fatima's older sister than her mother.

Dana could barely breathe through Fatima's squeeze, but managed to ask, "Can I come in?"

"Can you come in? You should ask if I'll ever let you back out! Oh Mom, what are you doing here?" Fatima had not expected Dana to return from her work in Malaysia for a few months.

"I heard my daughter might need me."

The news.

Dana saw Fatima's face cloud over. "Yes, Ali is pretty popular over there, in Malaysia. We hear everything." Dana gave a sheepish smile.

"But what about your work? You're not supposed to be back until September."

"I worked it out. After Ali called me, I talked to my supervisor and delegated some responsibilities. We have a first-class team, they'll manage."

"Wait, did you say Ali called you?" Fatima cut her mother off abruptly.

"Yes."

"When?"

"Monday morning."

"How did you get here so fast?" Fatima could not believe what she was hearing.

"He arranged that too." Dana stroked Fatima's cheek and gathered her hair, adjusting it behind her back.

Fatima was floored. She couldn't believe Ali had called her mother and arranged for her to come home so quickly, without saying a word. She had wanted her so desperately, but didn't have the nerve to call her and tell her what was going on. She was so grateful.

"What did he say to you?" They were now seated beside each other in the living room at the front of the house. The room was decorated in lavender and grey and had a wide sectional in the middle of the room.

Dana took her daughter's hand. "I think he told me everything. He told me about the letter coming and your reaction. He said he doesn't think he handled it properly and is not sure if he is supporting you in the best way. He is worried about you and the baby, and he said maybe it would help if you had your mom."

Fatima's heart ached. "He really said all that?"

"He did." Dana rubbed Fatima's hands between hers.

"Mom, what am I going to do?" Fatima felt like her mother could wave the mess away with the flick of her hand. One word from Dana and she would be all right, Fatima just knew it.

Dana stroked her daughter's head. "Keep doing what you're doing. Take care of yourself and your family, and prepare for your baby. Let Ali do what he has to, and let the rest take care of itself."

"I haven't even looked at what the news reports are saying."

Fatima closed her eyes and imagined tabloids with her family plastered all over them.

"I wouldn't if I were you." Dana tilted her head and looked at Fatima.

Fatima groaned and squeezed her mother's hand. Dana spoke quickly. "Interestingly enough, most of it is quite supportive, especially in the East. It's the hot topic on every corner, in the cafes and barbershops. I've become a celebrity over there, as the mother-in-law."

"You're kidding?" Fatima never imagined news about her family reaching the Far East, but since Ali was a professional athlete who was Muslim, it should not have come as a surprise.

Somehow, Fatima never quite got used to the lifestyle. She longed for the day they could live in quiet recluse.

Dana continued. "I'm serious. People have gotten into fistfights for suggesting that it might possibly, maybe, be a little bit true."

Fatima laughed with her mother and then got serious again.

"Mom, am I crazy to believe him? To believe that it's a lie and there is some explanation, reasonable or not?"

Dana paused for thought. "Based on the Ali we know...I would say no, you're not crazy."

"But...." Fatima encouraged her mother to continue.

"I didn't say anything about a but." Dana smiled at her daughter. "But it must be hard."

"Well, do you think it's possible that it's true?" Fatima held her lips tightly waiting for the answer.

"It's possible. Likely? Hmm, I don't know about that one. You know him better than anyone. What's in your heart?"

"I'm afraid to look."

Dana pulled Fatima closer and held Fatima's head next to her chest. "Oh my baby. It's going to be all right. No matter what, it's going to be all right. Believe that and you'll be fine. You are a strong girl. And when you can't be strong, I'll be strong for you. That's why I'm here, honey. That's why I'm here."

Fatima clung to her mother. "What do I do in the meantime, until I know for sure? How am I supposed to be with him?"

Dana pulled away enough to look Fatima in the eye. "Well, how does he treat you when you mess up?"

Fatima thought for a second. Yes, there had been times when she had made mistakes. "He's always the same. No matter what." Ali's famous line was, "Just because I'm upset, doesn't mean I don't love you." She smiled to herself when she thought of how often he had used it.

Dana's face showed concern and tenderness. "Take your cue from him."

Fatima sat up. "I need to call him." She reached for the phone and dialed his cell. She knew he would be practicing at this time. The phone rang five times and then went to voice mail. Just as Fatima was about to hang up, the other line beeped. Ali had called her back immediately. After reassuring him that she was fine and *not* in labour, he relaxed.

"What's going on?" Ali asked.

"Sorry to bother you, I know you're practicing." Fatima had difficulty keeping still.

"Come on, you're not bothering me. Everyone knows I'm on standby here."

Fatima walked over to the large window that faced the street. It was covered with white shutters and framed by lavender curtains. "Anyway, guess who's here?" Fatima couldn't keep the excitement out of her voice.

"Tell me."

"My mom!" She almost jumped again. "Ali, how did you know how much I needed her?"

"I know how much my parents mean to me, especially now, so it just made sense."

"Thank-you, Thank-you, Thank-you. I can't say it enough."

"No need Fatima. I'll talk to you later."

Fatima turned back to her mother. For the first time, she realized that her mother was without luggage. Dana reminded her that she had been pulled in too quickly to be able to move them from the porch.

After bringing the bags in, Dana pulled one into the living room and opened it up. "I brought you the most beautiful dresses. Wait until you see the prints."

The traditional dresses of the Malaysian Muslim women, *baju kurung*, were beautiful, and Dana had them in every imaginable colour. She had picked vibrant patterns of blue, green, pink and purple. She also had outfits in brown, beige, black and white.

"Mom, it's too much. Why did you do so much?" Fatima said as she hugged the dresses to her.

"I only have one daughter. Who else do I have to indulge but you and the girls? And yes, I have dresses for them too."

Dana shared pictures of Malaysia, showing Fatima all the beautiful sights, and dozens of pictures of her work in the Northern Region. They spent the rest of the morning catching up on all that had happened since Dana was last home, taking care of the girls and preparing for their afternoon shopping expedition. Fatima reassured her mother that she had taken good care of her house in her absence, as they picked up toys off the floor.

"I wasn't worried." Dana reached out and stroked Fatima's hair.

"You haven't gone there yet?"

"No, I came straight here. I'll bring my bags over later."

"Then you're coming right back over here. You have to stay with me, at least until Ali comes back on Friday," Fatima insisted.

"Of course, I'll stay with you. What am I going to do in that big house by myself when all my girls are over here? Now about this shopping expedition, are you sure you are up to it? The girls will be a handful for you."

"Oh no, I'm sure. I was going to do it alone anyway. Wait until you see Masuma in action. She is so mature and helpful. She really keeps the twins in line. And I won't be able to do this, again, for weeks to come." Fatima planned to take full advantage of the time after her baby was born. All she intended to do was rest and feed her newborn. Now that her mother was here, everything would be a breeze.

Chapter Eighteen

Ɔ

Rachel walked through the revolving glass doors of her office building, greeted the security guards and moved quickly to the elevator. She had a few early meetings followed by a full schedule. At noon she barely had time to eat, but she always made a point to leave the office at lunchtime. That break made such a big difference. Taking the day in two small portions was much easier than doing eight straight hours.

By four o'clock Rachel was exhausted and definitely looking forward to spending some down time with Fatima and the kids. She would wrap up her work in the next hour and go get her sons. After dinner with Fatima, she planned to meet with Shawn. She was nervous. She had no idea what to expect, but she would listen to what he had to say.

"Rachel, call on line three. They want to speak with someone *in charge.*"

"Thanks Jaz." Rachel looked around to see who she could give the call to, but everyone started ducking out. Rachel grudgingly pressed the flashing light. "Rachel Grant."

"Hi there." Rachel's body chilled at the sound of the familiar voice.

"What do you want?"

"Nothing, but I thought *you* would want to know that you don't need to worry about picking up the boys."

Panic seized Rachel. "What do you mean?"

"I have them. I'll bring them by later. Maybe." *Click*.

Rachel pressed the phone to her ear as she felt the adrenaline surging through her body. Her head was spinning. She couldn't think. What should she do? Maybe he was lying. She hadn't spoken to the boys or even heard them in the background. She would go to the daycare to pick them up as usual. Jamie was bluffing. He was just trying to unnerve her. He was wanted by the police. He wouldn't just go and pick up the boys. *Damn*. She would call the daycare and ask to speak to her sons, and then she could relax. She would find them there and that would be it. She had no idea what Jamie was up to, but he was not going to mess with her head. Not today.

Forty-five minutes later, Rachel was pounding on Fatima's doorbell. She hadn't called her, because she needed to speak to her in person. This was not a conversation for the phone. "Come on Fati." When Dana opened the door Rachel was stunned. "I'm so sorry. I didn't know you were here."

"Rachel darling, are you ok?" Dana reached for Rachel's shoulder and ushered her into the house.

Fatima came up behind her mother. "Rachel, so good you're here. Wait until you see what I got for the boys. You'll have to let them come to the wedding now." As Fatima got closer she could see the expression on Rachel's face. She knew only one thing could make Rachel look like death warmed over. "Oh no. The boys," she said breathlessly.

"Jamie has them." Fatima saw Rachel crumble before her eyes.

"Mom quick, bring her in here." Fatima threw the boys clothing to the side as Dana led Rachel to a seat in the kitchen. "How did this happen?"

"He called me and said he picked them up from daycare. I

didn't believe him until I called to check and they said it was true." Rachel had already started to cry.

"But *how* could he just go and get them. Don't they have a list of who can pick up the kids?"

Rachel dropped her head. "I never took him off the list."

"Rachel!"

Jamie had never given Rachel any reason to believe he would harm the children, and there was a time when he seemed to be showing interest in being an active father. He had been with her when the boys were first registered at the daycare. Above all, Rachel always remained hopeful that he would one day play a positive role in their lives. "I know. I know. He's never picked them up before. I just never thought it would be an issue." Rachel sobbed uncontrollably.

Fatima looked up at her mother and back to Rachel. "What exactly did he say when he called?"

"He said he would bring them by later, maybe."

"Did you call him back?"

"He called from a pay phone." He had covered all the bases. He had even given someone else's account number to the clerk who had answered the phone so Rachel wouldn't know who was calling. Rachel didn't have any of Jamie's current numbers. He tended to change them often and moved around a lot. He never had a permanent place to live.

"We're calling the police. Mom, pass me the phone, please."

"And say what? Their father picked them up from daycare and said he's bringing them home later?" Rachel said between sobs.

"Yes, exactly. I think the police kind of want to know where he is right now. What was he thinking?"

While Fatima was on the phone with the police, Dana called the Abatis from Rachel's cell phone. Within minutes they were in the house. Shawn arrived soon after.

By the time the police arrived, Rachel was in a daze. After taking her statement, the police moved to the front of the house. Due to his history, Jamie was considered to be armed and dangerous.

Within the hour the family had pictures of Jamie, Joshua and

Jonah circulating online. Police were going door-to-door questioning residents of the neighbourhood surrounding Rachel's home and the daycare. Papa organized a group to start distributing flyers.

Rachel curled up in a ball on one of the couches. "He has to bring them back. He has to." She looked at Fatima who had come to sit beside her. "You don't think he'll hurt them, do you?"

"No. No, I don't." Fatima held Rachel and silently prayed that she was right.

The hours passed with no word on the whereabouts of the children and no call from Jamie. At about 10 pm, the phone rang. Fatima was holding the phone in her hand and answered without checking the caller id.

"Fatima, I heard the news. What's going on?" Ali's voice was tense.

Fatima went through the entire story of the last few hours.

"How was he able to get them from the daycare?" She hesitated. "Fatima?"

Fatima cleared her throat. "It seems that Rachel never removed his name from the list of people able to pick them up."

"Oh, Rachel."

"I think she's heard that enough tonight."

"What's happening now?" Fatima could hear Ali knocking his knuckles against a table.

Fatima looked across the room at Rachel. "Everything that can be done is being done, I guess. We're just waiting and trying to keep Rachel calm."

"Ok, I'm coming home."

"What? You can't. You have another game tomorrow."

"It's done. I'm coming. I can get back here by tomorrow night if I need to. Once I know Joshua and Jonah are safe."

"What about practice?"

"*Practice?* This is Joshua and Jonah we're talking about. Coach will understand. In any case, I'm coming."

Before Fatima could reply, she saw lights outside. She moved to the front door in time to see Jamie pull up with Rachel's two sons. He stepped casually out of the car and waved to Fatima.

"Hey, Fatima how you doing? Looking good, as usual. Oh, looks like Ali's been busy. What is this now? Number four, or five?" Fatima turned away without responding.

The police immediately flanked him. Rachel rushed outside and embraced her two boys, hugging and kissing them. Fatima headed into the house, past everyone that had gathered at the door, as Rachel led the boys inside.

Emotionally exhausted, Fatima sat down on one of the couches in the living room before remembering the phone in her hand.

"Hello?" Ali was still there. She filled him in on the details of what had just happened.

"He dropped them off? Where?"

"Right in front of the house." Fatima rubbed her temples. She just realized that she had a headache.

"He drove in front of our house?"

"Yes, he just drove up and dropped them off. The police have him now."

"Are the boys ok?"

"Yes, they seem pretty happy actually. They're a little surprised to see all the people and police around." Fatima looked up to see the police talking to the boys in the hallway. "Everything is ok now. You don't have to come home."

"Is this the first time Jamie has been around the house?"

Fatima had dreaded the day this conversation would happen. "No."

"So, he's been coming around when I'm not there, and no one told me?" She could hear the rise in Ali's voice.

"It hasn't been often." Fatima knew that was no comfort to him.

"Did he see you?"

"Well, I went outside when I saw the car." Fatima racked her brain to come up with a way to divert the conversation.

"Did he speak to you?" Knowing there was no good way to answer this question, Fatima remained silent a little too long. "Fatima, did he speak to you?"

"He basically just said 'hello.'" She grimaced and put her hand to her forehead. She knew what to expect now.

"Basically." Fatima could hear Ali drawing in a long deep breath. When he finally spoke his voice was tight and caused Fatima to shiver. "Let me be perfectly clear; I do not want you going anywhere near him. I don't want you speaking to him. I don't even want you to look at him; because if he looks at you, never mind speaks to you, in the wrong way, God help him, if he touches you I'm going to-"

"Ok, Ali." Fatima deliberately cut him off. She didn't want to hear him say anything he might regret.

"Do you understand me?"

"Yes." He was perfectly clear.

"Put Rachel on the phone."

"Excuse me?" Fatima pulled the phone from her ear.

"Rachel. I want to speak to her."

Excited chatter flowed from the group that had congregated in the kitchen. Fatima moved toward them and extended the phone in Rachel's direction. "Ali wants to speak to you." Silence fell on the room and everyone present started shifting their eyes from one person to another. Rachel slowly took the phone from Fatima's hand. Fatima straightened her back. "I'm going to check on the kids."

Rachel put the phone to her ear. "Hello? Yes, I'm fine...No really, I was a little shaken but I'm ok now...Yes, they're perfectly fine. Yes, Jonah is fine...I think they were happy to spend time with him, actually...I know...I think everyone was worried...Thank you." Soon the conversation turned more serious, and Rachel, knowing her face was showing signs of stress, was becoming increasingly aware of the eyes on her and how quiet the others had become. She slowly moved from her position in the kitchen to stand just around the corner in the hallway. She knew they could all still hear her, but at least she didn't have the eyes to deal with.

Within a few minutes, Fatima had returned. She passed Rachel in the hall and took a seat at the booth in the kitchen. Rachel rounded the corner. "He wants to talk to Shawn." She released the phone into Shawn's hand. Rachel swallowed, and then said, "Ali said he's on his way home, and he wants me and the boys to stay here tonight."

No one dared to break the silence. Fatima was the first to speak. "Of course. Of course you'll stay with us. Naturally." She stood and rubbed Rachel's arm. "I'll go and fix the room for you guys."

Dana put her hand on Fatima's arm. "No, I'll do it. You've all been through enough today."

By the time the police had left, it was after midnight. All the children were asleep. The girls slept in their room and Rachel's boys slept in the guest room on the main floor where Rachel would later join them. Papa had insisted on staying until Ali arrived and had made himself comfortable in the family room.

Shawn was the last of the others to leave. "I'll be back in the morning. I have to go over some things with Ali." Shawn had already started paperwork for Rachel. She had agreed to file for sole custody, and she would put a restraining order against Jamie.

"Thank-you so much, Shawn, for everything." Fatima walked him to the entrance of the house. After seeing him out she turned to Rachel. "What a night."

"I have to keep slapping myself to believe it's real." Fatima offered her tea, but she refused. "I think it will be hard enough for me to sleep as it is."

"I know. Me too. Well, you just go and hold onto your boys and thank God they're safe in your arms."

Fatima hugged Rachel and watched her turn in. She then positioned herself on the couch to wait for Ali.

She had slipped into sleep but was awakened by the sound of Ali's key in the front door. She stayed still until she saw Papa leave, then she sat up and waited for Ali to join her on the couch.

181

"It was nice of you to come home so quickly."

Ali just raised his eyebrows and nodded his head slightly. "How are you feeling?"

Fatima shook her head. "Wow. It's been a crazy day. It started out normally. Rachel came over and we had a good session in the morning. After she left, my mom surprised me, so I was on a high all day. I was already expecting Rachel for dinner, but then she showed up in a frantic mess. Then the boys were gone and the police came. Now they're all safely in bed."

"Roller coaster." Ali lifted his eyebrows briefly.

"Yes, I'm exhausted. Mentally, physically, emotionally, everything." Fatima circled her tummy with her arms.

Ali looked down at her hands. "You didn't have to wait up. You shouldn't have, actually."

"I was too wound up to sleep well. And I wanted to see you."

Ali sighed deeply. He asked about the girls and was happy to hear that for the most part they were unaware of what was going on. Dana and Rahma had kept them out of the way, in the basement. After the police had left, they were put to bed.

Ali looked up. "They're really ok?"

Knowing he was no longer talking about his daughters, Fatima smiled and replied, "Yes, they really are ok."

"Where are they?"

"In the guest room." Fatima motioned towards the spare room on the other side of the kitchen.

Ali rubbed his chin. "I would have felt better if they were upstairs."

"Oh. Well. I'm sure they're sleeping by now." Fatima placed both of her feet on the floor.

"Could you check?"

Caught off guard and not having a decent response to such a request, Fatima simply asked for confirmation. "You want me to check if they're sleeping?" She enunciated each word carefully, hardly believing she was asking at all.

When Ali indicated yes, Fatima slowly stood and walked over to the room that Rachel occupied with her boys. She knocked softly and then a little harder, gently calling Rachel's name. When there was no reply she opened the door and saw all three huddled together on the queen-sized bed. She turned back to Ali. "They're out."

"All right… I'm just going to stay down here."

Fatima nodded slowly. "Is there anything you need before I turn in?"

"No, I'm fine." Ali leaned forward, staring straight ahead.

Fatima motioned towards the bag Ali had left beside the front door. "Should I bring your bag up?"

"No, of course not. Really Fatima, I'm fine."

"Well, I'm exhausted. I'm going to bed."

"Yes, you should," he replied without moving or looking up.

After Fatima went upstairs Ali checked all the doors and windows and then called the men he had stationed around the property. When he was comfortable that all was well he moved to the family room, at the back of the house, and seated himself in an armchair. He spent what was left of the night in that position. For the first time that he could remember, since he was a boy, the night passed and he did not sleep.

Chapter Nineteen

Rachel lay in bed. She hadn't slept all night. How could she? She had heard when Ali had come home and Fatima had entered her room. She was aware that Ali had spent the night downstairs. She was touched. She thought back to their telephone conversation. After being assured that she and her sons were fine, he had really torn into her. She always expected him to be honest and straight to the point, but this time was different. He had never spoken to her that way before.

She knew she had made a mistake. She knew Ali was frustrated with her and concerned about their well-being, but she had heard something else in his voice.

It was still difficult for Rachel to accept that people cared about her as much as they did. Ali had left his team to fly back home even after the boys were safe. Her boys. He had done it for them.

She wasn't going to work today. She was going to stay with Fatima and keep Joshua and Jonah close to her. Maybe she could help Fatima with something or at least watch the girls while she studied.

Upstairs, Fatima sat cross-legged in her bed waiting for Ali to emerge from the shower. She was still disturbed by something he had said last night and needed to address it with him. Shawn would be arriving soon, so she knew she didn't have much time.

Ali's side of the bed had not been touched. She didn't like that he had sent her to bed by herself, but considering the circumstances she thought it best to leave that alone. She wondered about how he had spent the night and what was on his mind now. She knew that she may never get the answers to those questions.

"Hey, come sit here. I want to talk to you." Fatima moved over to make room beside herself as Ali walked out of the closet that connected the bathroom to the bedroom.

Ali sat down and rubbed his head with a towel. "How are you feeling this morning?" he asked her.

"I should ask you. Did you sleep at all?"

Ali let out an abrupt laugh and shook his head. "You know I didn't. That girl Rachel is going to be the death of me." He seated himself next to Fatima, but did not look at her.

"Yes, she sure had us all going." In spite of his good-humoured facade Fatima could see that Ali was still on edge. "Anyway, I wanted to talk to you about something," she started carefully. "We all were scared yesterday and emotions were running high, but you said something about Jamie that really disturbed me."

"Really? What was that?" His eyes narrowed at the mention of Jamie's name.

"I know you were really upset and probably didn't mean it, but you sounded like you were suggesting that you might harm him in some way. I think that was a little excessive." She folded her hands in front of her.

Ali stiffened. "I didn't say that."

"No...Because I interrupted you, but that was the tone of your conversation." Fatima widened her eyes and tilted her head slightly.

"Well, I'm truly sorry if I disturbed you." Ali continued to look straight ahead.

"I don't care about being disturbed. I care about my husband, potentially, doing something wrong."

Ali dried in and around his ears and attempted to reassure her. "No need for you to be concerned."

Fatima was not satisfied. "I was hoping to hear something more along the lines of 'Oh no, I didn't mean that. I was just talking off the cuff. I would never do anything like that.'" Fatima kept her eyes on Ali.

When Ali didn't respond, she continued. "You keep saying that I don't need to be concerned, but things keep happening that concern me." She continued after a slight pause, "Listen to me. I can understand how you were feeling, but Jamie is not worth getting yourself in trouble over or getting hurt."

"Hurt?" Ali almost laughed.

"Ok, Superman. I don't know what you think you're planning, but *Allah* is the Best of Planners and you never know what He has in store for you. You need to watch yourself."

Ali adjusted Fatima's duvet. "You worry too much."

"What do you expect when I have my husband going around talking crazy?"

Ali threw the towel around his neck. Fatima knew he was absorbing what she was saying so she pressed on. "I know what you're thinking, 'It's not about him,'" she said, in a voice that mimicked Ali's. He chuckled at her imitation.

"And Ali, you're right. It's not about him. It can't be. It's about you and us and our family. That's what's important. Ali, look at me." She reached forward to turn his head so that he was facing her. "I just don't want you to do anything wrong."

He couldn't hold back his smile. "I won't."

"Can you promise me?"

"Yes," he teased her.

"Ok..." Fatima prompted him.

"I promise."

It wasn't enough. "*What* do you promise?"

"You're not letting me off the hook, are you?"

"No way. This is too important." Fatima held his face firmly

Ali finally gave in. "I promise you I won't do anything wrong."

"Thank you. Now that wasn't so hard was it?" Fatima released her hold.

"Extremely painful." Fatima had no doubt. Ali stood up. "May I get dressed now? Shawn should be here any minute."

"Go." Fatima leaned back into her pillows, feeling only minor relief. Ali had never broken a promise as long as she had known him. She hoped and prayed that wouldn't change now.

Rachel got dressed in a pair of jeans and a white shirt. She looked at herself in the mirror. "This is so Fatima's style."

She hadn't even thought about what to bring over last night and had just grabbed the first thing that she had seen. She decided to forego make-up and just brushed her hair into a neat ponytail.

Joshua and Jonah were still sleeping. All the children had gone to bed late, and Rachel hoped they would wake up late too. She wanted to spend some time alone to sort out some of what was on her mind. She wasn't going to work today at all, maybe not even tomorrow, and the boys would definitely not be going to daycare. She was not letting them out of her sight.

After she had called her workplace and then the daycare, she just sat and watched them sleep. They both looked a lot like Jamie, in different ways, but she never saw him when she looked at them. She just saw her babies.

They were always begging her to do things with them, but she never found the time. She never *made* the time. Yesterday, when she had thought she may lose them, she realized how much she was missing. Her friends, neighbours and Naomi's church family had filled in many of the gaps, but now she realized she had to make the best of each moment. She leaned over and kissed each of them.

When she heard the doorbell, she realized it must be Shawn.

"Rachel, good morning. You look much better than you did last night." Shawn stepped over the threshold.

"You think?" Rachel joked in spite of herself and closed the door behind him. "Come on in. I'm sure they'll be down in a minute. I did hear some movement up there." Rachel stepped aside allowing Shawn entrance into the foyer.

Shawn stood inside, but didn't move to the interior of the house. He was dressed for business in an olive suit. He was over six feet tall with a lean build. His hair was shortly cropped and he sported a well groomed moustache and goatee.

"Can I get you something?" Rachel asked.

"Oh, she's a hostess too."

"Well, I *can* make tea." She moved towards the kitchen.

Shawn wrinkled his brow. "Coffee?"

Rachel thought for a second. "You might be pushing it, but if you're adventurous, I'm willing to experiment."

Shawn agreed to take his chances and sat in the kitchen booth. Rachel set up the coffee maker and then sat across from him.

"Thanks for coming so quickly last night. Your support was tremendous and you got the paper work ready so quickly." Rachel was truly impressed.

"With good staff everything is easy."

When the coffee was ready, Rachel poured for him and waited for him to take the first sip.

"Perfect." He lifted his cup. "Thank you."

"Now I can add coffee making to my list of talents."

"That you can." Shawn rested his cup on the table. "How are your sons?"

Rachel exhaled and leaned back. "Fine. Still asleep."

"You're not working today?"

Rachel gave him a look that said, "Are you kidding?"

"No, I think I'll just hang out here today...Shawn, I know you can't talk about Ali's case, but I just hope everything is going to work out."

"No, I can't discuss it, but I'm certainly going to do my best for him."

Rachel fiddled with her fingers while Shawn finished his coffee.

"You guys will have a full house today," he said while looking around the lower level.

With four adults and five children the house would hardly be full. It was a spacious home with more than enough room for everyone. Rachel had not spent many nights there, but on occasion, when Ali was away, she and Fatima would hang out, slumber party style, talking or watching movies.

"Yes, I think we'll have fun." Rachel noticed Shawn's glances towards the stairs. "I'm sure they'll be down soon."

"Yes, we're right here," Fatima said, as she descended to the main floor. "Ali is right behind me."

Shawn greeted them both and he and Ali headed towards the living room. Fatima stayed with Rachel. "How are you feeling?"

"I'm good." Rachel always felt relaxed in Fatima's home. She told Fatima of her plans to visit her father and bring her sons with her. It would be the first time they had ever been to their grandfather's gravesite.

"That's a wonderful idea. Hey, Shawn can drop you off. I'll pick you up when you're ready, and we can go out for lunch."

"I have my own car," Rachel countered.

"I don't think you should drive. You've had a serious trauma these last 24 hours," Fatima fired back.

"Nice try, Fatima. I'm fine," Rachel leaned forward and whispered tightly.

Ali stepped back into the hallway. "I think she's right. You shouldn't drive. I can drop you off, and then Fatima will pick you up." He looked at Fatima, "But make sure you bring your mother with you. You're too far along to be going out by yourself."

Shawn appeared in the doorway and placed his hand on Ali's shoulder. "I'm sure you have things to do. I don't mind." He looked at Rachel. "Really Rachel, I would be happy to take you. It's no problem at all."

Rachel threw her hands up in defeat. "Fine, fine, I accept."

Ali nodded at Shawn. "Shawn is safe. We wouldn't allow it otherwise."

Fatima beamed. "Go get ready. I don't think we'll be too long."

When they were all seated, Shawn placed his bag on the table. "The judge has ordered the DNA test. I found a private lab, a little out of town. It's new, but I think it's the best choice."

"What's the first step?" Ali asked.

Shawn stretched his arm to expose his watch "A representative from the lab will be here in about 10 minutes."

"Here?" Ali didn't try to hide his surprise.

"Sure. I thought it would be better for you and definitely quicker. Otherwise we would have to go out there. It would take 90 minutes each way. They'll just take your sample and someone will be sent to do the same for the baby, and then it's 10 to 14 days to get the results."

Ali nodded. "Ok, let's do it."

"While we wait, take a look at these." Shawn laid some more photographs on the table. "We've investigated this woman. She's pretty clean, except for her connection to this guy right here." Shawn pointed at the person in the photograph. "His name is George Harmer, one of the best con man-scam artists around. The police have been after him for years, but can never get enough evidence to bring an indictment. This guy is as slick as they come."

"So what's the connection to this woman?" Ali leaned forward to get a better look at the pictures.

"It seems she is his brother's ex-girlfriend's sister."

"I don't get it," Fatima said.

"Yeah, where do I come in?" Ali asked.

"That is not clear yet, but George is the best in his business. If you need a job done, he's the man to call. The evidence they have against Ali would be nothing for someone like Harmer to put together. The woman is just someone who is squeaky clean and wouldn't raise any red flags. There would be no reason to suspect she's lying."

Shawn went on to explain, they could either get this woman to confess or keep gathering evidence until they blew the whole thing right open.

"Isn't this theory of yours somewhat of a stretch, Shawn?" Fatima challenged.

Shawn reluctantly agreed, "Maybe."

Ali looked at the pictures again. "When the DNA test results come back won't that be enough?"

"For the paternity case yes, but I'm concerned about more than that." Shawn took the pictures from Ali and shuffled them.

"His reputation."

"That's right. The DNA test can only prove that you're not the father. It can't prove that you don't know her..." Shawn looked at Fatima. "I think that's just as important. Then we can talk about pressing criminal charges."

Fatima spoke up. "What if you can't prove that?"

Shawn rubbed the back of his neck. "We have to try."

Ali interrupted them. "Ok Shawn, whatever you say."

The doorbell rang and Shawn stood up. "That would be the lab. If I may, I would like to get it."

Ali rose to his feet. "Please, go ahead."

Chapter Twenty

𝔍

"You really don't have to stay." Rachel sat on a large rock beside her father's grave. *Whoever thought to put this here really hit the mark,* she thought. Rachel looked around the cemetery and could see that a few graves had benches beside them. She made a mental note to do that one day soon.

Joshua and Jonah had spent the first ten minutes examining their grandfather's grave and headstone. They fired question after question at Rachel. Shawn had stood quietly to the side. Now the boys were exploring the cemetery and checking out all the other headstones.

Shawn took a few steps forward. "I don't feel right leaving you all here alone." It was still early and they had only passed one other couple in the entire cemetery. It was an enormous lot, almost a small town really, and was located about two miles in from the main road. A gravel road led to the main entrance and all surrounding land was undeveloped forestry.

"That's kind of you, but it can't be much fun. This isn't exactly entertaining." Rachel brushed some grass from her jeans.

"I really like cemeteries, as a matter of fact."

"Really?" Rachel had never heard such a thing.

"Yes. History was my favourite subject, and the cemetery is full of it."

"That's an interesting way to look at it." Rachel shrugged.

Shawn watched Joshua and Jonah studying a headstone intently. "Can they read?"

Rachel turned her head. "Joshua reads quite well, actually. Jonah just likes to pretend...You don't have any kids."

"No, not yet."

Rachel looked back at her father's grave. This visit had been much easier than the last time. She actually felt happy, somewhat peaceful being here. The old flowers were gone and fresh ones sat in their place. She felt like she should camp out to see who was leaving them.

She couldn't believe it had taken her so long to start visiting. The boys were fully excited. This was the first time they had been allowed to talk about their grandfather so freely. Whenever they had asked questions before, they had been brushed off. Naomi had difficulty even hearing his name, so it had been very awkward. Rachel noticed Shawn still had not made any movement to leave.

"So, why did you choose law?" she asked him.

"I wanted to put my father in jail."

"What?" Rachel jerked her head around and stared directly at Shawn. His face showed no signs of humour.

Shawn placed his hands in his pockets. "When I was a child I used to watch a lot of court TV, and I would see the lawyers at work. I figured if I became one, I could bring my father to court and get him locked up."

Rachel wasn't sure if she should, but she asked, softly, "Why?"

"I never knew him. I grew up feeling so much rage that he wasn't around. I figured I wouldn't be able to beat him up, so I opted to put him in jail."

"And now?"

Shawn nodded his head. "I figure one day I'll have my own children and just be the best father I can be. I'll be everything he wasn't." Shawn lifted his chin in the direction of the grave. "I'm truly sorry for your loss. At least you had him."

Rachel's eyes stung as she thought of a little Shawn growing up with the pain of having no father. Her own pain was unmanageable at times, but to think a father would not even want to see his own son grow up was inconceivable.

"You're so much like Ali," she said, before realizing it.

"Except, I'm better looking."

Happy to have the mood lightened a bit, she responded in time, "No comment."

"Oh! Brutal honesty." Shawn laughed, and then said, "He *is* serious competition."

They were both laughing when Rachel caught herself, and covered her mouth with her hand. "I feel guilty laughing over my father's grave."

Shawn immediately became serious too. "He would want you to be happy."

"I guess." Rachel stood up. "Anyway Shawn, thank you for bringing us here and keeping me company, but I don't want to keep you any longer."

"All right." Shawn stepped back. "Take care. We'll be in touch."

"Are you leaving?" Jonah came running through the headstones with Joshua by his side.

"Yes. Take care of your mom."

"Drive safely," Joshua piped up.

Shawn stopped his retreat to extend his open hand. "Hey, thanks, little man." Joshua placed his small hand in Shawn's palm. Rachel watched as Shawn slowly closed his hand on Joshua's, squeezing, and then releasing it. He turned his attention back to her.

"Ok Rachel, we'll talk later."

"Bye. Thanks again."

As Shawn walked away, Rachel pulled her sons close to her. They remained that way until Fatima arrived.

Fatima and Dana arrived together. By the time they reached the gravesite, Fatima was breathing heavily.

"Here, sit here. I know it won't be that comfortable, but it's better than standing." Rachel jumped up to let Fatima have a seat.

Fatima looked at the rock and shook her head. "I don't think so. I have a foldable seat in the car. I think that would be better." Dana returned to the car to get the seat for Fatima.

"So, Shawn just left?" Fatima asked.

"About thirty minutes ago," Rachel confirmed.

"No, I saw him drive out when I was coming in," Fatima insisted.

"Really? He did mention being concerned about leaving us here alone."

"He probably waited until he saw me coming. I told you he was a good guy." Fatima bumped Rachel with her shoulder.

"Where do you find them?"

"There are good guys all over. You just have to take your eyes off the losers long enough to see them."

Dana returned with the chair and Fatima sat down. "Beautiful flowers. Where did you get them?" Dana asked.

"They were here when I came.

"Really? No note?" Fatima adjusted herself on her seat.

"Nothing. There was a different set last time. It's a mystery."

"Sounds exciting." Fatima had that mischievous twinkle in her eye.

"I'll pass. I've had enough excitement to last a lifetime, thanks."

Dana moved through the headstones. "I'm going to walk around. I know a few people buried here."

As Dana walked away, Rachel turned to Fatima. "Hey, remember that time my dad had to rescue us from Christina 'Beaston?'" Christina *Easton* was a bully who Rachel and Fatima decided to stand up to together. They arranged to meet her after school and planned to teach her a lesson.

Unbeknownst to Rachel and Fatima, Christina had called her older brother and cousin for reinforcement and the girls ended up being out numbered and outmatched. They were sweating, until

Rachel's father had come looking for them when they hadn't returned home immediately after school.

Fatima laughed. "No, not really."

"Sure, play innocent now. We had our time."

"We made a pretty good team, didn't we?" Fatima nudged her with her elbow.

"Oh, selective amnesia, is it?'

Fatima sighed. "It just seems like a lifetime away."

"It's not that far away that I don't remember. I have to give it to you, girl, you could throw down."

Fatima giggled. "The best part was always seeing the shock on the faces of those who had underestimated me because of my size."

"Well, they learned fast. That's part of the reason I hung out with you. I didn't want to be your enemy."

"Come on. I didn't pick on people. I just defended myself." Fatima pouted.

"I don't think it makes a difference when you're lying on the ground with a bloody nose how you got there." Rachel laughed at the memories.

The girls continued to reminisce about their childhood and all the fun they used to have getting in and out of mischief, until Dana returned. On the ride to the mall, Rachel discussed her swim team. "I haven't told anyone, but an Olympic coach has been looking at Tracy."

Fatima pulled the car into the mall parking lot. "That's amazing. When are you going to tell her?"

"Soon. I just don't want her to get nervous. She's such a powerful athlete, but I swear her head is in the clouds."

Dana and Fatima exchanged looks and smiled. "I'm sure you can help her with that," Dana said. She also reminded Rachel that it wasn't too late for her to compete herself.

For many women her age it may have been, but Rachel had kept herself in condition. She swam whenever she was coaching, after the girls had left, and she timed herself once a week. She was still competitive. "I'll think about it."

It was still early, so they cruised through the mall until lunch. They made appointments to go to the spa the next day and when they returned home, Fatima carried bags of new clothes that she planned to wear after having her baby.

The women spent the rest of the day hanging out at Fatima's house engaging in what Dana called laugh therapy. Ali returned to meet his team and life resumed as normal. When Naomi was dropped off later that night, Rachel was home to greet her.

"Mom, have you lost a bit of weight?" Rachel asked.

"Certainly, and I have made a resolution. I am going to overhaul my diet and walk every day."

"Ok...no more fruit tarts?" Rachel asked.

"Well, they were always low fat. And *I* don't have to eat them."

Rachel laughed as they climbed the stairs together. Joshua and Jonah waited in the doorway. "Guess what Grandma?" Jonah started. Rachel, anticipating what he was about to say, widened her eyes and shook her head. Jonah stopped with his mouth hanging open. "Oh, maybe I forgot." If Rachel wasn't so nervous she would have laughed. The last thing she wanted was for her mother to know what was going on with Jamie.

When they got inside the boys spent some time playing with Naomi, but Rachel was relieved when their bedtime came. She was too stressed out that they might mention Jamie picking them up from day care. After tucking them in she made two cups of herbal tea and went to sit with her mother.

"You know Fatima has been doing a lot of research lately about natural remedies that could be good for your condition."

"Really? I think she did mention something like that." Naomi closed her hands around the cup of tea that Rachel handed her.

"I wrote down some things. Maybe we could try. It won't hurt." Naomi agreed that she would try just about anything. Mother and daughter sat in the living room and talked about Naomi's trip and natural health remedies until Naomi dozed off on the couch.

Rachel sighed. It was the first time in years that she had had such a long and pleasant conversation with her mother. She really missed her and had not realized it.

Rachel covered her mother with a blanket. When she was satisfied that Naomi was comfortable, she put some cushions on the floor, lay down and pulled a blanket over herself.

Across the street Fatima sat on the edge of her bed. This was the last night Ali would be away until next season. She couldn't wait until the following night. Then they could return to a regular life for a few months. Of course he would be engrossed in watching the playoffs, but at least he would be home. She never let him know how much she missed him during his absences. This was their life, for now, and she accepted it.

She looked at the table beside her. She had seven papers now. 7, *e,e,n,a ,h,t*. She continued to rearrange the papers until she was pretty sure of what the letters were spelling. Of course, she would have to wait until she found the other two papers to be sure. She wondered what her surprise might be. She didn't even care. She just wanted her husband home and her family to be together.

She was grateful the paternity case was starting to make a little sense, but they still had to get the test results. She just wished all this could be over with before she had their baby. She couldn't imagine going into labour with this on her mind. Giving birth was something that needed your full attention and focus. Painful distractions were not helpful. She had been in the hospitals and seen how stress affected the birthing woman. It could be a killer, literally.

As long as Ali was with her she would be fine. His presence was enough to block out everything else. Before she turned out the lights, she heard Dana's soft knock at her bedroom door. "Come in," Fatima said.

"I saw the lights. Everything ok?" Dana stood in the doorway dressed for bed, in light blue short-sleeved pyjamas. The soft lighting from the salt rock lamps filled Fatima's room.

"Sure. I'm just waiting for Ali's call, and then I'll go to sleep." Fatima turned in and pulled the covers over her legs, adjusting herself on her body pillow. It was a life saver during her pregnancies. She could never get a good night sleep without one.

"Ok, sleep tight. See you in the morning." Dana stood back and started to pull the double doors closed. "By the way, I love what you've done with the room." She smiled and closed the doors.

"Knock, knock." There was a heavy rapping on the door of Ali's hotel room.

Ali walked from the bathroom. "Who is it?" The knock became louder and more aggressive.

"Guess who?"

Ali arrived at the door and opened it.

"We're hitting the streets. You coming?" Rami and Jeremy, two of Ali's teammates, stood in the hallway.

"Where's Kirk?" Ali looked down the hallway. The three of them usually moved together.

Jeremy waved his hand. "Ah, you know he's boring as hell. He's probably sleeping or watching sad movies or something."

Ali leaned on the door. "I'll pass. I have to call the wife."

"Cell phone, baby," Jeremy prompted him.

Ali smirked at their persistence. "I want to be alone. Some of that might do you some good once in a while, Rami."

"Hmm. I'll pass. Anyway, how are Rachel and the kids?" Everyone was aware of why Ali had left to go home two days before.

"They're ok. They're with Fatima." Ali held his position in the doorway. "They're fine."

"They're fine. Is that what you think?" Rami laughed and moved closer to Ali. "Why don't you just marry the girl and put her out of her misery?"

Jeremy stepped forward. "Now, that's a religion I could get down with."

"Do you clowns ever talk any sense?" Ali started to close the door.

"Hey, after you put Fatima to sleep you're going to link up with us, right?" Rami held the door open with his hand.

Ali had been feeling sombre since his return. The paternity suit, the coming baby, and then the situation with Rachel had all put a strain on him. "I just might do that," Ali said.

"We'll be waiting, honey," Rami sang in a teasing tone.

Ali closed the door, pushing Rami and Jeremy back into the hall. "Rude or what?" Ali could hear Jeremy say.

"He's just edgy. You know he doesn't like to keep her waiting."

When she heard the phone, knowing it was Ali, Fatima did not even let it complete one ring. She told him all about her day and listened to his game highlights. Just his presence was soothing to her. They discussed what they planned to do over the next few days and weeks. Knowing Ali intended to sleep early, Fatima ended their conversation and went to sleep thinking that finally life may be returning to normal.

Fifteen minutes after Fatima had completed her call with Ali, the phone rang again.

"Fatima."

"Ali." Fatima, already asleep, had reached for the phone in the dark.

"I'm not going to sleep right now. I'm going to hang out for a little while. I just wanted you to know that." Ali knew that Fatima had the impression he was going to bed after their conversation. He didn't want her to feel that he had misled her, especially not now.

Fatima blinked her eyes in the dark and took a few breaths to feel alert. "Thanks…Ali…is everything ok with you?"

"I just need some fresh air."

Fatima only paused for a second. *It's his last night out.* "Ok…be good."

"Good night."

Chapter Twenty One

ॐ

"Ray, what are you doing here? Aren't you going to work to-day?" Rachel stood on Fatima's porch, casually dressed in a brown velour tracksuit. She eased her way through the doorway and closed the door behind her.

"No, I have some flex days, so I figured I would give myself a long weekend." Rachel chewed the inside of her lip as she rested her hands on the back of her hips.

"Makes sense. How is your mom doing?"

"Great, she had a good time, and she even lost some weight. She said she's going to start walking and eating better. "

Fatima raised her eyebrows. "Inspiring."

"Yes. She's just getting ready for your session later. Anyway Fatima listen. Not that I was snooping or anything, but when I was over here I did notice the photos that Shawn left, and I couldn't get something out of my mind. I'm positive that woman in the picture with Ali looks familiar."

"Are you sure?" Fatima was definitely intrigued.

"Yes, what do you think?"

Fatima sighed. Even though Ali had insisted the pictures were manufactured, she couldn't stand to see him so close to another woman. "I never really looked at them."

Rachel looked at Fatima in shock. "Girl, are you for real? Your man is in a photo all up on some woman, real or not, and you are not looking at it? I would be dissecting that thing." Rachel shook her head. "Thank goodness you married Ali. I don't know what would have happened to you otherwise." Rachel gently pulled Fatima's arm. "Follow me, dear."

"See, I know I've seen her before, but I don't know where." Rachel tapped one of the pictures Fatima had laid out on the coffee table.

"Shawn said they checked her out pretty well, and she's fairly clean. No big story." Fatima shrugged her shoulders.

"We'll see about that. Pull up your pictures on the computer. I want to go through them." Rachel pulled a seat in front of the computer and waited.

Fatima opened the file holding her photos, and Rachel started to go through them one by one. Fatima had all the pictures organized in different folders, so it was easy for Rachel to locate what she was looking for.

"That's it!" Rachel slammed her hand on the desk. "The birthday party. Remember the surprise party those guys threw for Ali a while back? She was there. Let's see if I can find her in any of the pictures."

"Are you sure? How can you remember that?" Fatima pulled her chair closer.

Rachel squinted and looked at each picture intently as she scanned the faces for the one she wanted. "I was checking out every woman there, honey, especially the ones that were checking out *your* husband. While you were playing the happy hostess, I was looking out. And it's a good thing too. See! There she is." Rachel pointed to a blurred image of a person in the background of one of the pictures. "I know you can't see much in this picture, but I remember her because she was never more than 10 feet away from Ali the whole night."

Rachel turned her chair to face Fatima. "He didn't recognize her from the picture?"

"No, he said he didn't." Fatima shrugged her shoulders.

How was that possible? "Hmm. There *were* a lot of people there," Rachel offered.

"Sure, whatever. Ok, so what are you thinking?"

"Maybe she was stalking him."

"She said she met him about 18 months ago. It was October, so the timing is right."

"All part of the plan," Rachel answered quickly.

"Whose plan Rachel?"

"That's what we need to figure out. Maybe I can find her and go talk to her."

Fatima shook her head. "That's definitely not a good idea. Remember we are in the middle of a lawsuit? What makes you think she would talk to you anyway?"

Rachel made a short laughing sound and pointed to the picture. "Look at her? You know I could get that girl to talk." She looked sideways at Fatima. "I could use some back-up, but you're in no condition."

"Oh please, I am not getting myself into trouble with you."

"I could take Dana."

"Now you want to drag my mom down? Why don't you start from the beginning and think this through again.

Rachel knew she could be persuasive. She could definitely learn something by meeting with this woman. Even body language could tell a lot. She tried to remember everything she could about that night. Yes, she clearly remembered having her eye on that woman. She had no recollection of who she had come with, or when she had left. But she was definitely trailing Ali.

"Fatima, what do you remember about that evening, after the party?"

"I left early. Remember the twins were sick and I felt like I was coming down with something? I just went to bed and slept until the next morning. I don't even know when Ali came home. I never asked him. I had no reason to question him about that."

Rachel tapped the desk in a rhythmic way while she thought things through. "Ok, I'm going to think about this. Let me sit on this for a while." Rachel paused, and then continued. "I wish I could see the info that Shawn has on her." She turned to Fatima. "Can I go through the other pictures?"

"Sure, look at anything you want. I'm going to shower and start getting ready for the meeting with Naomi."

Rachel spent the next hour going through Fatima's pictures and committing to memory every detail she found in Shawn's report about this mystery woman.

"Miss Naomi, you look great." Fatima walked up the stairs, from the landing at the front door, to arrive in Naomi's living room, and was surprised to see the obvious change in Naomi. She hadn't seen her in a few days. Naomi had definitely lost weight. Her complexion looked brighter, and she was smiling.

Even her style had changed. She wore a floral top in spring colors of light yellow, blue and white. She complimented them with a pair of white pants. She stood up when she heard Fatima's voice and hugged her tightly. Fatima had come over a little early hoping to have some time to talk to Naomi alone. At some time or the other everyone in the neighbourhood had come to Naomi for advice, or comfort,, or just to sound off. She had a unique way of seeing things and a special way of helping you get to the root of your problems.

"How have you been, Baby?" Naomi asked.

"You know, I'm hanging in," Fatima replied.

"Ali will be home for good today, isn't that right?" Naomi sat back on the couch and patted the seat beside her.

"Yes, thank goodness. I know I should be disappointed that they haven't done better this season. The competition was fierce, but really, I couldn't care less. I've been barely keeping it together and I honestly don't think I could stand him being away one more day. If anything else were to come up I think I'd lose it."

Fatima sat close to Naomi and shifted so that she was facing her.

"And the baby?"

"I can't even think about it. If I could, I would put the whole thing on hold and just wait until after this case is resolved.

"What would be different then?" Naomi asked.

Fatima was taken aback. "Well, I don't know. I just wouldn't have to think about it."

"Think about what?"

Fatima knew she shouldn't be surprised. Naomi was the same old Naomi. You could come to talk to her about one thing, but she never let you go until she forced you to get to the bottom of the real issue. She made you dig deep and admit things you didn't want to admit even to yourself. It was what Fatima had come for. She might as well go for it. She took a deep breath and started talking.

"Think about whether or not the accusations are true, whether or not he's lied to me, whether or not my life is what I thought it was."

"Hmm." Naomi nodded.

"It's so funny. All I can think about is my father. I don't know why. I just keep thinking about my childhood and how I spent all my time trying to please him, make him love me and I just never felt like I could. Then this lawsuit came up and I realized I still feel like that girl, only the leading man has changed."

"Have you spoken to Ali about your feelings?"

"No, I don't want to add any stress to him right now." Fatima looked at the wall that Naomi had decorated with pictures of her children and grandchildren.

"Is that so? Are you sure?" Naomi's face showed that she was doubtful about Fatima's real motivation. "What would happen if you told him how you feel?"

Fatima knew that Naomi was going to pull the truth out of her eventually. She might as well not fight it. "He would know that I have insecurities, and I don't want him to see me that way." Fatima considered Ali to be such a pillar of strength; she didn't want him to view her as weak.

Naomi smiled and held Fatima's hand. "Do you think he doesn't know? He knows you better than you think. He talks to me."

Fatima knew that Ali spoke to Naomi. They all spoke to her. She just had that special type of insight, and it was great to get that from someone who could be objective. Fatima wondered how couples that didn't have the kind of support system that she and Ali had actually survived. They knew of several couples who had lost their marriages over problems that were definitely resolvable. Without the proper kind of support, little things could become huge and big things impossible.

Naomi spoke again. "I am not a fortune teller. I certainly don't know what's at the end of the road in terms of this case. But I do feel that you two will be left standing, together. In the end how you two come through this will depend a lot on you. Ali may be the head of the home, but you are the heart."

Fatima squeezed Naomi's hand. "I'm not sure why, but that is such a comfort to me."

"Sometimes, we just need to hear someone say it's going to be ok." Naomi was silent for a moment before adding, "Ali has something big to deal with right now, and that's his thing. You have something of your own to deal with.

"You have to work through your own feelings, and they have nothing to do with your husband and what is going on in your marriage right now. The reality is, though, if you don't work through your own issues they can be a burden on your family and yes, then that would be a mess."

Naomi released the hold on Fatima's hands and let her hands slide up Fatima's arms until they reached her shoulders. "Ali is a man; no more and no less, but a good one. I've been around long enough to know. No matter what the results are, he's worth fighting for."

Fatima sighed. She felt like she had been fighting all her life. She didn't want a relationship she had to fight for. She didn't want love she had to fight for. Not anymore. She felt she had been doing a good job of keeping her feelings, her worries and concerns from having a negative impact on her marriage. She worked hard not to let one affect the other, but it was getting harder each day.

As if reading her mind, Naomi said, "The issues that we don't resolve in our relationships from our childhood, we will have to face in our subsequent relationships. The soul always yearns to fix what is wrong."

Naomi patted Fatima's hand. "Your angst really has nothing to do with Ali and this case. This is all about you. You have to stop being afraid. Everything I ever feared came to me. Your fears will come to you too. It's misdirected energy, Honey, but energy just the same, and it will all come back to you." Naomi wiped a tear from her eye, sniffed, and then straightened up, just as the doorbell rang and Susan pushed open the door.

"Hi everyone." She stopped when she saw Fatima. "Oh, Fatima." She hurried up the stairs and rested her long fingers on Fatima's shoulder. "How are you?"

Naomi and Fatima smiled simultaneously. Fatima reached out and held Susan's arm. She replied very seriously, "I'm fine. Thank you for asking."

"I saw the press conference. I noticed you weren't there." Susan squeezed in between Fatima and the arm of the couch, forcing Fatima and Naomi to move over. She wore a lime-green stretch-knit dress. She bent her head and looked at Fatima with wide eyes, as though looking over glasses, which she didn't have.

Fatima cleared her throat. "Well, I'd really rather stay out of the spotlight, and I *am* nine months pregnant."

"Of course. Of course." Susan squinted her eyes and broke out in laughter. "Girl, I don't know how you are living in that house with that man. I would have torn the whole place down."

Fatima had no idea what to say. She felt like defending herself and her family, but she couldn't. She couldn't create a defense for something that she was not even sure about herself. She just kept silent; anger and embarrassment burning inside of her.

One by one, the other ladies filed in and seated themselves. They continued catching up on the past week before starting with the topic for the day. Mama arrived with the other ladies. She hugged and kissed Fatima as though she had not seen her in weeks, although they saw each other every day.

"Dana didn't come?" Mama asked.

"No, she's staying with the kids."

"Please join us for dinner tonight. I'll do something special for Ali's homecoming." Mama's eyes held that special warmth that made you feel at home no matter where you were and made even strangers feel like family. Every day, since news of the paternity case had hit, she had shown Fatima more love than the day before, and had given her strong quiet support as only Mama could.

When everyone had arrived Sister Charles started with the first questions. "Fatima you were raised as a Christian. How could you turn away from the truth?"

This was a question that Fatima had heard many times. Everyone believed that their faith was the correct one and the only way to salvation. She always wondered, *why then were people guided to so many different paths?*

"I never turned away from anything," Fatima said. "I just learned more. The *Quran* is the final revelation of a number of revelations that God has sent to mankind. Islam was the continuation of the religion I had learned as a Christian, and it appealed to my sense of reason. The meaning of life became clear. Even though I didn't start to practice what I was learning at that time, I could still see the sense in it. I just knew I was Muslim. It was like discovering a hidden or lost identity."

"What do you mean, dear?" Sister Barclay asked.

Fatima thought back to the early days of meeting the Abatis. She had spent a lot of time at their home during the time they were studying Islam. In fact, she had learned right along with them. She was only eight years old, but the revelation brought by God's last Prophet(saw) had made sense to her, and she had known she was Muslim even then.

Dana had been very open to Fatima's interest in the religion. She had travelled the world and had a greater understanding of, respect and tolerance for world religions than the average person.

She had always felt that in the end there would only be two sides anyway, the side for God and the side against. Whether you had lived as a Muslim, Christian, Hindu, Buddhist or Atheist, in the end everyone would stand on one side or the other.

Fatima directed her answer to the entire group. "Imagine you had been born into a First Nations family, but were raised by other people. You never knew anything about First Nations people and their history. Indeed you had never seen such a person.

"Then one day you meet some First Nations people and start to learn about them. You realize that they look like you and share a history with you. You *are* First Nations. No one could ever say you *became* First Nations, you always were, you just didn't know. That's what happened to me. I realized I was Muslim."

"But you were so young," Susan said.

"I don't believe age necessarily matters. Actually the younger you are the purer your heart is, I think. Anyway, I wasn't ready to actually make a commitment and live completely as I should until I was about 17."

"Because of your husband?" Susan leaned forward in her chair.

"No, not at all. Remember, I knew I was Muslim when I was eight. I didn't know who my husband was going to be until many years later."

Fatima was accustomed to this line of questioning. People always assumed that she had become Muslim because of Ali or because she had wanted to marry him. Nothing could have been farther from the truth. She had been on her own spiritual journey and he had been on his. She liked to think that she had actually helped him to become stronger and more committed to his *deen*, though he would never admit it.

"You also were married quite young. Do you think that was a good idea?" Sister Edwards asked.

"Yes, I was almost 18. Was it a good idea? For me, yes. For others? It depends on who you marry. I think the best time to get married is when your spouse arrives. Age does matter, but compatibility, maturity, commitment, willingness to learn and true compassion, that counts for a lot more. I think I was ready...more importantly, *Ali* was ready. That made it all possible. We also have a large support system. We wouldn't have made it without that."

One woman, who had previously remained silent, now asked, "So, if you were going to break Islam down to the basics, what is it exactly?"

"That's a great question. It is the belief in one God, and the belief that His last Prophet was Muhammad(saw). Once you accept that, you are Muslim. Muslims believe that the *Quran* was revealed to the Prophet Muhammad(saw), through the Angel Gabriel, and is the final revelation from God to mankind."

"How do we know who the true prophets really are?" Susan asked.

"There are tests of a prophet. These are written in the scriptures. If you believe in the Bible, check it out. What does the Bible say are the tests? Then just apply the tests. Does he pass or fail? Study the *Quran*. Does it speak the truth or not?"

The room fell silent as the women considered Fatima's responses to their questions.

"What is the best way to really know what is true?" one of the women asked.

"This is only my opinion of course, but start with a pure intention. Make your intention to really discover truth, whether it is what you think it should be or not. Pray for guidance and then study. Eventually, you will see."

The questions continued and Fatima was amused by some of the questions the women asked, especially Susan. They wanted to know more about her personal life than anything else. What was marriage like? Did her husband help with the kids? Do house work? Was she allowed to work or go to school? What happened if she disobeyed him? Did they ever watch TV? Did she wear *hijab* at home? Fatima sipped a cup of tea while she and the others answered each question.

"What happens if you don't have a boy?"

Fatima almost choked. "Excuse me?"

"I saw this show on TV where a woman, I think it was in Bangladesh, was divorced because she didn't have a boy."

"Yes, some are beaten or even killed," another woman added. "They burn them, I think."

Sana interrupted the exchange. "Islam mentions nothing of the sort. Islam came to correct these sorts of injustices and has to a large degree. Unfortunately, injustice still exists in every part of the world. In Islam there is no favoritism of one sex over the other. In fact, it is said that if you must treat one child better, then it should be the girl."

"*Really?*"

"Fatima, you have three girls, right?" Susan asked.

"That's right, and my husband adores all of them." Even as she said it Fatima knew she sounded a little too defensive.

Finally, Naomi stood. It was getting late and time to wrap up the session. She promised to call about the next meeting, since Fatima's baby was due the following week and she might not be available. Oohs and aahs floated through the room as the women smiled and nodded.

"Fatima, how do you stay so active and fit when you are nine months pregnant?" Sister Charles asked on her way to the kitchen.

Fatima stood up and adjusted her red wrap-around maternity top that she wore over a pair of boot cut jeans. "Well, I *am* married to a professional athlete and have three active little girls. I need to keep up."

"That you do," Susan said as she slipped past Fatima.

"Do you still do yoga every day?" Sister Barclay asked.

"I do." Fatima had fallen in love with yoga during her pregnancy with Masuma. It kept her relaxed and grounded. Though it was a challenge to keep it in her schedule, she knew it was a must. Yoga had a host of additional health benefits and helped her to keep flexible and strong.

The group broke up and the women gathered in the kitchen to sample the food that was set on the table. Rachel had outdone herself. All the women were pleased, but none more so than Naomi.

After the meeting Mama invited Fatima to come and spend time at her house. She agreed out of politeness, but only stayed for a short time. Papa had gone to *Jumah*-Friday prayers and Mama liked to have company on the occasions that she stayed home. Fatima reminded Mama that she was expecting Ali soon and just wanted to be home when he arrived. She promised they would return in time for dinner.

If she could have she would have skipped across the street, she was so happy. It was Friday. The season was over and Ali would be home soon. Life didn't get much better than this.

Chapter Twenty Two

ℑ

Rachel tapped her foot on the tiled floor while she waited in the lobby of the hospital. She hated being here. There were too many bad memories. She had promised herself that she would just move on this time and not let the memories haunt her. She wouldn't wonder what her baby would have been, or what her life would have been like or if she had indeed done the right thing. She wouldn't beat herself up about making the same mistake again and again. *Easier said than done.*

Funny how no one ever tells you about these feelings. When Rachel was pregnant and had gone to the hospital clinic, the first thing the nurse had said to her after "you're pregnant" was "what do you want to do?" *What do you want to do?* Rachel had thought being pregnant meant you're going to have a baby.

The first time around Rachel had not even thought about anything, other than becoming a mother, until options had been presented to her. She had been so stressed out, and had no idea how she could ever tell her mother, that she just took what she thought was the easy way out. Nothing she had read or heard had prepared her for the range of emotions that erupted weeks and months after the procedure. *Why did no one ever tell you about that?*

Rachel pressed her hands against her eyes as if doing so could squeeze away the images that were flashing in front of her.

"Rachel? Hi." Brigitte's voice shocked Rachel out of her reverie.

"Brigitte, thanks for meeting me." Rachel shook her head and blinked her eyes to bring herself back to the present.

Brigitte was far too pretty to be a nurse. Today she wore hot pink scrubs and white sneakers. Rachel hadn't really looked at her closely before. Today she wore her thick curly hair in a tight ponytail and wrapped in a huge bun at the back of her head. Still, a few unruly ringlets refused to stay put and now framed her face. She had light brown eyes and a sprinkle of freckles across her nose. Her skin was the colour of almond butter. The woman in the picture could have been her twin, except Rachel was sure Brigitte was older.

Rachel had spent the morning at Fatima's going through Shawn's report. Some of the unremarkable information from the woman's file was that she had a sister named Brigitte. Rachel was sure that was the woman standing in front of her right now.

Rachel pointed to a bench in the corner behind a tall plant. "Let's have a seat."

They were in the children's section of the hospital. Rachel thought it would be more private there. They were surrounded by brightly coloured walls with fantastic designs, glass elevators and towering plants - all designed to cheer and lift the spirits of the children. Rachel was sure it worked for the parents as well. She always wondered why all hospitals were not like this. Adults needed comfort too.

Rachel had already given Brigitte a brief rundown of why she wanted to meet. Now she pulled out the pictures from her bag.

"Yes, she is my sister." Brigitte confirmed with her eyes downcast.

"So, what do you know about this case?"

"There doesn't seem much to know. My sister does have a baby and she says Ali Abati is the father."

"Have you ever seen her with him?"

"No, but I imagine he would have been discreet." Brigitte brushed her loose hair strands from her face.

"This just doesn't make sense to me. I know him really well. Something is not fitting. During her entire pregnancy, or before, you never saw her with any other man?"

"She has friends, but no one in particular."

"When did she first tell you about the father of her baby?"

"She never talked about it much until this all became public. She kept quiet about the pregnancy, too, almost until the end. She just said it was a complicated situation. We never pressed her. She's a very private person." Brigitte leaned back in her seat on the bench.

Rachel went over the details with Brigitte from every possible angle, getting as much information as she could from her. Brigitte didn't know George but conceded that another sister had gone out with his brother quite a few years ago. Brigitte finally told Rachel that she had met Jamie while he was visiting one of his friends in the hospital.

"He's such a charmer," Brigitte said.

Rachel tried to keep from rolling her eyes. "Indeed. Well, thanks for the information. I'm not sure what I'll do with it anyway."

"Oh, it was nothing." Brigitte stood up, said goodbye and started to walk away.

Rachel called to her before she had gotten too far. "Brigitte, please tell me nursing wasn't your first choice."

Brigitte smiled, showing perfect white teeth. "I wanted to be an actress, but my parents wouldn't hear of it."

"Are you in the driveway?" As usual when Fatima expected Ali's call she never let the phone ring more than once. She had been

215

waiting for him to come home, and when she heard his voice on the other line she assumed he was calling from outside their house.

"No."

The tone of Ali's voice made Fatima want to sit. She had been about to move to the front window, now she lowered herself back into the couch she had just jumped out of. "What's wrong?"

"Nothing. I'm just going to be late." Ali's voice did not sound like nothing was wrong.

Fatima responded slowly. "Ok…no problem."

"A day late."

"What?" Fatima felt her blood pressure rising.

"It's not a big deal, but I'll be coming home tomorrow."

"Why?" Fatima could feel her grip on the telephone tightening. *How could he say it was not a big deal?*

"I just have something to take care of."

"Did something happen? Is something wrong? Ali, please just talk to me." Even as the worlds formed and left her mouth, she knew they were futile. It seemed like Ali hadn't spoken to her about anything significant in weeks. She felt completely shut out of his life.

"Listen, it's nothing for you to worry about."

Fatima could barely contain her anger. "Again? 'Nothing for you to worry about?' Just be happy that your husband is staying out and can't tell you why."

"Fatima, I understand how you feel. Trust me, it will all make sense soon."

"No, I need it to make sense right now, because two days ago you dropped everything and flew home because Rachel was in a crisis, and now you're telling me, your pregnant wife and mother of your three children, that you are not coming home and you can't say why? This is not right, Ali."

"You think I came home just for Rachel?" Agitation grew in Ali's voice. "I came home because I was worried about all of you - you and the girls."

"Oh? That's why you sent me to bed, while you guarded Rachel's room all night?" When the silence between them grew heavy, Fatima continued in a softer tone.

"Ali why? Why are you doing this to me?"

"Fatima please, I'm not trying to do anything to you."

"I am pregnant and you are stressing me out!"

When her mother appeared in the doorway looking concerned, Fatima realized how loud she was getting.

Ali kept his voice even as he spoke. "Understand something. This last incident made me aware of how vulnerable you all are when I'm away. I couldn't sleep that night. If anything else happened I wanted to be up. That's all," Ali said.

She turned her back to Dana and lowered her voice, a little. "So what am I supposed to do now? Twiddle my thumbs all night wondering where you are and what you're doing? Does this have anything to do with the case?"

"No, not at all. It's nothing like that."

"Then *what* Ali? Say *something*! And why do you sound so strange? What about Joshua's soccer game tonight?"

"There's an assistant coach, and Shawn volunteered to go help out."

"Oh, so Shawn knows about this? And I guess your parents, too. Who else, Ali? Please, please tell me who else is on the list of people more important than your wife."

"You know there is no one more important than you."

As angry as Fatima was she didn't care whether he sounded sincere or not. His behavior was inexcusable and she wasn't accepting it.

"I'll be home tomorrow. We can talk about it then. Tell the girls-"

"Tell them yourself." Fatima got up, threw the phone onto the couch and called for Masuma. All three girls came running. "Your father is on the phone." Fatima walked past Dana, in the doorway, being careful to avoid her gaze. Before she continued down the hallway, she turned her head to look at Masuma. "When you're finished, hang up."

Fatima didn't stop walking until she entered the workout room and then slammed the door. The stepping machine was looking very good to her right now.

Rachel spent the rest of the afternoon wondering what to do with the information she had gathered. She really didn't have anything new except that the woman mentioned in the report was a nurse in town and she knew Jamie. *Coincidence?* Rachel didn't think so. But she had no idea what it meant. She would at least tell Shawn. He would know what to do with the information. Rachel wanted to do more investigating, but was not sure which direction to take next.

Now, she sat watching her son's soccer game. She had been surprised when Shawn had called her to say that he was filling in for Ali tonight because Ali would not be home until tomorrow. Rachel was sure that was news to Fatima, because Fatima had been very excited about Ali's homecoming. Rachel was sure she would be unpleasantly surprised to hear about his change of plans. *What was going on?* Rachel wondered.

"Joshua has some serious skills. Ali told me he was good, but I never imagined." Shawn stood over her lawn chair, partially blocking the setting sun.

"Oh, he just works really hard. He wants to impress Ali so much." Rachel looked up and shaded her eyes with her hand.

Shawn turned and looked towards the field. "No way, some things are natural. This boy has a gift."

Rachel had to admit that Joshua really did stand out on the field. She had played soccer as a child and could see that Joshua was talented. Her father would have been so proud.

Shawn motioned toward the other side of the field. "Looks like I'm needed over there."

Rachel pulled out her cell phone. She wanted to see how Fatima was doing. The phone rang four times before Dana answered. "Hi Dana, is Fatima home?"

"Sure Rachel, let me see if she can come to the phone."

"Hi Rachel." Fatima sounded drained.

"Hey, what are you up to?"

"Nothing, I was just resting. I'm actually expected at Mama's dinner table in about three minutes. How's the game?"

"Great, should be finished in about ten. Then we're heading

home. I can come over. My mom is at some church thing."

"Sure, meet me at Mama's."

"Fatima, I think I learned something new concerning the case."

"Rachel, please. That is the last thing I want to hear about right now, trust me."

"Ali's not coming home tonight, eh?" Rachel was really starting to wonder what was going on with this man.

"Do you see him at the soccer game that he's supposed to be coaching?" Every ounce of the sarcasm that Fatima intended came through the phone line.

"It must be important if he missed the game and is staying away from home an extra day."

"Are you sure he didn't hire you as his defence lawyer?"

"Fatima please, I'm just trying to help. Did he say anything at all?"

"No, nothing. I'm sorry. I know you're just trying to be helpful. Listen, I have to go. I'll see you later."

Clearly Fatima was not ready for the information just yet. Rachel thought maybe she should sit on it for a while and see what else she came up with. She turned it over and over in her mind. Before the end of the night she had decided to tell Shawn. He just nodded while he processed the information. "Definitely interesting," he had said. Rachel thanked Shawn for the ride home and focused her energy on the task ahead of her. She had one pregnant woman to cheer up and one paternity case to solve.

Later that night Fatima placed the last two papers on her night table. She had found an *h* and *v* in one of her textbooks. She played with the papers and moved them around until she spelled out, *7th Heaven.* Fatima scoffed and shook her head.

"Oh sure, right." Ali had often used the term to describe their life together. Though it had felt that way at times, her life was nowhere near paradise now. She had had such a wonderful conversation with Ali the night before and then he hit her with this.

She hated the constant questioning and wondered when it

would all end. She took one hand and swept all the papers off the table and crumpled them up. She slowly walked to the washroom, threw them into the toilet, and flushed.

The following week passed by without event. Ali came home to a very cool reception, and the atmosphere in the household was rather tense for a few days. He had tried talking to her about his delay in coming home, but she had told him that unless he was going to reveal where he had been, she didn't want to hear it. That put an end to that conversation.

As her due date approached she became a little happier. *It would not be long now*, she thought. She busied herself with studying and rested when she could. Ali took over most of the household duties and looking after the children. Mama cooked for them every day. Rahma came over many mornings, and Dana spent her days at Fatima's house to help with the children.

Rachel continued to come in the mornings for the *dua* sessions and Fatima visited the cemetery with her once. Again, there were new flowers at the gravesite. Rachel had wanted to share with her mother what she was doing, but somehow did not feel that Naomi was ready for it.

"Or is it you who's not ready?" Fatima had asked. Rachel had really thought about the answer to that question. She had been through such an emotional upheaval when she visited the first time. She anticipated Naomi would have a similar or even more profound reaction when forced to confront this issue.

"I feel really good now. I just don't want to go back, that's all," Rachel finally said.

The Thursday night before the wedding, Mama and Papa invited Fatima's and Rachel's families to their home for dinner.

"Since the girls are ready, I can take them over." Ali leaned in the doorway of their bedroom closet. He had made a conscious effort to avoid looking at the pile of clothes on their bed when he had entered the room. Fatima was just beginning to get ready.

"Fine." Fatima looked through her closet while she decided what to wear.

"I'll come back to walk over with you." He placed his hands inside the pockets of his organic cotton lounge pants. He wore a matching shirt.

"No." Fatima was still angry with him and was irritated by his constant attempt to engage her in normal conversation. Each day he got up and acted like nothing had happened the day before. She was incensed at the thought that he might be trying to wear her down. It would be out of character for him, but so many strange things were happening that Fatima didn't know what to expect. In the past few weeks she had questioned every aspect of her life with Ali. A few nice words and kind gestures were not going to erase the issues.

Through the corner of her eye, Fatima saw Ali's body language change in response to her "no". She quickly back-tracked. "The girls can be a handful. You should stay with them. I have my mom with me, I'll be fine." She never moved her eyes from the clothing she was rifling through.

Fatima grew increasingly uncomfortable when Ali did not move and did not speak. Finally, he shifted his weight from the wall. "All right, Fatima." He turned and left the room.

Fatima let out the air she hadn't realized she was holding and picked out a pale yellow floral maternity top and a black skirt. When she walked out of her closet, Dana was sitting on her bed. "Do you think you've punished him enough?"

"I'm not." Fatima laid her clothes on the bed.

"I think this is the most you've spoken to him since he came home. Be careful, Fatima. Ali has been back for almost a week. You could make better use of your time." Dana rose to her feet and walked towards the doorway. "I'll be waiting for you downstairs."

Fatima dressed and thought deeply about what her mother had said. Ali was patient when it came to her, but she wondered if she was making the situation worse by being so distant. No matter how much she wanted things to be back to normal, she couldn't pretend everything was ok when it wasn't. She certainly didn't want to set a precedent. She couldn't allow Ali to think it was acceptable to disregard her feelings whenever it suited him.

Before she left her room she walked over to the table beside her bed. She opened the drawer and removed the box that Ali had given her when he came home. She hadn't opened it yet. She knew he was hurt that she had just asked him to put it on her bedside table when he had offered it to her.

Inside was a stunning white gold bracelet set with seven rubies. Fatima sighed and closed her eyes. "Ali, Ali, Ali." She put it on her wrist, admiring its beauty. She then closed the drawer, grabbed her *abaya* and went downstairs to join her mother.

Fatima and Dana met Rachel and her family in front of the Abatis house. Since the door was unlocked, they just pushed and entered. Rahma met them in the foyer.

"*Sorella*, we were waiting for you. Why didn't you come with Ali?"

"I wasn't ready." Fatima made sure to avoid looking at Dana while she slipped out of her shoes.

"Ali doesn't look so good," Rahma leaned in and whispered to Fatima.

"He's just tired." Fatima rubbed Rahma's back reassuringly. She suspected that Ali was hurting as much as she was, she just didn't understand why he didn't do something about it.

"Rahma, I heard you're planning to travel this summer," Dana said.

Rahma looked around before answering. "Yes, I'm going to Italy for the summer."

"Looking for me?" Ali leaned over the railing on the second floor. "There is no way you're going to Italy by yourself, so you can forget that," he said, as he made his way down the stairs.

"I won't be in Italy by myself. Our family is there. Anyway, it's not up to you." Rahma poked Ali in his chest as soon as he hit the landing.

"Is that what you think? We'll see about that." Ali fell in line behind the last person as they all moved toward the voices coming from the back of the house.

"Who are they talking to?" Rachel asked, referring to Mama and Papa.

"Each other," Fatima said.

"Why am I hearing two different languages?"

"That's how they usually talk to each other when they're alone. You must have heard them before."

Mama was speaking Kinyarwanda, and Papa was speaking Italian. In their most intimate moments they would speak in the language that they could best express themselves. They understood each other perfectly. Papa, of course, had learned the indigenous language of the country he had lived in for 15 years. Mama had learned Italian within eight weeks of her marriage. She had made it her top priority. Since she was already fluent in French, had a gift with languages and was highly motivated, it had been easy. She had been on Fatima's case to learn as well.

"I guess I never noticed. That is so cute. They're so adorable," Rachel gushed.

As they all approached the dimly lit room, they could see Mama seated on the couch and Papa lounging in the armchair to the left of her. The chair was a special one. Mama rarely let anyone sit there. She would occupy it on occasion, when she was deep in thought, otherwise it would remain empty. The fact that Papa was there now was a testament of Mama's good mood.

After dinner and a few short *duas*, they made their presentation. "For our very special lady," Mama said.

Fatima's baby was due the next day, and Papa had carved a plaque with a Rwandan saying on it. *Umukobwa Ni Nyampinga-* A girl is a palace of wealth.

Tears came to Fatima's eyes. She knew that Papa had been

spending weeks working on a wood carving but had no idea it was a gift for her. He had learned the ancient art in Rwanda and usually had one or more projects keeping him busy.

Although she had not expressed it, they all knew how much she wanted a boy. It was never mentioned, but it was in everyone's eyes tonight.

In their own way, Ali's parents were telling her that no matter what she had, she was blessed, and they would all be happy. She wished she felt the same.

Chapter Twenty Three

R achel sat in her rocking chair and looked out the window. For
the first time in many years she felt some peace. She was
visiting her father regularly and feeling good about it. Naomi was
in good spirits. She was eating better and walking as often as she
could. She could go up and down the street alone, although
someone was usually available to walk with her.

Rachel was putting more hours into training her swim team. It
also gave her more of an opportunity to swim as well. The time she
spent in the pool was like time in another world. When she dove
into the water she left everything behind her. As much as she had
loved competing she didn't feel the desire to do so anymore. Knowing she *could* was enough for her. Now coaching, that was special.

Rachel never thought about how good she was at it. She just
knew she loved bringing out the best in others. She could see the
strengths and weaknesses in another person easily and had the
special talent of being able to build them up. If only, she thought,
she could do the same for herself.

Rachel was regularly complimented on her expertise, and her
girls were the best in the province, but she never connected their

achievement to her own self worth. She did know how much she enjoyed working with them. Helping to push the girls to do their best, while fine-tuning their technique, was exhilarating. There was nothing more thrilling than being able to share some useful tip, see it applied and then observe how the swimmer's performance improved.

Yes, life seemed somewhat normal. Ali was home and had called off "the dogs", as Fatima liked to call the security people he had enlisted to watch the house while he was away. Fatima had felt it was unnecessary. They had good neighbours, a top of the line security system and were close to a police station. What else did they need?

It was close to 4 a.m. when the lights went on across the street. Rachel would pray now too. It gave her a feeling of comfort to pray when Ali did. She didn't feel so alone. She knew that his parents were dedicated to saying the night prayers. When Ali started to get up regularly during the night, she knew he was doing the same thing. She had heard about the benefit of praying in numbers. This was her way of taking advantage of those benefits while still keeping her prayers private. Somehow she felt God would be more likely to hear her if she approached Him with someone else.

Just as she reached for her list, a scream from her sons' room caused her to freeze in mid-motion. Rachel raced out of her room and met her mother at the door of the boys' bedroom. Rachel threw open the door and flipped on the lights. Jonah sat on his bed shaking and crying. "I saw a man in the window."

Rachel rushed to the window, but saw nothing out of the ordinary. The rooms were on the second floor. It wouldn't be easy for a man to be in the window.

Rachel sat on Jonah's bed and cradled him in her arms. "Jonah, I think you had a bad dream."

Fatima and Rachel had painted a sky mural on the wall of this room. It had clouds, birds and kites. When Jonah started to have regular nightmares Rachel had hoped that would help to calm him.

"No, I was awake. He was in the window."

"Who?"

"I don't know!" he wailed. Sweat beaded his face and the room was warmer than usual.

"Ok, honey. It's ok now." Rachel rocked him on her lap while Joshua continued to sleep next to her on the bed. He had stirred when Rachel entered the room but had not woken up.

The phone rang and Naomi picked it up. "Yes, it was Jonah. It seems like he had a bad dream."

"It *wasn't* a dream," he insisted.

Rachel took the phone just as pounding started on the front door. Fatima's concerned voice could be heard over the line. "Rachel, we heard that scream all the way over here. Ali's at your door."

"I'm coming!" Rachel ran down the stairs still holding Jonah in her arms.

She opened the door to see Ali standing on her porch, wearing jeans and a long sleeved t-shirt. She knew from the time she had spent living at the Abati house, after the death of her father, that Ali always kept street worthy clothes next to his bed in case of an emergency. She smiled when she thought about how little he had changed through the years. He wore sneakers that were not tied up, and she wondered whether he had bothered to put on socks.

"What happened?" Ali's eyes quickly scanned Rachel and then the room behind her.

Rachel silently pointed at Jonah, who had jumped into Ali's arms as soon as Rachel had opened the door. She rested her head on her hands to indicate that Jonah had been dreaming. She relayed to Ali what Jonah had said about a man in the window. She winked to show that she was humouring him.

"I should check around the house," Ali said. "Jonah, stay with Mommy. Rachel, close the door. Just keep an eye on the front."

When Ali turned to walk away, Rachel noticed that in addition to the flashlight she grabbed from the hall closet, he had something in his back pocket. She immediately recognized it as his nun chucks. She silently prayed that she was right and there was no one out there. She knew how dangerous Ali could be with that weapon. He had never lost a competition since the age of 16. More than one opponent, who had made a mistake on the floor, had ended up in the hospital. Skill paired with his intensity was a deadly combination. She paced the floor inside until she heard his footsteps on the porch.

By the time Ali had returned, Jonah had fallen asleep in Rachel's arms. "There's nothing out there."

"I'm sure he was just dreaming. It's been happening a lot lately. I'm going to put him down." Ali waited at the door for her to return.

"And Joshua?" Ali asked, as Rachel descended the stairs.

"He never woke up. I think he is so used to these incidents that he doesn't bother." Rachel, suddenly conscious of her pyjamas, pulled her arms across her chest.

Ali looked past Rachel into the home. "It'll be daylight in a couple of hours, but I could walk you through the house if you want."

"We'll be fine, Ali. I'll make sure everything is locked up. Thanks for coming. I'm sure Fatima is worried. I'm really sorry to be such a burden on you guys."

Ali paused on his way out. "No, don't ever say that. I wouldn't be here if I didn't want to be." He then backed out into the cool stillness of the night. "Good night, Rachel. Call us if you need anything." Ali stepped off the porch. "Or yell," he added with a smile.

His smile was contagious. She thanked him, and when he had crossed the street she closed the door. She immediately called Fatima to fill her in and let her know that Ali was on his way home. Just as she had told Ali, Joshua had not woken up, and Jonah was fast asleep, again, under his covers. Naomi sat in a chair beside their bed. As Rachel said she would, she checked all the doors and windows. Just before she closed the blinds in her sons' room, she noticed something she had not seen before. The window was cracked open.

Fatima heard when Ali reentered the house and locked the doors behind him. She heard him remove his shoes and pick up the phone. He had called his father to let him know that he would not be coming over this morning. He was going to pray at home. When she heard him calling the *adhan* she got up to join him. After the prayer and their usual *salaams*, with perfunctory, "May *Allah* accept your prayer," they returned to bed. Just before Ali turned out his lamp, Fatima spoke to him.

"Ali, I was thinking-"

"Oh. You're talking to me now?" Ali leaned up on his elbow to face Fatima from his side of the bed.

"I always talk to you." Since her conversation with Dana, Fatima had tried to be more responsive to Ali. Still, it was not easy for her to pretend she was all right when there were so many unanswered questions looming in her mind.

"Yes. No. Whatever. Is that how you talk to me now?" Even in the dim light Fatima could see the sadness in his eyes.

Fatima knew the truth would not be pleasant, but it was all she had. "I didn't know what to say to you."

Ali sank back into his pillow and looked up at the ceiling. "I see." Fatima watched the rise and fall of his chest as he inhaled and exhaled deeply. With heaviness in his voice he said, "That hurts."

Fatima had never heard him speak like this before. He never used negative words to describe his emotions. They all knew that he felt deeply, but he rarely shared those feelings.

"You're hurt because of me?" Fatima asked.

Ali didn't answer her question directly. "I just can't give you what you need right now." Keeping his gaze on the ceiling, he said, "I guess every marriage goes through a rough spot."

Fatima felt like she had been hit. She tried to turn to face him, but quick movements had become difficult for her. "What exactly does that mean?"

"We've had almost seven years of bliss; I guess we're due for a little shake up."

The pain that Fatima felt at hearing those words was agonizing. An image of Ali on their wedding day flashed across her mind. He had been so happy. She had always felt a secret pride that Ali was so pleased with his marriage and family. The thought that she may have been wrong was devastating.

"Is that what this is?" Fatima folded and unfolded the corner of her silk nightgown.

Ali locked his fingers together and placed his hands behind his head. "I don't know. I guess it'll be whatever we allow it to be."

"I don't know what else to do. I feel like I'm reaching out to you and you're just not there. You say you're not keeping secrets from me, but there's something going on in your life that I don't know about, and that hurts me."

Fatima kept her hand on her abdomen, feeling the waves her baby was making. She remembered, with her first pregnancy, how she and Ali couldn't wait until night to just sit and watch Masuma move. 10 p.m. was the time she usually started to get active. They would stop everything and sit waiting for their nightly show. "I just don't know what to do. Sometimes it scares me."

Ali turned to look at Fatima again. This time his eyes were filled with compassion. "You don't have to do anything except ace your exam tomorrow and get ready to have a baby. I can handle the rest."

A momentary feeling of relief and comfort came over her at hearing his simple words. In spite of everything she had been through in the last two weeks, Fatima still wanted to believe that he could.

"So tell me, what were you thinking?" Ali asked, while he still faced her.

"Nothing." *He still had said nothing.* "It was nothing." Fatima reached to turn out her lamp, and they both settled in to get a few more hours of sleep. Fatima's exam was at 10 a.m., but there was no way she could sleep now. It definitely had not been lost on her that, for the second time in little over a week, Rachel had been successful in completely upsetting Ali's schedule.

Chapter Twenty Four

𝔍

"Wow, Ali you look great." Rachel had expected Fatima to open the door, and was slightly taken aback to see Ali greet her, dressed in full white.

"Thanks, come on in. Fatima's right here." Fatima stepped out of the kitchen where she was preparing snacks for the children.

"You're dressed too? The boys aren't even ready yet," Rachel said.

"That's ok, just bring them over and do it here."

It was the day of Abbas's wedding. Mama and Papa had gone ahead to help with the final preparations and Rahma had stayed behind to help Fatima with the children.

"Once we're all ready we can take some pictures. By the way, how was Jonah this morning?" Fatima asked.

Rachel looked despondent. She felt so helpless when the topic of Jonah's nightmares came up. She didn't know how to help him and it was the worst feeling a mother could have. "He was really quiet. I didn't mention anything about last night. Neither did he, but he started to really freak out when I said I was coming over here."

"What did he say?" Ali asked from his seat on the stool beside the kitchen island.

"The same thing he always says. Bad men come when I go away."

Ali and Fatima exchanged looks. When Fatima had returned from writing her exam, they had heard that the con man, George Harmer, had been taken into custody on unrelated charges. He had died the morning before, after being restrained by guards. A fight had started at lunchtime, and he was in the middle of it.

Jamie had been in custody since the daycare incident and was supposed to be transferred from the same facility that morning. No word yet on his exact location. Shawn had been trying all afternoon to get an update. He had a hunch that Jamie had orchestrated the daycare incident to intentionally get himself arrested. That idea was starting to sound very plausible.

Ali stood and moved past Rachel. "I'll get the boys."

After Ali left, Fatima turned her attention to Rachel. She asked Rachel to wait while she returned to the kitchen, reached into a cupboard and pulled out a gift bag.

Rachel's eyes misted instantly. "In all of this, you remembered my birthday?" Although Rachel had refused to celebrate her birthday since her father's death, Fatima always gave her a gift on that day.

"Of course I remembered. We have to make new memories. Good ones." While Rachel started opening the bag, Fatima burst out, "They're the earrings you saw in the mall. You loved them."

"Thanks for letting me be surprised." Rachel rolled her eyes. She knew, well, how impatient Fatima could be.

"There's something else in there."

Rachel reached in and opened an envelope containing a gift certificate. "Rock-climbing? I know *you're* not planning to go with me."

"You've always wanted to go, and you can take anyone you want."

Rachel stuffed the envelope back into the bag. "Fatima, will you just stop. I know what you're trying to do. Anyway, I'm just going to wait a few months and drag you with me, or your mother. Dana will be up for this."

"Why do you always have to be such a party-pooper? Every time I try to point you in the direction of someone half decent you shoot me down." Fatima leaned against the kitchen counter and crossed her arms over her extended middle.

Rachel allowed herself to be distracted by the return of Ali and her sons. She smiled sweetly at Fatima and escaped to open the door for the boys. Ali offered to dress them and when they disappeared, Fatima pulled Rachel into the kitchen and sat across from her in the booth.

"Why Rachel?"

"What?" Rachel shrugged off the question.

"Why do you always reject any possibility of a decent man in your life?"

"I have a lot of things to deal with now, I can't focus on that. Really Fatima, you may not understand, but I have some major issues in my life right now. I don't feel like I'm in the right place to bring someone new into my life. I have quite a few things to work out first."

Fatima leaned back and studied Rachel. As usual when this topic came up she refused to meet Fatima's gaze. Enough was enough and Fatima was feeling bold, so she charged ahead. "Really? Is that all? Or is it because you love someone else?"

Rachel's lids flew upward and she looked directly into Fatima's eyes. "*What* are you talking about?"

Fatima folded her hands and stared at Rachel, giving her a look that said, "You know exactly what I am talking about."

The shock in Rachel's eyes gave way to a calm resolve.

"We are not having this conversation."

"Yes, we are," Fatima insisted. "Right now."

Rachel blinked rapidly. She felt like she was suffocating. Her mind went blank. She was completely unprepared and had no idea how to respond to Fatima. She just knew that she had to go. She had to leave immediately. She couldn't have this conversation. Rachel stood to leave, but Fatima was in front of her before she could escape.

"Why are you running from this? No more, Rachel. Really, it's time we talk about it." Fatima's eyes were soft but her voice was firm.

"There is nothing to talk about." Rachel reached for the door, but Fatima had already covered the handle with her hand. Rachel pressed her thumb and forefinger to her eyes and took a stabilizing breath. She could barely get the words out. "Fatima please, you are my best friend. I love you more than anything. I won't let anything come between us. I know what you're getting at and I'm not going to do this. I'm not talking about this. I'm not even going to think about it."

"But you do think about it." Fatima continued carefully, steadily. "You think about it every time you're in my home. You think about it every time Ali comes to your house to do something for your boys or your mother. You think about it when you see my children and every time you hold yours. You think about it every time Jamie breaks your heart. And you think about it when you are sitting in your room watching my house."

Rachel gasped. Her hand flew to her mouth.

Fatima stepped back. "Ali has a regular bedtime. I don't."

The tears Rachel fought to hold back flowed freely now. "No, Fatima it's not like that. You know I just think a lot, and I can't sleep. Sometimes I just don't know what to do, and the rocking chair is just by the window, that's why you see me there. It's not what you think."

"Rachel, just stop. I know everything and I'm saying that we need to deal with it."

Rachel sat down on a bench in the foyer. She had been caught off guard by this line of questioning. Had she been prepared she may have lied or denied everything more adamantly. Still, it wasn't all what Fatima was thinking. She really did have trouble sleeping sometimes; and then there were the prayers. She wasn't ready to talk about that yet. All she could think about now was the effect all this would have on her relationship with Fatima. "Fatima, I'm sorry. I'm so sorry."

Fatima sat beside her friend and dropped her shoulders. The weight of what had just been revealed rested heavily on her. "I can't believe you, Rachel. I just can't believe you."

She knew Rachel had had a crush on Ali when they were children. Everyone did. After Rachel had become involved with Jamie, and Ali had proposed to Fatima, they had never spoken about it again. Fatima did wonder, from time to time, if those feelings had died. Over the years there were enough signs to indicate that they had not. After all, how easy was it to change your feelings?

"Don't say that, Fatima, please. I'm sorry. I've never done anything to hurt you and I never would. Let's just forget all this." Grief stricken, Rachel remained motionless, unable to breathe, never mind move, while she waited for Fatima's next words.

Rachel had spoken the truth. She had never done anything inappropriate or threatening, and Fatima was not going to fault her, now, for what she had always known to be true. Everything was out now. The issue was what to do about it. Fatima had been turning this over in her mind, and it was time to voice her thoughts. "Actually, I've been thinking about this for a while. I think we can work it out," Fatima said.

"What do you mean?" Rachel's eyes were wide. "I can't believe this. You must hate me."

Fatima scoffed. "How am I going to hate you?" She looked down and said, thoughtfully, "How could you not love him?"

Fatima lifted her eyes and studied Rachel. She was her dearest friend. She knew Rachel would do anything for her. She loved Rachel like a sister. Rachel *was* her sister. She knew Rachel felt the same way about her, and as much as Rachel was loathed to admit it, Fatima knew she was in love with Ali. She wiped Rachel's tears and held her hands. "I don't think it's one-sided either. It's time we deal with this."

"Fatima, please don't even say that to me. I can't handle this." Rachel sobbed as her heart pounded in her chest.

"It's obvious, Rachel. You only have to say 'ouch' and the man is upside-down and inside-out. I have lived with him long enough. I know what I'm seeing, what I'm feeling." Rachel ran her fingers through her hair and shook her head. Fatima continued. "Ali has a big heart. I've been thinking-"

"No." Rachel put her hand up to cut Fatima off and then stood up abruptly. "Fatima no. This is your husband and your family. I won't do it. I won't hear of it."

"Just listen to me."

"No. I am officially *not* listening to you. I don't even want to think about what you're getting at. This whole conversation is creeping me out."

"Mommy, Mommy, look at us!" Joshua and Jonah came bounding down the stairs.

Rachel turned away in an effort to save face. "They can't see me like this." She headed towards the front door, "I'll be back in a minute."

Ali arrived behind the boys with Rahma and the girls trailing behind him. He looked out the kitchen window. "Is everything ok?"

"Yes, she'll be back in a minute." Fatima turned to look at her family, all dressed in white and green. "Let's take some pictures."

When Rachel returned they continued to take pictures and Fatima asked Rachel to take one of her family with Rachel's sons.

"I really wish you were coming with us," Fatima said. Ali held the twins, and Masuma stood beside Fatima, while Joshua and Jonah stood in the front.

"You guys look beautiful!" Rachel took picture after picture. Suddenly, loud noise and yelling could be heard from outside. "Did you hear someone call my name?" Rachel asked.

Ali quickly moved to the window and looked out. He tightened his lips and formed a fist, pounding the wall beside the window.

Rachel stood behind him to see what was going on outside and nearly passed out when she did.

"Jamie! How?!" Jamie marched up and down the driveway of Rachel's house yelling. He obviously thought she was home.

"You think you're going to put a restraining order against *me*? And take custody of my kids?" He yelled, "Joshua, Jonah! Get out here now!"

Fatima immediately sent all the children to the back of the house with Rahma and asked her to keep them in the basement where they would be away from the chaos ensuing in front of their home.

Jamie continued to rage outside. "*You* take my kids? A murderer like you? You don't even want kids!"

Ali turned and headed up the stairs. "Everyone stay inside this house." When he was half-way up the stairs he turned back. "Rachel, do *not* go outside."

Rachel felt a cold ball in her stomach, while her face burned with anger and humiliation, as she listened to Jamie ranting outside. He had no idea that she was watching him from across the street. She just wanted to die knowing that Fatima and Ali were hearing every filthy thing that Jamie was saying about her.

Watching him and listening to him expose and degrade her in front of the people she loved the most, built a rock solid hatred in her heart. She had a pretty strong arm and she felt like taking a kitchen knife and lancing it right into the back of his neck.

Fatima positioned herself on the other side of the kitchen window. "Your mom must be terrified. You should call her. I'm sure Ali's gone to call the police."

Rachel had completely forgotten that Naomi was home alone. Dana had taken her to the doctor early in the morning and had brought her back home, leaving again to do some work at the reference library downtown.

With shaking hands, Rachel managed to dial her home number from Fatima's cell phone. "Mom, yes I'm fine. No, no, it's going to be all right."

Fatima could hear Naomi's speech, loud and animated, through the phone line. Her heart went out to her. *How dare he frighten this poor woman?*

Jamie was clearly uncontrollable. After he had said everything he could possibly say, in an attempt to disgrace Rachel, he picked up a stone from the carefully tended garden and sailed it through the front window. The entire window came crashing down. Rachel was out the door almost before she opened it. Fatima tried to grab her, but Rachel was too fast.

"Here I am! You're looking for me? Who do you think you are? Messing with my mother and my kids! It was you last night at the window, wasn't it? You animal!"

Jamie looked bewildered for a moment. He couldn't have expected Rachel to come at him from behind. Now Rachel stood before him, defiant humiliation flaming in her until it turned into an inferno of rage.

All these years she had loved him, trusted him, believed in him, hoped that he could do and be better. She thought of the children she had because of him and the children she didn't. Now he would dare to stand in front of her home, in front of her friends and call her names, talk about their most personal affairs, terrify her mother and threaten her children, his children, destroy her property, and then expect her to want him? What kind of monster was he? None that was worthy of her, that was certain. "Get off my property," she said as she glared at him.

Jamie stepped towards her. "Not yet." Then he rammed his hand against her throat.

"Where is Rachel?"

Fatima turned to see Ali standing behind her. Before she could answer him they both witnessed Jamie grab hold of Rachel's neck and throw her to the ground. Ali tore out the front door and Fatima flew behind him, grabbing his arm in an attempt to stop him. She could feel something hard in his hand but refused to look. She immediately recognized the feel of his nun chucks. She held his arm with both hands. "Ali, please. Don't. You'll kill him," she whispered.

The cool evening breeze blowing through the trees was a stark contrast to the pounding of Fatima's heart in her chest. Her blue jay screeched as it flew overhead.

"I'm just going to talk to him," Ali said so calmly that Fatima almost believed him.

"Ali please, I'm begging you." Ali had never had a conversation with Jamie, and Fatima certainly couldn't see him having one now, not with nun chucks, and not after seeing Rachel thrown to the ground.

"Go inside the house," Ali said, while he kept his eyes focused on his intended destination.

Fatima stood firmly in front of him, trying to push him back towards the house as he moved forward. She could see and feel that every muscle in his body was tense. In desperation, her mind raced to come up with something that may affect him. "Think of the children," she pleaded.

"And shut the door."

Chapter Twenty Five

ℐ

Fatima stepped back while keeping her eyes on her husband. She was going to do exactly as he had said. *Go inside and shut the door*, but the reality made her sick and she kept her mouth tightly shut to keep from throwing up. She now realized what she had feared all these weeks. The constant feeling of anxiety that she couldn't eliminate and could not find the reason for; it was all culminating into this moment. Fatima knew that she could not stop what was about to happen and she started to pray it would not be the horror that she was expecting.

Jamie stood over Rachel as she struggled to get up. Her nose was bloody, and even from the distance Fatima could see that her lip had been cut when she fell against one of the stones framing the garden.

Jamie caught sight of Ali approaching from across the street. Fear flashed across his face before he caught his footing. "Oh the 'Big Man', just who I've been waiting for." Even before he reached behind his back, Fatima knew what he was about to do.

The way he had spread his legs and opened his shoulders told her everything she needed to know.

"Ali!" The sound escaped her before she could stop it. She had not intended to distract him.

Ali turned in the direction of his house and in doing so he blocked Fatima's view of Jamie. Before she could inhale, the sound of one single shot rang through the air.

Fatima had never heard a gunshot before, and because she didn't actually see Jamie pull out a weapon she hoped she was wrong, but when she saw Ali stagger backward and tumble over the bushes at the end of her front yard, falling onto the sidewalk, his white robe quickly turning red, she knew.

Fatima didn't even recognize the scream that exploded from her. Although she felt completely unhinged, she knew she only had a few seconds to make all the difference for Ali. She had to keep her head on. Struggling to continue her own breathing and steady her racing heart, she moved as quickly as she could to get to his side.

Jamie walked slowly towards Ali with the gun still aimed at him. Fatima did not care. All she could see was Ali's heaving chest and his clothes quickly being soaked with his own blood.

Hysterical, Rachel ran and jumped on Jamie's back, hitting and scratching him. The neighbours came out of their homes and Jamie started to retreat. He shook Rachel off and ran. Some of the men started to chase him before he quickly jumped into a waiting car while the driver sped off.

Fatima searched Ali's clothing for the bullet entry point and tried to rip the cloth. She couldn't. It was woven too tightly. "Damn!" She wondered about the value of quality clothing and was incredulous that she ever decided to buy this outfit. *Oh Allah, don't let this be his shroud*, she thought. She tried applying pressure where she thought the wound was, but her hand was getting so bloody she knew she wasn't finding the right spot. "I need scissors! And petroleum jelly!" she yelled into the gathering crowd.

"Ali breathe, please just breathe." Fatima struggled to keep him still and hoped that her words would comfort him and keep him focused on the difficult task of moving oxygen through his body.

A scream pierced the air, and Fatima closed her eyes preparing herself for the ugly scene she expected. She knew it was Rahma, and could see neighbours struggling to hold her back from getting closer. She was hysterical and was giving them the fight of her life. It took three people to hold her and they still couldn't drag her back to the house. "Get off me!" she screamed, while trying to pull away, throwing kicks and punches at anyone who dared come close. "I need to see my brother! Please, just let me see him! Oh God, I just want to see him!"

Fatima didn't want Ali to be aware of his sister's distress. She turned to Rachel who was sputtering and coughing while she cried beside Fatima. "Oh my God, Oh my God, what have I done!" Rachel gasped.

"Listen to me. You pull it together. Go calm Rahma down, get her inside the house, and then get back here. *Fast*. I need you. Bring towels. Any. And do *not* let my children come out here!"

Fatima continued talking to Ali while she tried to put pressure on the site she thought the blood was coming from.

"Scissors! I need scissors!"

She knew Ali had a chest injury and she had to seal the wound to prevent air from entering his chest cavity. She had no idea when help would arrive and she wasn't going to wait. Finally, a neighbour handed her scissors and a tub of petroleum jelly. She sliced Ali's shirt in one clean motion and located the entry point of the bullet. It was on his left side just below the midpoint. She cursed Jamie's good shot.

Rachel returned, calmer this time, kneeling down on the pavement. "I called the ambulance. They already had several calls from the neighbours." She looked at Fatima's blood covered hands. "What should I do?"

"Cut a piece of his shirt so I can dress this wound." While giving Rachel instructions, she used the towels to create a barrier between Ali and the cold pavement.

Rachel's hands were shaking. "How big?"

"Four by four, roughly, doesn't have to be exact."

Fatima kept her hand on the wound and frantically looked up

the street while straining her ears for the sound of sirens. A person could bleed to death in minutes if an artery were hit. She tried not to think about where the bullet may have lodged. She couldn't locate an exit wound, indicting it was likely still inside.

"Line three sides with petroleum." Rachel took instructions and worked quickly while Fatima sealed the wound with additional petroleum. The bleed was slowing. *Not necessarily a good sign.* She took the dressing from Rachel and placed it over the hole while she asked Rachel to check his pulse.

"It's weak."

Fatima had not thought it was possible to feel any more dread than when she had first seen Ali fall, but after hearing Rachel's pronouncement she felt her insides turn to ice. "Ali, stay with my voice please. The ambulance is on its way. Please, please Ali just listen to me and keep breathing." Fatima kept talking to him and reciting *Quran* over him until the paramedics arrived. She stepped aside and prepared to enter the ambulance with him.

When Rahma saw Ali on the gurney she ran outside. She stroked his head and kissed his face. "I love you, Ali. You have to be all right. You have to." When she broke down again, Rachel led her away. She quickly returned and stepped behind Fatima. "I'm coming."

Fatima held onto Rachel's shoulders. "No. Your mother needs you. The kids need you. And please contact his parents. I'll call you from the hospital."

"This is all my fault." Rachel's face collapsed with guilt and grief.

Fatima shook Rachel's shoulders. "That's not useful right now. You have to focus." She motioned in the direction of the house. "They all need you now. Go, and I'll call you."

Fatima released Rachel and followed Ali into the back of the ambulance.

Fatima paced the floor in the small waiting area, oblivious to her constant back pain and the increasing pressure in her lower abdomen. She didn't seem to notice her swollen feet and the fact that her legs felt like lead. She had managed to wash her hands and face and now was wringing her hands while she replayed the scene in her head over and over.

Could she have done anything to prevent this? Did she do everything she was supposed to after the shooting? Did she act quickly enough? Did she get everything right? Ali's life could depend on it. Those first few minutes were crucial.

When she turned and saw Ali's parents quickly approaching her, with their friend, Nargis, steps behind them, she felt a mixture of relief and anxiety. She was relieved that she was no longer alone, but their presence reinforced the gravity of the situation.

When she saw Mama's and Papa's formal wear she remembered that today was someone's wedding day. Ali was supposed to be reciting at the wedding. The image of men reciting *Quran* over Ali's body flashed across her mind. She quickly pushed it aside. She had to remain positive.

Papa often used a cane when he had to be out for long periods of time. He had several that he might choose from depending on the occasion. Even though the family sometimes lovingly teased him about being an old man, they were obviously proud of the way he had come by his injury, and Papa never felt insulted by them. "If you don't live long, you can't get old," he would simply say. Although he didn't have the cane now, he moved swiftly to reach Fatima's side.

Upon seeing Fatima's blood-soaked clothing, Mama's usually serene face contorted, but only for a second. Then she blinked and put her arms around Fatima. Feeling the love close around her, Fatima relaxed, but when Papa enclosed both of them in his embrace, and Mama's hold on Fatima tightened, Nargis bit her lip and Fatima finally let out everything she had been holding in from the time she had felt the nun chucks in Ali's hand.

"He's in surgery," Fatima said between sobs. "I tried to stop him...I tried." She clung to Mama as she struggled to catch her breath.

"There's nothing you could have done," Mama whispered.

Papa added, "We know our son. He wouldn't be Ali if he had done anything differently."

"That Jamie is just a born thug!" Nargis said.

"I could see what he was going to do, but it happened so fast..." Fatima cried into Mama's shoulder.

"Hush, hush," Mama cooed.

"Fatima!" Fatima released herself from the Abatis' hold to see Brigitte running toward her. "I just heard! I can't believe it! What happened?" Brigitte's eyes were wild with panic.

"Brigitte, what are you doing here? Fatima looked at the baby blue scrubs and understood. "You work here now."

"Yes, I have for about two years."

"I had no idea."

Brigitte shook her head. "Anyway, I know Ali's been shot, but what happened?"

Fatima finally sat down. "Our close friend has a complicated relationship with the father of her kids and Ali kind of got in the middle of it."

Nargis mumbled under her breath about wayward young people.

Brigitte sat beside Fatima. "What's his name?"

"Jamie Weston."

Brigitte's hands flew to her face. "Oh no, oh no," she kept repeating.

Mama and Papa moved closer to the two women, listening intently without saying a word.

"You know him? How?" Fatima asked breathlessly.

Brigitte just nodded and then said, "When I first started here, he was visiting a patient and-" She broke off crying. "I can't believe this has happened."

Fatima and the others exchanged knowing looks. They didn't need to hear any more. Jamie had always been popular with the ladies. Brigitte straightened her back and vigorously wiped her face. "I promise you I will do everything possible to make sure he gets the best care. I am personally going to see to it." She blinked her eyes rapidly.

Fatima almost felt sorry for *her*. "Thank-you. We appreciate it."

Brigitte turned to Mama and Papa. "I'm so sorry. I promise you he will be taken care of." Then she stood to leave. "I'll try and find out some details. And Fatima...I did always like you."

Fatima reached for her hand. "I know. Thank-you."

As soon as Brigitte left, Rachel rounded the corner holding a bag. "I brought you some clothes. I knew you would be spending the night, so I grabbed some toiletries too."

"Great, I'm dying to get out of these. What's happening at home?" Fatima took the bag onto her lap.

Rachel put up her hand and shook her head. "No, tell me about Ali first."

"He's in surgery. We're just waiting. It might be a few hours before we hear anything."

"Everyone at home is ok. The kids never left the basement so they don't really know what happened. Rahma is a mess. My mom is with them. I told Rahma, when Dana gets there, she can come to the hospital. I'll call her in a little while and she can just take a cab. I'll meet her downstairs."

On hearing about Rahma's condition, Mama and Papa left to phone her. Nargis took a seat in the corner of the waiting room next to a large potted plant.

Rachel continued to fill in Fatima. "My mom has started a prayer chain and I think some sisters will be meeting at the house soon. They'll be praying all night. No one will be able to sleep anyway."

Fatima recalled hearing about mothers in some Asian countries who would "bow" all night before their children's university entrance exams, to ensure good results. She often wondered why more Westerners didn't take that approach to addressing their needs.

Rachel lowered her voice. "So you know that nurse?"

"Yes, her husband used to be one of Ali's teammates. He never played, but I got to know him and Brigitte very well. He was eventually transferred to another team and we fell out of touch."

"That's it? No other story?" Rachel knit her eyebrows and sharpened her eyes.

"Like what?" Fatima sat a little taller in her seat.

"Well, I don't know if this is the best time to bring it up, but her sister is the one bringing the paternity suit against Ali. I recognized her name in the report and I confronted her. She admitted as much."

Fatima was floored. Nargis leaned forward in her seat. "We did have a falling out," Fatima admitted.

"I knew it. What happened?" Rachel put her hand on her hip and waited for Fatima's response.

Brigitte had befriended Fatima, like many of the wives had, and had confided in her about her issues with her husband. Her husband had made up for his inactivity on the court by being very busy off court. Many nights Brigitte had called Fatima looking for him and trying to find out information about his social activities.

"I told her the same thing I told all the others. I'm not looking after anyone's husband except mine, and I can't discuss anyone's business. I mean, if you have to be asking, that's the first clue you have a problem."

Rachel smiled. "No wonder those guys love you so much. So, do you think she's the revenge type?"

Fatima didn't think so. "It would take pretty elaborate planning, don't you think?"

"Hmm, I guess we can just give Shawn this information and see what he thinks about it."

"Shawn!" Fatima threw her hands to her head. "We haven't called him. Rachel, could you please? I can't break the news." Fatima held onto Rachel's arm.

"Of course. You better get changed. There are about 200 people downstairs waiting to talk to you, and at least six really big guys pacing in the parking lot. I think they all want to see you."

Fatima stared in astonishment.

Nargis moved from her place in the corner. "When we had to leave the wedding, many of the guests just followed us, including the bride and groom."

"Oh, no." Fatima was overwhelmed by the outpouring of affection and support. "They didn't get married?"

"Oh no, they made sure to get married. Then they came." Nargis was the first to start laughing.

"I better get changed and go see them," Fatima said.

Nargis volunteered to go with Fatima when Mama and Papa had returned. Fatima quickly put on the clean clothes and a brave face. She and Nargis headed to the main floor of the hospital to see the friends and loved ones who were eagerly waiting for information on Ali's condition.

"The next twenty-four hours will be critical. We'll know by then how he has responded to the surgery." The bullet had missed Ali's heart by a hair, the doctor said. Fatima's quick attention had been a critical factor in increasing his chances of survival. "He is a very, very lucky young man. The angle of his body when the bullet entered is what saved him. Had he been facing the shooter, we might not be having this conversation."

Rahma, Mama and Papa, Rachel and Fatima hung on the doctor's every word. "He's not out of the woods yet. We'll be watching him very closely for the remainder of the night."

"Can we see him?" they asked in unison.

"One at a time, and just a few minutes please. He really needs to rest."

When Fatima entered the room she felt the full weight of her pregnancy for the first time since the tragedy had unfolded. She knew she had to keep it together for Ali's sake and for her own sanity. Seeing him attached to various tubes and equipment and hearing the beeping and surging of the machines supporting his life, made her want to run and scream. She knew if she gave in to that feeling she may never be able to stop.

After all the family members had seen Ali, Rachel approached Fatima. "I know it's a lot to ask, but could I have a minute with him?"

Fatima turned to look at Ali's room and then back at Rachel. "Ok, one minute. I'll be right here."

Rachel took a seat beside Ali's bed, and as she watched his chest tremble with each breath, the tears started and she felt her throat closing as she struggled to speak.

"Ali, it's Rachel. I'm so sorry. If only I had listened to you, all the time, any of the time, you wouldn't be here right now. I was so selfish, so childish and so blind. Now you have to pay for it. Your family has to pay for it." Rachel felt like she was choking, but she had to continue.

"I was running after what I thought was love, when the love I needed was right in front of me; my mom, my dad, my sons, you and Fatima.

"Now you're here and you have to hold on. You have to come back to us. I've learned my lesson. I promise. Everything will be different. I will be different. I promise. I promise." Rachel's body shook with wave after wave of tears, but she continued.

"If we lose you, if I lose you, I can't forgive myself. If Fatima loses you, I can't live. Ali, I can't live." Rachel broke down sobbing at the side of Ali's bed. She was broken and drowning in grief, while facing the realization that she could possibly lose her childhood friend and Fatima could lose her husband. How could they go on without him? She needed him and Fatima needed him and she wasn't going to let him go. Yes, she accepted that she was to blame for his injury, but there was no way she was going to watch him die.

"You listen to me, Ali. You're strong. You're healthy, and you're alive. You're fighting with every breath. Each minute that passes brings you closer to perfect health, and back to the people that love you. Ali, do you hear me? I will be by Fatima's side until you walk out of here. I promise you...I promise. I'm so sorry. You were right...you were right."

Rachel dropped her face into her arms and when the last tear had fallen she lifted her head to see Fatima standing on the other side of the bed, tears streaming down her face. She walked over to Rachel and put her arms around her. "We have to go." As she led Rachel away she said, "Thank-you for being here. I know it means the world to him."

Rachel and Fatima spent the last hours of the night at the hospital locked in the memories of their childhood. The other family members spent the time talking, laughing, crying and praying together, affirming to Ali his strength, their love for him and encouraging him to hold on and come back to them.

Chapter Twenty Six

ℑ

Each day that passed saw Ali becoming a little bit stronger. The surgery was successful and he was healing as expected. He was fortunate not to have any lead poisoning, which was one of the greatest dangers after a shooting. Without that concern, he was on a clear road to recovery. After a few days he was able to sit up and move around in a wheelchair. He had a steady stream of visitors and he managed to entertain and uplift them all.

Rachel kept her promise and went to the hospital every day with Fatima. She stayed outside Ali's room to talk to and update the many visitors who didn't want to ask Ali too many personal questions. Jamie was still on the run and Rachel swayed between praying that she never saw him again and wishing she could meet him alone on a dark night.

Each day she dropped her sons off at daycare and returned to pick up Fatima to go to the hospital. She had taken time off work and was seriously considering whether she wanted to return at all. Dana and Rahma took care of Ali's and Fatima's children and Naomi's house was filled with women who came to pray. They prayed in shifts so that the prayers continued around the clock.

Mama and Papa's friends would also meet there since they spent most of their time at the hospital.

This particular morning the song of the blue jay lifted Rachel's spirits as she stood on Fatima's porch, but when Fatima opened her front door Rachel immediately knew something was wrong.

"What?" she asked, with her heart in her throat. Fatima looked down and Rachel followed with her eyes to the envelope she held in her hand.

"The results of the paternity test." Rachel held her breath until she realized the envelope was unopened. "It was here when I came home yesterday. I was just looking at it."

Rachel stepped inside and closed the door behind her. "Are you going to open it?"

"No." Fatima stepped back and brushed her fingers across her brow. She had her hair neatly braided in eight long cornrows. She looked like she was sixteen.

"Why not? Just put yourself out of your misery."

"It's Ali's mail. He should open it..."

"Ok, then let's go and have him open it." Rachel reached for the door handle behind her with one hand and Fatima's scarf and jacket with the other.

"...when he comes home."

Rachel stared at Fatima, wide eyed. She knew waiting for the results had been killing her. "You're insane." Rachel let go of the door handle and reached for the letter.

Fatima pulled back her hand. "I can't do this today. Let's just go, and don't say anything about it yet. Please."

"This makes no sense. You guys have been suffering for so long. You've been waiting for this." Fatima fidgeted but didn't answer. "I think we need some good news right about now."

"Not today. I was just going to put it in my room," Fatima replied without looking up.

Realizing Fatima was clearly strained, Rachel decided to back down. "Fine, whatever you want."

When Fatima returned, they left in Rachel's car and for several minutes drove along in silence. Out of the corner of her eye Rachel could see Fatima smoothing the same area of her dress over and over. "Any other new developments?" she asked her.

"Brigitte hadn't mentioned that she divorced her husband two years ago. Shawn found out. She had been seen with Jamie, on occasion, up until about a year ago when it seems she cut contact."

"Lucky her." Rachel stopped at a red light. "I haven't seen her at all at the hospital."

"She comes around. She usually checks on Ali at least once day."

"How do you think she's involved in this?"

"That's not clear yet. There are so many variables." Fatima turned to look at Rachel. "We just have to keep looking."

"Or get it out of her." Rachel raised an eyebrow.

Fatima gave her a warning look.

"You said she's coming around every day. She must feel guilty about something." Rachel turned left and continued toward the hospital.

"We were really friendly. She may be concerned."

"Sure, about herself."

The car entered the hospital parking lot and Rachel took her parking ticket and turned into a spot close to the entrance. Fatima turned to Rachel and held her arm before she left the car.

"Please, don't say anything about the results coming."

Rachel put her hand to Fatima's cheek. "I won't say anything. I already told you I won't. By the way, you look beautiful today. You look like summertime." Fatima wore a black and white summer dress with a white jacket. "You're the only person I know who can make black and white look so stunning."

Fatima nodded. "Thank-you. For everything."

Rachel dropped her hand to Fatima's shoulder. "Change of topic. Fatima, I have to ask. Do you think that Ali would consider taking some kind of revenge?"

Fatima sighed heavily. "I'm sure he's thinking about a lot of things."

"That's exactly what I'm afraid of. Not that Jamie wouldn't deserve it, but it's Ali I'm concerned about."

"He has his dad. They've been talking a lot. I think he'll be ok." Fatima opened her door. "Let's go."

When they arrived on the floor, Mama and Papa were already in Ali's room. Ali sat in a chair looking out the window. The room was filled with flowers. Each day there were more, and Mama and Papa had to take some home every night.

"*As-salaam alaikum*," Fatima greeted all of them.

"*Wa alaikum as-salaam wa rahmatullahi wa barakatu*," Ali and his parents replied.

They were all pleased to see Ali doing so well. "Aren't you a sight for sore eyes?" Rachel put her purse down on the table beside Ali's bed.

"You should have seen me walking earlier." Ali smiled slightly, and Papa squeezed his shoulder.

The nurse walked into the room as if on cue, "I think he's planning to walk out of here holding that baby in a few days. At this rate he just might."

The nurse was pleasant and cheerful with an eastern European accent. She looked to be in her mid-thirties. "Ok, Mr. Abati we have to run some tests. Say goodbye to your family for now."

She helped him into his wheelchair and out of the room leaving Mama, Papa, Fatima and Rachel together.

"How is he doing this morning?" Fatima asked Mama just before sitting in Ali's chair beside the window.

"He's been quiet so far. He did have a little walk, as he said. He really is determined to get home as fast as possible."

"Looks like he's going to do it," Rachel said. They all nodded in agreement. "But, I would enjoy the down time if I were him. It'll be chaotic by the time he gets home."

"At least he'll be home." Fatima looked out the window.

Rachel touched the bouquet of flowers closest to her. "Who sent these?"

Mama came to her side. "There's no card."

"There are so many coming, who can keep track?" Papa answered from across the room.

"They look similar to the arrangements at my dad's grave." Rachel touched the petals gently.

"They *are* common spring flowers," Mama said.

Papa came to Mama's side. "Let's go get something to eat before our boy comes back. You haven't had anything this morning." Papa took Mama's arm and started towards the door.

Rachel grabbed her purse. "Good idea. Fatima?"

"No, I think I'll just wait here." Fatima closed her eyes and rubbed her hands over her face and up over her head.

The others raised their eyebrows and exchanged looks. Mama walked towards Fatima and felt her face. It was cool and moist. She then felt her pulse and held it for a few moments. When she lowered Fatima's hand she looked concerned. "Fatima, why didn't you tell us you were in labour?"

"She is having regular uterine surges but has not dilated much at all. It's unusual for a third pregnancy." Dr. Wilson sat back on her stool and removed her gloves.

"She has been under a bit of stress lately, and her husband is also a patient here. He was shot." Mama stood next to Fatima stroking her head.

"Yes, that would do it," Dr. Wilson said. "There is really nothing more for you to do, right now, except relax and wait. You know how it is." She looked directly at Fatima. "The more relaxed you are then the easier this process will unfold, literally." Dr. Wilson stood up. "The baby is doing well and everything looks fine, so it's safe to wait for a bit, or we can take some steps to start speeding things along since you're already past your due date."

"I'll wait."

"She'll wait." Mama and Fatima responded at the same time.

When the doctor left, Rachel peeked in the door. "Can we come in?"

"Of course." Fatima motioned with her hand for Rachel and Papa to enter the room.

"Has anyone called Ali?" Rachel sat next to Fatima's bed.

"I don't want to worry him prematurely."

Papa stood beside Mama. "I called. He's not back in his room yet."

"Nothing is happening yet, anyway," Fatima said.

Mama stroked Fatima's arm. "She just needs to relax. She's not dilating, most likely due to stress."

"She's just waiting for her own doctor to be available to deliver her baby," Rachel joked.

Fatima reached for Papa's hand. "Don't tell Ali I'm here yet. I don't want him to worry. Let's just wait and see what happens."

Rachel blurted out, "Wait for what? You *are* having this baby tonight. He needs to be here."

"Maybe you'll relax more easily if you can see him, or talk to him at least," Papa suggested.

"Not yet."

Rachel reminded Fatima, gently, that Ali would wonder why she hadn't returned to his room.

"Think of something. Tell him I went to rest. *Anything*. I'll just call him later." Rachel, Mama and Papa looked at each other without saying a word.

Fatima had anticipated this day for so long. Her baby was about to be born and they finally had the results to the paternity test. Yes, she agreed they needed good news. But what if it wasn't good news? She couldn't deal with that now; not when she was about to give birth and not while Ali was still in the hospital. When they were all home she would give Ali the letter.

Her thoughts went to her baby. "Oh little one, what a time for you to be born." She stroked her tummy. "I do love you, no matter what." A few short days ago she had almost lost her husband. Now nothing was more important to her than Ali's recovery, the safe delivery of this baby and being at home with her family again.

Fatima spent most of the night in the same condition. Uterine surges came at five, four, sometimes even three minute intervals, but they were not strong enough to increase dilation.

Fatima thought about Ali when she wasn`t sleeping, but she knew that each day was critical for his recovery. She didn't want to hinder that. He needed his rest and she would only call him when absolutely necessary.

In the morning Fatima's primary care doctor was in, and after examining her, Dr. Grant insisted that the time had come to start moving things along, as the baby was starting to show the early signs of distress. Fatima finally agreed to call Ali.

Initially, there was silence on the other end of the phone. "I'll be right there."

"Why didn't you call me yesterday?" Ali sat in a wheelchair next to Fatima's bed. The room was also furnished with a reclining armchair and a sofa.

"I didn't want you to worry without reason."

"I was worried. I've been calling you since last night, and everyone kept giving me the run-around."

"You also need your rest. I didn't want to wear you out."

"How are you feeling now?"

Fatima shrugged.

The phone ringing interrupted their conversation. Ali held the receiver to Fatima's ear.

"Fatima?"

"Daddy." Fatima threw Ali a surprised look.

"Hi Pumpkin."

"How did you know I was here?"

"I'm your dad. I keep informed. So this is number four?"

"Yes."

"Another little princess?"

Fatima glanced at Ali. "I don't know. I guess we'll find out soon."

"I won't hold you up. You take care, and I'm going to try and get out there this summer. I can't believe it's been seven years." Fatima hadn't seen him since her wedding. "I can't wait to see my girls. They remind me so much of you when you were small. Any of them handy with a wrench?"

"Batool definitely." Fatima had not sent him any recent pictures, but she didn't wonder for a second who had been keeping her father updated. They said their goodbyes and Fatima turned her attention to Ali.

"Thank-you."

"For?"

"I know you called him. How often do you speak to him?" Fatima knotted her loose braids and tied them into a bun at the back of her head.

"Once in a while."

"Is a *while* a year? A month? A week?"

"Something like that. Anyway, forget that. I'm here now, and I want you to put everything out of your mind except relaxing and allowing our baby to come out to meet us."

Dr. Grant cleared everyone out of the room except Ali. "Ok, let's give them some time alone and see what happens. I'll be back in 15, 20 minutes tops."

Outside the room Fatima could hear the doctor say, "If there is no movement by that time, we will have to intervene."

No way, Fatima thought.

Dr. Grant returned in exactly 15 minutes. She was all smiles.

"You look relaxed."

"I am," Fatima replied.

Dr. Grant started her examination. "Amazing... four cm...almost four and a half. Things are moving right along. Good job, Mom." Dr. Grant patted Fatima's leg. "We can move you to the delivery room now. You're progressing quickly, so we can't take a chance."

Fatima continued to labour through the day, making steady progress, with Ali by her side. Mama, Dana and Rachel were in and out of the room and tried to relieve him on several occasions, to allow him a chance to go and rest, but he refused each time.

"Ali, you really should get some rest," Dana insisted. "Remember, you're still a patient too."

But when Fatima tightened the hold on his hand, he knew he couldn't leave.

"I'm not going anywhere, Fatima. You can ease up now." Ali teased her.

All humour was lost on her. She was past the point of being able to appreciate it. She was now showing the face that Dr. Grant had said she wanted to see. Intense, sweating, no more time for talking and laughing. When she started to shake with each surge it was clear she was getting closer to complete dilation.

"Mom...just...count...for me," she asked, breathlessly. Somehow, a woman's voice was much more soothing at this point. She didn't want to hear Ali speak at all. She couldn't imagine what he could say that could help her. She just needed to know that he was there.

Dana watched the monitor and as each upward line began, she started counting to help her daughter focus on her breathing. "1...2...3...4..." Through each surge she counted to 10, four times, while Fatima inhaled a long and slow breath each time. Then she released and prepared for the next one.

Ali tried to wipe her face in between each surge with a cold cloth, but when she shook her head violently, he decided to leave the nursing to the women. When Dana took the cloth from him and gently wiped Fatima's face, she instantly relaxed.

At the end of the next surge, Fatima lay limp on the bed. "I need to go to the washroom."

Ali tried to stand. "I'll help you."

"No! Don't come near me."

Dana and the nurse helped her to the washroom. "Call us if you need anything, Fatima. We don't want that baby in the toilet," the nurse said.

Dana had barely closed the door before the force of another surge threw Fatima onto the floor with her moaning, "I can't do it...I can't do it."

"You *are* doing it, Honey." Dana's voice soothed her. "Your baby is almost here now. It's almost over."

"When?"

Dana reminded her that when she felt like she couldn't possibly go on, it was near the end. That was a small comfort now. Somehow, she was helped back into bed just as another surge started.

"I'm feeling a lot of pressure," Fatima said as another surge swept through her body.

"You're just seven cm. Don't you start pushing yet. Otherwise you will have a swollen cervix and a baby with a very bruised head," Dr. Grant said as she reentered the room.

"I think...I need to."

"Just breathe it out." Dr. Grant came closer and stroked Fatima's back.

"Really...I can't.

"Let's see." Dr. Grant sat in front of the bed to check Fatima and was shocked to see the baby's head emerging. "The head is out! I can almost see the forehead."

The attending nurse was fully unprepared. No one had expected Fatima to go from seven cm to birth in less than fifteen minutes. The doctor got so close to Fatima's face that Fatima could feel her breath and see every colour in her iris. "Do not push! Just breathe, *he he hoo, he he hoo.*"

Chapter Twenty Seven

ℑ

Fatima tried to hold back, just as the doctor had said. There was no way she could. She was vaguely aware of the nurses trying to remove the bottom portion of the bed and shift her lower. Unable to stop herself, she released her hold on her baby and felt it slip from her body. She suddenly had difficulty catching her breath. She tried to hold up her head to see the baby, but couldn't. The entire room started to spin. She could hear frantic voices but couldn't make out the words. There was rapid movement around her and she felt Ali let go of her hand but could not tell where he had gone. She was so weak she couldn't turn her head anymore or even lift her hand. Again she tried to open her eyes, but this time she couldn't. Her head was pounding and then everything was black.

Fatima could hear footsteps and voices, but they seemed far way. She opened her eyes slightly, only to have bright lights force them closed again. Everything was a blur. She was not sure where she was or what had happened. She put her hand to her belly. It was soft. She blinked and opened her eyes. The first thing she saw was Ali's face. His expression was gentle but grave.

"What happened?" she asked in a whisper.

"You're in the hospital." His eyes searched her face for some memory of what had just transpired.

"I can't remember anything." Fatima continued to blink under the lights.

"Good, I don't need you to ever remember seeing me lose my cool," Ali answered her delicately.

"You? I would never believe it." Fatima started to laugh, but found she didn't have the strength.

Ali tucked back a piece of hair that had slipped into her face. "Perfect, let's keep it that way."

She could see that Ali was sitting in a chair next to her bed, and she was in a room she didn`t recognize. She must have been moved. She strained herself to make sense of her surroundings and current situation. "Where's your wheelchair?"

Ali shook his head and exhaled. "I don't even know where I left that thing."

She reached for his hand. "Did I scare you?"

"I was so scared."

Fatima had never heard him speak like this. *What had happened?* Everything was still so foggy. "I'm sorry, I think I was really mean to you," she said.

"No, no, you're going to be fine. That's all that matters."

Then she remembered. *The baby.* She tried to get up. Panic seized her as the memories tumbled over each other in her head. "What happened to the baby?"

Ali leaned forward in his chair to push her back. "Shh, don't move. He's fine."

He. "What did you say? What is it?" Fatima grabbed Ali's arm.

"It's a boy." His face remained stoic.

"We have a son? Really?"

"Yes. Yes, we do." Ali finally smiled.

Fatima leaned back and closed her eyes. The feelings rushed

through her, overwhelming her, and she couldn't imagine what to say or do. "I need to see him."

"He's in the nursery. His temperature was a little low. They're keeping him warm. I'll go in a few minutes to check on him."

"He's ok?" Fatima asked, with desperation in her voice.

"He's perfect. 8 lb 10 oz"

"A big baby for a little lady like you." The nurse entered the room and walked over to check Fatima. "So, you're awake? You gave us all a scare."

"What happened?" Fatima tried to sit up.

"You lost a lot of blood, your blood pressure dropped suddenly and you went completely limp. You had us jumping," the nurse replied.

"I still feel so weak."

"You will for a while." The nurse checked all her vitals and gave her some pills to take. "Did your husband tell you how amazing he was in the delivery room?"

"No." Fatima glanced at Ali sideways. Ali lifted his eyebrows and shrugged. The nurse continued. "Everything happened so quickly, we were a little short-handed. He really helped us out. You're a lucky lady." She patted Fatima's shoulder. "I'll bring you some food."

"I don't think I can eat anything." Fatima ran her hands over her hair. Her head was still damp.

The nurse paused at the door. "How about some soup?"

"I'll try."

"Will do. I'll be back in a minute."

Fatima turned her attention to Ali. "I thought you lost your cool."

Ali lifted his chin. "She's exaggerating."

"I can't wait to see him."

"Fatima, wait. We need to talk. Our son is healthy and I'm thrilled that you both came through ok, but all this was wrong."

Fatima fixed her gaze on a spot on the bed. She knew what he was about to say, and she knew he was right.

"This pressure you put on yourself to keep trying for a boy was wrong, and I was wrong for allowing it. When he was born I couldn't even be happy. One second I heard I have a son, and the next second I realized that your life was in danger. I thought, *what will I do with a boy if I don't have you?*"

"I know. I just so much wanted for you to have a son." Fatima raised her eyes to meet Ali`s gaze.

"Boy or girl never mattered to me. I'm sorry if I made you think otherwise. I don't want our girls to ever think that it matters to me or you."

"No, it wasn't you. It was all me. I just couldn't believe that you didn't care about not having a boy." She leaned back into her pillow.

"But why?" Ali searched her eyes for the answer. He couldn't believe that her insecurities about her father had pushed them to this point and that he had been so negligent as to not see how serious the issue was and where it was leading. He didn't even want to think about what could have happened in that delivery room.

Fatima closed her eyes and simply shook her head, and waved her hand in front of her. She couldn't talk about this now. She had been scarred by her parents' breakup. Deep down she feared that if she didn't have a son, Ali's commitment to her and the family would not be complete, but she could never admit that to him.

Ali brushed away her tears. "Listen, just focus on getting well so we can all go home. I should be the one apologizing to you. I know I added a lot of stress to your life these last few weeks. I'm sorry for all of it. I know I can't make it up to you, but I'm going to spend my life trying."

"It wasn't your fault," Fatima said from her position on the pillow. She looked up at the ceiling for a few minutes without speaking. "There's something else I should tell you." She lifted her head from the pillow. "The results from the paternity test came."

Ali sat straight up in his chair.

"It came on Monday. I didn't open it. I figured you could do it when you get home."

The nurse returned to the room with the soup. She then turned to Ali. "Could you help her?"

"Sure." Ali adjusted the tray and took out the spoon.

The nurse returned to the room pushing a wheelchair. "Look what I found."

When the nurse left, Fatima said, "I want to see the baby."

Ali insisted that she finish eating before he would get him.

Within a few minutes Fatima finished her soup and Ali had returned with their newborn son in his arms. The nurse held the door open for him. "I've seen your daughters. They are all lovely, but I think you saved the best for last. Enjoy."

Ali kissed his son and placed him in his mother's waiting arms.

Fatima unwrapped the blanket to examine his whole body and then swaddled him again. "It's Mama. I love you." She kissed his cheek and held him to her chest. "He is so beautiful. I think he looks like your father."

"Yes, I think so," Ali agreed.

"And a little bit like you."

"Lucky boy."

"Yes, he is." Fatima looked at him again. "So lucky." Then she looked at Ali. "Like his mom."

Rachel held Fatima's son in her arms while the whole family stood around. Fatima looked across the room towards the window, seemingly, far away in her thoughts. Rachel wondered what she was thinking about.

"Congratulations. Now you have everything you ever wanted."

Fatima barely smiled.

"Don't tell me you're still not happy? What do you need now, twin boys?" Rachel teased.

"No, I just haven't seen Ali, yet, today, that's all." Fatima looked concerned.

"Did you call him?" Papa had just entered the room.

"Yes. He wasn't in his room, but I expected him to call or come down by now."

Papa moved to the phone and dialed Ali's room. He moved as far away as he could and spoke in hushed tone. Rachel strained herself to understand his Italian. She leaned into Fatima and whispered, "What are they talking about?"

Fatima wore a guilty look and shrugged her shoulders.

"I bet you're kicking yourself that you didn't listen to Mama and learn Italian," Rachel scolded.

Papa hung up the phone and turned to the ladies. "He'll be here. Soon."

Rachel heard footsteps in the hallway and turned just in time to see Brigitte moving away from the door. "Here, hold your son." She placed the baby in Fatima's arms and rushed into the hallway.

"Brigitte."

Brigitte stopped and turned around. "I'm kind of in a hurry. I have an appointment."

"No, I don't think so. Looks like you were about to come in." Rachel caught up to her and stood blocking the hallway. "Fatima said you visit them every day. I found it funny that I always miss you."

When no reply came from Brigitte, it confirmed Rachel's suspicions that Brigitte was avoiding her. "So, how is your sister, Leanne, doing?

Brigitte stiffened before replying. "Please, just leave her alone. She's not doing well right now."

Rachel wondered how far she could bluff her way through this. "I guess she got the paternity results also."

"Please, just leave her alone. None of this is her fault." Brigitte turned and walked away.

"No you don't." Rachel stepped in front of her. "Leanne started this mess and my friends have been suffering as a result. So, no, I am not going to *leave her alone*. People who want to be left alone don't file paternity suits against rich married men. As a matter of fact, I'm sure you're involved in this somehow too."

Brigitte's eyes grew wide. Rachel continued. "It doesn't take a genius. There are just too many coincidences. Let's see, you know Jamie, very well it seems. He just happens to have a vendetta against all of us. You were married to one of Ali's teammates and you seem to have reason to be ticked off with Fatima."

"You don't know what you're talking about. You don't know anything about us." Brigitte's lower lip started to tremble. She tried to keep her voice down since the two of them were starting to attract attention from the nearby nurses' station.

Rachel decided to take advantage of her weakness. "Well, I suggest you fill me in, or else I will go straight to Ali's lawyer. They uncovered quite a bit of juicy information on you and your family from their private investigation. I don't think you will be looking too good at the end of all this."

Brigitte pulled Rachel into an empty kitchen. "It...it's my father."

Rachel blinked in shock "Your father? What does he have to do with this?"

"All he cares about is money. As soon as we were old enough to make money for him, we did. However he wanted us to."

Rachel listened intently. She had no choice. She was speechless.

"He introduced my sister to Matt." Brigitte, obviously tormented, started to talk very quickly.

"That was George's brother, the con artist." Rachel prompted.

"Oh, George was nothing compared to Matt. George was just more notorious." Brigitte pulled Rachel deeper into the kitchen.

"Matt kept everything under wraps, but he was definitely bigger than George. He made a lot of money doing everything you could think of and my father saw an opportunity to get something out of having a beautiful daughter. I'm sure he was involved in other business with Matt as well."

"I can't believe this," Rachel whispered.

"Well, she got tired of being used and just disappeared for a while. Matt didn't even bother to look for her, he just moved on to someone else. But my dad was angry. That's when he set me up with my ex-husband. That was a nightmare. I don't think he ever really wanted to be married. And his career didn't go where my father expected, so that flopped all round."

"That's when you became friendly with Fatima and Ali?"

"Yes, I really liked them. I just lost it when Fatima wouldn't give me any information. I knew she must have known what my husband was up to."

"You know that it wasn't her place to do that?"

"Of course, and I didn't want to put her in the middle, but I just had no one else to talk to. I was desperate. When we got divorced and I moved back home my father started plotting again. Leanne, she's the youngest and so easily influenced. She just went along with whatever my dad wanted."

"Which was..."

"I met Jamie here at the hospital, and when he met my dad and they both realized that they had a connection to Ali they got excited."

Rachel's heart started to beat faster. She wasn't sure if she was going to like what she was about to hear.

"My dad decided that Leanne should go after Ali and Jamie promised he could help with all the details."

"But he's married, what did your father expect to happen?"

"Well, he figured every man has a weakness and that if Leanne could get close enough to him he would at least be willing to pay her to keep quiet or go away. That was the plan."

"So what happened?" Rachel tried to sound casual.

"I brought her to his birthday party. She was on her own after that."

"Did you see her talk to him at least?"

"I really couldn't bear to watch her. I know how it feels to be in her position. But you've seen her; she's not someone that goes unnoticed."

"Ali said he doesn't remember her." Rachel crossed her arms.

Brigitte laughed. "I doubt that...and what would you say if you were in his position?"

Rachel ignored the question. "And the baby?"

"I just know what she told me."

Rachel opened her arms. "I could just wring your neck. You're still trying to convince me that that is Ali's baby? Where is your sister now?"

"She was just admitted to the hospital, and she is not having any visitors."

"Why? What happened?"

"I think the stress got to be too much for her. She just broke down."

"Really? Well, you must have a picture of your nephew."

Brigitte pulled out a photo of Leanne's son.

"Let me see that." Rachel studied the photo for a few minutes and her temper cooled. He was just an innocent child, and he reminded her so much of her own little boys when they were babies.

"This baby has nothing for Ali Abati, at all." She thrust the picture back at Brigitte.

"Not every baby looks like the father. He looks more like Leanne." Brigitte took the picture from Rachel and placed it back in her wallet.

"Ok Brigitte, I think I've heard enough. For now. I suggest if you have anything more to confess you do it soon, because this is about to blow up, and you do not want to be in the middle when it does." With that, Rachel turned and left the kitchen, nearly bumping into a housekeeping cart on the way out.

Rachel hurried back towards Fatima's room. Fatima was being discharged today, and Rachel had to act quickly. She now had to shadow Fatima and make sure that she did not open the results of the paternity test.

Chapter Twenty Eight

"Who is this answering Fatima's phone?"

"Who do you think? And don't even think about getting it wrong," Ali replied.

"Who are you, the guard dog?"

"Come find out."

"Oh, now you have big talk."

"Kirk, what's up?" Ali was thrilled to hear from his teammate. "Fatima is in the nursery right now."

"Congratulations, man."

"Rami. Who else is on the line?" Ali asked, leaning back in his wheelchair beside Fatima's bed.

"Jeremy here. So this is number four, in five years. What are you trying to do, show off?"

"He always was a big shot," Kirk said.

"He does make pretty ones though. You have to give him that," Jeremy said.

"Wait until you see this one," Ali said proudly.

"We can't wait. What's his name?" Kirk asked.

"Ismail."

"Got that?" Rami asked. Kirk always had a difficult time remembering names.

"Got it. Like it." Then to Ali, he said, "We're trying to get up there and see you all next week. Until then, give Fatima our love."

"And next time let her answer her own phone. We didn't call to talk to you," Jeremy teased.

"Isn't that just like him to land himself in the hospital to try and steal all the attention?" Rami spoke again.

"Totally."

"Thanks guys. I'll pass on the congrats and see you all soon."

"You take care of yourself and the little guy," Kirk started to say his good-bye.

"See, he forgot the name already!" Rami and Jeremy howled with laughter.

Ali laughed and disconnected the call.

Rachel went downstairs in the lobby to make a call from the pay phone. "Hi Shawn, this is Rachel. Please call me as soon as possible. Very important."

"Did you really need another bath demonstration?" Ali watched as Fatima entered the room and placed their sleeping baby in the bassinet.

"Well, sometimes you forget something, and it's fun. I find it interesting." She turned to face Ali. "Can you believe they wanted to use our baby for the demonstration? They already said he was cold, and then they want to have him on display? I don't think so."

"Go ahead, Mommy." Ali was always proud of the protectiveness Fatima had for their children.

"Don't tease me." Fatima tossed her head.

"Listen, sit down. I want to talk to you." Fatima sat on the bed facing Ali. "You're going home today. Since I won't be home for a few days, I want you to open the letter."

271

The colour drained from Fatima's face as she looked towards the floor.

"Fatima, we both know what the results are going to be. I am not that child's father, and it's killing me to see what this has been doing to you. Just open it, and put an end to all of this, for yourself."

Fatima looked Ali directly in the eyes. "I don't need to. I believe you."

Ali frowned. "If that were 100% true, you wouldn't turn grey every time the topic comes up. Just open it. I'll feel better."

She finally agreed, more to end the conversation than because she was really in agreement with Ali.

A playful look spread across Ali's face. "Then call me and remind me what a wonderful husband I am."

Fatima laughed. That she could do.

After making the phone call, Rachel headed back to Fatima's room. She was startled and slightly worried when she found her room empty. She questioned the nurse on duty. "Where is Fatima?"

"She was discharged. She left with her mother-in-law about five minutes ago."

"Thank-you." Rachel turned away. "Shoot." She debated whether she should go and talk to Ali or go directly to Fatima's house. She decided to head to Fatima's house with speed.

Mama dropped Fatima off in front of her house and lifted Ismail out of the back seat. They met Dana at the front door. "You're earlier than I expected. I was just going to the store. Will you be fine until I get back?"

"Yes, I'll just get settled in." Papa was out with the girls to give Fatima the afternoon to herself. Fatima stepped inside and kissed Mama good bye. After closing the doors, she lifted her son from his car seat and headed upstairs to her room. She opened the double doors to her bedroom and sighed. The smell of roses warmed her senses. There was a fresh bouquet beside her bed. It was so good to be home.

She put Ismail into the bassinet beside her bed. When she lifted the blanket that was folded in the corner of the bassinet, to cover Ismail, a tiny piece of paper fell out. Fatima's heart soared. *How did he do it? When did he leave this one?*

Fatima opened the paper. *For all you do…thank you.* Fatima had to sit down. She had never told Ali how much these notes meant to her, how much they added to their marriage. This small expression of appreciation meant more to her than she could say.

She had been running herself ragged since the day Ali was shot. She had lost track of the days. Before Ismail's delivery, she had been running back and forth between the hospital and home. She hadn't been sleeping well and only ate when some member of the family got a hold of her and forced her to. Although Ali had written and placed this note long before now, the timing of its appearance was perfect.

She looked at Ismail sleeping in the bassinet. She always felt like she didn't know what to do with herself when she came home with a new baby, and this was the first time being home without Ali. She breathed deeply and said a silent thank-you that he would be coming home at all.

She admired Ismail's face, his smooth cheeks, cute nose and sweet baby lips. His profile looked just like Ali's. *The letter*. She remembered what Ali had asked her to do when she got home. She might as well get it over with it. She reached into her dresser drawer and pulled out the letter.

"Am I getting every red light, or what?" Rachel pounded the wheel in frustration. When her cell phone rang she reached into her purse, grabbed it and answered before the second ring.

"Rachel?"

"Shawn, thank goodness. I really need to talk to you." Rachel leaned on her horn just to release her pent-up frustration.

"What's happening?" Shawn sounded hurried.

"It's about the paternity test, but I need to speak to you in person. I'm on my way to Fatima's house now."

Shawn exhaled slowly. "They received it, I guess."

"Yes, the day Fatima went into labour. She didn't open it yet. I have to make sure she doesn't."

Shawn's voice piqued. "Why do you say that?"

"That's what I have to talk to you about, but not on the phone." The light turned green and Rachel floored the pedal.

"If this wasn't so serious, I would laugh. I just got some information a few seconds ago, and it seems like it's old news to you."

"These people are important to me. You know I would stop at nothing for them." Rachel rounded the corner leaning her body into the turn.

"I think I should hire you. I could get rid of a couple people if I had you."

"We can discuss that later. I think you should meet me at Fatima's house."

"I need to speak to Ali," Shawn said.

"Fatima has the letter. That's where I need to be."

"Good point. I'll meet you there." Shawn hung up.

Fatima decided to sit downstairs. Ismail could sleep without her. When she was comfortable in her favourite chair in the living room, a cream-coloured armchair currently wearing a charcoal and cream slipcover, she turned the envelope over. "I only need to do it once. I might as well get on with it." She used the letter opener she had picked up on her way to the living room. She sliced open the envelope and unfolded the paper.

Reading the document, she felt like all the blood had drained from her body. Her diaphragm tightened. Even the thought of breathing was painful. "Oh God, this can't be real." But there was no mistaking what she had just read. Ali was the father.

"Oh no!" Rachel pressed the brakes to decelerate but knew she was too late. The police officer stepped into the road and waved her to the side. "Agh!" she groaned out loud. That hill always got her. You had to accelerate to get over it, and if you didn't pay attention you would be sailing over well past the posted limit of 50 km. It wasn't the first time she had been caught here. Today she wasn't even thinking. The only thing on her mind was getting to Fatima's house.

Rachel stopped and rolled down her window. "Hi." She smiled. The officer was close to her age and looked friendly, so she hoped for the best.

"You were going way past the limit, more than 20 km over. It's a school district, so I have to give you a ticket, but I'll see if I can reduce it for you," he said.

Wow, just like that? Rachel wasn't complaining, but she *was* watching the clock. Maybe she should call Fatima? No. It wasn't a good idea while she was waiting on the officer to do her a favour.

"Ok, Ok, buddy let's go." Rachel tapped the armrest in her car.

Finally, the officer finished writing up her ticket and let her go with an additional warning. At least she wasn't going to lose any points. When she was well on her way she picked up the phone to call Fatima. The phone call went straight to the voice mail.

"Who could she be talking to?"

Fatima had called Ali's room four times without getting an answer. She decided to call the nurses' station to try and locate him. After a few minutes the nurse came back on the line. "He's not in his room." *No kidding.*

"Please ask him to call home immediately. I need to speak with him." Fatima disconnected the call and had the sudden urge to smash the phone into the wall. *No point, I would just have to replace it.*

Fatima couldn't imagine what she could say to Ali on the phone, but she couldn't wait to speak to him. She would have preferred to see his facial expression when she told him that he was the father, but she had no patience with urgent matters such as these. She didn't know whether to laugh, scream or cry. She felt like she was in a dream, a nightmare actually. Was this really happening? *Was her husband the father of this child?*

Of course he was. The test proved it. But how? How could he be? How could he have lied to her, knowing that it would come out in the end? It just didn't make sense. *Was he crazy?* Or was he trying to make her think she was crazy? She had heard about men like this. They were better than professional actors. They would lie elaborately even in the face of obvious facts. But Ali wasn't that kind of man. Was he?

Maybe he was scared, she thought. He was just too afraid to tell her the truth. She had been pregnant, and he had just been afraid to tell her. *How had he planned to work his way out of this?* He probably had convinced himself that he wasn't the father. That's why he had the nerve to tell her to open the letter. He had hoped that it wouldn't be him and that would be the end of it. Fatima was familiar with situations like these. As long as there was a possibility that it could be someone else's child, the man in question would not accept responsibility.

No. Ali was not that man. She had known him since he was 10 years old and, for the life of her, she could not think of a lie that had ever passed his lips. As for not taking responsibility for women and children? No way. He cared about people too much. He was honourable. He could never do it. She was so confused.

Fatima walked around the room. She couldn't sit still. Adrenaline was coursing through her. *Where was he?* She hated this mysterious behavior he was exhibiting lately, and she hated even more, the suspicion that it fostered in her. If there was a possibility he was the father why hadn't he just confessed weeks ago? She would rather have dealt with it then. How could he put her through this? Frustration, anger, fear and humiliation got the best of her. She sat down on the couch, dropped her face into her hands and started to cry.

Rachel drove up Fatima's long driveway. She parked and rushed up the steps to the porch and took a breath to appear calm. Before she could ring the doorbell, Fatima opened the door. The look on Fatima's face told her she was too late. "Fati?" Rachel stepped inside. Fatima didn't respond but stepped back to allow Rachel to enter the foyer. She returned to her seat on the couch and sat down curling one leg underneath her. Rachel followed her but was afraid to speak. Finally, she sat down and asked, "Where's Dana?"

"At the store," Fatima answered mindlessly.

"What's wrong?" Rachel ventured.

Fatima put her hand to her forehead and rubbed. The worst had happened. Even though she had prepared herself for it, nothing could have steeled her for the jolt that went through her upon reading those words. She still had not heard from Ali, and the fact that she had not been able to confront him was eating her alive. "The results say that Ali is the father." She couldn't even think about what it would mean to her life. She was completely numb. *The children.* How would she explain something like this to them?

Rachel couldn't imagine how Fatima must feel. She had to admit to herself that there had been many times she had envied Fatima for her seemingly perfect life. This was not one of them. Still, if she could take the pain Fatima was clearly feeling and transfer it to herself she would. Even though she had known what the result was going to be, seeing Fatima's devastation was unbearable for her. She had told Brigitte that the baby looked nothing like Ali, but she couldn't lie to herself about what she really saw in that picture.

Ali returned to his room and saw the note next to the phone telling him to call home. He sat on the bed and dialed his home number. The phone didn't even ring; it went directly to the voice mail. While he still held the phone in his hand the nurse entered the room. "Mr. Abati your wife just called. She wants you to call her right away. Oh, did you get the message already?"

Ali lifted his hand and nodded and the nurse ducked out of the room. When Ali didn't get a response on the home phone he called Fatima's cell. Still no answer. "Where could she be?" More than her whereabouts he wondered about what had happened. What could be so urgent? He decided to call his parents. Then he remembered. *The paternity test.*

Rachel moved closer to Fatima and could feel the nervous energy radiating from her. She had obviously been crying and looked completely worn out. How could Rachel begin to explain this crazy mess? She herself didn't really understand it. From the time that she had first learned about the paternity suit she had been in Ali's corner. She had never believed that he had fathered a child outside his marriage *and* lied about it. She definitely had not been prepared for what she had learned today. She wasn't sure how to handle it and now she had to tell Fatima. Shawn didn't seem to be taking it well either.

"He has to do the test again," Rachel said.

Fatima scoffed. "Again? Why?"

Before Rachel could open her mouth, Shawn stepped through the open front door. He had heard their conversation from the porch and was ready with the answer that Fatima needed. "Because he is not the father. We have good reason to believe that Jamie might be."

Shawn started to explain. Just as Brigitte had said, her father had set up Leanne to meet Ali. When she was not successful in getting his attention, Jamie devised a more devious plan. When Leanne had her baby the plan was to switch Ali's DNA sample with one from Jamie.

"How could they do that?" Fatima asked before she dropped into the seat behind her.

Shawn shook his head. "They did their research. The director of the DNA clinic had a few skeletons in his closet. It was straight blackmail."

"How did you find out?" Fatima asked.

"The director got nervous when George ended up dead. He must have realized Jamie was housecleaning. It seems he feared Jamie more than the law. He went to the police and spilled everything." Shawn turned to Rachel. "Jamie definitely planned to be arrested. Using Joshua and Jonah to get to you was a bonus. He wanted to be in with George. I guess to make sure he was taken care of. He set everything up, and then he got out of there."

"But how?" Rachel knew Jamie was capable of almost anything, but he had surprised even her this time.

"When you have people on the inside and the outside you would be surprised at how easy it can be. I'm sure he has a few police officers on his payroll as well; maybe a whole station."

"So the baby might actually be Jamie's?" Fatima leaned against the arm of the chair.

Shawn and Rachel both nodded. Shawn directed his next question to Rachel. "How did you figure it out?"

Rachel sat on the arm of the couch closest to the door. "I saw the baby's picture and I just knew. He does look like his mother, but there was something about him that looked like my sons, and he had a cleft in his chin. I knew if Jamie was involved, somehow that test result would be positive."

"Oh Rachel, I am so sorry." Fatima's face wore the five different emotions she had gone through in the last minute.

Rachel waved her hand. "I'm sorry for Leanne, and that boy. But it would have been far more devastating if it had been the other way around."

Shawn explained that they had a signed confession from the director. All that was needed to settle the case was a new DNA test.

"Are you sure?" Fatima actually sounded hopeful.

"Surer than I have been for weeks. This is the first time anything about this has made sense. Finally." Shawn then let himself out to go give Ali the news while Rachel stayed with Fatima.

"Time to celebrate." Rachel went to the kitchen to whip up a huge pot of cornmeal porridge.

Chapter Twenty Nine

ℑ

The porridge just couldn't be finished. Rachel and Fatima ate, all the children ate, Dana, Naomi, Mama and Papa ate and there was still almost half a pot left.

"Rachel, you can cook for us anytime. There certainly was a lot of blessing in that porridge," Fatima said.

All the adults were seated in the kitchen while the kids played in various rooms of the house. Each floor had one or two children on it and they continued to run up and down the stairs as they liked.

"*Attenzione*! Rahma please, *le figli*. Be careful. The children!" Papa was starting to feel nervous, as he usually did when he thought the children might be in danger.

"*Si* Papa." He was usually the one to occupy the children, but tonight he was sticking close to Fatima. They all were. Everyone was relieved that their ordeal was coming to an end. Fatima was in a permanently good mood, and the air was jovial and light in her home.

"I better go check Ismail. It's about time for him to wake up, and in all this noise I'll never hear him."

"I don't understand why you don't use a baby monitor," Rachel said. She, Dana, Mama and Papa sat around the booth in the kitchen and Naomi sat on a chair close by.

"I don't believe in them. They just make you more anxious. I don't want to hear every little sound. If he needs me he'll cry loudly enough." Fatima disappeared up the stairs.

"Hurry with my grandson, my arms are itchy." Papa's eyes danced. It had been almost 27 years since he had held a new born boy from his bloodline, and he could not have predicted how delightful it would be.

When Fatima returned with Ismail, Naomi held out her hands. "I haven't seen him yet."

"Certainly." Everyone smiled at the use of the word 'see.' Naomi still spoke as though she had full vision and many people were none the wiser. She had never accepted her health conditions as limiting. She always acted as though perfect health were just around the corner for her.

Naomi held the baby and stroked his cheek. Then she held him close, nuzzled her nose into his neck and inhaled deeply. "Don't they just smell delightful?"

Fatima stood in the doorway and watched with deep satisfaction. She was deliriously happy since learning the truth about the paternity case and having the entire family in her home was the proverbial icing on the cake. She was particularly moved to see Naomi, or anyone for that matter, loving her children. Ismail had so many people to love him, and she prayed that he grew to be just as wonderful as his father and grandfather.

Naomi smiled. "Look at that, he has Ali's dimple." Silence fell on the room.

"Ma, what did you say?" Rachel came to her feet.

"His dimple, it's like his father," Naomi said in a matter-of-fact way.

"Who told you that?" Rachel had risen from her seat and moved to her mother's side.

"No one had to tell me, Rachel. It's right there." Naomi carefully placed her finger in the indentation in Ismail's face.

Fatima's hands covered her mouth as she watched the unfolding scene. Rachel lowered herself before her mother's feet, rested her head on her knees and started crying. Mama turned her eye's upward and whispered *Alhamdulillah*. Papa simply nodded his head and Dana laughed out loud. "How long were you going to keep this secret?" she asked.

"I don't know what all the fuss is about. I told you my sight comes and goes. It has just been coming more often and staying longer these days." Naomi kept her focus on Ismail and placed her free hand on Rachel's head.

Rachel laughed through her tears. One by one all the women hugged and kissed Naomi. Papa took Ismail and walked out into the family room to give the ladies time alone. They bombarded her with question after question about her sight and the progress of her condition, "How? When? Why?" she was asked in rapid succession. Naomi's answer was simple and to the point. "Good living."

Chapter Thirty

Each day Naomi would spend a portion of her time outside on her porch. Today was a perfect day for it; warm and sunny. Many of the neighbours had been in and out frequently this morning and Fatima knew why. Word had gotten out that Ali was coming home today. She had wanted to sit out on her porch as well, but didn't feel like making a spectacle of herself. Not wanting to see or talk to anyone, she decided to wait in privacy.

She had not told her daughters that Ali was coming home. She didn't feel like hearing, every fifteen minutes, "When is Daddy coming?" So, she had opted to make it a surprise. She had asked Dana to take them out for a while so she could have some time alone with Ali. Ismail was proving to be an easy baby. He barely cried and he ate and slept regularly. She didn't expect him to be a problem.

When the sound of Papa's car came close, Fatima jumped to her feet. She looked out the front window and saw that almost every house, as far as she could see, had someone standing outside. They were waving and cheering and sending best wishes to Ali and his family. Fatima had planned to be strong, but this scene moved her beyond what she had expected.

Ali stepped out of the car and leaned on his walking cane. Fatima moved to the front doors and opened them to receive him. She had to brace herself against the door to resist the urge to move forward and help him. She and Papa both knew he had to do this on his own. Papa stood back and held onto the open car door. Fatima suspected that, like her, he was using it as a form of support at this emotional moment.

Ali took his time, but his steps seemed as strong and sure as they always had been. Fatima wondered if he was thinking the same thing that she was. The last time she had stood at the door and watched him was the day he had fallen at the hands of Jamie and his gun.

Fatima's eye shifted to the sidewalk where Ali had fallen. The neighbours had spent hours scrubbing the area clean after the police had finished collecting evidence. By the time Fatima had returned home there was not one spot of blood to remind her of that horrifying moment.

Ali made his way up the stairs. He had lost some weight and his face looked slightly gaunt. Fatima had bought him new clothes to wear home because she hadn't wanted him to feel bad about the loose fit of his old clothing. She also wanted him to feel like he was embarking on a new beginning.

He had smirked when he looked at the size. He hated to lose weight, but knowing him he wouldn't keep it off long. Fatima had bought blue jeans and a navy jersey. She had originally gravitated to the same shirt in white. She thought it was his best colour, but she didn't know when she would ever be ready to buy him anything in white again.

When Ali reached the doorway Papa followed, placed Ali's bag inside the house, hugged and kissed him, kissed Fatima and then returned to his car.

"We'll see you later tonight, Papa," Fatima called after him.

"*Si, Piccolina*. Enjoy. And keep him out of trouble."

"Definitely." As soon as Ali was safely inside Ismail started crying. Fatima threw her head back and moaned. "Oh! What timing."

"No, it's perfect. Do you want me to get him?" Ali picked up his bag and moved towards the stairs.

"Are you kidding?" Fatima wrestled the bag from his hand and pushed him away. "Go and sit down somewhere."

"I'm not an invalid." He sounded serious, but since she could see his dimple she knew he was playing.

She paused on the bottom step and turned around. "When I'm around, you are. Now go sit. I'll be right back with your son."

By the time Fatima returned, Ali was standing in the family room at the back of the house, looking outside at the birds playing in the backyard fountain. Fatima sat in the couch facing the window and started to nurse Ismail. "It's so peaceful watching the birds, isn't it?"

"Yes, I could do it for hours. You wouldn't imagine how much personality a bird could have or how much you could learn from them." Ali turned around. "I was thinking of building a solar-heated birdhouse, for the birds that stay in the winter. I noticed some of them on the roof trying to stay warm this past winter and the idea came to me." Ali joined Fatima on the couch. "What do you think?"

"I think that's a beautiful idea." Fatima always found new reasons to be proud of him. She knew he would have found some project to immerse himself in upon returning home. He wasn't able to work out, so Fatima knew he would have to find some way to deal with the emotions he must be having surrounding the shooting. She just hadn't thought he would delve into something so quickly. He hadn't been home for five minutes.

Ali adjusted himself in his seat and looked at his son for the first time in days. "He's changed so much already."

"I took pictures every day; morning and night." She looked down at Ismail. "Are you sorry you didn't do the slaughter for his *Aqeeqa*?"

Ali stroked Ismail's head with one finger. "No, I didn't want to delay it, and it was fitting that Papa do it." He smiled. "Maybe I'll do it for my grandson one day."

"Or your other sons." Fatima waited for Ali's reaction.

"Fatima..." Ali warned.

"Just joking!"

Ali appeared relieved. "Feed your baby. And behave yourself, or I may have to move into the guest room."

Fatima snapped her head. "Just you try it." She could see Ali suppressing a laugh. She had no reason to hold back her emotions anymore. For the first time in almost two weeks she let out a fully satisfying laugh, straight from the heart.

Chapter Thirty One

𝔍

"I can't believe a father would do such a thing, use your own daughters just to get money?" Fatima, Ali, Shawn and Rachel sat in Shawn's office discussing recent events.

"It's shocking, but true." Shawn stood in the middle of the room. It was after hours and he was dressed casually in a charcoal sweater and grey pants.

"I can't believe she wants to meet us. What for?" Fatima questioned.

"Well, I suppose she has some things to say." Shawn brushed imaginary lint from the sleeve of his sweater." Leanne had requested a meeting with Ali, Fatima and Rachel, which had been arranged at Shawn's office. When she arrived, they seated her in an armchair and waited for her to speak.

She looked so fragile, Fatima thought. She shuddered when she thought of this beautiful young woman being abused by her own father in this way. Leanne wore a jersey dress in a paisley print of blue, green and white. Like her sister, she had a beautiful head of thick dark brown curls that hung well past her shoulders. She was stunning and so sad.

"Can we get you something to drink?" Fatima offered.

"No. No, I'm fine. Thank-you for allowing me to come. I felt I owed you some kind of explanation and apology. I know that it may not be worth anything to you after what you've been through, but I felt I had to do something."

Shawn crossed his arms and leaned against his desk. Rachel sat across the room and Ali and Fatima sat together on a couch facing Leanne. They all waited patiently for her to continue.

"I never meant to harm anyone. I just went through the motions and just did what I was expected to do."

"But to lie about your child's paternity? You could have ruined Ali's and Fatima's life, not to mention your own son," Rachel said.

"I didn't know it was a lie."

Eyes darted around the room. "Explain," Shawn said, while quickly stealing a side glance at Ali to gauge his reaction. Ali didn't even flinch.

Leanne breathed deeply. "Maybe, I will have a glass of water." Immediately Shawn stood up. He went to the cooler and returned with water for Leanne. She gulped, and then started to speak slowly.

"The night of the party, Jamie had someone put something in my drink. When I started to feel sick I looked for Brigitte, but she was gone. Someone offered to help me. I don't even remember who. The last thing I remember is getting into a car. When I woke up, Jamie was with me and he filled in all the details. I didn't remember anything. I just went along with what Jamie told me had happened."

Ali's eyes darkened. "You know how ridiculous that sounds?"

Leanne hung her head. "I know. But you may have heard, I have a history of mental illness, and he took advantage of that. He had pictures and I just believed him."

"Pictures?" Shawn asked.

Leanne hung her head and her face turned deep red. Shawn looked at the others then prompted her gently. "Take your time."

"Now I realize they were doctored, but at the time I had no idea it was actually Jamie." Leanne sat with a film of moisture covering her face and arms.

Silence sat on the entire room for one full minute. "Why didn't you go to the police? If you were drugged and didn't remember anything, you must have realized a crime was committed," Fatima said.

"I was scared and so embarrassed, and Jamie and my dad kept saying that I had gone to the party with a goal and everything had worked out fine. When the director of the clinic confessed, I realized what had happened. Then, I just broke down. I couldn't take anymore. I had no clue that Jamie was actually the father of my son. Now, my father is just complaining about all the money we're not going to get."

"This is horrifying," Rachel said.

"Now, I have to do another paternity test to confirm that Jamie is really the father, and I just don't know what I'm going to do. My father is a con artist, and now my child has worse than that for a father. At least my father only hurt his own kids."

Fatima was in shock. "What could be worse than that?"

Ali cleared his throat and stood. "Excuse me, I've heard enough."

As he left the room, Fatima stood to follow him, but Shawn put his hand up. "Let him go." She sat back down and focused on Leanne.

"I have a question for you. We all live in Toronto. Why did you use a lawyer in Ottawa for this case."

"Jamie again. He had been trailing Ali and when he saw that he was making frequent trips to Ottawa he figured a lawyer from that city would be appropriate. Jamie found a lawyer that he could manipulate and just went with that."

Shawn tightened his mouth and shook his head slightly. He leaned forward and onto his feet in one smooth motion. He thanked Leanne for coming and told her that they didn't want to take any more of her time, making an effort to get her out of the office as quickly as possible.

"Frequent?" Fatima asked, ignoring Shawn's attempt to silence Leanne. "How frequent?"

"I don't know, at least once a week, I guess," she said innocently.

Fatima scratched the back of her neck through her scarf. "I see."

After Leanne's last comment, Shawn hurriedly ushered her out of the office.

After she had left, he turned to Fatima and Rachel, who had moved to stand next to him. "Fatima, you can relax, finally. You have your life back now," he said to her.

"Are you sure about that?" Fatima held the handle of the door.

"Yes, I'm sure. Listen, it's getting late. We'll have to catch up later. Tell Ali I'll call him."

When they arrived at the elevator Fatima turned to Rachel. "Can you believe that Jamie would actually do such a thing to someone?"

Rachel had a flashback to the night Jamie had confronted her on her porch, threatening to force his way into her house. She shivered and rubbed her arms. "Yes, I can."

"Oh honey," Fatima moved in and circled her arms around Rachel's waist, holding her tight. "It's over now."

Rachel rested her face against Fatima's head. "Not until he's caught."

"These flowers are dead."

"So they are." Rachel stood beside Joshua. She felt the crisp leaves and petals in her hand before they fell to the ground. These were the same flowers that were at her father's grave the last time she had been here. She wondered what had happened. She had a strange feeling of being concerned about the person who was leaving flowers anonymously. She wondered if they were ok, and if she would ever get to meet them.

Joshua and Jonah wandered through the cemetery. Rachel wondered what they could possibly find new and exciting on each visit. After a short time, Rachel was startled to hear the grass close to her crunching beneath footsteps. No one had been in the cemetery when she arrived. Her father's grave was deep into the site and there weren't too many other plots this far in.

"It's quite late to be here by yourself."

Rachel turned her head to see leather boots less than five feet away from her. She slowly lifted her gaze to see Ali standing in front of her. Relieved, she relaxed.

"What are you doing here?" she asked.

"Same thing you are, it seems. When did you start coming?" Ali kept his hands in his pocket.

"A few weeks ago." Two lines deepened between Rachel's brow. "You've been here before?"

"Sure."

Rachel couldn't hide her surprise. "When? Why?"

"From time to time. Your father was good to all of us. I was taught to remember those who have died. I never think of them as gone, just away." He stepped closer to the plot. "I usually come before I leave town or before I return home." Ali's head moved up and down. "It reminds me."

"Of what?" Rachel tilted her head. Ali had such a unique way of looking at things. She always learned something from conversations with him.

"What life is all about. What our end will be. It keeps me grounded." His eyes remained fixed on the grave.

Rachel thought about the fact that many of Ali's loved ones were also buried, but so far away that he could never visit them.

She wondered if he thought about that when he visited her father's grave. *Of course he did.*

Wanting to change the subject, Rachel asked, "You came alone?"

"No, actually I didn't." Ali stepped aside. A few metres down the hill Rachel saw Naomi standing and holding a basket with two bouquets of flowers. Stunned, Rachel didn't know what to do.

"Maybe, you could help her up the hill," Ali prompted. When Rachel walked down the hill, Ali headed to his vehicle to wait.

"Mom, it was you? Why didn't you tell me? How long have you been coming?"

"I've always come."

"But you always seemed like you were...you couldn't even stand the mention of his name."

"That was because of you. I could hear the pain in your voice. I could see how much you were suffering. I couldn't add to that."

"I couldn't imagine who had been leaving the flowers."

"Oh, that wasn't me."

Rachel was more confused than ever. "Then who?"

Naomi smiled as tears crowded her eyes. "Your father."

"What?" Rachel felt like she had been punched in the stomach.

Naomi took Rachel's arm and started walking towards her father's grave. "Months before he died we had gone to a funeral. He noticed the flowers that people kept bringing and was moved at the immense grief of the family members. He decided that after his death he wanted to give something to those who came to remember him. He arranged with the flower shop, that we always used, to have fresh flowers placed every month. It's paid for from his estate.

"Some other flower shops learned about his 'legacy of love', as they called it, and also donated so that fresh flowers could be here every week, sometimes more frequently."

Rachel pointed toward the grave. "But these flowers are old. What happened this week?"

"I called the flower shop and asked them to hold off. I wanted to bring the flowers this week," Naomi said.

Rachel was overcome with love, grief and joy. Her father had always thought of others and how he could show love to them. To think that he was concerned about the feelings of those who would visit him after his death was astonishing. She missed him even more. She hugged herself, trying to rid herself of the ache she had for him.

"Mom, I'm so sorry. It was just so hard."

"I know, Honey. I know. What changed things for you?" Naomi squeezed Rachel tightly.

"I just needed him, so I came."

"And he was here for you?"

"As always." Tears rolled down Rachel's cheeks as she thought about how long she had neglected her father, when each week there had been flowers sent by him, for her and all those who loved him.

Yes, he had always been there for her. He had always given her the strength that she needed. If only she could gather it for what she had to do next.

Chapter Thirty Two

ℑ

"What are you doing out here so early?" It was barely daylight, but Ali was in the backyard surveying the property. After putting Ismail to sleep, Fatima had come out to join him. She was still in her nightclothes and had put on her favourite *abaya* over them. It was blue and had a built in headpiece. She always kept it handy for occasions like these.

Ali looked at her sideways without turning his head. "Don't you have children to look after?"

"What do you think my mother is for?" she countered swiftly.

Ali chuckled, "Oh, you're quick this morning." Ali was naturally witty, but it had taken Fatima years of practice to be able to keep up with him."

The weather forecast had predicted a high of 27 C. Already there was humidity in the air. The sound of birds chirping, while they cooled themselves in the fountain, brought a special serenity to the backyard. Fatima took a few steps forward. "Seriously, what are you doing?"

Ali leaned forward, onto his cane. "I was just thinking about the aviary. How it would work. Where I would put it." Like all the others on the street, their home had a large backyard. None of the properties sat on less than half an acre. Ali stood between the fruit trees that were starting to get their first buds and looked around. He held a measuring tape in his hand.

Fatima sat on a nearby bench. "Don't you ever rest?"

Ali lifted his chin. "I'll rest when I am dead."

"*Inshallah.*" At the mention of Ali's death, Fatima felt chilled. The images that she fought to keep out of her mind, daily, came flooding back. The look on Jamie's face just before he pulled the gun, the sound of the shot, Ali falling on the cold sidewalk, the smell of his blood, the tortured look on his face as he fought for each breath, Rahma's screams. It was all too much.

As if just realizing what he had said, Ali turned towards her. "Fatima, I am so sorry." He approached the bench and placed the measuring tape in the back pocket of his jeans before sitting beside her.

Fatima rubbed her arms as if trying to brush away the memories. "I'm fine. If you're ok, then I guess I should be too. After all, it was your experience." She lifted her hand to scratch her face and saw that it was shaking.

Ali took her hand in his. "It's not the same as being a witness. I know that from being at the hospital with you." He pursed his lips and shook his head. "It was a careless slip. Beat me."

Fatima cracked into laughter. It was just what she needed to release the nervous energy that was building in her. So much had happened in the last few weeks. She sometimes felt that if she really thought about it all, she would be one breath away from insanity. She tried to compartmentalize each issue and only deal with what was on hand at the time.

Right now she thought about the conversation she had wanted to start with Ali the night that he had returned from Rachel's house, after Joshua's scream. She hadn't the guts to continue then, but she figured now was as good a time as any.

"Ali, I was thinking-"

"Again..."

"I'm serious. I was thinking about Rachel." She was surprised to feel her own pulse quicken.

Ali became serious. "Ok, what's up?"

"I think she needs a husband."

Ali relaxed and chuckled. "Ok."

"What do you think?"

"I think that's her business." Ali stretched his legs in front of him.

"For sure, but I think she has kind of given up hope." Fatima watched Ali carefully as he listened.

Ali shook his head. "She's too young for that."

"I'm serious."

Ali leaned back and watched Fatima intently. Fatima continued. "I think she needs someone special."

"Fine…I know some good men who want to get married. Since it seems like you're set on playing matchmaker, you can introduce them, but I'm out of it. That's not my thing."

"I don't know about that." Fatima wrinkled her nose. "She needs someone exceptional; someone who will really cherish her and be patient with her; someone who will understand her special relationship with her mom and definitely someone who will love her boys. Joshua and Jonah are a primary concern in this."

Ali stood and straightened his clothes.

"Don't you think?" Fatima pressed.

He looked at Fatima for an uneasily long time. "Why don't you ask me the real question?" he asked slowly.

Fatima answered more slowly. "I thought I did."

Ali leaned his head back and rubbed his eyes. "I don't think this is something you need to worry about."

Fatima was suddenly flustered. "Oh, I'm not worried. Not at all."

Ali half smiled. "Sure, and it's not April, and we're not in the backyard, where you are sitting and telling me how much Rachel needs a husband."

Fatima felt her cheeks heat. Ali leveled his shoulders and rested his hands on his lower back. "Listen Fatima, don't worry about it. Rachel will work herself out."

Fatima folded her hands in her lap.

"Are you satisfied with that?" she asked.

Without missing a beat, Ali replied, "Yes."

Even though she was becoming increasingly uncomfortable with the topic, she had opened it up and she could not stop until it had been thoroughly thrashed out and resolved. Although, at this point, she was no longer sure about what kind of resolution she wanted.

Fatima looked up at Ali. "What if she never gets married?"

Ali sniffed the morning air, and Fatima could see his jaw tighten. "I don't spend that much time thinking about it, Fatima. My focus is my own family."

Fatima looked at the fence that surrounded their property. Every few boards had a small stenciled pattern on it. Rachel and Fatima had spent weeks creating the original stencils and then spent the entire summer completing the boards. Rachel had complained every day, but had still been there each evening and all day on the weekends to help. Ali had complained that he had been reduced to being a single parent, but everyone had been proud of the effort when the project was complete.

There were replicas of the fruit trees planted after the birth of each child, images of the family's favourite foods and activities. Of course, there were flowers of various types. One board in the centre of the fence, at the back of the yard, held an image of a scroll with writing on it. Across the scroll lay a pen. The image represented the lists that they all had used at some time or the other to approach *Allah* with their requests.

Rachel had been a part of it all. She was definitely a part of their family.

Fatima was through with hedging around the topic. "Ali, I can see what's going on here. Can you just talk to me honestly? Just be straight with me."

Ali was taken aback. "You can see what's going on. What are you suggesting?"

"No one makes you jump like Rachel, and this thing you have with Jamie, it's more than, 'oh he's just a bad guy.'"

Ali blew out into the morning air and dropped his head. When he spoke his voice was strained. "She's our friend. I thought you wanted to help her. I thought I was doing what you wanted." He sighed deeply. "If any of this was a problem for you, you should have told me."

Fatima looked at her hands in her lap. "It just hit me all at once. I didn't really think about how I felt before."

Ali turned towards her. "What do you want me to do?"

"Tell me how you feel." The scene was becoming more emotional than Fatima had expected. She had not anticipated it unfolding like this.

When the silence was too much to bear, and the tears started to build behind her eyes, she asked point blank. "Do you love her?"

Ali moved to stand in front of the bench, directly facing Fatima. "I love *you*. I love our children, the family I have with you."

The chatter of the birds competed to dominate Fatima's and Ali's conversation. It usually happened when they spoke outside. A bird landed on a branch of the cherry tree, and a breeze blew cherry blossoms towards the pear and apple trees that Ali had planted for their children with his own hands.

"I *know* that. I don't doubt that. I never have." Fatima held her head back and blinked to hold back her tears. "That's not what I'm asking. Tell me you don't love Rachel."

Ali sat back on the bench beside Fatima, watching her eyes fill. "I don't."

Love her! Fatima screamed inside her head. "Well, what you're not saying is coming through just as loudly as what you are saying." She gave up trying to hold back her tears.

"Fatima, listen to me. I love you. I love *you*. That's all there is to it. You brought this up, but we don't have to discuss this again. We can leave this right here. If you think I'm paying too much attention to Rachel and her family, I'll stop. It's that simple. You are what's important to me. If I had known this was a problem I would have changed everything. I never meant to give you the wrong impression."

Fatima wiped her tears and breathed heavily. Birds danced in the water fountain just as they did every morning, but this was not like every other morning. Everything was different now. "I don't know what I really expected to hear from you." She sighed again. "You just staying away from Rachel is not the solution. If you start avoiding her it's going to be awkward for me. It will just remind me of why your relationship has changed with her." She wiped her cheeks and faced him directly. "This is what I want you to do. Take time and think about your feelings. Really think about what you want, and tell me honestly. Then we can put it to rest, one way or the other."

"This is nonsense. I already told you-"

Fatima stopped him with her hand. "I appreciate you trying to spare my feelings. Really, I love you for that, but this is too important for you to take lightly or brush off quickly. She is too close for us to ignore this issue. I can't continue living like we are until this is resolved."

Fatima thought about all the time they spent in each other's homes, the amount of times a week or a day that Rachel was in her house or she was in hers. If Ali wasn't at home or with his parents, for sure he was doing something with, or for, someone in Rachel's family.

Fatima continued, "I need to know how you feel about Rachel and I need to know what you intend to do about it. It's not just about you or us. She is so close to us and she is clearly in need. When you're ready to be completely transparent with me, we can talk about it again. Don't say another word until you think about it and are ready to really talk to me."

Ali leaned back on the bench. "There is nothing to resolve. I don't need time, and I don't need to think about anything. In fact, I don't want to hear anymore about this. You are my wife and this is my family. We just had a new baby and you're talking to me about Rachel? *This* is my family. I know what I want. If you don't accept that, if you don't believe that, then maybe you don't know me at all.

"Ali-"

"Ismail is crying."

Fatima could hear Ismail whimpering through the open window. She had just fed him so she knew he wasn't hungry. He would likely settle down in a few minutes. Still, Ali excused himself, under the pretense of checking on him, when Fatima refused to move.

Fatima sat wondering what she had just done. *Was she crazy?* No, she wasn't the one who had started this. What woman would create a situation like this? It existed and she was not going to hide from it. Yes, she was stirring it up, but that was better than waiting for it to boil over.

"I can't believe you just gave your husband permission to consider another woman. Did you injure your head, sweetheart?"

Nargis and her new daughter-in-law, Zahra, sat across from Fatima and Mama at the table in Mama's sunroom where they were enjoying tea and Nargis's delicious desserts. She had prepared blueberry lemon coffee cake, pecan tarts and fruit kabobs.

"Well, it is his right," Zahra said, as she forked a strawberry. Zahra and her husband had just returned from their honeymoon in Kenya. They had spent two weeks visiting relatives and touring the country, going on Safari and enjoying the breath-taking landscape.

"Spoken like a true newlywed," Nargis replied.

They all laughed. "Ali is smart. He'll make the right decision," Mama said with confidence.

Nargis lifted her eyebrows. "Well, let me tell you something. Ali is a wonderful man. Really he is, but if he wants to take his right, then you demand yours. Do you hear me? You want to be *paid* for your work in the house, for taking care of *his* children. Aren't you breastfeeding? Well, you need payment for that. Can't you ask for back pay? You already nursed three babies. Otherwise, you don't lift a finger in that house. Do you understand me?"

Fatima giggled. "I don't think any of that would be a hardship for him."

"Hurting your feelings would be," Mama said, before pouring herself another cup of tea.

"Well, that's what you get for marrying a rich man. Either you pick the poor ones or you make sure you keep his bank account low. Do you ever see me in the same outfit twice? When I'm finished with my husband, he has no money to even support a pet, much less another woman," Nargis said.

Fatima held Ismail over her shoulder and reached for the blueberry lemon coffee cake. "I just want him to be honest with me. I want to know what he's thinking."

"*You* tell him what to think! You don't *ask* them anything." Nargis shook her head. "You poor young thing. Honey, this is like choosing to eat dessert. You have already finished your dinner. You don't need dessert. You don't really want it, didn't even think about it, but since it's offered to you, you just figure, 'why not.' That's what you just did. You offered your husband dessert."

Nargis lifted her tea cup. "If my husband ever let me know he was considering such a thing, I would become such a big 'B' that he would have to rescind, Honey. Not to mention the shopping I would be doing. I would redecorate my whole house!"

"Or he could just leave you," Mama teased.

Nargis snapped her head. "With eight children? How?"

Fatima continued to eat in silence. Her thoughts drowned out the chatter. The temperature was already close to the day's high and the warm breeze wafted the scent of gardenias towards her. She inhaled deeply. She hadn't planned to discuss the issue with Ali's family, but Rahma had overheard the early morning conversation and relayed everything to her parents.

Surprisingly, Fatima felt some degree of relief at not having to carry the burden alone. She was unprepared for how intense the conversation had become and the range of emotions it had stirred in her. Had she made a mistake by bringing up the topic of Rachel to Ali? She didn't think so. It was in her face. She couldn't ignore it anymore, and she certainly was not going to wait for it to take its own turn.

What if he decided in Rachel's favour? Could she really live with it? She loved Rachel, and she was secure in her marriage. She loved Ali and trusted him to be fair. It was too late to turn back now anyway. She would just wait and see what happened. Knowing was better than not knowing. That she was sure of.

Ali had been shocked by the suggestion and even a little angry that Fatima had pushed the point, but she knew when he calmed down he would consider what she had said. He would have to. At the very least, he would wonder if he could provide, for Rachel, the stability and security of a family that she so desperately needed.

No matter what he had said to Fatima, he would think about it. She knew that.

Chapter Thirty Three

𝔍

Ali walked every day at 11 a.m. Fatima usually went with him. Sometimes, they would take the children and wear them out before lunch. Upon their return, the children would eat and then go right to sleep. Fatima and Ali would have a couple of hours of quiet time, if Fatima did not sleep at that time also.

Dana was still with them and would likely be until June when she would return to Malaysia until September. No one knew where her next project would take her. Having her mother here these few weeks reminded Fatima of how much she missed her when she was away.

It was interesting that the people Fatima loved the most were never with her on a full-time basis. She used to think that she didn't mind, but now she realized how much she hated it. She wanted love full-time, not on a part-time rotating basis.

Today, Fatima planned for the whole family to go walking. She helped the girls put on their shoes and prepared to send them outside on the porch. She hated Ali being ready before her. Watching him wait for her made her feel rushed. She would rather be early and take her time getting ready so she could relax. She opened the doors to put Ismail's stroller outside and nearly ran over Ali's father.

"Papa!" Batool shrieked and pushed past the stroller to jump into his arms.

"My sweet, you are almost getting too big for me." Papa beamed as he looked into Batool's face.

"Papa, how are you?" They all knew Ali's schedule, so Fatima knew Papa had come for a specific reason.

"I'm fine. I came to walk with Ali today. Why don't you take the kids to the park?" He reached into his pocket. "Buy them some ice cream." When Fatima hesitated, he added, "We can take Ismail. Will he be all right for about an hour?" Papa asked.

Fatima was relieved. Ismail was only weeks old and she still felt insecure when she had all the kids outside by herself. She worried about being able to manage all of them on her own. "I think that would be fine."

"What will be fine?" Fatima felt Ali standing behind her before he spoke. "*Papa, tutto va bene*?-Is everything ok?"

"*Si, Si*, I came to walk with you and Ismail today. Fatima is taking the girls to the park." Ali nodded knowingly. Fatima excused herself and walked with her three daughters down the stairs. She felt strange without her baby, but she knew he was in good hands.

Ali helped the girls get buckled into their car seats and watched as Fatima drove their van up the street. "They'll be exhausted by the time they get back," Papa said.

"That's the plan. Ready to go?" Ali asked his father.

"*Si.*"

Ali and Papa headed up the long street pushing Ismail's stroller. It had rained the night before and the ground was still wet. Beads of water clung to the buds on the trees and the fences that framed most of the neighbours' properties. The air was cool and moist. Ali wore a blue and grey fleece sweater as extra protection against the elements.

"How are plans for the aviary going?" Papa asked.

Ali rubbed his chin. "Good. It will be small. I took all the measurements, and I'll see about getting the material one day this week.

I started a few days ago, but Fatima saw me and came out to talk to me. I had to finish when she was sleeping."

"She distracted you?"

"A pleasant distraction, but a distraction nonetheless."

Papa smiled. "I always knew you two would end up married. You always acted like a married couple, even when you were kids. Your mother and I used to talk about it all the time."

Ali was surprised. "Really? I never knew that."

"Oh yes, remember how Fatima used to check up on you? Did you do your homework? Did you eat? Did you sleep? Don't be late for school."

Ali remembered. He always pretended to be annoyed, but deep down he had been pleased.

"And you used to always leave food for her." Papa pointed at Ali. "If we had something special or some treat that you knew she would like, you would leave her share because you knew she would be coming by. I think she was there almost every day. Of course, we never told her that it was from you, but she knew. She was never as happy as when she was eating that food."

"No one ever told me that." Ali imagined his parents watching this interaction and talking about them in their private moments.

"It wasn't time for you to know."

They continued up the street with Papa pushing Ismail's stroller, and waved at the neighbours as they passed them.

"Yes, we could see something special about you two. It was there from the beginning."

"All three of us were close growing up, Fatima, Rachel and me."

"You were. It was a different dynamic, though. You know what I'm talking about. You and Fatima rarely made a move without considering each other. You were like two puzzle pieces."

Ali nodded and continued to listen. Papa spoke again. "Rachel is a wonderful girl. We love her. You know that."

"Of course." Ali waited patiently for the rest of what he knew Papa had to say.

"Son, sometimes in life we have seemingly difficult decisions to make, but it can be easier if we think about the long-term

305

implications. Choose in favour of long-term benefit as opposed to the short-term."

"Yes Papa." Ali stepped to the side to avoid a large puddle.

"Marriage is an enormous responsibility, as you know. You are still a young man with a young family. You have no idea what it's like to raise children until you have *raised* children. If you are thinking about taking on more responsibility, you have to heavily consider the future implications. I understand your caring about Rachel, but understand this; it is not enough to make a good decision. You have to make the *better* decision."

"You don't think I can handle it?"

"I know you can. Do you want to? Do you need to? Those are the questions you need to answer." Papa stopped at the top of the street and turned right onto the main street, pushing Ismail's stroller. Ali followed.

"I just worry about her so much."

Rachel may have appeared needy, and perhaps now she was, but Ali knew she was more than that. He remembered the years she spent living in his home and the time they spent playing, talking and sharing with each other, especially during his teenage years when he had strategically distanced himself from Fatima because of his growing affection for her. He had always regarded Rachel as his family.

He may have done a lot for her, but she had supported him on numerous occasions too. She was always attentive, kind and thoughtful. She knew when something was on his mind, or when he was dealing with an issue, and she had a gentle persuasive way about her that allowed him to eventually open up. And, of course, she was always eager to help.

Whenever she listened you could just see the wheels turning in her head as she tried to figure out a solution to your problem. She was always eager to fix things. Ali had never allowed himself much thought as to why that may be, but she *had* made an impression on him. Because they had lived under the same roof, there was a side to him that Rachel had known long before Fatima had the opportunity to.

Ali ran his hand over his head. "Maybe I can make her life better."

"Maybe."

Ali waited and listened. He knew more was coming.

"You have always made excellent decisions. I know whatever you decide will be right, and you will have my full support." Papa's eyes held that twinkle that they did when he was feeling mischievous. "My opinion is just my opinion."

Both men laughed. "Okay Papa...let me have it." Ali put his arm around his father's shoulders. "What's your opinion?"

"You don't have to do everything. You don't have to be every-thing to everyone. There *is* a man out there for Rachel. If I thought it were you, I would tell you so." Papa lifted his hand and brushed Ali's chest with his thumb. "I would have told you already."

Ali stepped in line with his father. "What if you're wrong?" Papa's steps halted. Ali took one more step and then stopped to turn and look back at his father. Papa studied his son for a moment before asking him, "Do you think I'm wrong?"

Ali looked away, searching himself for the answer to his fa-ther's question, and then refocused on Papa's intense gaze. "There's always a first time."

They continued walking and talking about their families, Ali's recovery and his plans for his summer. Three times they stopped to talk to neighbours who were excited to see Ali out walking with his new son. When they returned home Papa hugged and kissed him as he always did. Ali knew that was the last time Papa was going to bring up the topic of Rachel. He only gave advice once. Then he left you to meditate on what he had said.

Before Papa left, he pulled Fatima aside to speak with her. As they stood on the front porch a blue jay chatted over their heads. "You've been working hard with this one."

"Yes, I never understood how people could be so attached to animals, but I do now. I think he's actually jealous. He gets like this when I speak to anyone else."

Papa went straight to the point. "Fatima, Ali has a lot to deal with, now, since the shooting. He feels like he let you down."

"What? *Me?* How?" Fatima grabbed Papa's arm.

"To be gunned down in front of your home, in front of your wife, it can really do an assault on your ego."

"Oh, yes, of course." Fatima had known Ali must have some issues. She just didn't know exactly what or how to address them. She never could have imagined this. There were several times she had seen him staring at her intently, when he thought she was unaware, but each time that she turned to meet his gaze, questioningly, he simply looked away. She never knew what to say in those moments.

"I know he wouldn't ever say anything to me, and that's why I didn't know how to deal with it," she said. "I didn't want to bring up the shooting, in case I stirred up bad memories for him."

"This is why I'm telling you. The bad memories are there. They are not going away. The thing that is most difficult for him to deal with, now, is wondering what his wife thinks of him."

Fatima put her other hand to her chest. "But I'm so proud of him. We all are so proud of him," she insisted.

"Yes, we are. Yes, we are." Papa patted Fatima's hand that still rested on his arm. "I'll leave you with that, *Piccolina*. I'm sure you can take it from here?"

"Yes, of course. Thank-you, Papa."

Dana had lunch ready when they returned. She had prepared a vegetable lasagna and salad, a favourite of the children. She also made Fatima's favourite potato rolls. While they ate, Ismail continued to sleep in his stroller.

Fatima started thinking about the time when her mother would leave. "Mom, I don't know what I'm going to do without you." Dana had not only been helpful with the children but constant company and support for Fatima.

"Don't worry about that. I'm here now and now is what matters. Just enjoy the moment." Fatima certainly had had enough practice doing that over the last few weeks. Focusing on "now" had helped to keep her marriage and sanity intact.

Dana helped Laila to eat her food. Masuma and Batool were doing well on their own. When they had finished eating Dana took the girls to wash their hands and faces and get ready for their naps. Ali and Fatima cleared the table.

Fatima stacked the plates. "How was Papa today?"

"Good. Do you know Rahma may really go to Italy?"

"I heard about it. She wants to volunteer with 'Children of Rwanda.' I think it's a great idea." Noticing Ali's scowl, she asked, "Does that bother you for some reason?" Fatima packed the dishwasher while Ali cleaned the table.

"I'm just wondering what the big attraction is."

"Are you serious? Italy in the summertime? Why wouldn't she want to go?" Fatima turned and leaned against the counter. "Your grandparents will take care of her. They're more strict than Mama and Papa. Your grandmother goes to mass every day."

"They're old. Rahma will tie them in knots." Ali threw the cloth he was using into the sink.

"So what? You want to follow her?" As soon as the words left her mouth Fatima realized how good they would sound to a protective older brother.

"Do you want to?" Ali crossed his arms.

"You can't be serious." Fatima didn't try to mask her astonishment.

"Why not? It'll be fun. The fact that I can keep an eye on her will just be a bonus." Ali raised one eyebrow.

"I don't know how much fun it will be with you in spy mode. What are you so worried about anyway?" Fatima knew how fiercely protective Ali was of all the women in his family and she certainly did not want to be a party to this mission.

"She spends a lot of time online. What if she met someone?" Ali looked fretful and Fatima wondered, with all that he had on his plate how he found time and energy to conjure up ideas about Rahma.

"In Italy? She would have told your parents, don't you think?"

Ali reached for the broom closet. "You never know. Think about a trip to Italy."

"What about your studies. I thought you were thinking about taking some courses this summer." Fatima had not mentioned it, but she had been hurt that he had gone back on what he had said about taking the summer off.

Ali looked puzzled. "No, I told you that I wasn't. I'm going to help you with the kids."

Fatima turned back to the dishes. "But you were looking at the calendar that day."

Ali sighed. "When the letter came and you reacted the way you did, I just felt confused. I thought I should focus on finishing my degree and start building another life outside of basketball, but I'm going to stick to what I had said in the beginning. This summer is for the family. Now I have to focus on recuperation and rehab anyway, so it wouldn't make sense to take any courses.

"Is that what you and Papa talked about today, Italy?" Fatima took the opportunity to steer the conversation back where she wanted it.

"No." Ali started sweeping the kitchen floor. "You know he just wanted to give me his advice."

That was exactly what Fatima had known when she saw Papa at the door. "How do you feel about that?"

"Fine. I wondered when it was coming." Ali paused and leaned on the broom. "One thing about Papa, he never disappoints." Fatima raised her eyebrows and nodded slightly. Ali became serious again. "Fatima, this is ridiculous. We don't have to drag this out. We can talk about it now."

"No, I want you to take your time. I'm only going to discuss it once."

Ali placed the broom back in the closet and brushed his hands against each other while focusing on Fatima. "Fine. What are you going to do right now?"

"I'm going to rest down here, since Ismail is in the stroller. I expect him to wake up soon anyway."

"Ok, let's go."

Ali followed Fatima out of the kitchen, across the hall and into the sitting room. When they sat, she turned to him. "Ali, I never said anything before, because I didn't want to bring up bad memories for you."

Ali's chest constricted as he imagined what she might say.

"That day of the shooting, you did such a great thing. You stood up for Rachel and protected her. If you hadn't gone outside when you did, God knows what Jamie would have done to her. Maybe that bullet would have been for her."

At the mention of the word "bullet" Ali flinched, but he kept quiet while Fatima spoke.

"Jamie might have seriously injured her or worse, and who knows if she would have recovered from that. If you hadn't been there, I certainly would never have stood by and watched that. You protected all of us, not to mention Joshua and Jonah, and I am so very proud of you. We all are. You have to know that."

In that moment everything became right in Ali's world. "Thank-you. It means a lot to hear you say that. I can't tell you how much."

"You never doubted that I felt that way, did you?"

Ali lifted his shoulders. "I'm human."

"I forget."

They shared a laugh and then Fatima stretched out on the couch. Within seconds she was sleeping. Though he was the picture of composure, joy danced wildly in Ali's chest. *She was proud of him.* Ali listened to her breathe as he watched her. She wore white jeans and a coral-coloured baby doll top. It was hard to believe that a few weeks ago he would have seen the large movements of a baby inside her as she slept. Now, that baby slept in a stroller, just a few feet away.

She had given him so much, his own family, four children, the love and support that enabled him to do what he did on a daily basis, all while keeping it down at home. As a first born child who was very close to his mother, he knew how much effort went into organizing and running a family. Yet, no matter what was on her plate, Fatima was always, first and foremost, his wife. A few minutes ago she had made him feel ten feet tall. She did all this and she was still so young. Remarkable was what she was.

His mind came back to the decision she was pushing him to make. *How had it come to this?* Whoever said women were unpredictable had made the understatement of the year…decade actually.

Ali knew what he was going to do. He knew it was the right decision, but still he worried. So many lives were at stake.

Chapter Thirty Four

ت

It was unusual for the phone to ring before 8 a.m.

"Hey Fatima, how are you?" Kirk's voice rang through the phone line.

"I'm good and you?" Fatima sat on her bed nursing Ismail.

"Great, I'm in town with Rami and Jeremy. We want to come by today. What's Ali's schedule like?"

"He'll be home until 11, and then he usually takes a walk. He comes back for lunch at noon. I don't know if he has anything planned for the afternoon." Fatima put Ismail on her knee to burp him.

"Great. We're going to jack him up today. We'll be there by 10:45 to take him out for brunch. Make sure you pack his meds, he might have a breakdown after having his schedule messed up."

"He'll be fine. He's not that rigid." Fatima loved these guys and they felt the same way about her. Kirk spent many nights with Ali when they were on the road. Jeremy was rarely to be found after a game and Rami could go either way. He often had to be reined in, and Kirk and Ali were just the ones to do it.

Fatima could hear Kirk blowing air and Jeremy and Rami adding their comments in the background. "He needs to loosen up. He just came home from the hospital and he's on a schedule already? What's wrong with this guy? I thought marriage and family would change him, but he's getting worse."

Fatima smiled into the phone. "To be fair, he has more to do now, so the scheduling is more important."

"Normal people don't move like that. Remind me never to get married."

"I didn't think you were in danger of that."

"Got that right. We'll see you at 10:45. Don't tell Ali. We want to surprise him."

"Got it."

As soon as Fatima put the phone down she heard voices at the door. She put Ismail in his bassinet and moved to the top of the stairs.

Rahma, who had been over since *fajr* time, was now blocking Rachel's entrance into the house. Rachel was coming to see Fatima before going to work. When possible, they still kept up their prayer meetings. Fatima turned back to grab her *abaya* and then rushed down the stairs.

"Hey guys, what's going on?"

Rahma turned around, furious. "I can't believe she would show her face over here." She turned back to Rachel.

Fatima had moved to Rachel's side and pulled her into the house so she could close the door. She didn't want the neighbours to hear what was happening.

"First you almost get my brother killed and now you're trying to mess up his marriage? You're sick! If you need a companion why don't you get a dog and a good security system? Just leave my brother alone!"

Rachel was speechless. With Rahma glaring at her, Rachel had difficulty finding her voice. "Mess up his marriage? What are you talking about? I would never do that." She looked at Fatima in confusion.

"Rahma's just upset," Fatima offered.

"Just upset? Everything is her fault. *Sorella*, your friend is nuts. She almost made you a widow. Now she wants Ali? Why?" She stepped towards Rachel. "So you can put him in his grave?"

Rachel recoiled. "What? Now I think you're the one who's sick. *And* you need to back up."

"Rahma, that's enough. You need to calm down." Fatima stood between the two women and turned Rahma towards the back of the house.

"Just get out of here!" Rahma screamed over Fatima's shoulder at Rachel.

Ali had heard the commotion and came in from the backyard just in time to witness Rahma's last outburst. "Rahma, stop it," he said firmly. Rahma stood shaking, with her fists balled at her side. "You need to go home."

She faced Ali, with Fatima standing behind her, but refused to meet his gaze, her chest heaving as she breathed heavily.

"Now," Ali said.

Rahma stepped away from Fatima and walked towards the front doors, where she grabbed her running shoes. She made sure to open the doors wide enough to hit Rachel on her way out.

Rachel, Fatima and Ali stood still. Rachel looked down at a dish she held in her hand, tears already clouding her vision. She was hard-pressed to remember ever feeling so humiliated. "I should leave too." She lifted the container without looking up.

"Mom made these tarts this morning. I know how much you guys love them-" Her voice cracked, and her face grew red. She dropped the dish on the bench, turned and hurried outside.

Fatima started to follow, but Ali stopped her. "I'll go. Call my parents and tell them what just happened."

Ali stepped onto the porch and called Rachel back. She was already inside her car, but she couldn't drive. She was crying uncontrollably. Sure she had not heard him, Ali advanced to the vehicle. She was oblivious to his approach.

"Pull yourself together. No one is blaming you." He placed his hands on the roof of the vehicle and leaned in. "I'm not blaming you."

"I was just called out by a 15-year-old, and she was right, completely right, except about me trying to ruin your marriage. I would never do that." Rachel sobbed her heart out. All the guilt she had felt since Ali's shooting surfaced. Rahma's outburst just confirmed what Rachel was sure everyone was thinking.

"Rahma is young and, understandably, upset." Ali paused as the physical sensations of the shooting came back to memory. He remembered the shocking impact of the bullet hitting his body and then the terrible burning. He remembered the coldness of the ground and Rahma's screams.

As Fatima had frantically worked on him, he had thought, *Are these my last moments? How do you actually know when you are dying? Is this how it feels? Can I stop this somehow?* Ali shook his head. "It was traumatic for all of us. She'll get past it. No one else is blaming you. And we know you're not trying to interfere with our marriage."

"You told me to stay inside the house. If I had listened to you none of this would have happened." Weak from crying Rachel rested her head on the steering wheel.

"You were concerned about your mother. That trumps listening to me." Ali smoothed imaginary lines on the top of the car. "What happened wasn't your fault and feeling sorry for yourself is not going to change anything."

Rachel drew in deep breaths to steady herself. "With all the other stuff she was saying, I don't know what you guys are thinking of me." She wiped her face, being careful to avoid looking at Ali. "I don't want you or Fatima to think you can't trust me."

Ali nodded slowly. "Of course we trust you. Nothing has changed. We'll talk to Rahma later."

Ali leaned off the car with one hand and glanced at the house. He knew that Fatima would be close by. He called her name and when she appeared in the doorway he asked her to bring a glass of water for Rachel. He turned back to Rachel. "Don't worry about me and Fatima. We're solid."

Rachel looked up at him. His eyes were so reassuring that she relaxed instantly.

When Fatima arrived with the water, she accepted it gratefully. "I am so sorry about all that in your house."

"Everyone is emotional these days. We'll talk to her later." Fatima leaned against the door.

"That's what Ali said." Rachel inhaled deeply. After drinking half of the water she handed the glass back to Fatima. "Ok, I'm heading off to work now." Ali and Fatima stepped back. "Another drama filled day with Rachel." Rachel tried to lift the sides of her mouth.

Ali moved forward and put his hand on the open window. "Rachel, stop talking like that. Stop thinking like that. There is nothing drama filled about Rachel."

Rachel looked straight ahead. "You're right. Thanks. You guys have a good day."

"You too." Ali and Fatima said in unison. They stood together in the driveway and watched Rachel drive away.

Ali turned to his wife. "All this before 8:30? I'm starting to think I could retire and film a reality show around here."

"Well, put me on a plane, honey. It's enough living through it. I don't want to be able to watch it over and over again."

"I'm with you on that one."

At 10:45, on the dot, the doorbell rang. Ali was surprised but thrilled to open the door and see Kirk, Jeremy and Rami on his doorstep.

"Park your running shoes. We're taking you out," Jeremy said.

"After we see Ismail. Where is he?" Rami stepped through the doorway. On cue, Fatima brought Ismail and placed him in Rami's arms.

"*Bismillahi Rahmani Rahim. Allahumma salli ala Muhammadin wa ali Muhammad,*" he said as he lifted the baby. "Poor kid, he looks just like his dad."

"No way, I'm seeing Papa in there." Jeremy looked over Rami's shoulder.

Fatima interjected. "They're related, so I'm sure it's a mixture."

Kirk patted Rami's shoulder. "We have to get going. We have reservations." Then he turned to Fatima. "Fatima, does Ali have a nap time?"

Everyone laughed, including Ali. "No, he can go all day long," Fatima replied.

"Too bad. We were hoping to mess that up too," Jeremy said.

"Mrs. Abati, don't wait up for him. We are keeping him out late." Kirk bowed in Fatima's direction while Rami handed Ismail back to her.

"No problem. Just keep him safe," Fatima said. "Oh, you can't leave without seeing Mama," she added.

"Done did it. We stopped there before we came over here," Jeremy said.

"Let's go. Let's go." Kirk motioned impatiently with his hand.

After the men filed out of the house Fatima closed the doors and leaned against them. It was a beautiful sunny day and she was going to let her children spend the rest of the morning in the backyard while she watched them from inside the house, curled up against her mother.

"How was your day?" Naomi had just finished making dinner and was ensuring that everything was cleaned up and put away. She had a church meeting and would be gone for the rest of the night.

"Besides Rahma bawling me out in front of Fatima and Ali, I'd say it was pretty good." Rachel sat on one of the kitchen stools and watched her mother work. Now that Naomi's eyesight had improved, she took longer to do everything. She was so used to feeling her way around that now couldn't find anything. Yet, she refused help. She insisted on learning on her own.

"Yes, I heard about that. I'm sorry, Baby."

"I'm fine. I guess it's understandable. He's her brother. She loves him."

"We all do." Naomi dropped her sponge and moved closer to Rachel's seat.

Rachel sighed heavily. "Yah."

Naomi let Rachel's last sentiment hang in the air between them. After careful consideration, she said what was on her mind. "You don't have to deny your feelings. Just accept them for what they are. Give yourself permission to feel. Find the lesson that feeling or experience is trying to teach you so you can move on. After you have learned the lesson, you no longer need the experience. Sometimes, the more you fight something the stronger it gets."

Rachel twirled her earring in silence.

"Ask yourself. Are you prepared to act on your feelings? If not, just feel it, accept it, and then shelve it. There are many people in this world, ready and available to accept your love. Once you find your own, it will hurt less."

"Sure, Ma."

Naomi patted her leg. "Things are coming together for you. You're finding yourself again. Your swim team is getting set to break more records. I can see the old you emerging."

"Really? Who's that?" Rachel cracked a walnut from the bowl of nuts Naomi always had on the kitchen table and tossed her hair over her shoulder.

"The Rachel I know, the one I see now, is vivacious, full of life and fun. She is ambitious, talented and strong. She is loving and kind, and she is fiercely loyal to the ones she loves. I'm happy you're coaching. You have a lot to offer those girls."

Rachel smiled when she thought of the girls on the team. "I do love it."

"Tracy called today. She said she met Coach Corlis and she really likes her. She's going to start training with her in a few weeks. She was so excited. She bubbled right through the phone."

Rachel sat up. "That's amazing. I'm so happy she's going to do it. There's no reason she can't make the Olympic team."

Naomi pursed her lips. "And finally that Jamie is out of our lives. I don't know what you ever saw in him. If your father had been alive..."

Rachel scoffed. "I think about that a lot. Actually Mom, I never saw anything. He saw something in me. It just took me this long to finally shake him."

"Well, I'll tell you this. Now that I am getting my footing back, he better know, if he comes around trying to cause trouble again, he will have me to deal with."

Rachel smiled. She completely related to her mother's feelings. When you let someone take a little of your power they would never stop until they took all. There had to be a time when you were ready to stand up, come what may. She was definitely there.

Too bad it had taken nearly loosing Ali for her to arrive.

Naomi moved forward and stroked Rachel's cheek. "I can hear my ride is here." Naomi kissed Rachel. "Love you. Lock up."

Rachel relaxed in front of the TV while Joshua and Jonah played upstairs. She felt nervous hearing them tumble and jump around on the floor. Sometimes she swore they would come right through the ceiling.

When things became quiet for a while, she figured she better go check on them. That was usually a sign they were in some sort of trouble.

"Josh! Jonah!" Rachel called as she climbed the stairs.

"Yes Mommy," Joshua answered her. By the shakiness in his voice she figured that her guess was right, they were in trouble. At the top of the stairs she could see their bedroom door was open. As she got closer she saw them crouched against the wall huddled together. They were scared.

"It's ok, just tell me what happened." Before they could answer, Rachel heard the floor boards creak. She knew she hadn't moved. A cold feeling started in the pit of her stomach before she straightened her back, preparing herself for what was coming. By the time she heard his voice, she was ready.

"Rachel, how nice to see you."

Rachel whipped around to see Jamie standing less than two feet away from her. "What are you doing here?"

"Who me? Oh, I'm going to kill you," he said calmly. "Don't worry. I'll make it look like an accident."

Jamie flexed his hands that were covered in black leather

gloves. Rachel had to think quickly. She could hear her children sobbing. They used to scream and cry when Jamie fought with her, but not this time, they were completely broken now. She stepped back far enough so she and Jamie would not block the doorway to the children's room. At least they could run. They would need to go get help.

With one lunge Jamie was on her, his hands forming a vice around her neck. She knew he meant it. He was going to kill her. She could feel him pressing his thumbs deep into her neck. She started to feel dizzy. She knew she would pass out in seconds and that would be the end. "Too bad you won't remember any of this. We're going to have fun." Jamie smiled.

He was going to kill her. He was going to kill her in front of her children. If he didn't kill her he was going to show them that their mother was weak. She couldn't take care of them. She couldn't protect them because she couldn't protect herself. She knew that if she lived through this ordeal she could never face her children again.

That was what he wanted. He wanted to break her, destroy her in the eyes of her children and reduce her to the garbage that he had been telling her she was for years. *Never*. She would never let it happen.

He was the criminal. He was the abuser. He was the one that had come from the dysfunctional family and allowed his past to define his future. He was the one who choose the low road all the time and refused to be better than what he was now. That was not her. Not Rachel.

She was smart, talented, beautiful and strong. She had good friends and a loving family. She had Ali and Fatima who would give their lives for her. She had two beautiful boys who loved her, depended on her and were huddled against a wall, sick with fear, broken, crying, with no one to help them. They were watching their mother, their lifeline, being abused and threatened with death. This was not going to happen. She was going to come through for them.

Rachel decided in that moment, just as her head felt like it was going to explode with the pressure, that she was going to die fighting. The last memory her boys would have of her would not be a scared woman being terrorized by this demon, but a lioness who would put down her life for the sons she loved so much.

As Jamie pushed her backward over the railing, she held onto his hands that were around her neck. It was now or never. Rachel curled one foot around the railing behind her, let go of Jamie's hands and held onto his shirt with her left hand while pulling her right hand back. She positioned her fingers and aimed right for his eyes. He roared and loosened his grip on her neck. She had hit it.

Jamie, searing with pain, staggered backward. That was all the time she needed. She brought her foot up, aiming to get him between the legs. He couldn't see well, but he must have anticipated that move, because he shifted just in time. He was mad now. She had to act before he came back to himself.

She slammed her fist against the side of his head. When he buckled, he grabbed her. As they fell, Rachel brought her fist down on his collarbone with all the force in her body. She imagined her hand going right through him, straight to the ground. Her goal was to split him in two. *Crack!* She had him now.

Jamie's left arm hung limp at his side. Rachel pounced on him, causing both of them to tumble to the ground, and started beating his face. She slammed his nose upward with the bottom of her palm and dug her knee into his solar plexus, making sure to lean to side of his broken collarbone. Jamie howled and tried to flip her over, but he was hurt, his face was covered with blood, and she was a mother on a mission. She wasn't giving him an inch.

She had trembled when she felt his nose turn to mush under her hand, and the blood was making her stomach roll, but she couldn't stop.

She screamed at her boys, "Run! Go to Auntie Fatima's." She prayed to God that Fatima was home. *Didn't she have a doctor's appointment today or was that tomorrow?* It was late. She must be home by now. Could the boys cross the street? She had never let them do that before. The road wasn't that busy, but they were only four and five years old. *Oh God help me!* She cried inside her mind.

She continued to beat Jamie, pummeling fist after fist into his head. He continued to flail his hand, trying to block her hits or grab hold of her with the one arm he could move, but she was loose. Each fist came down as payback for years of pain and frustration, all the hurt he had caused her, all the tears she had shed, all the humiliation she had suffered, the fear she had lived with, all her shattered hopes and dreams, and Ali, what he had done to Ali.

She knew she had let out enough on Jamie. He was barely able to move now. He just moaned in pain, but she feared if she stopped he would overpower her and kill her. What was she going to do? Where were the boys? "Oh God help me!" she cried out loud this time.

Just then she heard Fatima's voice. "Rachel! Rachel!"

"Help me!" she screamed.

Fatima rushed up the stairs with a phone in her hand. "Stop! You're going to kill him!" Rachel felt Fatima pulling her off of Jamie. *Thank God*. There was no way she could have stopped. She was on auto pilot.

"We've already called 911." Fatima returned to the phone to give an update.

Rachel looked around. Her hands were covered with blood, as was her shirt and face. Fatima was on the phone again. "We need an ambulance at 108 Greenlane Court."

Joshua and Jonah stood, wide-eyed, at the bottom of the stairs. Rachel ran down to meet them. She bent to meet them at eye level.

"How did you cross the street?"

"We held hands and looked both ways," Joshua said.

Tears came to her eyes as she looked into the faces of her innocent boys. "How did you know to do that?"

"Uncle Ali taught us." She squeezed her eyes shut, causing tears to stream down her face.

"Mommy, did you kill Daddy?" There was a flicker of excitement across Joshua's face.

"No, no, I hope not." Rachel was sure she saw disappointment in Joshua's eyes.

"But you got him good?" Jonah asked.

"Yes, I got him good." Rachel couldn't help but giggle. The pride she felt was reflected in her sons' faces. The boys started to smile, then they started to giggle and then the giggling turned into uncontrollable laughter. They were happy. Rachel laughed too. The three of them sat at the bottom of the stairs laughing hysterically.

"Rachel." She was snapped back into the moment by Fatima's serious tone.

"The boys should go back to my house. My mom is there, and I'm going to call Mama to come home and stay with them too." It was Thursday night and Mama and Papa were at the *masjid*. "I'll take them and be right back." As she passed by Rachel, she whispered. "The police are on the way."

"For what?"

"Someone has been assaulted."

The realization of what she had done finally sank in and Rachel suddenly knew the meaning of "blood ran cold." When Fatima returned Rachel said, "I have it on tape."

"Have *what* on tape?"

"After the shooting, I had cameras installed around the house."

Fatima held Rachel's shoulders. "Don't say anything about the tapes until Shawn gets here. He's on his way. Actually, don't say anything, at all, until you talk to him about it. *In private*." Fatima ran up the stairs to check on Jamie. She let him know the ambulance was on its way and he should try to stay still.

Rachel could hear his whimpering which was soon drowned out by the sirens of the approaching emergency vehicles. She wondered about the boys seeing all of this from across the street.

No, Fatima would have put them in the basement to play.

Fatima returned and stood beside Rachel while she spoke to Dana on the phone. "Don't worry, the kids are in the basement. They won't see anything," she reassured Rachel.

Rachel was happy to hear her boys were safe and felt relief to see Shawn arriving seconds after the police had pulled into the driveway.

Chapter Thirty Five

J

"Girl, you really messed him up." Shawn was obviously impressed. "I may have to rethink hiring you. Never mind if we put a file in the wrong place."

Fatima squeezed Rachel tightly. Ali's eyes gleamed with pride. "I always knew she had it in her, but I was beginning to doubt my teaching abilities."

Shawn shook his head. "If you were her teacher, I'm telling you right now, you could make a fortune. This woman has skills."

"And heart," Ali added.

The ambulance had taken Jamie away, and the police had completed their questioning. Shawn had refused to let Rachel say anything except that Jamie had attacked her. He was referring her to his associate who specialized in domestic abuse cases, in the event that Rachel had to go to trial.

"It may not come to that, but just to be on the safe side."

They all stood around in Rachel's home. Naomi had not returned from church yet, and Fatima had wanted to help Rachel clean up before she got there. They didn't want to alarm her more than was necessary. They had all waited while Rachel had showered and put her sons to bed.

"Are you going to be all right sleeping here tonight?" Fatima asked.

"Of course. I think, for the first time in a long time, I will sleep really well," Rachel answered.

Shawn stepped towards the door. "I better get going. Rachel, here's my home number and my personal cell. Call me anytime." He handed Rachel a card.

"Thank-you. I really appreciate that." Rachel took the card and placed it in her pocket.

"Good night, people. You're all too exciting for me." Shawn headed outside with Ali following him.

"Shawn, can you come over sometime within the next few days? I need to talk to you about something."

Shawn stopped short of stepping off Rachel's porch. "Sure, what is it?"

"It can wait until I see you. It's nothing urgent, but still important."

Shawn searched Ali's face for a hint of what he may want to talk about but found nothing. "Sure. How is Saturday morning, around 10?"

"Perfect, I'll be waiting."

That night after Rachel checked on her boys and ensured Naomi was sleeping peacefully, she lay awake in her bed for a long time. She kept replaying the events of the evening like a movie in her mind.

Jamie had intended to kill her. She was sure of it. He would never accept her rejection of him. The fact that she had put a restraining order against him and filed for sole custody was a slap in the face. He wanted to make her pay. He hadn't changed much since he was a teenager.

He had come from an average family with hard-working parents. He had one older brother who was a record producer in

Vancouver. Rachel had been surprised that his family didn't take more interest in her sons. They did seem happy whenever they saw them, but never called or took the initiative to visit. They left the contact up to Jamie.

Jamie had always played the tough guy. He would fight at the drop of a hat, but he was lazy in other areas. He never wanted to work for anything, not grades or money. He just wanted everything easy.

She thought about the fight she had given him. What had made this time different from all the others? Why was she able to fight back now but not all the other times? She had always had the physical ability. She had the training and skill. Ali had made sure of that. So what was the hitch? *Fear*. All the other times, she had let fear overpower her. She had always been afraid of what Jamie might do to her. He might hurt her, or her children might wake up, or Naomi might find him in the house, on the many occasions he had forced his way in.

In the past she had been paralyzed by fear. She had even feared hurting him or killing him, then having to face the consequences herself. This numbing fear had controlled her, and had given Jamie all the power, allowing him to control her.

But tonight she had known she was going to die. She had no doubt about Jamie's intention. All the other fears had paled when she was staring into the face of death. The decision she made to die fighting had propelled everything into motion.

Naomi had always told them not to have fears. Until now Rachel had not realized how debilitating fears were and how liberating putting them aside would be. Imagine, she could have kicked Jamie to the curb years ago. *Literally*. She laughed out loud. *He must be mad as all hell*. She didn't care. She felt like a champion.

Rachel looked around her room. She had wanted to make changes years ago, but had always put it off. Tomorrow she would start. She would take down the wallpaper and start looking for new furniture. She definitely needed an updated room. She felt like she had just broken out of a box. She wanted everything in her life to reflect that.

She looked at the card she had held in her hand since entering her bedroom and removing it from her pocket. *Shawn's home number and private cell*. She already had his office number and cell number that he used for business. She didn't even want to think about why he had offered her these numbers now. She really didn't have a lot of experience reading men. Besides Jamie, the only other man she had ever been close to was Ali, and he was definitely safe.

What could Shawn's intentions be? She knew he had been Ali's friend for years, but didn't know much about him personally. Ali would never have a close friend that wasn't a decent person, of that she was sure. Fatima wouldn't have encouraged Rachel to get to know him if he were treacherous. Still, it was hard to feel certain.

"Come on Rachel, he wouldn't have made the gesture in front of Ali and Fatima if he had ill intentions." She directed her statement to the teddy bear that always sat on her bed. Shawn knew their standards.

Rachel remembered what Shawn had said when he gave her the card. *Call me anytime*. "Let's see if he meant it."

Rachel picked up her phone and dialed his home number. She hated calling people on their cell. You never knew where they were or what they were doing and she always felt like she might be interrupting something. Not that she might not be interrupting something now, but he *had* told her to call. "You're thinking this through too much. You just stared into the eyes of a killer. What's a phone call?" she asked Teddy.

She wondered if Shawn had call display. She knew a few people who still didn't. As soon as he answered the phone, she knew the answer.

"Rachel."

"Yes." She tried to keep her voice steady.

"Are you ok?" She could almost see him coming to attention.

She had to swallow before she could speak. "Yes, I'm fine. You said I could call anytime...I was just testing." She held her breath waiting for his response.

A slow, deep chuckle melted all her fears. "Did I pass?"

"I'm not sure yet." She sat up in her bed and held Teddy for support. "Did I disturb you?"

"Not at all, I was just reading and watching a movie."

"You can do both?" Poor Teddy, Rachel was twisting his ear into a tight knot.

"The movie is just for background noise, to keep me company."

For the second time, while talking to Shawn, she felt a tug on her heart strings. It sounded like such a lonely way to spend your time. "Do you usually stay up this late?"

"Often. I catch up on sleep on the weekends, if I need to. Otherwise, I boost myself with caffeine.

"It must be difficult to get up in the morning." Rachel was starting to see the value of Ali's strict scheduling.

"I don't need that much sleep, and a cold shower usually does the trick. It's also good for the circulation."

"Yes, but you should alternate hot and cold water." She hoped she didn't sound too brazen.

"So you know about hydrotherapy? Why am I not surprised?"

"My best friend is a health guru who likes to share information." Rachel was feeling more relaxed with each sentence.

"Lucky for us." Shawn's voice was so soothing. Or was that just because it was deep into the night? "How about you?" he continued. "How are you feeling right now?"

"Pretty good." Rachel smiled when she recalled why.

"You should be proud of yourself for what you did tonight. Your sons are lucky to have you as their mother."

"My boys were there. I had no choice."

"We always have choices. What you did tonight was awe-inspiring."

Rachel could not remember the last time she had had a conversation like this with anyone, but talking to Shawn seemed like the most natural thing in the world, and she felt like she could go on for hours.

"Well, Shawn I don't want to keep you. You must have missed a chunk of your movie by now."

"I paused it when I saw your number."

Why did that make her so happy?

"Listen, I'm glad you called, and Rachel, you can feel free with me. I never had a problem taking tests."

Rachel was relieved Shawn was not able to see her at that moment, because she could not wipe the silly grin from her face after hearing his last comment. "I hope you don't think I was forward in calling you this late."

"I'm the one who told you to call. That would make me the forward one."

Okay, I need to get off this phone right now! "Thank-you Shawn, for everything. Good night.

"Good night, Rachel.

Rachel put down the phone and almost jumped out of her skin. She had never called a man before. Ever. Well, she didn't plan to make it a habit. She was just testing. He had seemed sincere enough. Not that she was the best judge when it came to the character of men.

"That's not true," she said, shaking Teddy. She had not been that into Jamie. Yes, he had been attractive and fun, certainly cool and popular in some circles, but she had known he wasn't long-term material.

Even when she was a teenager, on first meeting any man, she would always imagine him as a potential husband and father of her children. If he didn't meet the grade, she would dismiss him, no matter how appealing he was.

Jamie had not measured up. She would never even have spent any time with him if he hadn't been so persistent. She had heard about relentless people, but had never met one before or after Jamie. He never backed down.

After the boys were born, she kept hoping that he would change, grow, anything that would make her dream of giving her sons a family, a reality. He had potential and Rachel had felt it was her personal responsibility to help him reach it. Her sons deserved that. They had not chosen their father, she had. She owed them her best effort.

She had grown up in a two parent family. All her parents' friends, relatives and associates were couples. That was all she knew. She just couldn't wrap her head around being a single mother. She couldn't give her sons less than what she had had. *Wasn't each generation supposed to do better?*

As time went on and Jamie showed more of his deviant side, Rachel withdrew more and more. Each rejection was met with abject hostility and more force. The more she pulled away, the more he pushed forward. He was like a spoiled child who threw a temper tantrum when he didn't get what he wanted. He had no idea how to handle his emotions, and Rachel had no idea how to handle him.

Most times she would give in. It was just easier than fighting. She had grown up in a peaceful home. The kind of arguments and fights that Jamie introduced were alien and unnatural to her. She shuddered at the memories. Each time she promised herself it would be the last.

Finally, after years of battling with herself, the last time had come. He had bulldozed his way into her life, and she had allowed it because of her weakness. She was over that now.

She had judged Jamie correctly. She just hadn't acted on what she knew. She had judged Ali correctly too. She always knew that he was good. So she *was* a good judge of character, and Shawn was good. She kissed Teddy and drifted off into the most peaceful sleep she had had in years.

Over the next 24 hours the transformation in Rachel was evident. She got up extra early Friday morning and went jogging, and then she went to Fatima's house for a prayer meeting. Her list was getting shorter and shorter. It seemed that each time she looked at it there was something else to cross off. She asked Fatima if she could use her weight room sometime, around Ali's schedule, of course.

"Sure. He usually works out in the morning, so if you don't mind using it in the evening, that's fine."

"Can I borrow Dana for a few hours tonight? I need to take down the wallpaper in my room."

"Really? You've had that forever." Fatima was visibly excited.

"I've wanted to change it for a while. I'm pumped now. Hey, do you want to go shopping on the weekend? I'm looking for new bedroom furniture."

"I'd love to. Ali is meeting with Shawn on Saturday, so we can go then." Fatima's eyes sparkled.

"Great, I'll see you later and thank-you so much for everything. I couldn't ask for a better friend."

Fatima looked forward to the opportunity to shop for Ismail and herself. She hadn't bought anything new since his birth. She laughed to herself when she remembered Nargis's comments about keeping the men poor. She wondered if men had any idea how calculating women could really be.

On Saturday morning Rachel called early to remind Fatima to be ready. She wanted to be at the stores when they opened. She had worked late into the night, cleaning her walls, and wanted to pick new paint as well.

"Don't worry, I'll be ready." Fatima pulled the pillow over her head to muffle her conversation so she wouldn't wake Ismail.

"What are you planning to buy today?" Ali asked from across the room.

"I didn't even know you were up here." Fatima put the phone back in place. "I'm not sure. Are you worried?"

"No…" Ali answered slowly, while moving towards her. "I was actually thinking about all the walking you would have to do. Are you sure you're up to it?" He stopped at the edge of the bed.

"I feel good, but I'll rest if I need to." Fatima had continued yoga up until giving birth and now did two or three poses each day to help with her post partum recovery. "So, what are you and Shawn meeting about today?" She shook her tousled hair out of her face and reached onto her dresser for a claw-clip to secure it on top of her head.

"Men stuff." Ali turned around and headed toward the closet.

"Sounds interesting." Fatima sat up and folded her legs beneath her.

"I expect it will be."

When Shawn arrived at 10, Rachel was right behind him. She yelled to Fatima, "Honey, we're *late*. The stores are opening now!"

"Ok, ok, I'm ready." When Fatima lifted Ismail's car seat, Shawn immediately took it from her and walked her to Rachel's car.

When Shawn returned to the house, Ali was waiting for him at the door. "Do women always look that happy when they're going shopping?" Shawn asked Ali.

"It depends on how much they have to spend." Ali was amused by the worried look on Shawn's face. "Take my foolish advice, save as much as you can now. After marriage, it's a whole different world."

Ali led Shawn to the library, behind the staircase leading upstairs. The room was lined with books and had two huge full length windows that looked out on the backyard. It was sunny, like most rooms in the house and decorated with white furniture and soft colours. The walls were painted a light blue.

"Sit. Make yourself comfortable." Ali pointed to a padded swivel chair.

"I haven't been in this room in a while. Should I be nervous?" Shawn sat and ventured a smile which Ali did not return.

"I don't want the girls to come looking for me." Ali sat across from Shawn with a desk between them. "I'm going to be straight forward. I want to talk to you about Rachel."

"Is there a problem?" Shawn lifted his hand as though to loosen his tie. When he didn't find one, he simply ran his hand down his chest, smoothing the black pin striped shirt he wore over black jeans.

"How do you feel about Rachel?" Ali asked him, leaning back in his chair.

Shawn answered cautiously. "I like her. She's nice."

"Nice? Come on, Man. Ice cream is nice. We're talking about a woman here." Ali let his hands slide across the edge of the desk.

"Maybe, if I knew exactly where you were going with this, I could be more specific."

Ali straightened his arms and pushed away from the desk. "Rachel is very special to me, and I want what's best for her. I get the feeling you may be interested in her, and I think that may be a good thing. I want to know what your intentions are. Specifically."

Shawn didn't even think about not be being straight with Ali. He knew how Ali was when it came to women. He was serious about protecting them. He never accepted any kind of insolence in his presence. Maybe that's why he had so many of them in his life or vice versa.

Shawn brought his hands together. "I like her. I would like to get to know her better."

"I can tell you everything you need to know. She's beautiful, as you can see, smart, ambitious, loyal to a fault, caring, generous. You've been in her house. You know her family and friends."

Shawn put his hand up to stop Ali. "Ok, what else can you tell me about her? What about this guy Jamie? Do you think she's over him?"

Ali scoffed. "She beat him to sickness. What do you think?"

Shawn shook his head. "I've seen a lot of strange things in court. Believe me, that doesn't necessarily mean anything."

"So what? You think she's crazy or something?" Ali was immediately defensive.

"Not at all, but she has a long history with him, and they have two kids. Do you really think she's finished?"

"Yes, I do. I think she's wanted to be for a long time. She's just soft-hearted, and he took advantage of that. I think with the right kind of support, she can easily move forward. Look, she has every quality you could possibly want in a woman. The only question mark is you." Ali always was a straight shooter.

Shawn stared at Ali. "Fine, you're telling me all these incredible things about her. Tell me some of her faults."

Ali straightened in his chair. "She's impulsive, she tends to act first and think later. Other times she thinks too much. She tends to live in the past...she's a risk taker for sure. Not that that's all bad..." Ali was silent for a moment. "...and she doesn't know her true value."

Shawn cleared his throat and looked away. "Ali, don't worry man, everything is cool." Shawn gestured with his hand and then rested it on his knee.

Ali got up, walked around the desk and leaned back on it, all the while keeping eye contact with Shawn. "Nothing is 'cool' here. Rachel is our family, so hear what I'm saying. She doesn't need a *boyfriend* or a *playmate*, so if you don't know what you're doing then *next*."

Shawn could feel the tension building in the room. He held up one hand. "Ali, you know me. I didn't mean anything like that. Calm down."

Ali knew that Shawn was a decent man. And he knew he would be a good match for Rachel. He wouldn't be having this conversation with him otherwise. But when it came to Rachel he was protective. They had been friends since childhood, and he had seen her go through so much pain. "She's been through a lot. I don't want to see her hurt anymore."

"I'm clear on that. Really. I wouldn't hurt Rachel. Ali, you're acting like you don't know me." It was Shawn's turn to be irritated. "Anyway, she's stronger than you think."

Ali raised an eyebrow. "You think you're telling me something I don't know?"

"Just give her some room, she'll be fine. I know she's vulnerable right now. She needs time. I understand that."

Ali became pensive. "I don't think she needs that much time. What she needs is a good man, one that will make a good husband. If you're not thinking along those lines then just shuffle on along." Ali's usually soft, warm eyes were severe and chilly.

Shawn thought about all he had just heard and then stared at

Ali for a hard minute. "You're in love with her."

Ali came to his feet and walked towards a window. "She's my sister. I want what's best for her, that's all."

"Bro, I'm not asking you, eh? I know it wouldn't be acceptable for you to give me any other answer." Shawn inhaled sharply. "Listen, I get it. Rachel is special to you, so if I'm not serious then leave her alone, right?"

"Right." Ali kept his gaze outside while he leaned on the window sill.

Shawn cracked his shoulders and leaned back in his chair. "I'm serious."

Ali turned around. "Do you mean it?"

"Yeah, it gets lonely in that downtown condo." He was clearly trying to lighten the mood with a joke.

Ali pulled a chair closer to Shawn and sat down. "She has two sons."

"I noticed."

"And some baggage."

Shawn shrugged. "I'm strong."

"She won't leave her mom."

"You didn't leave yours. Fatima still puts up with you."

Ali's face finally cracked into a smile.

"Suburbia looks good on you. I could try it."

"*Try* it?" Ali tilted his head.

"I could do it. For Rachel I would do it. I kind of like this village thing you guys have going on here. I think I would fit right in. You need another man around here anyway." Shawn watched as Ali lowered his gaze, completely lost in his thoughts.

Ali looked up. "What if she doesn't want to have any more children?" He watched Shawn closely for his response.

"If things get that far, I guess it's something we would have to talk about. It's been years since I've met a woman as dynamic as Rachel. If I had her and Joshua and Jonah, then I would consider myself fortunate."

"Don't play. I'm serious." Ali rubbed his temples to relieve the pressure he was feeling in his head. He couldn't imagine what it would be like facing the men that would be interested in his daughters. This was pure punishment.

"So am I. If we are meant to be together, with or without more children, that's how it will be. She has two. If she doesn't want any more, I'll deal with that."

Ali's face reverted to the tender expression that he so often wore with those dear to him, and his eyes revealed the deep emotion he was feeling at that moment. "Could you love her?"

Shawn smiled so naturally that Ali could have predicted his response. "With ease."

"And be faithful to her?"

"Of course I would."

Ali believed him. "Ok."

Shawn reached over and put his hand on Ali's shoulder. "Don't worry. I'll handle her with care. I wouldn't even consider it otherwise."

Ali exhaled and rubbed his hand over his head. He felt like he had just unveiled a precious heirloom, all the while worrying if it would be damaged or not.

"Ali, I have a question for you."

Ali lifted his head.

"Two questions actually. Can you let her go? And if things work out, can you be happy for me? For us."

Ali realized that he had been playing the role of surrogate husband and father to Rachel's sons. He would indeed have to let go and step back if Shawn entered the picture. Ali's smile was automatic. "Yes. And if you stand by what you just said to me, I'll be happy for you and even happier for her."

It was Shawn's turn to challenge. He leaned back in his chair and swiveled. "What if she's not interested in me?"

"You have to figure that one out. Can't help you there. I already have my wife."

"I hope you realize how lucky you are," Shawn said, with sincerity.

"Now more than ever." Ali absorbed his own words and thought about how much Fatima meant to him, and how grateful he was that she had pushed them all to this point. He could never have expected things to end the way they had, but he could not say he was disappointed. "Now more than ever."

Chapter Thirty Six

𝕴

When Fatima returned from shopping with Rachel, Ali was on the front porch, reciting verses from the *Holy Quran*, with Masuma, Batool and Laila. Each girl competed to outdo the other and gain their father's most coveted pleasure.

Fatima lifted Ismail out of the car before Ali noticed her. His voice never failed to have a mesmerizing effect on her. She could have listened to him into eternity. When she stepped onto the porch she could see that Ali and the girls had previously been playing a game of marbles.

"How was the meeting with Shawn?" she asked, when Ali paused and looked up at her, breaking the spell.

"Perfect." Ali was obviously pleased. She had missed seeing his dimple this week. "And your shopping?"

"Do you have to ask? The trunk is full. I'll bring the bags in later." She kissed the girls, who had crowded around her to "coo" and "aah" at Ismail. She actually had to fan them away. "They're acting as though they've never seen him before."

Ali sat up. "It's been a few hours. You know how they are when they go through withdrawal."

"I'm starving. I'm going to find something to eat." Fatima turned and entered the house.

After more than an hour, she returned to find her family right where she had left them. She watched them for a while before clearing her throat.

"You have a son, too, you know," she teased.

Ali stood up and moved to stand in front of Fatima. He stroked Ismail's tender head. "I know, but right now I don't have what he needs."

"Oh? Is that because he can't run and jump?" Fatima looked up at Ali.

Ali lowered himself into a chair and extended his hands to receive Ismail. "You know I don't care about those things." He kissed Ismail's forehead, his cheeks, his nose and then his little chin.

Fatima took the seat next to him. "No? Mr. Professional Athlete? It's just your whole life."

Ali looked at Fatima, searing her with his eyes. "*You* are my whole life. Everything else is just a means to an end."

Fatima held his gaze for a few seconds. She didn't doubt that he meant every word of what he had just said. She could hear the songs of the birds, as they bounced from branch to branch, mixing with the laughter of her daughters. Everything else was still, as she basked in the bliss of this moment. She was completely comforted and at peace with the love and adoration she felt from this beautiful man, who was her husband, and the joy at being surrounded by his children. It was perfect. Almost.

Locking him with her eyes she said, "Just before I came out, your phone was ringing."

"My cell? Who was it?" Since the shooting everyone knew that Ali was home and called him on the home line.

It took everything in her not to look away. "Private caller."

Ali looked straight ahead. The silence grew between them like waves pulling away from a shore, each second increasing the distance between them.

"Fatima, would you excuse me for a minute?" Ali asked, without looking at her.

"Sure."

Ali stood and placed Ismail in her arms before entering the house. After the door had closed, the smell of soap, rosemary, ginger and tangerine remained. Fatima regularly experimented with different essential oil combinations, and Ali was her usual test subject. She had recently been trying some oils that she expected would help with his recovery.

Normally, this kind of awareness of him made her feel content, at peace and reassured. Now, it just made her feel dejected and empty. She held Ismail to her chest and reveled in the feel of him as his breath moved his little body up and down. She settled into her seat as she watched the girls play. She knew Ali wouldn't be coming back.

Chapter Thirty Seven

ﺝ

"What will you lovely ladies have for breakfast this morning?" Dana was usually cheerful, but today she was over the top. The three girls ran into the kitchen, all speaking at once, trying to make sure their breakfast orders were the ones heard. They still wore their sleeveless nightgowns, except Laila, who never left her bedroom without being properly dressed. Fatima stood in the doorway.

"Where's Ali?" Fatima had slept after *fajr,* and when she woke again he was gone.

"He left quite early. He said he'd call you later." Dana had started cracking eggs to meet Masuma's request for French toast.

Fatima stood still while her thoughts charged ahead. Since the phone call on Saturday afternoon Ali had been rather quiet. He had spent most of Sunday on the computer or in the library. Still Fatima couldn't imagine where he could have gone before 9 am on a Monday morning. When breakfast was ready Fatima sat with her family and pushed her food around on her plate.

"You're breastfeeding. You need to eat," Dana said, over her glass of juice.

Fatima held up her full water bottle as a defense.

"The fact that it's still full means you're not drinking much either, so you're still on the hook." Dana stood to let Batool leave the table. Masuma and Laila had already returned to their rooms to play. "Do you want to talk about it?"

"Not really. There's nothing really. I was just wondering where Ali could be."

"Does he have to report his every move to you?" Dana asked, hoping to draw a smile from Fatima's worried face.

"No, of course he doesn't, but he usually does, and he's just been acting so mysterious lately." Fatima finally took a bite.

"Maybe he's planning a surprise for you." Dana sounded hopeful.

Fatima pondered the idea for a second. As much as she would have loved to believe that, she knew that wasn't it. "No, it's not a good kind of mysterious. Something serious is on his mind. He is so heavy these days. I'm trying not to be concerned, but it's hard." She looked out the window and saw an elderly couple going for a walk.

"I'm sure you'll hear from him soon." Dana stood up and rubbed Fatima's shoulder. "Until then you have a lot to keep you busy."

She sure did. Now was a good time to have a look at her books and organize a study schedule for her last exam. It had been deferred to July, and Fatima had decided to start studying as early as possible so she could make the most of her preparation time.

She went upstairs and first started to collect clothes for the laundry and then began organizing some books she came across in her closet. She found some old cookbooks that she hadn't used for ages.

"Maybe I'll cook something different tonight." She sat on her bedroom floor immersed in the books and didn't even realize the passage of time until the phone rang.

"Hello?"

"*As-salaam alaikum.*"

"*Wa alaikum as-salaam.*" Fatima wasn't sure whether she should be happy or not at hearing Ali's voice.

"Fatima, do you have some time for me today?" Ali's voice, as always, was deep and rich.

"Of course."

"What were you doing right now?"

Fatima closed the book she was looking at. "I was planning dinner, and then I was going to put in some laundry and do some studying."

"Forget the dinner, I'll pick up something. The laundry we can do later. How much time do you need for studying?"

"I was just going to have a look at the books and kind of get organized, so maybe an hour."

"45 minutes?"

Fatima laughed. "Ok," she agreed. "What's going on?"

"I'll be home in 40 minutes and waiting for you. I want you to come somewhere with me."

"What about Ismail?" He was sleeping, as usual.

"Bring him of course. Can your mom keep the girls?"

"Yes, I'm sure."

"See you then."

Fatima quickly put away the cookbooks and pulled out her textbooks. It seemed like a lifetime away since the last time she had looked at them. Her last exam had been the Friday morning that Ali was shot. She shuddered as she tried to shake the memory. It had been before Ismail's birth, before her phone call from her dad, before Naomi's eyesight came back and before Rachel whupped Jamie.

She snickered to herself. She knew Rachel's fierce side had just been waiting to come out. Fatima had sparred with her in the past and knew she was strong. She just held back all the time. Now she was out. And so different. It's like the old Rachel had been released from some kind of prison. Fatima could see prayers having an effect on Rachel's life. There was definite movement. She hoped Rachel could see it, too, and was putting the credit where it was due.

Fatima put her focus on her books for a full 30 minutes. She completely plotted a study schedule for the next eight weeks. She broke down everything into sections and knew what she was going to study at each time. She even scheduled review time.

"Piece of cake," she said, closing her books. She made a mental note to discuss her schedule with Ali, so he would know when she would be unavailable.

She dressed in a teal and grey crocheted dress. She covered it with a long lambskin vest. She pulled on her favourite knee-length brown leather boots. She was ready and waiting when Ali pulled into the driveway.

"What got into you today?" Ali asked Fatima when she slid into the passenger seat.

"What do you mean?"

"You're actually ready. On time."

Fatima couldn't admit how eager she was to see what he wanted to show her. She had felt so shut out of Ali's life over the last few weeks that she literally jumped at the chance to be included in something he was doing. "I guess it wouldn't do me any good to ask what's going on. Where are we going?" she asked him.

"Trust me, you'll find out soon enough."

Fatima kept silent for most of the journey. She kept running possible scenarios through her mind. Could they be going somewhere, going to meet someone, see something? *What?* Ali was reserved, focused, a little nervous. *What did it all mean?* Fatima reclined in her seat and closed her eyes. She would know soon enough.

When they started following the signs leading to the airport Fatima sat up. Ali wouldn't take her away suddenly, without any preparation. "Are we meeting someone?"

"Fatima please, I know this is hard, just be patient. We're almost there."

Fatima had to bite her lip to keep quiet. They parked and entered the airport. She did realize they were on the arrivals side. *Who was coming?*

"We're early. Do you want a cup of tea?" Ali asked.

"Yes, actually I would, if you're going to join me."

It had been a while since she had enjoyed a cup of tea with Ali alone. Not that they were really alone. Fortunately, Ismail was an easy baby. Being the fourth child, he must have realized it was best for him to keep a low profile, and he did so beautifully.

Fatima looked at her sleeping baby and then up at Ali who was just returning with their drinks. "Do you love him?" she asked playfully.

Ali expected this question. She asked him the same question about all their babies. He always gave the same simple answer. "Yes."

She looked down at the baby again. He was wrapped in her favourite pale blue microfiber blanket. She loved it because it was lightweight, very warm and so soft. "I love Papa, and it's nice that Ismail looks like him..."

"But..." Ali pulled a seat next to her and sat down.

"A little sun would do him some good."

"Does it really matter?"

"I prefer tall, dark and handsome," Fatima said, as she reached for her tea.

Ali lifted the cover off his cup. "You already have a husband."

Fatima laughed quietly. Of course she didn't care about the complexion of her children. She just relished any opportunity to play with Ali. She lifted her cup and tried to forget that she had no idea what she was doing in the arrival section at the airport.

She had almost finished her peppermint tea when Ali looked at his watch. "Do me a favour. Sit over there and wait for me, ok? Do you have your cell phone with you?"

Fatima held up her phone.

"Good, I'll be back soon."

Fatima finished her tea and took a seat where Ali had indicated. She watched the throngs of people moving through the airport. She always loved coming here as a child. Her mother or father was always travelling somewhere. *Maybe that's why their marriage didn't work.* They were always running in different directions.

Fatima tried to imagine where the people were going, who they were and what their life story was. *There must be a million stories here today*, she thought. After some time Ismail needed to be fed. She nursed him, covered him with his blanket and put him back in his car seat that rested in the stroller.

When she heard Ali's voice, she jumped and turned to see him standing almost beside her. It took about five seconds to register what she was seeing. Then the rush of emotion was overwhelming. She lifted her shaking hands to her mouth in case she made an inappropriate sound. Slowly, she rose to her feet. There was no need for Ali to make an introduction. The resemblance was too great.

"Fatima, I would like you to meet my grandmother, the original Mama." Ali stood with his arm around his grandmother's small shoulders, and she held onto him so tightly that the sight pinched Fatima's heart. She smiled warmly at Fatima.

She was a slightly smaller, older version of the Mama they all knew and loved. She was dressed in a blue and white dress with matching head wrap. Fatima moved towards her and encircled her in her arms, then stood back and kissed the two sides of her face.

"I am so pleased to meet you," she said, with tears glistening in her eyes.

"She doesn't understand much English. You'll have to brush up on your French." Fatima knew, from the stories Mama had told, that her mother had been a school teacher and, like Mama, was fluent in French.

Fatima hugged her again, "Ali, how did you do this?"

Ali sighed and rolled his eyes. "It wasn't easy."

"Alessandro, *elle est très belle*-she is beautiful," Grandma said, addressing Ali by his birth name. They had been separated before the massacre. She would not have known him by any other name.

Ali looked at Fatima. "I'm sure you understood that."

Fatima couldn't let go of Grandma. She held her all the way to the car. Ali put Ismail in the backseat and helped his grandmother in beside him. When he closed the door Fatima was still standing.

"Does your mother know?"

Ali had a strange expression on his face. "Not yet."

"Are you worried?"

"It will be a big shock. I just couldn't say anything before, because I never knew how things were going to turn out. I didn't want to get her hopes up again. That's why I never told you what was going on either. I couldn't talk about it. It was so stressful; I didn't want to deal with it any more than I had too."

Fatima had long ago decided that when it came to the matters of Rwanda she would let Ali deal with them however he saw fit. She could never imagine what he had gone through and how it continued to affect him, so she just stood back and tried to support him however he needed.

"Ali please, don't say anything more. You don't have to explain anything to me. I understand. Just forget it, and let's get her home. She must be dying to see your mother." Fatima looked through the window at Grandma, who smiled and waved a tiny hand at her. "She is so cute! Ali please, let's just get her home."

Chapter Thirty Eight

T

R achel stepped off the elevator and walked towards the law-yer's office. She had an appointment with Lauren Lowry, the lawyer specializing in domestic violence cases. She would find out today whether or not she would have to go to trial. She had prayed all night for a miracle. Literally. She surely couldn't or rather didn't want to have to deal with a trial, but couldn't imagine how she could avoid prosecution. Self-defence was her defence, but she *had* gone overboard, hadn't she?

She knew it was likely that she would see Shawn since he worked for the same practice. As a result, she had been stressed out about what to wear. She wanted to look smart and sophisticat-ed, but not like she was trying to impress anyone. *Did men even think that far?* Anyway, she had chosen a white mock croc jacket and slate-coloured pants. She had blown dry her hair and wore it parted on the side, smooth and straight back, falling several inches past her shoulders.

She took a deep breath and entered the office. Lauren was at the reception desk waiting for her. Two large flower pots sat on either side of the desk. "Come right this way, Rachel. I'm pleased to see you."

Lauren put her at ease right away. She was young and stylish. She had warm kind eyes but was obviously all about business. She got into the matters of the case right away.

"Good news." Lauren went on to say that the Crown Attorney had been after Jamie for years. He had a string of charges that had not been able to stick. The lead prosecutor on her case was looking for a promotion and did not want to leave office prosecuting a woman who had been stalked and abused by her children's father.

"And...Jamie has insisted that he doesn't want to press charges. He has confessed to breaking into your house and attacking you. He said you defended yourself." She went on to explain that Jamie was still in the hospital, with broken nose, facial bones and collar-bone. He was in police custody and would be transferred for booking when he was released from the hospital.

Rachel blinked. "What? Are you sure?"

Lauren nodded. "Absolutely."

"So that's it?"

"You are free and clear, darling." Lauren smiled across her desk.

"I don't even know what to do with myself." Rachel rubbed the arms of the chair she was sitting in.

Lauren stood up and went to get a glass of water for Rachel. "Take a minute to absorb it all, and then go have some lunch." Lauren patted Rachel's shoulder and then left her alone in the office, closing the door behind her.

Rachel finished her water and stood to leave. *Could it really be true? Was it all over now?* Each day she was getting more and more of her life back.

She left Lauren's office and was just saying goodbye to the receptionists when Shawn opened his office door. "Rachel, could I speak to you for a minute?"

Rachel turned and headed into Shawn's office. He closed the door behind her and led her to one of the chairs facing his desk. She had a beautiful view of downtown from her seat.

"How was your meeting?" He leaned against his desk.

"Great." She filled him in on the details. While he listened he just smiled and nodded.

"I'm really happy for you, Rachel."

"Thank-you. You can't be happier than me." She looked around Shawn's office. He had more books than she had ever seen anywhere, other than the library. "Are these all legal books?"

"Most of them. There are some other things too. Everything is catalogued. You can go through them sometime, if you like. I know you like to read."

"I don't have that much time these days. But I would like to see what you have. Have you read all of these?"

"Pretty much. Some are reference books." Shawn kept his focus on Rachel.

With all the knowledge he would have acquired from reading he must be an interesting conversationalist, Rachel thought. *I would love to pick his brain.*

"What are you thinking about?" Shawn was definitely perceptive.

She was almost ashamed to say. "Jamie never read anything at all. I tried to give him a book, once, that I thought he might find interesting, and he never even touched it. He literally left it exactly where I put it. He never talked about anything except what he could learn about from TV."

Shawn stood up and flexed. "Good thing you don't have to worry about that anymore."

Rachel closed her eyes, realizing she had made a mistake talking about Jamie in that way. Wanting to change the subject, she said. "I never did thank you for continuing to work with Joshua's soccer team. I know he and Ali really appreciate it. Me too, of course." Rachel suddenly felt shy.

Shawn noticed the change in her and smiled. "I've been having fun. I know Ali is eager to get back to it, but I told him to take some more time."

"He could always come out to watch," Rachel offered.

"Are we talking about the same Ali?"

"You're right. He better stay home a while longer." Rachel moved forward in her seat, thinking it was about time she excused herself and let Shawn get back to work.

Noticing her movements, Shawn asked, "Have you eaten lunch?"

"No, not yet." She had been too nervous to even have breakfast.

"Good, I've been waiting for you. Are you ready?"

"Sure, but you must be busy. Are you sure you have the time?" Rachel stood and put her hand bag over her shoulder.

Shawn raised his brow. "Do I have time to eat? With you?" He reached across his desk to shut down his computer, turned off his cellphones and walked over to where Rachel was standing. "Let's go."

Rachel could have bounced all the way out the door.

Chapter Thirty Nine

𝔍

The entire ride home, Grandma talked and sang to Ismail. He gave her his full attention. Fatima tried hard to maintain conversation with her and had to keep asking Ali to translate or remind her how to say certain things. She was going to have to pull out her French/English dictionary as soon as she got home.

Ali had a peace and contentment about him that Fatima had never seen before. She thought how amazing it was that you could know a person for so long but seeing them in a new situation or facing new challenges still brought out new aspects of their personality and character. Life, particularly marriage, was a process of learning, growth and development.

When they pulled into the driveway, Fatima could see that Ali had tensed. She reached out to him. "You've done a great thing. Everything is going to be fine." She had never been prouder than that very moment to call him her husband.

Ali sat still. The enormity of what he was about to do filled him. Mama had no idea if her mother were dead or alive. She had not been able to get conclusive information about her during their years in Canada. Mama had not seen, spoken to or heard of her mother in more than 15 years. How would she react to seeing her now? Would the shock be too much for her? Maybe he should prepare her somehow.

"Ali?"

Ali released the steering wheel. "I think I should go and get her first."

Fatima understood what he must be going through. "I'll wait here."

Ali entered and walked to the back of the house. Both of his parents were in the garden. He greeted them and called them inside the house.

"Mama, I have a surprise for you."

"That's unusual. What is it?"

"It's outside. It's a big one, but it's good. I don't want you to be too shocked. "

"Ok, let's go see." Mama removed her gloves and followed Ali outside.

Papa patted Ali on the shoulder as he passed him and then he stopped to call Rahma from her room. When they arrived on the porch, Ali asked Mama to wait. He went back to his vehicle and opened the back door to help his grandmother out. She stepped carefully as her eyes focused on her daughter, standing just feet away from her.

Mama squinted, trying to focus on what she was seeing. "No, no." She grabbed at her own neck. "It can't be...no, it's not." She turned to look at Papa. He smiled at her and nodded, reassuring her that what she was indeed seeing was correct.

"Mama? Mama. Mama!" Mama dropped to her knees. "Mamaa! Mamaaa! Mamaaaa!" she screamed over and over. Grandma hurried as fast as she could to reach her daughter's side. Each step she made was punctuated with Mama's screams that came louder and louder, climbing higher and higher.

Mama crawled toward the older woman, crying and beating the ground, barely able to support her own weight. Her body weakened by pent up grief, overwhelming need and undying love. By the time Grandma reached her, Mama was shaking and holding her head, unable to move forward anymore. Her voice was already hoarse. She barely whispered, "Mama, Mama, my Mama."

All the years of waiting and wondering, the years of sleepless nights and waking up drenched in sweat from nightmares that outlined the insidious things that may have befallen her mother, the years Mama had held her children and grandchildren and wondered if she would get to once again hold the woman who had given her life. All those years had now culminated into this one blessed moment. Her mother was once again about to be in her arms.

Grandma bent down and held onto Mama, cradling her in her arms. "*Shu, Shu, Mama est ici, Mama est ici*-Mama is here." Mama clutched her mother and cried until there was no sound left in her body. One by one the neighbours came outside to see what all the commotion was about. The message passed through the crowd. "It's her mother. It's her mother." By the time Ali and Papa were able to gather the two women and bring them into the house, there was not a dry eye on the street.

Mama could not stop holding, hugging and kissing her mother. It was as though she didn't believe she was real or leaving her side might cause her to disappear. One minute Mama was laughing, one minute she was crying. Grandma sat in Mama's special chair, surrounded by her surviving child, grandchildren and great-grandchildren.

Dana had come over with Fatima's daughters and Grandma could not get enough of them. She laughed and hugged and kissed them and they kept clambering to get more of her attention. Everyone else was so excited, they certainly weren't going to be left out.

Grandma studied them individually and commented on each girl. Holding Masuma's face she said, "*Elle est très intelligente*." For Batool she said, "*Elle est forte*-she is strong." When Laila stepped forward Grandma smiled and simply said, "*Ooo la la*."

Rahma relished her position at her grandmother's feet. Like everyone, she was completely caught up in the rapture of the moment. She didn't know what to say, but just wanted to take in every single detail about her and this moment.

"You all will have a beautiful summer, finally," Dana said, from her position on the arm of the couch.

"*We* will be in Italy." Ali leaned casually, in the doorway.

Rahma shot to her feet. "What? Papa!"

Papa was nonchalant. "Your brother is a grown man. I can't control where he takes his vacation."

"Don't you have therapy and stuff to deal with?" Rahma panicked.

"I can do that anywhere." Ali seemed to enjoy unnerving his little sister.

"Oh Papa! Please! He's going to ruin everything." Rahma fired Ali a vicious look.

"That's my job," Ali said.

"*Sorella!*"

Fatima attempted to sooth Rahma. "Honey, it will be fine. We'll all be busy doing our own thing, but we'll be there if you need us. Ali's just watching out for you. You may not understand it now, but girls do need protection. We'll all have fun. I promise."

Rahma sulked until Grandma pulled her closer. Rahma resumed her position at Grandma's feet and allowed her to soothe her by stroking her head of thick brown curls.

Fatima sat and nursed Ismail, and then put him to sit in the baby seat that Mama and Papa kept at their house. She asked Dana to watch him and went back to Ali's side. She needed to talk to him.

When she pulled his sleeve, he lowered his head to hear what she had to say. "Do you think we can escape this lovefest for a minute? I want to talk to you."

Ali nodded his agreement and backed out of the doorway. Fatima pulled him toward the front door. "Let's go home." When they were inside their home, she said, "I'm so proud of you. I can't believe you pulled this off. You have to tell me how you did it."

Ali told her that through the years there had been various leads, but nothing had materialized. He had been travelling to Ottawa because there was an organization there that specialized in reuniting Rwandan families. Finally, Grandma was found in the USA. She had been sponsored by an American church, along with some other Rwandan refugees, after spending years in a refugee camp.

"Oh my God, a refugee camp, at her age." Fatima pulled off her scarf and shook her hair free.

"Yes. She insists she was fine." Ali rubbed his head. "I don't know - the things I know about those camps."

"Ali, she's safe now. Now is what matters. And she is so happy." Fatima tried to look positive. Ali simply nodded.

Fatima still hadn't mentioned what was foremost on her mind when she had asked to speak to him.

"Ali, I'm sorry about everything. I'm sorry about doubting you and being angry with you. You asked me to be patient and give you time, but I just couldn't do it. I never had any reason to distrust you, but I still did, and all the time you were carrying this enormous burden of not knowing whether you were going to find your grandmother and bring her home. I am so sorry." Her face showed that she was tormented and her eyes were heavy with remorse.

Ali's eyes slowly lit up. "Is that a plea for forgiveness?"

The light in her eyes matched his. "Yes."

He lowered his head. "I'll think about it."

"Ali!"

"Ok, you're forgiven. Not that you need to be. I knew I was asking you for too much. I know it was a burden on you. I just couldn't handle anything else at the time. I couldn't talk about it. I don't know how to explain it."

"You don't have to. Just forget it. Now we can focus on our family, our new family with all its additions." Then she remembered.

It had been a week since they had spoken about Rachel. Neither of them had any idea what the other was thinking. Ali had given no indication either way and Fatima had not mentioned it either.

Noticing the sudden change in her, Ali asked, "Fatima, what just happened?"

"Rachel." Fatima waited for a response. "What about Rachel?"

Ali moved into the living room and sat on the arm of the closest chair, pulling Fatima with him.

"There is no Rachel. There is just you, me and our family."

"Really." She eyed him cautiously.

"Of course, really."

Fatima pulled back, crossing her arms in front of her. "I'm not sure, Ali. There has been a lot going on that would belie that statement."

Ali frowned. "You're right, and I was wrong for all of it. I never stopped to think about the message that I was sending to you or even Rachel, for that matter. I never want you to think that there is anyone, other than you, in my life, on my mind or in my heart."

Fatima pushed his shoulder. "Why did you take so long to discuss it?" she scolded.

"Girl, don't drive me crazy. I tried speaking to you days ago."

Fatima studied him for a few moments, trying to read his thoughts. "Was it difficult for you to confront this issue?

Ali *had* thought seriously about Rachel, but from his initial reaction to his final decision his intention had always been the same. "No, I have always known what I want."

"You were so pensive this whole week, and on the weekend it was like you were completely emotionally absent. I didn't know what to think."

"I had a lot on my mind. My grandmother was coming and it still didn't seem real to me. Until I actually saw her and touched her I couldn't allow myself to believe it." Ali exhaled deeply. "I was concerned about Rachel too."

"In what way?"

"I wondered about her future, whether or not she would be taken care of, whether she would be happy. I also thought about the possibility of me influencing her with Islam."

Fatima unfolded her arms. "What do you think now?"

"I think she'll be fine. If *Allah* wants her He will call her, and it will be up to her to answer, not me. I was so busy trying to take care of everyone that I didn't think about how things must look to you. I was so caught up in feeling needed, that I didn't even consider how I was making you feel. I took you for granted, and I'm sorry. I won't make that mistake again. You are my wife, my responsibility is to you. If I ever slip, call me on it. Every time."

Fatima was incredulous. She was stuck after the forth sentence. *I was caught up in feeling needed.* Was Ali suggesting that he didn't feel needed by them? Could he be serious?

Fatima was very independent. As an only child with busy parents it came naturally. The fact that Ali was away so much made it necessary. She never told him how difficult it was for her because she didn't want him to worry about them while he was away. Now it seemed her desire to save his feelings and actually help him had backfired on her.

"And *we* don't need you?" she asked.

An emotion flashed across Ali's face that Fatima didn't recognize. Was it anticipation, hope, fear or a mixture of all three? "Do you?"

He was really asking. Fatima's mind raced to find the right words to express all that she had never told him, to give him just what he needed at that moment. The only thing that came to her mind was the only thing that made sense. She hoped that the sincerity in her eyes and voice would be enough.

"Yes. Yes, we do. More than anything, we need you, Ali."

Ali nodded slightly. "It's good to hear it sometimes."

Fatima was touched by all that he had just said and by his sudden, unexpected display of vulnerability. "You are absolutely, positively, incredible. Do you know that?"

Ali laughed. "You may have mentioned it before, but you can repeat." And so she did, again and again and again.

Chapter Forty

Rachel opened the piece of paper in her hand. Her list. It seemed like such a long time since she had written it. Now most of the items were crossed off. She had prayed over the list for so long, and it seemed like nothing was happening. Now she realized that things were always happening; she just couldn't see them. All she needed to do was be ready.

In the last few weeks everything seemed to come together at once. She couldn't deny she was thrilled. Finally, her prayers had been answered. So many of them. The past week was a beautiful one. Fatima and Ali were back to normal. Mama's mother fit right into the family as though she had always been there. Indeed she had been in spirit; now she was in the flesh.

Rachel looked around her room. It was crisp and cool. She had painted it a light greenish grey shade called "caper." She and Fatima had hunted for unique pieces of furniture, all in light and neutral shades. Taupe pillowcases wrapped full-sized pillows. Crisp white sheets and a bright citrus throw covered the bed. It felt like springtime in her room. Rachel inhaled deeply trying to soak up the feeling and hold it inside.

Joshua and Jonah were home. They both had claimed to be sick in the morning. Five minutes after Rachel had called the daycare, they were running, jumping and playing. Instead of chastising them, she had decided to take the day off. Since the incident with Jamie, they wanted to spend more time with her than usual. She couldn't deny them that. Today she planned to take them to the park with Fatima and her children.

When the doorbell rang, Rachel was surprised. Fatima was early. Rachel took her time getting to the door, just to tease her friend and was stunned when she opened her door to see Shawn standing in front of her.

Rachel was immediately apologetic. "I'm sorry, I thought it was Fatima...do we have an appointment?" Naturally, she knew that wasn't the case. She would not have forgotten an appointment, and Shawn always dressed for business. Today he was wearing dark blue jeans and a black mock turtle neck.

"No, actually..."

"Excuse me, that's for me." Naomi pushed past Rachel and stepped outside.

"I beg your pardon?" Slightly confused, Rachel looked from Shawn to her mother.

"Since Fridays are usually quiet days for me, I told your mother I could walk with her sometimes."

Rachel raised her eyebrows in amusement. "I see." Shawn was certainly full of surprises.

Shawn stepped aside to allow Naomi to pass him. "Rachel, when we get back, would you allow me to take you both to lunch?" Shawn asked.

"I'll have to ask my mom."

"Certainly." Shawn put his hands in his pockets.

"It's fine with me." Naomi was already on the sidewalk.

"Oh, I forgot, my boys are home today." Rachel couldn't hide the disappointment she felt.

Shawn lifted one hand. "The more the merrier. We can go to a kid-friendly place and then hit the park. I have a few hours free."

A slow smile etched across her face. "Sounds great." Rachel

knew Fatima wouldn't mind the change of plans. "Maybe I should meet you. We can't all fit in one car, not with their car seats." Shawn drove a Jaguar XKR convertible.

"Taken care of." Shawn moved aside to reveal the brand new Infinity Truck he had driven.

Rachel stepped outside and put her hands on her hips. "You didn't have that the last time I saw you."

"I work quickly." Shawn watched for her reaction.

"That's a big commitment for a day at the park."

Shawn answered with care. "Well, I've been thinking about it for a while. If it passes approval, I'll keep it."

"And if it doesn't?"

Shawn smiled mischievously. "I might still keep it. It's a nice ride."

"Wow, cool!" Joshua and Jonah rushed past Rachel to admire Shawn's new purchase.

He turned back to Rachel. "Three down, one to go."

"The most important one."

"Undeniable."

"She can't be pressured."

"I wouldn't dream of it."

Rachel nodded and looked away. Suddenly feeling chilled, she pulled her arms close to her body. "Enjoy your walk. We'll be ready when you get back."

She watched Shawn and her mother stroll up the street and shook her head in amazement.

"What's going on here?" Fatima had crossed the street to speak to Rachel about what she had just witnessed from her house.

Rachel threw her hands up. "He's walking with my mother and look, he bought this truck."

"Wow, he has it bad." Fatima looked at the driveway then turned and grabbed Rachel's shoulders. "I'm ecstatic!"

"You would be." Rachel rolled her eyes.

"What's that supposed to mean?"

"You're always trying to set people up." Rachel looked down her nose at Fatima.

"I just want everyone to be as happy as I am," Fatima answered innocently.

Rachel snorted. "Oh, now you're happy? A few weeks ago you were ready to offer Ali to the highest bidder."

Fatima lowered her chin. "I've learned my lesson."

"I told you so. And yes, I am very pleased to be able to say it." Rachel poked Fatima lightly in the shoulder.

It was good that Rachel was feeling so positive about her future, Fatima thought, but there was still one thing they needed to clear the air about. "Listen Rachel, about the conversation I started a few weeks ago, concerning Ali."

Rachel put up her hand to stop Fatima. "Forget it. I don't even know what to say. I guess you said it all. Ali is a wonderful man. But I would never do anything to hurt you guys. Your friendship means more to me than anything else."

"I know that."

"And I would be the first in line to take down anyone who threatened your marriage."

"So we see."

"I'm sorry if I behaved in some way that made you both uncomfortable. I can't even imagine what Ali must be thinking. Until you confronted me, I never realized what energy I might be putting out. This is all so embarrassing. Maybe it was what I needed to shake me up. I was so wrapped up in the past I couldn't even see clearly. All that's different now. Now that I've shifted my focus, the future and its possibilities have become so clear."

Fatima held her hands together. "We can put it behind us. I was hormonal and frustrated, and the three of us do have a unique relationship. I just really wanted the best for you and your boys, and I know Ali cares about you all as much as I do." She waved her hand. "But you know Ali is like a rock. Nothing fazes him. Everything will be just like before. We wouldn't ever let you go as a friend, and we do trust you. I trust you."

"Thank-you, so much."

"Enough about me. What about you? And Shawn?"

"I don't know." A smile crept over Rachel's face. "I think he likes me."

"You think? Men don't make the decision to park their sports cars lightly." Fatima pulled Rachel into a chair and sat beside her.

"So what do you think?"

"I think he's amazing. *And* I'm just taking one day at a time."

"Great." Fatima stifled a squeal. "I better let you get ready. I heard something about going to lunch?"

"Yes, and we're going to the park after. You could still bring your kids." Rachel felt a little guilty about standing Fatima up.

"No way, they can play together anytime. I didn't tell them we had plans." Fatima stood up and hugged Rachel. "You have come such a long way. I am so proud of you. I love you, and you deserve the best. You know that, don't you?"

Rachel thought about that question for a long moment. There was definitely a time when she did not believe she deserved anything good. Now, she looked at her boys running around the shiny new truck in the driveway, and her eyes surveyed the street where she lived, where she had grown up and built the most treasured friendships and extended family unit possible. Then her eyes travelled to the two specks up the road that were her mother and Shawn.

Her hands slipped into her pocket and she fingered the piece of paper that contained her list. Everything she had asked for, she had received. She had only one more thing to cross off, and she realized she could do that now, if she decided to.

She focused on Fatima and answered her question, "Yes, I do." Then she turned into her house to get ready.

Epilogue

ℑ

"You're not getting cold feet, are you?" Fatima put the finishing touches on Rachel's makeup and took a tissue to blot the sweat from her forehead, nose and top lip.

"No, no of course not. I just feel so nervous." Anxiety travelled from her stomach all the way to her throat." I don't think I'll be able to stand, never mind walk."

Rachel touched the fabric of her dress that lay on the bed beside her. The dress was simple and elegant. It had a pleated empire bodice that moulded perfectly to her body. The hand-beaded crystal circles under the bodice made the dress unique. Metres of silk chiffon created a splendidly flowing skirt.

It hadn't taken her long to choose the dress. Instead of spending hours in bridal shops, she found exactly what she wanted in a magazine and just went directly to the store to order it. It was beautiful, romantic and ultra-feminine. Fatima had given it her stamp of approval.

"Well, don't stand too close to the microphone, because no one will be able to hear you say, '*I do*'. All I can hear now is the thumping of your heart."

Rachel looked at Fatima to see if she was serious. When she realized that Fatima was making fun of her, she had to laugh at herself. "What am I going to do, Fati? How am I going to make it through this day? With everyone looking at me? You know I can't stand being the centre of attention. What will Shawn think? I can't stop shaking."

"He will think he is the luckiest man in the world, to be marrying you today, that's what. Everything will be fine. Trust me."

"Were you this nervous?" Rachel linked her fingers to keep from wringing her hands.

"Not quite. But I was nervous. Don't you remember? I couldn't eat anything all day? Not even at the reception. By the time I got back to the hotel, I was starving."

"Yes, I remember. Ali ran all over town trying to find you a *halal* chicken sandwich. What a way to spend your wedding night."

"Well, it was a cute way to break the ice. And he proved himself to be a patient and caring husband."

Rachel started to wipe her face with the back of her hand. "No you don't." Fatima said, handing her a tissue. "Just blot. Here, sit in front of the fan. It's already like an icebox in here. I don't know how you are still sweating."

It was October, but still warm enough to need air conditioning. Fatima was helping Rachel get dressed in her bedroom in Naomi's house. The ceremony would be in her home and the reception for 100 would be under a tent in the backyard. Fatima was her matron of honour, although she had balked at the idea initially.

"**Are you sure?** Remember I have *hijab*, and then there is the issue of the best man?"

"The best man is Ali, so that's not a problem. And you can make the dress however you want. We can select the material together and the other girls are all wearing long skirts so you just do the top anyway you want and then put on your scarf. Please? I need you. I can't do it without you by my side."

Fatima had reluctantly agreed, but now was truly enjoying her role as the matron of honour. She had helped to organize everything, from choosing the decorations for the house and the backyard to the menu and cake.

"Every time I think of my dad missing this day I can't stop crying." Rachel dabbed at her eyes.

"If you mess up your makeup you're on your own." Fatima pointed a blush brush at her.

"I know. I know. I'll be fine." Rachel fanned her face vigorously.

"Listen, don't think that your dad is not here. Imagine that he is and he is seeing everything. He's here with you and is so happy that you have chosen an excellent man for your husband and father for your boys. You know he would love Shawn and be so proud of you. Just enjoy your day."

Rachel sobbed. "And what about you guys? Now, I'm going to be living so far away. I can't just run across the street any more. And the boys won't see my mom as much. This is the last time I'll be in this room and I put so much time into fixing it up. Now, what's it going to be? A guest room?!" Rachel blew her nose violently.

Shawn had spent months canvassing the neighbours on the street. He had come to know each one personally and let them know that he would be ready to purchase as soon as anyone thought about selling. The fact that a house had not been for sale on the street in the past two years hadn't discouraged him.

"The distance might be good for you. You two will have some privacy and you'll feel like you're really starting a new life. Anyway, it's not that far. It's not next door, but number 10 is just up the street. You can still see us whenever you want. It'll be good exercise for you."

"What about when it's raining?!" Rachel started to wail, until a loud knock at the door startled her.

"Oh, I hope that's not my mom. I can't take all her crying," Rachel said, before blowing her nose again.

Fatima smiled as she moved to open the door. Rachel was so upset she apparently hadn't noticed the obviously male voice behind the door. When Fatima cracked open the door, Ali was on the other side.

"What are you doing here? No one can see her yet," Fatima said.

Ali was fully dressed in a black tuxedo with platinum vest. "I'm not the husband." Ali motioned behind Fatima with his chin. "Anyway, she's not even dressed."

"Ali!" Fatima squeezed the door towards the frame and looked over her shoulder to see how much of the room was visible.

"Relax. I can see the dress on the bed. I just came to tell you guys to hurry up. You have less than 10 minutes to be downstairs. Everyone is getting antsy."

"How is Shawn doing?" Fatima whispered.

"He's fine, just hurry up." Ali turned to walk down the hall.

"Ok. And don't say anything about the dress."

"Already forgotten," he said over his shoulder.

Fatima closed the door and turned back to Rachel. "We had better get you into this dress."

"So lovely." Mama, Dana, Naomi and Fatima all stood around admiring Rachel. She wore her hair in a smooth roll with a crystal headband tiara. Her veil fell behind her back, reaching the floor.

When everyone had left her, she sat on the bed with the door open waiting for her cue to make her entrance.

"I should have eloped."

She fanned her face and took long breaths in an attempt to slow her heart rate. Then she caught sight of herself in the full length mirror and smiled. She was beautiful. The dress was perfect. Her hair and makeup were perfect. She felt like a princess. Now, if she could only make it down the stairs and down the aisle.

All the furniture had been moved out and the main floor had been decorated with lilies, Rachel's favourite flowers, and candles of all sizes and shapes. It was already evening and soon the candles would be the only light they would have for the ceremony.

The staircase had also been decorated with flowers and the ceiling had layers of white fabric attached to it, cascading down the walls. She couldn't believe it was her house. She felt like she was surrounded by clouds.

When Rachel heard the start of her song, she knew she had to go. "Ok Daddy, this is it." She took one last look at her room and stepped into the hallway. Her bouquet in hand she moved forward, and when she arrived at the top of the circular stairway, she saw Shawn waiting for her at the bottom. He wasn't supposed to be there, but she couldn't deny that she was relieved and comforted to see him. She wasn't going to have to make the walk by herself.

She slowly made her way down the stairs, stepping gently on the white rose petals under her feet. When she arrived at Shawn's side she looked up at him. He wore the same tuxedo as Ali and the other groomsmen, with a slightly darker textured vest. Rachel thought he looked so handsome and not at all nervous.

"You're not supposed to be here," she whispered.

"I thought it would be easier for you," Shawn replied.

She could barely get the words out. "Thank-you."

"Are you ok?"

"No," Rachel admitted.

Shawn lowered his head. "Change your mind?"

Rachel's eyes widened. "Are you serious?"

"Serious." Shawn's dark eyes were resolute.

Rachel nipped her bottom lip. "What if I did?"

"It's your call."

Shawn had asked Rachel to marry him one month after the day he had shown up in her driveway with his new truck. She had never second guessed her decision even once. He was the best thing that had happened to her and she knew it.

In the month before his proposal he had won her heart with his kindness and gentle open manner. His attentiveness to her needs, as well as those of her sons and her mother, was unrivalled. Ali and Fatima had assured her that this was no act. Shawn was always this considerate. It was his nature. Although he was extremely busy with his growing practice, when he was with

Rachel and her family he made them feel like he had nothing else to do in the world.

After she had accepted, Shawn had worked overtime trying to secure a house on the same street as her current home, knowing how much it would mean to her. Finally, Mr. Marinos had been put into a senior's home, and his son had called Shawn to offer him the house before putting it on the market.

The interior of the house was outdated, so Shawn and Rachel had started renovations as soon as they had signed the papers. It would still take a few weeks to be complete. While they waited, Rachel and Shawn would stay in his condo and the boys would continue living with their grandmother until they all moved into the new house.

Change my mind? "Of course not."

"Pheeew." Shawn let out a long breath and relaxed his shoulders. "That was your last chance. Let's go, our guests are waiting."

Rachel giggled softly and smiled all the way down the aisle.

On either side of them were their closest friends and family members. Each one of the 100-plus chairs was wrapped in fabric secured by a floral arrangement at the back. Rachel's brother and sister, who had come home for the occasion, both sat beside their mother and Naomi could not have been happier. By the time Rachel arrived at the altar, she was completely relaxed.

Surrounded by her dearest loved ones she could not have been more content. Fatima's three daughters were her flower girls and wore identical white dresses. Fatima wore a platinum-coloured dress covered by a chiffon bolero with extended sleeves. Joshua and Jonah stood proudly by Shawn's side.

The entire ceremony was a blur to Rachel. All she knew was that she was wrapped in more love than she knew what to do with. She stood in this home that held so many wonderful memories for her, as she was about to step into a new life; a better life than she could have ever imagined a year ago.

When the minister asked her the question she had been waiting for and dreaming of hearing for the last four months, she almost laughed at the derision of the question. "Do you take this man?"

Clearly she did. "Yes, I do."

When she saw the smiles on all the faces around her, Shawn, the wedding party, her mother and all the guests, she knew she had made the right decision. Nothing could have taken her higher, except hearing Shawn's answer to the question "Do you take this woman?"

"I do."

She was his wife. It was a new life and she was elated and grateful to be entering into it. She thought about how close she had come to not having any of this. All it had taken was her believing and then having the courage to reach out, just a little.

When the minister declared, "I now pronounce you man and wife," Rachel looked fondly at her husband. For the first time, she couldn't think of one thing to write on her list.

Glossary of Terms

Throughout the text, some Arabic words have been used. This guide has been included to help the reader understand the context.

Abaya Modest dress, often worn over clothing to preserve hijab

Adhan call to prayer

Alhamdulillah All thanks be to God

Allah God

Aqeeqa Ceremony that involves sacrificing a lamb or goat on behalf of the child. It is giving thanks to Allah for the gift of a child. The meat is distributed to the poor, or it can be used to arrange a feast to which the poor as well as relatives and friends are invited.

Bismillahi Rahmani Rahim. Allahumma salli ala Muhammadin wa ali Muhammad In the Name of God, The Most Beneficent, The Most Merciful. God send blessings on Muhammad and the family of Muhammad

Dua Supplication

Eid Celebration, two of the biggest Eid celebrations are Eid ul-Fitr,
after the month of fasting, Ramadan, the month of fasting, and
Eid al-Adha, occurring after the yearly Hajj, the pilgrimage to
Mecca.

Halal Lawful or permitted. In this case, food that is lawful to be
eaten. In order for the meat to be halal, the animal must be
slaughtered according to Islamic law.

Hijab Covering, often used to refer to headscarf

Imam Ali(as) (on him be peace) the cousin of the Prophet Mu-
hammad(saw) and the husband of daughter of the Prophet Mu-
hammad(saw), Fatima. He is accepted by Shia Muslims as the
rightful successor of the Prophet Muhammad(saw), as ordained
by God, and the first of twelve successors or Imams.

Muharram the first month of the Islamic calendar. It is one of the
four sacred months of the year in which fighting is prohibited. The
tenth day of Muharram is called Yaumu-l 'Ashurah, which is
known by Shia Muslims as "the day of grief", due to the sufferings
and slaughter of Husayn ibn Ali and his household on the day of
Ashura by Yazid ibn Muawiya. Husayn is the son of Imam Ali(as)
and the Fatima, the daughter of the Prophet Muhammad(saw).

Rasoolullah Messenger of God, referring to the Prophet Muham-
mad(saw). It is favourable and beneficial to send Him salaams –
peace when entering your home.

Wa alaikum as-salaam, wa rahmatullahi wa barakatu response
to **As-salaam alaikum** translated as "and onto you be peace,
and the Mercy of God and His Blessings." It is favourable to
return a greeting with a better greeting than the one received.

About the Author

Marjorie Dawn Tulloch was born in Jamaica and raised in Toronto, where she currently lives. She accepted Islam in 1997. She loves reading, cool summer nights and good conversation. She has published one children's story, The Night Prayers, under the pen name S.A. Tulloch.

www.ingramcontent.com/pod-product-compliance
Lightning Source LLC
Chambersburg PA
CBHW021521250626
47154CB00006BA/1925